Always Faithful

Julie Miller

LOVE SPELL BOOKS NEW YORK CITY

LOVE SPELL®

April 2000

Published by

Dorchester Publishing Co., Inc.
276 Fifth Avenue
New York, NY 10001

ISBN 0-505-52374-4

Printed in the United States of America.

For Tom Binger.
Every girl should be lucky enough to have a big brother
like him.

With thanks to the two Georges in my life.

I've learned about the character it takes to be a
United States Marine from you both.
I thank you for letting me ask questions and listen to your
stories and observe you in action as veterans
and family men.
Any mistakes in my fictional world are my own.

Semper Fi

****

I dedicate the characters of Emma, Jas, and BJ to their
real-life counterparts—Kimberly Opie McKane, Becky
Owenson Kilpatrick, and myself—the Young Bag Brigade.
And to their inspiration—the Old Bag Brigade —Barbara
Binger, Ginny Taylor, and Fritzi Hazelrigg—for showing
me what long-lasting friendship is all about

"Nothing in life is more wonderful than faith—
the one great moving force . . ."
—Sir William Osler

Prologue

An unknown time in a place with no name

"Send me back!"

Piercing blue eyes nailed Faith with such intensity that she shivered. The man before her formed an imposing silhouette against the bright light. His anger would have made the walls shake, if they had walls about them.

"It's not that simple, Colonel."

"I've been wandering around here for days. Make it simple!" He barked the order, and Faith snapped to attention in her seat.

The man had every right to be angry. She had made one hell—er, pardon—of a mistake on her first solo assignment, and knew of no sure way to fix it. She'd tried to explain that she wasn't cut out for this kind of work, but her superior hadn't listened.

And now, despite her best intentions, her gross incompetence had pulled Lieutenant Colonel Jonathan Ramsey from earth before his time.

She flipped through the pages of the wordless book that floated in the air beside her, telling the life story of her charges. So much was left to be written. She prayed that an answer would show itself. But she'd been so eager, she hadn't realized . . . "I just wanted to save you the agony. The explosion caught us all off guard."

"My men will be looking for me. I have to be there."

She shrugged, suspecting he wouldn't understand her explanation. "Your comrades won't find you. Your fate is determined."

"But I saw Hawk. I talked to him . . ."

Her silence transformed his confusion into anger. The colonel grabbed the tattered remnants of his bloody shirtfront, thrusting the material toward her in frustration. "I've survived worse than this. I always make it home!"

Faith shrugged her shoulders in mute apology. In her effort to spare the noble career soldier a painful death, she had snatched his spirit the moment the grenade detonated.

Unfortunately, she had snatched him too soon. She had cheated him of his final moments on earth.

Now Jonathan Ramsey, respected leader and family man, stood before her just as the other man in the blast, a notoriously elusive arms-dealer limped his way through a similar process in a very different, much darker place.

The colonel pulled something from the pocket of his jungle fatigues and moved closer. "Look, lady"—

his tone softened and cracked in a way that made her heart turn over. "Ma'am."

He unfolded a nylon wallet and stuck it between her and the book. "I'm married to the sweetest woman in the world, with legs so long and fine a man can't even begin to describe them."

Faith looked at the picture, seeing it through his eyes, understanding the longing in his voice.

"We have a little girl who'll be two on December twenty-fourth. I bought a swing set to put together for her in the spring. I promised them I'd be home for Christmas to celebrate with them. I don't want to disappoint my little girl."

The serenely beautiful woman in the photograph held an infant with sable curls like her mother's and the clear blue eyes that she had inherited from her father.

Faith swallowed back tears she wasn't allowed to shed. She glanced at the colonel's sorrowful expression and on up into the bright nothingness above her. "We're talking Christmas," she pleaded.

The light from above spun around them, flashing with tints of blue and yellow. Faith returned to the book. She turned back two pages. Inspired. "I may know a way."

"How?" The colonel pocketed his wallet and looked over her shoulder. She doubted he could make sense of the images swirling across the translucent pages. But he concentrated on them anyway, as alert and intense as a man who led others would be before a decisive battle.

"I'm not sure I should do this." Faith sat back, debating the wisdom of her decision. "But maybe if I help the other one redeem himself, that will make up for . . . Oh, I don't know if I can."

The colonel knelt beside her, his deep, calm breathing steadying her own. "You have to try. You have to give me a chance."

Faith frowned at her dilemma. "There's a rule about balance. Two men died down there. I'd have to send two men back. I'd have to send him back, too."

"The Chameleon?" The potential menace of the dealer who had chosen to take his own life instead of surrendering, and had taken the colonel with him, became evident in the cold narrowing of the colonel's eyes.

"Maybe we can save him, redeem him," Faith said. "but I've never done this before." The heavenly light that surrounded them began to dim. "I know it's not an easy decision. But it has to be made quickly."

"We'd arrive after the explosion?"

Faith nodded. "You can't go back and change what's already happened."

The colonel pushed himself to his feet. "My unit tracked him down once. We could do it again."

The light around them wavered. "Hurry, Colonel. Decide."

He rubbed his palms against his eyes, his shoulders sagging in a moment of defeat. "Em has so many responsibilities. I haven't always been around when she's needed me. But the Chameleon . . . A lot of people have died because of him. It took us so long to catch him—I don't know how long it would take to do it again. I'm the only one who knows what he looks like. How many people might die?"

Faith looked at the fading images in her own book. His question hovered in the air. Then the colonel straightened, steeling himself. "Send me back."

Faith nodded.

14

"Is there anything I should do to help?" he asked.

"Pray."

He closed his eyes. Faith felt strengthened by the power of his simple wish, but this was still a complicated process.

She pressed her palms together, feeling the air between them grow warm. When it became more than she could bear, her hands parted and a circle of light emerged. It swelled and brightened like a thousand suns, glowing intensely and triggering a low humming sound, a life force blossoming in the air around them. It swirled into tornadic spirals, escaped from her and seized the colonel in its midst. Faith shielded her eyes as he vanished in a burst of white-hot lightning.

An instant later, she could breathe again. She opened her eyes, once more alone in her citadel at the outer reaches. She leaned back, amazed at the complexity of the whole ordeal.

The atmosphere changed, bleeding color into a place that knew no sunset. She understood the message even though she heard no audible words. "I know. No wings today."

A piercing light beamed onto the open page, reflecting into her eyes before the book slammed shut. Faith gasped at what she had seen. "Oh, my God. What have I done?"

The air around her blinked. She looked up. "Sorry."

Faith dropped her face into her hands, dismayed by her inability to do her job right. She'd broken the rules and screwed up badly—again. And now a good man and his family would pay the price.

She shifted her hands into a gesture of supplica-

15

tion. "By all that's holy, I swear to protect everything the colonel loves to the best of my ability."

If he knew what she'd done, the colonel might have refused Faith's assistance. But with the future she'd just given Jonathan Ramsey, he'd need all the help he could get.

Chapter One

Drew Gallagher shifted on the cold stone bench, stretching his long legs into a more comfortable position. After five hours on stakeout, he felt about as comfortable as the men who had worn the suits of armor on display in front of him must have.

He'd already studied them in detail. He'd memorized every hinge, every clamp, every bit of protective shielding on those figures hours ago. Just as he'd analyzed and catalogued every visitor, volunteer, and employee who strolled along the black marble halls of the Nelson Art Gallery in Kansas City, Missouri.

He sighed. This sorry case he was working on didn't fall into his usual area of expertise. Anybody could do a simple stakeout. He preferred the chal lenge of going undercover, assuming a new identity, becoming whomever he needed to be. At that, he was an expert. The charge of danger electrified him, gave him a focus, made him feel alive.

Lying in wait for a suspect who might not even show up was a tedious assignment by comparison. It gave him too much time to think, too much time to ask questions. And too much time to realize how few answers he had.

The D.A.'s office must be falling behind to hire a freelancer like himself. And since his own private investigation business had slowed during the post-holiday season, he'd taken them up on their offer. He didn't need the money. He needed the favor in his portfolio. He'd made a couple of questionable moves on his last case, and a little brown-nosing with the county courts might ease their scrutiny of his work.

Otherwise he wouldn't be here. All Drew had to do was wait for Stan Begosian to show his face, then record the man's activities for the alleged child pornography case they were putting together against him.

"Here we have examples of medieval suits of armor." The tour guide's voice broke into his thoughts, the over-rehearsed monologue a slight distraction in his continuing surveillance of the room. It was the third group of students to come through in the last hour. First- or second-graders, judging by the size of them. About the same age as Begosian's usual victims.

"Are these ch-children's sizes?" A dark-haired girl, front and center of the group, whispered the question.

"No." The guide laughed. "This armor was built

for full-grown men, the warriors of their time. The average size of humans has increased over the years."

"Are they from the eleven hundreds?" one boy asked.

"I believe so. You know, around the time of King Arthur."

The dark-haired girl tipped her head back. "The real K-King Arthur lived in the s-s-sixth cent-ch-ury. My Aunt Jasmine saw where he and G-G-Guinevere are buried in G-Glastonbury, England."

"Yes, of course."

Drew felt himself sitting up a little straighter, worrying for the little girl stuttering through her explanation. He silently applauded her for sticking to her guns in the face of the guide's sugary condescension. She might have stumbled over some of the big words, but she knew her stuff. Smart kid.

"Kerry." A woman's voice, soft and throaty, sounded beside him, and a figure in a navy blue suit walked past to join the students. "You can ask more questions later. We need to move along before the next class comes through."

"Oh-kay, Mom."

"Thank you, Mrs. Ramsey." Drew hunkered back down on his bench, watching the cool way Mrs. Ramsey ignored the tour guide's fawning. Drew listened as she talked to her daughter, and he found himself drawn to her voice. It was seductive. Not that it was lewdly overdone like a woman making a come-on. She still sounded like a mother, all right. He just liked the sound of it, a lot.

The woman joined three other parents to herd the thirty or so students through the doors at the opposite end of the room. Drew enjoyed the view.

Now, she was something that could truly distract him. He adjusted his glasses, peering through the gold-wire rims to get the best view possible. The woman had *legs*.

Great legs that ran all the way up to her tight little bottom. A picture made even more appealing by the fact she tried to camouflage her sleek curves beneath the sensible cut of a navy pinstripe business suit.

Everything about her spoke of sensibility. She was taller than most women, almost his height, in fact, though she wore low-heeled pumps to try to play it down. Dark, rich waves of hair that must feel like soft silk to the touch were pulled back by a clip at her nape.

She had money. He could tell by the expensive leather purse she carried. But she didn't advertise it in any other way. No artful fingernails. No fancy jewelry. Just a plain gold wedding band with a diamond solitaire on her left hand.

Moving nearer, Drew leaned back against a stone pillar and watched unobtrusively until she vanished into the next room. She was nice. Very nice. But not his type. Definitely not his type. The whole air of the woman, in addition to the Grace Kelly figure, said wholesome suburbia. Class. Culture. Respectability.

Pure trouble for a guy like him. Not that he didn't enjoy playing out of his league every once in a while. There was a perverse satisfaction in knocking one of those class-acts out of her Ferragamos. He felt occasionally obligated to wake them up to reality, proving that he wasn't so far beneath them on the social register as they might think. Or as close to the seedy world of the streets as he might feel.

But he drew the line at married women.

Look, but don't touch.

The sign near the room's entrance mocked him. "As if you need the reminder, Gallagher."

Drew sighed and rolled his neck to loosen the muscles cramping there. He'd enjoyed the show while it lasted. Mother Pinstripe would never know how closely he'd scrutinized her. It was time to get back to work.

"That place on his boot is shiny because all the boys and girls rub it for good luck."

Drew turned at the high-pitched tenor of a man's voice. He'd slipped. A man in a brown tweed overcoat with its collar turned up to his ears had moved into the room without being spotted. The man's face remained hidden, but Drew's hackles shot up, and a time-tested sixth sense that alerted him to danger pushed him to his feet.

Kerry. The name stuck in his head as something familiar. Mother Pinstripe had used it. Kerry, the intelligent little girl with the stutter, had slipped away from her class to study the armor more closely. Mr. Tweed Coat sauntered in her direction, speaking calmly, knowledgeably.

"Upstairs, the museum has tapestries that were made in the Middle Ages. One of them portrays the legend of Arthur and the Round Table. Would you like to see them?"

Though she sidled a few steps away, Drew crept up close enough to see Kerry turn her big blue eyes on the man. "My Mom says I shouldn't t-talk to s-strangers."

21

Smart kid. Drew relaxed a fraction and pretended an interest in a fourteenth-century mace on display. Mr. Tweed opened the front of the coat and flashed some sort of name badge. "I work here. I'm just coming back from my lunch break. Your class is headed upstairs right now. I can show you a shortcut so you can meet them up there."

Drew's hands itched with the urge to grab the man by the scruff of the neck and toss him out into a snowbank. "Don't buy it, kid," he whispered under his breath.

"You don't want to get in trouble with your mom, do you? For wandering off?"

Drew rammed his fists deep into the pockets of his black suede jacket. He patted the reassuring bulk of his Glock 9mm, holstered at his waist.

The girl looked up again, past the man, at the ornate headpiece of the armor in front of her. "Are you sure?" she said to the armor. "Mom won't like it."

She spoke so clearly that even Drew turned to look.

The man in tweed hesitated an instant and turned to check the room for whom the girl addressed, giving Drew a good look at his scuzzy face. Begosian. The man's confused frown changed into a smile before he looked at Kerry again. "I'm sure."

She lowered her gaze to Begosian. "All r-right."

Drew clamped down on his scream of frustration. Dumb kid. Begosian took her hand and led her to the same exit the class had used, but once out, he turned in the opposite direction. Moving at the casual pace of any other museum guest, Drew followed.

* * *

"Kerry?" Of all the dark heads scattered throughout the miniatures room, none belonged to her daughter. Emma choked down the swell of panic. A second survey of the room confirmed her worry. No Kerry.

Emma quickly retraced her steps toward the main concourse. Her daughter had led the way in, while she'd brought up the rear. But then she'd gotten to talking with Mrs. Simmons about arrangements for the class's Valentine's Day party, and she'd lost track of her daughter.

Calm in a crisis. Emma Ramsey had earned that reputation running the administrative side of LadyTech, a software communications corporation she owned with her two closest friends.

She'd be damned if she'd lose her composure now just because her little girl had wandered off. Kerry was bright. Curious. And Emma worried about her only child way too much. She trusted the girl to be sensible. To stay safe.

It was all the other bozos and maniacs in the world she didn't trust.

The armor room had several patrons milling about inside. But it was empty of the one person who counted.

And that man.

She'd felt his presence when she'd entered the hall earlier, felt the cool weight of his eyes on her.

Blond, she remembered. Longish hair, with a lock that fell beside his temple. Glasses. An artist, perhaps. No? Too much danger, too much mystery. Despite his golden good looks, some darkness hung around him like a cloak.

A chill raced along her spine, knowing he'd

watched her. A chill matched only by the heart-numbing fear of knowing he'd now disappeared, along with her daughter.

She alerted the security guard at the entrance, giving him a succinct description of Kerry. While he radioed his staff, Emma walked back to the main concourse in Kirkwood Hall, turned in a slow 360-degree arc, then waited for some instinct to tell her where to look.

She imagined a tap on her shoulder, nudging her feet into motion. She started walking, searching for either the blond man or her daughter. The museum had two large wings, three floors and a basement. A lot of square feet for a little girl to get lost in—or for a dangerous man to lurk in.

The sculpture garden would be closed because of the snow, so she didn't bother to look there. Something urged her up the stairs to the west.

Fear hastened her steps. Her world had shattered five years ago when her husband, Jonathan, disappeared. Lost on a mission, she'd been told. MIA. The authorities had given her no body to bury. No culprit to blame. He was just gone.

She'd rebuilt her life and heart around her only tangible link to Jonathan—their daughter.

She couldn't survive losing Kerry, too.

"Th-th-this isn't the way to the t-tapest-try room."

Drew hurried down the deserted marble hallway, following the little girl's halting voice. He coached her beneath his breath. "That's it, kid. Tell him off. Make a scene."

It was his duty to save the girl. Despite the D.A.'s instructions to simply observe, he intended to take Begosian downtown. But if Drew showed himself too soon, the dirtbag would bolt—maybe escape. And the knowledge that he'd be free to molest some other child, especially if they were all as gullible as this one, burned in every chivalric bone in Drew's body.

Where were the damned security guards who swarmed all over the first floor? He unzipped his jacket and unfastened the catch on his holster before stepping into the Modern Art wing. Large paintings of stripes and geometric figures and cans of soup lined the walls, and unfortunately placed partitions blocked his view through the center of the room.

"Are y-you real?"

The girl had stopped in front of a strikingly life-like figure of a patron staring at one of the murals. Drew had read of this famous sculpture, and how startled visitors often apologized for getting in its way before realizing it was one of the artworks on display.

Drew rounded a partition and walked straight over to the girl. Begosian jumped in his shoes, alarmed as if Drew himself was a statue come to life.

"Put your hands where I can see 'em, Stan." He pulled out his wallet and flashed his ID at the little girl without taking his eyes off his prey. "I'm here to help you. Get over here behind me."

Instead of obeying, the little girl stopped beside Drew and reached for his hand. Startled by the unexpected touch, he glanced down. The brief distraction was enough to send her stocky abductor running toward the far exit. Drew's instinct to pursue jolted through his legs, but the girl's trusting grip around his fingers anchored him in place.

He bent his knees and hunched down to the girl's level. "You need to find a security guard," he said softly. "Tell him you're lost and you have to find your mother. He can call her name over the intercom."

Drew straightened, took a step. But Kerry tugged at his hand. He glanced over his shoulder, saw Begosian near the archway. He turned back.

"Are you a g-good guy?" The little girl batted her eyelashes, her curious blue eyes watching him.

He shifted impatiently on his feet. "I try to be, kid."

"Faith t-told me I'd meet a g-good guy today."

Drew squatted down, took the girl gently by the shoulders, and fought to comprehend how a child's mind worked. "Is Faith your mom?"

Her sable curls bobbed around her cheeks as she shook her head. "She's my friend. Mom can't t-talk to her because she d-doesn't b-believe she's real."

Drew frowned and looked at the exit. Begosian had vanished. Recalling the presence of his pint-sized companion, Drew swallowed his curse. An invisible friend? What the hell would his psychologist tell him about such childish fantasies? Well, this girl had been kidnapped and rescued—both by strangers. That should be enough stress to trigger a busload of imaginary friends. Drew lifted his glasses and rubbed the bridge of his nose. He was way out of his league with children.

"Are you oh-kay, m-mister?"

Drew nodded. He even dredged up a rusty smile for the girl. "Let's go find your mom."

"Oh-kay."

"Let go of her!" A Louis Vuitton purse loaded

with bricks slammed into Drew's arm, knocking him off balance.

"You stay away from her!"

Falling to one knee, he felt the girl snatched from his grasp. He reached for his gun, but the brick bag struck him in the face, sending his glasses flying.

"Help! Security!"

Fortunately, his astigmatism didn't prevent him from seeing the bag hurtling his way for a third time. He deflected it with his arm, twisted the straps around his wrist, and yanked the offending weapon toward him.

Ms. Navy Blue Pinstripe came with it. They tumbled backward, crashing onto the marble floor, her long legs twisting with his. There was no time to enjoy the fantasy that sprang to mind. In a split second she shifted, and Drew guessed the direction her knee was headed.

"Dammit, lady, I'm on your side!"

He rolled over, pinning her to the floor beneath him. She struggled valiantly, a sinuous, writhing, dangerous opponent whom he dared not release if he intended to be physically able to chase down Begosian.

"Mom! He's the g-good guy I told y-you about. He s-saved me from the bad man! He's a policeman."

The girl's words stilled her mother's struggles. With wary precision, Drew shifted the lower half of his body off hers and knelt beside the woman. He helped her to a sitting position, but she quickly jerked from his grasp, adjusting her clothes as she scooted away from him.

"Show me your badge." Her throaty voice contained more venom than sex appeal at the moment, and Drew judiciously obliged.

"I'm not a cop. I'm a private investigator working for the district attorney's office," he explained. He pulled his wallet from his pocket and opened it so she could match the picture on his I.D. to his face.

All at once, Drew's world stood still. Face to face, up close, he looked into eyes of deep smoky blue. She had porcelain skin dusted with freckles, high cheekbones, and a regally straight nose. Her perfect oval face, framed by dark brown hair, looked familiar. *Felt* familiar.

"Have we met before?" He heard his own voice as little more than a rasp in his throat.

Her eyes narrowed. She studied his photo, then looked at him. She scanned him from head to knee, from the crown of his shaggy blond hair to the faded threads where his jeans had worn thin.

Then her gaze met his, guarded and dismissive. "I don't think so, Mr. Gallagher."

She curled her legs beneath her. Drew stood and extended his hand to help her up. Once on her feet, she pulled away as if his touch might transfer some horrible disease. She circled her arm around her daughter, the ewe drawing her lamb into the fold. "Thank you for helping Kerry."

Drew choked back his annoyance. As verbally polite as leggy Ms. Priss might be, she'd relegated him to the status of public servant. Though what had he wanted, really, an invitation to dinner? "Sure. You'd better have a talk with her about strangers, though."

The woman released the girl and squatted in

front of her. "How many times have we talked about trusting people you don't know?"

Kerry shrugged. "Faith said it was oh-kay."

Her mother bristled. Her deep, controlling breath made Drew wonder what she might have said if he wasn't standing there. "Sweetie, you shouldn't listen to Faith if she tells you things you know are wrong. Use your common sense."

"Faith s-said she'd protect me." The girl grew agitated in her defense, and her struggling speech became almost incoherent.

"Kerry! She's not real. Angels don't . . ." The rest of the reprimand disappeared behind a cool mask of control that slipped onto her face like it had been there all along.

She stood and faced Drew, a woman of backbone and grit. With a quivering chin. That acknowledgment of her emotion was fleeting, and quickly hidden with an arrogant thrust of her jaw. "Sometimes my daughter's imagination gets the better of her."

Drew wondered why she fought the display of weakness. Most moms would be sobbing with relief or cussing up a storm by now. But not this one. Maybe her detachment had nothing to do with him, after all. Maybe she'd keep all her feelings locked up no matter whom she was with, whether it was a smooth talker in a three-piece suit or a cynical bum like himself.

"No problem. Just glad I was here."

The woman's expression softened a bit. "I'm Emma Ramsey. Do you need me to file a report?" Even in this clipped, businesslike demeanor, her voice had a sexy undertone.

He fought the nagging feeling of recognition. Where would a no-name like himself run into a class act like her? Only in his dreams. He shook off his confusion. "I'll take care of it. I'd better see if he's still on the premises."

Emma nodded. "Thanks again."

"You'll need these t-to c-catch the bad guy." Drew looked down and found Kerry offering up his glasses.

"Thanks." Acting on an unusual impulse, Drew reached out and cupped the girl's cheek. Her childishly soft skin reminded him of home. At least, it reminded him of the kind of place he wished he could call home. The gentle touch earned him a shy smile that warmed him despite her mother's frosty dismissal. "You listen to your mom, you hear?"

"Oh-kay."

Drew put on his glasses and gave a mock salute to Mrs. Ramsey. She clutched her daughter in front of her protectively. He turned and walked toward the exit where Begosian had disappeared. This do-gooder stuff wasn't exactly his thing. The reluctant gratitude shining in that mother's eyes and the wide-eyed trust placed in him by that little girl were undeserved. And unwanted.

He came out at the top of a back stairwell. Begosian was a cockroach kind of criminal. He'd keep to the dark, try to blend in unnoticed if people were around. Drew pulled out his gun and slipped down the stairs, noiselessly closing in on his prey. The cockroach might not have escaped yet. He had probably moved slowly, not wanting to draw attention to himself. Drew had no intention—

"Freeze! Drop your weapon!"

A door swung open and a security team swarmed in. Surrounded, Drew slowly lowered his gun to the floor, keeping his free hand raised in surrender. "Easy, guys, I'm with the D.A.'s office. I have a permit."

One of the guards thumped him on the back, forcing him to the floor. "Face down and stay put!"

The clock ticked away as Drew seethed with indignant frustration. Several guards frisked him. One found his wallet and identified him.

But Drew's opportunity had passed. The guards returning his gun and I.D., dusting off his jacket, and apologizing repeatedly did little to reverse Drew's darkening mood. Begosian was long gone, and by now the trail would be cold. He'd botched what should have been a textbook assignment for a seasoned pro like himself.

Nope. This was definitely not a good day. Sweet little girls and sensible mothers weren't just out of his league. They were bad luck, pure and simple. They'd never mix with a man like Drew Gallagher.

Emma waited for the school bus to pull away before hurrying across the parking lot to her customized Chevy Astro van. After talking to the police, it had taken a considerable degree of willpower to let Kerry get on the bus with her classmates. What she really wanted to do was bundle the girl up in her arms, take her home, lock the doors, and stand watch over her.

But Kerry had begged to finish the day with her friends, and Mrs. Arnold—her teacher—had assured Emma that maintaining a normal routine would be beneficial to her wayward daughter. So Emma had waved good-bye and buried her fears deep inside.

She concentrated on reviewing the rules of self-defense that Jonathan had taught her, and she made a mental note to reinforce those same precautions with Kerry. She had her keys ready as she approached her van, and casually scanned the area, alert to spots that offered hiding places for the kind of man who would steal a child from her mother. Or detain a woman with bad come-on lines.

Have we met before? She allowed herself one, short laugh. She'd heard all the lines—good and bad—and had turned them all down. She was a married woman, after all. Though her heart might be gathering dust on a shelf, it still belonged to her husband.

A voice inside her said he was still alive somewhere, struggling against captors or injury to find his way home. The men Jonathan Ramsey had served with continued to pursue any leads on his whereabouts. She'd traced him through military channels. Foreign embassies. Police. Private investigators.

But in five years, she'd found nothing. Nothing but heartache and loneliness and a dying faith that he would one day return to her.

Emma glanced beneath the frame of the neighboring car and her van before stepping between the vehicles. She fought off a feeling of guilt. Somehow, that Gallagher man had diverted her attention long enough for her to lose track of Kerry. He was lanky and lean. So intense, so unpredictable. With those incredible eyes. Behind his glasses, Mr. Gallagher's eyes reminded her of rough-cut emeralds—deep green, without a tinge of blue or gray.

She'd been wary of him. Yet he'd helped Kerry, and for that she was grateful. But she couldn't shake the way his eyes had stared at her. Hungry. Pleading. He'd made a silent request of her, but she hadn't understood the question. Maybe they *had* met before. But she'd have remembered a man like him—so polished beneath his coarse veneer, with fluid strength and precise movements. He was coiled, cautious.

She had barely unlocked the van door when it was yanked from her fingers. "Get in!"

A leather-gloved hand pushed her inside.

"Move over."

Emma obeyed the breathy commands. Shock clouded her ability to think clearly, but she reacted on instinct. She jumped to the other side of the vehicle, and her fingers worked like a broken toy, struggling to open the passenger door handle.

"Don't."

The man's fingers clamped on to her elbow and twisted it behind her back. He leaned over her, pinning her with his heavier weight. Flight would not be possible. Out of breath, the man's heavy panting fogged up the windows, leaving Emma to wonder if anyone could see her plight. She schooled her panic.

"Who are you?" Her own breath caught on a strangled whisper. "What do you want?"

"My name doesn't matter." She craned her neck to study his face. She saw sweat beading on his forehead, despite the chill of the day, and his wild gaze darted from the back of the van to the windshield, looking for something neither of them could see. She flinched when his gaze landed on her. "I didn't intend to hurt your girl."

"*You* took her?" Fury swelled in her, overriding her fear. Emma jerked against his grip, but the movement only angered him.

"You listen to me!" He yanked her arm in its socket, forcing her down onto her knees in the space between the two front seats. Emma yelped at the pain shooting through her shoulder, but chose not to struggle. She gritted her teeth and listened to his coldblooded offer.

"I have a computer disk with proof your husband is still alive. For twenty-five thousand bucks I'll deliver it to you."

"My God. You were going to give that message to my daughter?"

She didn't know whether to scream or cry. To deliberately involve Kerry in this cruel scheme as bait or incentive to ensure her cooperation sickened her. But Jonathan? Could this bastard really know something about her husband? The possibility beckoned her. But her husband would never want her to be a part of something like this. He'd made a career risking his life to save the world from conscienceless predators like this lowlife.

"Where is he?" She heard herself ask the question, five years of grief and despair overwhelming the morals of a lifetime.

His hot breath lapped against her ear as he bent closer. "For another twenty-five, I'll tell you. Deal?"

The driver-side door wrenched open.

"Having car trouble, Mrs. Ramsey?"

The deadly quiet voice startled her assailant. His grip slackened, and a blast of cold air swept over her. Pulling her arm down and cradling it against her stomach, she could turn just enough to see a silver handgun pointed right at the man's temple.

She looked beyond his dazed expression to see the predatory gleam stamped on the taut features of Drew Gallagher's angry face. "Hands up, Begosian."

The eyes of her assailant dulled as he slowly turned and placed both hands on the steering wheel. With his gun still resting against her attacker's scalp, Gallagher spoke. "Let me help you out."

Drew dragged the man from her van, and Emma scrambled to her feet and climbed out after them. He hauled the man by the lapels of his brown tweed coat into the open parking lot and shoved him onto his knees upon the asphalt.

"Face down," he ordered, following the man down to frisk him for weapons and handcuff him. Then, with his knee squared in the middle of the guy's back, Drew pulled a cell phone from his jacket and punched in a number.

Emma huddled inside her coat, chilled by the cool efficiency of Drew Gallagher's actions as much as by the damp January wind. The shiver drew his attention, and he finally looked at her. His strange eyes narrowed. "You hurt?"

"Nothing serious." She dropped her gaze to the dirty slush that stained the hem of her coat where she'd been forced to kneel on the floor of the van. Had she been rescued a moment too soon? Was the chance to find Jonathan about to be bundled

35

off to the police station? "I thought you weren't a cop."

"I'm not." His short answer surprised her. "I'm just doing a favor for the D.A.'s office."

Before she could redirect her question, his party answered and he stepped away to conduct his phone conversation in hushed, efficient tones. Emma plunged her hands into her pockets and shifted her curiosity to the man lying handcuffed on the pavement. She had to raise her voice to be heard over his cursing and muttering about his rights.

"Do you really know my husband?" she asked.

"I'm not saying nothing now! You're screwed. He's screwed. Hell, I'm—" He spat the words at her, and in an instant she found Drew Gallagher's strong back positioned between them, protecting her from her assailant's spew of foul language. She could see neither Drew's face nor the man's, but suddenly the man fell silent.

"Anything else you want to say?" challenged Drew. His lanky height topped Emma's by only a few inches, yet an indefinable energy radiated from his broad shoulders, making him seem bigger and brawnier. He shielded her, made her feel feminine. He made her feel safe.

"What's this guy's interest in your family?" asked Drew, taking her elbow and guiding her several feet away, but not so far that he couldn't keep watch over the man in handcuffs.

Her personal life was none of his business, but, unnerved by the unexpected warmth that radiated from deep inside her at the protective gesture, Emma answered. "He says he has a computer disk that can help me locate my husband."

"Your husband? How long has he been missing? Have you reported it to the police?" He slipped his hands into the pockets of his leather jacket.

"He's been gone five years." Her tone silenced a chain of professional questions he no doubt wanted to ask. The same questions she'd answered more times than she could count. "And there's nothing the police can do to help me."

"Five years?" He said the words and an odd transformation took place. The intensity in his cat-like eyes wavered, and suddenly Drew Gallagher was miles away from her.

Realizing the hopelessness of her situation, she tried to draw him back, to show him the validity of her concern. "How can I know if he's telling the truth? If he has that disk hidden somewhere, I may never get a chance to see it."

Suddenly back, he drilled her with a look that made her feel silly. "That's Stan Begosian. He's wanted in an investigation for creating and distributing child pornography. You want me to release him before the cops get here so he can give you a disk he may or may not have? For all we know, it's a scam. That disk—if it does exist—might contain nothing more than pictures of children he's taken. It could have been a picture of your little girl."

"That's enough!"

"I'm not trying to be cruel, but whatever he claims . . . don't believe it."

Emma bristled at his easy dismissal of her last shred of hope. "He knows who I am. That has to mean something."

"It means he's a conniving lowlife." Drew

Julie Miller

splayed his fingers across his hips and stepped closer. "Look, the cops will search his place. Ask them to look for the disk."

Emma tipped her chin to look him in the eye. "Apparently your goal is simply to get your man, regardless of the cost his actions or yours have on anyone else."

He pressed his mouth into a grim, flat line. Emma clenched her toes inside her pumps to keep from backing away from the disquieting intensity of his eyes. "I rescued your daughter today from that creep. I just saved your butt. And now *I'm* the bad guy?"

Two black-and-white units pulled up, giving Emma an opportunity to sneak a breath she wasn't aware she'd been holding. With their hands on their holstered guns, the officers hurried out and surrounded Begosian. Drew turned to acknowledge them, then raked his fingers through his hair, shaking loose his mane of wheat-gold waves. His shoulders rose and fell in a deep breath before he turned back to her.

"This has been more fun than I can stand, but we have to stop meeting like this."

Her heart thumped in a funny rhythm at the veiled disapproval in his voice. Maybe she hadn't properly thanked him. But, savior or not, he'd cost her a lead in finding Jonathan.

More than that, she couldn't be around a man whose simple eye contact made her pulse pound in her veins. The instantaneous awareness felt too much like betraying her husband.

"No, Mr. Gallagher. We have to stop meeting, period."

Chapter Two

Drew inhaled deeply, the sharp winter air freezing the salty taste of sweat at the corner of his mouth. He raised his shoulders, pushing his right palm slowly forward. Then, stepping out, he thrust his left hand in the same precise, controlled manner.

Sleep had eluded him yet again. Or rather, the nightmares had failed to elude him.

His spare loft-style condo, in a reclaimed building near downtown Kansas City, suited his early morning kata. A second-degree blackbelt in Tae Kwon Do, he routinely worked through the inexplicable images that haunted his sleep by performing the ritual exercise of form known as kata.

Even in winter, he stripped to the waist, opened the windows, and exorcised his demons through the meditative routine. Turn. Kick. Punch. Breathe.

The stifling air of the jungle sucked the breath from his lungs. And still he ran.

Drew lunged to the side, stretching his arms like graceful wings. He narrowed his eyes, pushing the scene from his mind with the same controlled force.

The stamp of booted feet hounded his steps. Palm fronds with stalks as thick as his forearms snapped into place behind him. While he chased his quarry, he, too, was being pursued. He was both men.

He cocked his elbow and jabbed in slow motion. He kicked to the side and focused on his peaceful center.

"Stand fast or I'll shoot!"

"No, you won't. You'll never take me alive." The grenade pin sailed into the endless gulf of jungle foliage. *"We'll both die."*

The nightmare never varied. The one memory branded into his subconscious mocked him with his inability to understand it. He was at once both killer and victim.

Awake, Drew forced the hellish images back into the abyss of his past. The low temperature in the loft chilled his skin. He breathed deeply through his nose and released it slowly through his mouth, creating a cloud of frosty air.

Nearing the end of his kata, he concentrated on the controlled perfection of his movements.

Listen.

He ignored the command just as he ignored the other meaningless images in his mind.

"May I help you?"

Drew stumbled, his form slipping for an instant. The ever-present chaos of his jumbled memories had never included a woman's voice. Not that voice. Not her voice.

Yet it was there, clear as the brisk winter air surrounding him.

"Sir, may I help you?"

Drew stopped in mid stride, cursed himself, then quickly apologized. He bowed to the sunrise, toward the honor of his sensei. He grabbed a towel and wiped his face, then tossed it around his shoulders to absorb the dampness there. His morning routine hadn't erased the odd snippets of dreams from his mind. He couldn't tell if he was insane or clairvoyant. Were the disturbing images from his past or future?

Funny how amnesia could make a man question everything—even his gifts. He either had one hell of a memory trying to break through, or one hell of a psychic ability that he had forgotten.

The irony of his situation failed to make him laugh.

He crossed to the kitchen and poured himself a mug of hot coffee. He spread strawberry jam on wheat toast and sat down to read the next chapter in his dog-eared copy of the Andrew Gallagher detective novel he'd picked up at a flea market. The series of cheap pulp fiction books provided easy reads. His lone bookshelf overflowed with the paperbacks he'd collected, not because they had any antique value, but because they reminded him of where he'd come from and whom he had chosen to be.

He'd spent a lot of months healing in a Central American hospital. He knew that. Books printed in English had been hard to come by, but a sympathetic nurse had brought him some novels from her brother who'd gone to school in the States. With nothing in his head to miss or look forward to, he'd filled the time reading every last Gallagher novel. The cagey fictional detective used too much hardware to solve his cases for Drew's taste, but he always landed more on the side of good than evil by the story's end. With no other inspiration to guide him, Drew had adopted the hero's name and profession, and dedicated his life to solving the biggest mystery of all.

Himself.

"Sir, may I help you?"

The voice, along with smoky blue eyes, drifted into his thoughts and made it impossible to concentrate on the story he was reading. Instead of fighting the image, Drew gave up. If work was all he had, then he'd better get to it. He went to the table beside his bed, turned on the lamp, and picked up his notebook.

Thumbing through his daily notes, he found the address he had looked up yesterday. Emma Ramsey, Executive Director, LadyTech. Mrs. Pinstripe, with the brick-loaded purse, and legs that belonged on a Rockette, ran a corporation.

How the hell had she gotten into his head? She'd said that they'd never met. Was her appearance in his mind a real memory, or an image projected there by errant hormones?

No. Definitely real. She hadn't spoken those words to him at the museum. Yet he recognized them.

He remembered them.

Drew expelled his breath with a sigh, and felt the sting of the December air on his skin. He closed the windows, shed his sweats, and stepped into a hot shower. But the knowledge that he was on the edge of an important recollection lingered, chilling him.

Five years with nothing but a nightmare remaining from his former life. Until now. Until her.

Why?

He stuck his head under the full blast of the water and let the wet heat beat down on his scalp. Outside, the sun breaking the horizon teased him with the promise of hope for a new day. But until he pieced together the shattered remnants of his past, he had no hopes, no future. How many special sunrises had he forgotten? How many promises had he failed to keep?

Emma Ramsey seemed to be a key to unlocking at least one of those hidden answers. Or his subconscious seemed to think so. But after her icy dismissal yesterday, he'd need some kind of bargaining chip to prompt her to talk.

The solution that came to him seemed too easy. Drew turned off the water, grinning. He ran his fingers through his hair, squeezing the excess water from the shoulder-length strands and wringing the lingering doubts from his mind.

With enough purpose to finally begin his day, he wrapped a towel around his waist and shaved with an electric razor. Maybe he'd done enough good deeds yesterday to make up for his one little misdeed.

Once he had dressed and donned his holster, he went to the coatrack and reached into the pocket of his padded leather jacket. He pulled out the three-and-one-half-inch computer disk that he'd palmed from Begosian in the parking lot yesterday.

At the time, he thought it might be evidence for

the D.A.'s case, and had planned to give it to the boys in blue. Then, he'd been tempted to hand it over to Mrs. Ramsey; she'd sounded so desperate for any clue about her husband. The possibility of any lead, no matter how unlikely, slipping through her fingers had made a chink in that ladylike armor of hers and revealed a soft, vulnerable woman.

An alien impulse to shield her from that kind of hurt had spurred Drew to protect her, to try to talk some sense into her. He'd wanted to hold her, tell her she didn't have to always be so strong. But then she'd regained that icy superiority and told him in no uncertain terms that she didn't appreciate his brand of help. He patted the disk and enjoyed the empty victory of denying her what she wanted.

The fictional Drew Gallagher wasn't above using a bit of blackmail to find the answers he wanted, and neither was he. He pocketed the disk and shrugged into his jacket.

He knew Emma Ramsey. From somewhere in a murky past he couldn't remember. Maybe, with this bit of leverage to persuade her, she could figure out where she'd asked him so politely for help. It couldn't hurt to try to break through that snobbish reserve of hers and force some cooperation from the woman.

For a man with nothing to lose, it couldn't hurt at all.

Emma inhaled for five steps, exhaled for five steps. Never once losing her rhythm, she power-walked the perimeter of the LadyTech warehouse. Arms pumping, she clutched a five-pound weight in each hand, squeezing out her frustration on the spongy foam-rubber handles.

Criminy! She should be concentrating on the disaster that had nearly taken Kerry from her forever. Or lining up the questions she wanted to ask Kerry's counselor about Faith, her daughter's imaginary friend who convinced her to take foolish chances. At the very least, she should be reviewing her encounter with the man who had said he could help her find Jonathan, and consulting LadyTech's legal staff to find out more about Stan Begosian and his background.

She shouldn't be obsessing over dangerous-looking private eyes who thought they knew her.

To Mr. Gallagher's benefit, instead of working on the Consolidated Technologies buyout, Emma had frittered away most of her morning brainstorming ideas on where they might have met. It certainly couldn't have been at a P.T.A. meeting. And he didn't appear to have the means or even the interest in being a client of LadyTech. Her company worked at the wholesale level worldwide, supplying businesses with communications technology and products for retail.

Maybe he was somehow connected to her husband. But if Gallagher had served with Jonathan, he'd lost the swagger and clean-cut looks that marked a soldier, even in civilian clothes.

That stuck her with only one unsettling option. Upon his resignation at age thirty-five, Jonathan had remained with Marine Corps Intelligence as a consultant. Though he revealed little about the purpose and destination of his missions, Emma knew he'd worked with some very dangerous, very powerful people. Criminals. Terrorists. Spies. Subversives.

Any one of which fit Mr. Gallagher's looks and demeanor a whole lot better than a soldier.

So who was the good guy in all of this? The nervous man who'd forced Emma into her van, claiming he could help find her husband? Or the man with the transfixing eyes and gallant ways who had cost her a chance to discover the truth?

"Oooh!" She articulated her frustration on one five-step breath. She wished she could just walk away from yesterday and return to her dull, predictable routine. She'd made a good life for herself and Kerry, living like a loyal wife instead of a widow, waiting for Jonathan to return one day.

But last night Andrew Gallagher had filled her dreams. Today, he nagged her conscience, forced her into taking two extra laps of after-lunch walking just to purge his image from her brain so she could get some work done.

Why were these sensations coming to life again within her? She shouldn't be worrying about lion-haired mystery men whose intense gazes stripped her to her very soul, and whose callused handshake left her quaking with some unnamed and raw physical attraction. Andrew Gallagher had been aggressively, unapologetically male, with none of the gentle edges she had loved in Jonathan.

That was what disturbed her the most, she realized. That a man so unlike her husband should be the first to again stir to life her own feminine awareness. An awareness of physical and emotional needs that had fallen dormant over the years.

One, two, three, four, five. Inhale. Emma concentrated on her stride. She didn't want to feel. She didn't want to care about another man again. Not now. Not ever.

"Mrs. Ramsey?"

She screamed and whirled, fists poised to protect herself.

"Whoa!" With his palms raised in surrender, Andrew Gallagher stepped out from between the stacks of crates behind her.

"Damn you." The thumping in her chest verified that her heart had indeed started beating again.

His chiseled stone face softened with the hint of a smile. He'd clearly caught her off guard, and seemed to be enjoying the advantage. "Let me guess. You carry those weights in your purse, don't you?"

Emma frowned. "I carry everything in my purse."

Then she got the joke. Of course. She'd clobbered him yesterday. Relaxing her defensive posture, she lowered the weights. And raised her guard. "I can have Security here in sixty seconds."

That took the grin off his face. The unforgiving stamp of pride that replaced it made Emma wish she hadn't sounded so harsh. He stepped toward her, backing her against a crate. He reached out, resting his hand on the wooden frame beside her head.

He never touched her, but he trapped her just the same—more effectively than the superior strength Begosian had used against her. His arm blocked her on one side, his tall, lean body on another. He left her an escape. She could simply

47

step to the left and be free of his consuming presence and the heady leather-and-male scent of him.

"It'll take longer than that. They're responding to a silent alarm in one of your outbuildings."

"But the computer codes . . ."

". . . were impossible to override."

Emma's partner, BJ, programmed computers more powerful than the national defense system. LadyTech's security chief—and BJ's husband—Brodie Maxwell, through unique skills of his own had made it his business to protect people for a long time. It should be harder to break into the LadyTech warehouse than into the White House.

"Then how . . . ?"

"I have my ways." It was a statement of fact, not a threat. His apparent cunning only reinforced her suspicions of him. There must be more criminal than savior in this man.

The chilling surety of his actions sparked Emma's self-preservation instincts. She straightened to her full height and stood her ground. Whatever trickiness he'd used to misdirect the security guards wouldn't work on her.

"What do you want?"

"Is there someplace private we can talk?"

"You could have made an appointment for that."

Laughter rumbled deep in his throat, a sexy, warm sound. He stepped back, shoved his hands into his pockets, and broke the spell that bound her. She hadn't intended for her sarcasm to be humorous, but when he relaxed, so did she. A fraction. Enough to continue the conversation without bolting.

He seemed every bit as dangerous today as he had yesterday. Leather jacket, black jeans, wheat-gold hair tumbling past the collar of his shirt. Even his professor's glasses fit him like a mask, an attempt to civilize the rangy lion hidden beneath.

But his laughter humanized him. "That wasn't the impression you gave me yesterday," he said.

Emma averted her eyes, shamed by the accuracy of his observation. She owed him something for rescuing Kerry. And the idea of trusting a man like Stan Begosian to lead her to Jonathan showed just how desperate she had become. Desperate and ungrateful. She prided herself on having more sense than that. Jonathan himself had always complimented her on her level-headedness. But since yesterday's field trip she'd done little more than react to her gut instincts.

She breathed deeply and summoned the Emma that Jonathan would want her to be. "Show me your license again."

She looked straight into his eyes while he pulled his billfold from a back pocket. His gaze never left hers. His expression never wavered. He placed the open wallet in her hands and watched her study each line of information on his I.D. He didn't protest when she flipped it over to read the personal data underneath.

Thirty-eight years old, she calculated. Six-three. Two years as a licensed private investigator. She closed the billfold, and he returned it to his pocket. "Okay, Andrew Gallagher, what is it you want?"

"An exchange of information. I brought you a peace offering from our friend Begosian." He unzipped his jacket and reached inside. "I borrowed a bit of evidence from Stan's coat you may be interested in."

"You stole evidence?" She sputtered in a flare of

indignation. "Unorthodox is one thing, but illegal is something else altogether. I'm grateful for what you did for Kerry yesterday, but you can't involve me in this."

She waved him aside and strode toward the main concourse, angry with herself for even having considered cooperating with him. If she walked fast enough and far enough . . .

"Take your nose out of the air and look."

His raspy voice, low and deep, stopped her in her tracks. A biting remark froze on her lips when she spun around and saw the black computer disk held between the first two fingers of his right hand.

"The disk!" Forgetting her precious scruples, she lurched forward to take the proffered gift. But he swept it behind his back, and her fingers instead brushed against the soft suede of his coat and the harder leather of the holster he wore underneath. The solid breadth of his chest stopped her forward momentum. Emma snatched her hand back and retreated as if she'd been burned.

He had her at his mercy, she could see that now. She'd never once had the upper hand.

"You're a cruel man," she accused, drawing on every bit of shattered heart and endless fear and incompleteness she lived with each day of her life. "You don't know what it's like to lose someone you care about, to have that part of your life ripped away from you. You don't know how desperate a person can become or you wouldn't tease me like this."

"I know what it's like to lose, Emma." His pupils shrank into tiny black dots in a sea of emerald ice. A chill shimmied down her spine at the absolute void in his voice and expression.

"What are you talking about?"

"Answer some questions for me and the disk is yours."

He'd deliberately avoided her question. "How do I know that isn't a fake?"

"How do I know you'll give me straight answers?"

The challenge lay between them like a gauntlet thrown down before a duel. He left her no choice but to pick it up. "We can go to my office."

He waved his hand to the side and dropped his chin in a mocking bow. "Lead the way."

Drew followed Emma into the tailored simplicity of her Colonial-style cherrywood office. Before offering him a seat, she hurried to the wet bar and poured herself a cup of coffee. "Would you like some?"

"Sure. Black, please."

He recognized a challenge when she presented him with a delicate china cup and saucer. She carried her own over to one of a matching pair of pale rose loveseats. He let her have the time and space she needed to gather her strength and collect her thoughts. He'd more than startled her in the warehouse. Breaking in had been no easy task, and he had no doubt that finding an unwelcome stranger on the premises came as a real shock.

He waited patiently, intrigued by her long-limbed grace. He pretended an interest in the first-grade works of art proudly displayed on one wall while he covertly watched her perch on the edge of the seat and slip out of her tennis shoes and cotton socks. He outright stared when she stepped into a

51

pair of high-heeled pumps and ran her hand up her calf to her knee, smoothing her hose.

He imagined his own hand following that path, exploring even higher. Her husband had to have been kidnapped or killed, he thought. No healthy male would leave a pair of legs like hers voluntarily.

Even as the thought hit him, his gaze settled on the brass-framed photograph sitting on the corner of her desk. The thumbprints that smudged the glass and metal indicated a much-handled, well-loved picture. He set down his coffee and picked up the photo.

"Is this your husband?" he asked, feeling a twinge of envy for the dark-haired man in Marine dress blues holding an infant girl in his arms while a younger Emma curled her arms around his waist and laid her head on his shoulder.

"Yes." Emma crossed the room in three long strides and took the picture from, him, setting it back on the desk with gentle reverence. The Emma before him now had the tiniest of crow's-feet crinkling beside her eyes. The woman in the picture had a smooth face, lined only with the dimples of laughter.

She must have suffered a great deal over her husband's disappearance. Drew felt like a heel for taking advantage of her loss, but he had something equally important at stake.

She'd said her husband had been missing for five years. Five years gone from her life. An incredible loss for a young wife and mother to bear. But five years was all he knew. Five years to claim as his own. And she might be the only person who could provide a clue to that missing prelude to his meager life.

Yes.

An echo of a voice whispered in his ear. He ignored the plea and buried it along with his reservations deep in his conscience. He went to the picture window on the west side of her office and looked out at the gray sky and snowy landscape. From three stories up, he could see over the parking lot past an orchard of leafless dogwood trees to a park area. "Quite a view from here," he said.

"LadyTech sits on two hundred acres of land, giving us room to expand." Emma followed him to the window "Jas—our marketing and PR director—is partial to open space. So we bought enough acreage to keep a good portion of it undeveloped as well."

Her white silk blouse and gray wool skirt reflected the same cool elegance of the room, but the tight clench of her jaw revealed what this show of patience and civility cost her. Drew decided that now was as good a time as any to press her for answers. She didn't look as if she wanted to get any friendlier.

"Have you always been on top, Mrs. Ramsey?"

"Excuse me?" A rosy blush dotted her cheeks, pushing that cool composure of hers right out the window.

"Sorry. I phrased that badly." Did she remember their tumble at the museum yesterday? He didn't think he'd ever forget that moment. His body had kicked into overdrive and responded to the imprint of long, soft female sprawled on top of him. A simmering heat licked through his veins now at just the memory of it. He'd been alone too long for his body to react so quickly to the mere thought of touching the woman beside him.

He crushed that notion by refocusing on his missing past. "You run a corporation here. Did you start off as a secretary?"

"Oh." She tucked a strand of sable hair behind her ear. She wore it down today, and he could see the thick waves fell past her shoulder blades. "No. LadyTech is BJ's brainchild. She and Jas and I were roommates in college. We banked our skills in design and marketing and management, got a loan, and created our own company. Jas had the idea to take it global eight years ago. We opened it to outside investors a few years back, and its been growing by leaps and bounds ever since."

The image of a younger Emma, seated behind an office desk and making an innocently seductive offer to help him, blipped into his mind. "Did you ever work as a secretary?"

"I've done my share of office work. I clerked through college at a local hospital. Became an office manager before I met my husband and moved away. What did you do before you became a private investigator?" She slipped in the question with a sly finesse he admired.

"Odd jobs," he answered honestly, allowing her that much satisfaction while maintaining the upper hand in this silent contest of wills. "Bummed around the country a bit. Felt at home her in K.C., so I decided to stay. What about you? Is this where you and your husband settled? Or did LadyTech bring you to town?"

Emma's cup rattled on its saucer when she set it

down. "Is this what you wanted to discuss? My work history? I'll give you a copy of my resumé if it'll get you to show me that damn disk!"

"All right." Drew relented a fraction. Maybe she truly didn't remember him. Or maybe she was so obsessed with finding her husband that she couldn't concentrate on anything else until he gave her a glimpse of the information on the disk. "Here."

He barely had the disk out of his jacket before she snatched it from his grasp. Mildly curious about the contents himself, and profoundly hopeful it didn't contain any of the smut Begosian liked to put on the Internet, Drew followed Emma to her desk and watched her load it into her computer. With her hands pressed together in a praying position, she held them to her mouth. It seemed the most natural thing in the world for Drew to put his hand on her shoulder and give it a squeeze of reassurance. He held his breath along with her as she scrolled through the menu of files.

"It's encrypted."

Drew felt the tension in her dissipate beneath his hand. He pulled away, surprised at the apologies he wanted to make for playing a part in her disappointment. "Can you open and read any of it?" he asked.

"No. But I know someone who can." She ejected the disk, rose, and pushed past him. Watching his leverage zipping out the door with Emma's revitalized determination, Drew followed. She hurried down the corridor to the next office, knocked, then pushed the door open, announcing herself as she poked her head in.

"Beej, can you decode these files? They might have something to do with Jonathan."

"Seriously?" The voice that answered was bright, and Drew wondered to whom Emma had turned.

"I need to find out." She walked in.

Drew scanned the name on the door before he followed BJ KINCAID-MAXWELL, CREATIVE DIRECTOR. In stark contrast to Emma's tidy office, this one held a clutter of toys, pillows, and books. It also had a crib stashed in one corner, empty now, but clearly it was a focal point in the room, judging by the path made through the plethora of stuffed animals in, under, and around it.

He hovered inside the doorway, awed and unsure of the energy he felt in this room. A life force that reminded him of sunshine radiated from the curly-haired blonde seated at the old oak desk between two computer terminals.

Drew could see and appreciate the sensibility Emma provided to the leadership at LadyTech.

"Who's your friend, Em?" the blonde inside asked while loading the disk and typing a series of commands on her keyboard.

Emma stood behind her, hugging her arms at her waist. A frown of impatient concern marred the classic lines of her face.

"Drew Gallagher. He's the man who rescued Kerry yesterday." Her focus seemed entirely on the monitor, leaving Drew to feel like little more than an afterthought.

The blonde continued to type as she stood. "Pleasure to meet you, Drew. I'm BJ." She looked away from the screen for a moment and extended her hand across the desk. She greeted him with a smile that offered the first real sign of welcome he'd had at LadyTech. "Thanks for helpin' out."

"No problem."

She sat back down and studied the results of her work. "It's not as complicated as it looks. But it'll take me a while so that you can make sense of the text." She turned and glanced up at Emma. "I can work on it this afternoon and bring it over tonight when we come for dinner."

"I can't leave without that disk," warned Drew. Without it, he'd have no excuse to press Emma about their past connection.

"Oh, you'll leave." A deep, dark voice rumbled through the air behind him. Drew's eyes narrowed a fraction, the only outward sign of surprise that someone had somehow gotten the drop on him.

He stiffened his fingers, tamping down the surge of adrenaline that made him want to curl his hands into fists. Drew turned to face the reckoning he'd figured would find him sooner or later when he'd first slipped through LadyTech's security. He centered his weight on the balls of his feet, ready to fight, if need be, ready to . . .

Drew settled back onto his heels as he looked into the icy gray eyes of the craggy-faced giant in the open doorway. Despite the flannel shirt and jeans the man wore, Drew recognized a warrior. Knowing he himself was the villain here, he backed down from his defensive position to bide his time until he could either talk his way out of trouble or make a break for it.

"Nice diversion you created on the loading dock. Fortunately, nobody got hurt. But I'm not so easy to get around."

"Brodie—" BJ tried to say a word in Drew's defense.

"Not now, darlin'."

Darlin'? No wonder the guy took such a personal interest in getting rid of Drew. That was a problem with women like Emma, he thought abstractly. They always had friends. Lots of them. And this particular friend looked as if he wanted to take Drew's head off for entering his *darlin's* office. The man looked as if he could.

And Drew had no ally to help him.

He hadn't for a long time. His allies had vanished when his past did. When he'd awoken in that hospital all alone. When nobody, not one person, came to see him who wasn't on the staff.

Drew was painfully aware of Emma's silence. She'd gotten what she wanted from him, and now she probably couldn't wait for this Mack truck of a man to haul him away.

So much for finding answers.

Since this was a battle he couldn't win, he wisely retreated. "I guess I'll be going, then."

"Em, you want to press charges?" asked the big man.

"No." BJ interceded when Emma would not. "He brought us a lead on Jonathan."

The man's eyes narrowed when BJ came to Drew's side, but the giant remained on guard. "Move away from him."

"You have to excuse my husband, Mr. Gallagher. He tends to be a little overprotective." Drew understood that *he* was the threat here. He respected Brodie's skill and alertness—and admired his taste in women.

"I don't blame him," said Drew. "It's easy to see

why he'd want to keep you safe." Drew nodded his thanks to BJ and stepped toward the giant, deferring to the man's authority without bowing to his will. "After you."

"I don't think so."

Drew let the corner of his mouth curve into a wry smile. "After me, then."

The man stepped aside, and Drew walked into the hall. Before the hulk could push him on his way, he turned for one last look at Emma. One last look at the closest thing to a link to his past he had. "You're welcome."

But satisfaction at getting the last word didn't come. Instead, he wished he could retract his sarcasm and change the words to "I'm sorry."

She stood alone, staring at the computer screen with such sadness in her eyes that he moved toward her. The need to wrap her in his arms, to promise her that hope still existed, was as overpowering as it was foreign. She shouldn't hurt like that. He didn't want her to hurt.

But a large, unyielding hand on his shoulder stopped him. "This way."

They walked all the way out to Drew's Jeep at the far edge of the parking lot before the big man spoke again. His warning was unmistakable. "I don't know what you're up to, Gallagher. But you do anything to hurt that woman or her little girl, and you'll have me to answer to."

Drew nodded and climbed into his Jeep. The other man waited until he had the engine warmed up and had shifted into reverse before he backed away from Drew's door and headed toward the main building.

Drew looked up to the third-floor windows. The

glare of sun and snow reflecting off the glass prevented him from seeing inside. But he couldn't
help wondering if Emma was there, watching him,
worrying about him the way he seemed predis-
posed to worry about her.

He wondered if it was possible for a man to feel
more alone than he did at that moment.

He imagined he heard the sound of gentle weeping, but the tears weren't his own. He dismissed
them as another sign of madness and drove away.

Chapter Three

"I'm sorry there wasn't better news with the disk," said BJ, the frustration evident in her voice as she walked to the front door with Emma.

"Don't blame yourself, Beej. You'd think by now I'd be able to tell the difference between a legitimate clue and a scam." Emma's self-deprecating laugh echoed in the two-story entryway of her Mission Hills home. "I'm such an idiot to get suckered in by an opportunist like Stan Begosian! He was just looking for a way to weasel into LadyTech and get his hands on some of my money. Why does the world think a wealthy woman without a man in her life is an easy target?"

"I guess we've been down that road before." BJ's expressive eyes dimmed at the memory. "I'll never forget the last time."

Emma offered an apologetic smile, wishing she

could retract her unthinking comment. "I'm sorry. I didn't mean to compare my situation to what you went through when Damon Morrisey tried to take LadyTech from us."

"I know you didn't. But he almost destroyed us." BJ's smile returned with a twist. "I guess we haven't had much luck with father figures, have we."

"No, we haven't,"—she tried to boost BJ's spirits, and her own— "but we've thrived in spite of the pain they caused us."

"Got that right." She beamed down at her daughter, strapped and sleeping in her carrier. "I'm just ticked off that slime tried to use Kerry to get to you."

Emma swallowed past the lump of shame in her throat. "Even knowing that, I still wanted to talk to him. I hoped he might know something about Jonathan."

She held the baby carrier while her friend shrugged into her parka and wrapped a Kansas City Royals knit scarf around her head and neck. Brodie had gone outside several minutes earlier to warm up their Ford Explorer.

"You loved him," BJ reminded her unnecessarily. Emma surprised herself by not jumping in to change the verb to present tense. "Go easy on yourself. I can't imagine any of us giving up on someone we care about."

"Always faithful, huh?"

BJ smiled. "Semper Fi. That's what we get for loving former Marines."

Emma tucked the blanket more securely around BJ's seven-month-old daughter, Katie, and recalled performing the same attentive action for Kerry when she was an infant. By this time in her life,

Emma had envisioned having three or four children to care for. Jonathan would have assumed an administrative position with his task force, she would have phased herself out of the day-to-day running of LadyTech, and they would enjoy being homebodies together.

But Jonathan hadn't come home.

She hadn't had more children.

And "Iron Maiden" had become a term she heard in whispers behind her back after particularly grueling negotiations, or the firing of a crooked employee, or defending her right to full disclosure of any information related to her husband's disappearance.

She could be tough when she needed to be. It made her very good at her job. It had helped put her company on the Forbes 500 list. But being tough hadn't been enough to help her mother survive. Being tough hadn't made growing up any easier for her. And being tough didn't give her a wink of assurance across a crowded room. It didn't hold her when she cried. It didn't make the cold nights alone feel any less an eternity.

"Em?"

A gloved hand on her arm stirred Emma from the downward plummet of her thoughts. She mustered an unnecessary smile. BJ and Jasmine were the only friends she'd never had to pretend with. "I'm disappointed, but I'll be okay."

BJ squeezed her arm. "Look on the bright side. Maybe you've been handed a missing Sir Arthur Conan Doyle manuscript, and you can sell it for a million dollars."

Emma laughed. The rusty sound grated along her vocal cords. "What I think I got is someone's poorly copied homework assignments. I'll probably erase and reformat it so at least I'm getting a new disk out of the deal."

BJ's answering laugh boosted her spirit. "There you go."

Emma handed Katie to her mother and opened the thick oak door that guarded her foyer. A chilly wind that served as a prelude to the oncoming winter storm seeped through the glass storm door, and Emma shivered. "You guys drive safely. It's not icy yet, but the snow's on its way."

"We'll be careful." BJ wrapped her free arm around Emma and traded a hug. "Tell Kerry good night for us."

"I will."

BJ leaned back, her green eyes narrowing with concern. "I know you're the Rock of Gibraltar and all that, Em, but I'm calling you in the morning to check on you, anyway."

Emma rubbed her hands together and clutched her arms to her chest. BJ's promise provided the only warmth she felt at that moment. "Do that."

With a parting smile, BJ ventured out to the driveway, where Brodie took the baby and secured her in her car seat. Emma responded to his quick wave and waited until they had pulled into the street before closing and locking both doors.

Emma sighed and leaned her forehead against the cool oak. The roomy house she had designed and decorated with such love echoed with a lonely silence. She'd left Kerry in the study, watching an animated video about a streetwise boy who discovered a magic lamp that turned him into a prince.

Unbidden, Drew Gallagher's image popped into

her mind. With his tattered jeans and shaggy mane of hair, he could be the poster boy for "streetwise." He hadn't cowered when Brodie had shown up in BJ's office to throw him out. He'd kept his wits about him, falling quiet, pulling back from a sure confrontation as if biding his time. Learning the opposition, waiting for the right moment to assert himself.

Did that mean he'd be coming back?

Emma squared her shoulders and straightened the hem of her mustard-colored tunic sweater. He'd said he needed that disk. Probably to save his butt with the district attorney's office. He didn't seem to be quite aboveboard in the honesty department.

She grumbled to herself and headed into the study. She'd be smart to keep reminding herself of Drew Gallagher's shortcomings, since he seemed to keep springing into her thoughts without a proper invitation.

He might mesmerize her with those catlike eyes, he might intrigue her with the enticing scents of brisk air and worn leather, he might make her feel feminine and sheltered and out-of-sorts, but he wasn't her type of man.

He wasn't Jonathan.

"Hey, sweetie." Emma sat on the plush navy print sofa and hugged Kerry to her side. Her love for her daughter was one of the few constants that remained in her life.

"Aladdin j-just saved J-Jasmine." Kerry tucked the doll she sat with under one arm and lifted her lavender blanket. Emma curled her legs beneath it, sharing their warmth and their love as they watched the last few minutes of the movie together. Just as they had for so many nights the past few years.

"Okay." When the genie signed off at the end of the movie, Emma pressed the rewind button and stood. "It's after nine o'clock, young lady. Time to get upstairs and brush your teeth."

Kerry whined like any self-respecting seven-year-old. "But, Mom, I don't have s-s-school tomorrow."

Emma smiled and shooed her across the hallway to the carpeted stairs. "Saturday we have gymnastics and run errands. You need your beauty sleep so you don't scare away your teacher!"

"Mom!" Kerry's low-pitched belly laugh never held a trace of her stutter. "You're the one who n-needs beauty s-sleep!"

Emma opened her mouth in exaggerated shock. "Me?" She took one step and the chase was on. Kerry squealed and bolted up the stairs with her mother in hot pursuit. Her breathless laughter lightened Emma's mood, and soon they were tumbling onto the Minnie Mouse comforter of Kerry's white canopy bed, tickling and laughing and being kids together.

Emma heard the chime of the doorbell like a stern reprimand from her father, warning her to be quiet or he'd make her.

She sprawled on her stomach, breathing hard from the healthy exertion. Kerry lay on top of her, ending the game a few seconds after her mother went still.

The bell chimed again and Emma sat up, rolling Kerry onto the bed with her doll. Made of an old pillowcase and quilt scraps, Angelica, as Kerry called her, had seen better days. One arm hung by a few threads, and some of the yarn used for hair had worn away and left a bald spot beneath her bonnet. Emma felt like doing the same kind of damage to the unwanted visitor.

"Sorry, sweetie. You go on and brush your teeth. Remember to get the ones in the back, too. I'll be up to read you a story in a few minutes."

Emma marched down the stairs, stiffening her posture and finger-combing her hair into controlled order. She couldn't do anything about the flush of heat in her cheeks, but would let her unexpected guest attribute the color to her slow-burning temper at having her evening routine disrupted.

She threw back the dead bolt and fixed her most authoritative expression on her face. She opened the door, and her bravado dissolved on a puff of air.

Between the white Colonial columns on her brick front porch stood Drew Gallagher. With his shoulders hunched up against the cold, and the north wind whipping tendrils of his hair against his cheeks, he looked like a stranded motorist who had walked up to the house to ask for help.

He lifted his chin from the warmth of his suede collar and transfixed her with those cutting green eyes. Emma realized there was nothing lost or hesitant about this man.

"Mrs. Ramsey." She acknowledged his curt nod by clasping her arms across her stomach and steeling her will against his.

"Mr. Gallagher." She raised her voice to be heard through the glass of the storm door. "It's a little late to be paying a visit."

"I had to wait until they were gone. That guy, your guard dog, even walked up and down the block once. Probably knew I'd show up."

Apparently Mr. Gallagher couldn't take a hint. "Whatever it is, call my secretary on Monday. We can talk at the office."

He reached inside his jacket and pulled out a folded manila envelope. "You may not want to wait until Monday." He held out the envelope like a peace offering. "I have a pretty good idea where Begosian got that disk."

Emma wavered in her urgent need to dismiss this man. Still, she didn't want to be partner to another of his questionable attempts to help her. "Does the district attorney know about this?"

The stern granite of his face softened into a cagey smile. The cocky charm of his grin danced along Emma's resolve, making her feel teenager-ish, as if he were sharing a tantalizing but harmless secret with her. "Where do you think I got the information?"

Emma felt an intimate energy rising within her, but caught herself before her lips curved into a smile.

"All right," she relented, unlatching the door. She opened it only far enough to take the envelope. "Thank you. I'll read through this and give you a call on Monday."

Before she could pull the door closed, a black-gloved hand shot in and grabbed the frame, blocking her ability to shut him out. Drew leaned forward, his aristocratic nose mere inches from her own. "Don't you want to know what's in it?"

Emma's pulse quickened. He could easily over-power her and wrench the door open, or, she realized with belated chagrin, he could simply shatter the glass with a blow of his fist or foot. If he wanted to get into her house, there was nothing she could do to stop him.

He stood close enough to the slim opening for her to smell the worn suede of his jacket, and the woodsy scent of his after shave or cologne. Yet he didn't force his way in. He held his ground; he would not be shut out in the cold night by her. But he waited for her invitation.

This man who held a superior position gave her power over him instead.

"I'm smart enough to figure it out," she said.

Drew's smile had flattened into a grim line. "Em, unless you have contacts in the world of organized crime, I doubt you'll recognize the significance of some of those names."

"Organized crime?"

"Look, I know I'm not a welcome guest. But give me fifteen minutes to talk and then I promise to get out of here. To get out of your life." His gaze strayed to some faraway place that Emma couldn't see or understand. Then, as if by sheer will, he hardened his expression and forced his gaze back to hers. "I don't like leaving things unfinished."

Something about the distance he seemed to have traveled to find his way back to her struck a resonant chord within her at that moment. Her whole life had become unfinished business since Jonathan's disappearance. Drew might simply be talking about a case in the D.A.'s office, but she had an inkling that he referred to something more.

So, forgetting her promise to stay away from Drew Gallagher, she pushed open the door and invited him inside.

The surprised look that flitted across his face did more to reassure her of the safety of bringing him into her home than any words he could have said. He stamped his booted feet and rubbed his hands together while she shut and locked the doors. But when she held out her hand for his coat and gloves, he froze and studied her in mute surprise.

How many other times had he forced his welcome? she wondered. He didn't seem to expect the simple courtesy she would extend to any guest. That surprising revelation humbled and empowered her enough to give him a gentle mom's smile. "Those things are damp. I'll hang them in the kitchen so they can dry a bit before you get chilled through."

"Em . . ." Her shortened name in that raspy baritone did funny things to her feminine psyche. Like wish she'd stopped to put on regular shoes with her jeans and sweater instead of fuzzy blue slippers.

"C'mon," she insisted. With wary obedience, he slipped off his gloves and jacket and placed them in her free hand. "If your boots are wet, take them off and leave them on the front rug."

He obeyed her second command with a little less reluctance. When he traipsed down the hall behind her, she noted how very silent his movements were. She wouldn't have known he was there, except for the uncanny awareness she had of his presence.

"You can wait in here." She went into the study and set the folder on her desk. "Make yourself comfortable. I need to check on Kerry. Then I'll be back."

She watched the slow movement of his mouth as he formed words that seemed unfamiliar to those flat, male lips. "Thank you."

Emma tucked his jacket through the crook of her arm, turned, and barreled into a pint-sized dynamo in a Minnie Mouse flannel nightgown. She snatched Kerry by the shoulders to keep from knocking her to the floor. "Sweetie, you're supposed to be in bed. I said I'd come up."

Without conscious thought, she positioned herself between her guest and her daughter, blocking him from view. But Kerry peeked around her mother and smiled as if she'd spotted Santa Claus. "Faith wants him to r-read us a story."

"Kerry Doreen . . ."

"Please." The pitifully long wail almost negated the irresistible wish in Kerry's bright blue eyes.

But using the tools at her disposal, she stepped aside, giving her daughter a clear view of the tall, lean man in a black ribbed sweater and jeans. Hopefully, Gallagher would take the hint and say something to end the little crush Kerry seemed to have on her rescuer. And surely even he possessed enough class to let her down kindly.

He hooked his thumbs into his front pockets and shrugged his shoulders. "Sorry, punkin. I don't know how to read stories."

Emma flashed him a smile of thanks, but his focus dropped to the waist-high girl who frowned up at him. "Y-you can't read?" She tugged on her mother's hand. "Then I n-need t-to read to him, so he can go to s-s-sleep."

Seven-year-old compassion stumped both adults. Gallagher found his voice first. "I can read. I

71

read a lot, in fact. I just don't know how to read to, um, little girls."

Kerry's bottom lip pouted outward in a sigh of relief. She took his hand and pulled him toward the sofa. "It's oh-kay, I'll show you."

Held captive, he glanced over his shoulder, a look of distress widening his eyes. He mouthed the words, "I can't," to her mother. But Kerry sat him down, turned on the reading lamp, planted Angelica on his lap, and covered his legs with the lavender blanket, all the while giving instructions like a patient schoolteacher.

If she noticed the awkward confusion of either adult, she paid no attention.

"I'll, uh, put on some coffee. Decaf," Emma added, as if the most amazing idea had come to her. In actuality, she'd never been at such a loss to explain Kerry's instant allegiance to Drew Gallagher. "Since it's so late," she explained to no one. The other two had already tuned her out, her daughter from excitement and purpose, and Gallagher . . .

A slight smile tilted the corners of her mouth. The man had faced down a kidnapper with a gun, Brodie Maxwell when his temper was riled, and herself on prime defensive mode. Yet she'd never seen this burnished man of mystery with such a look of consternation on his face as when Kerry had climbed up into his lap and snuggled beneath the blanket with him.

Tamping down her natural instinct to protect her daughter from any slight or rejection, Emma slipped from the room. Kerry's unique combination of intellectual curiosity and her struggle to express herself clearly required a great deal of patience. Some adults, like the guide at the museum yesterday, patronized her. They listened and nodded their head without really hearing what she had to say.

But Emma gave Gallagher credit. Patience seemed to be one virtue he had in abundant supply. And though he claimed ineptitude at dealing with children, she placed a shaky trust in him to protect her precious girl.

She sat in the kitchen and listened. More than fifteen minutes passed before the silence of the house registered. Sudden alarm blended with the guilt of dropping her guard and propelled her out of the kitchen at a run.

The even cadence of Gallagher's raspy voice had taken over from the halting rhythm of Kerry's reading as he learned the lesson that the main requirement in reading a book to a child was simply an interest in spending time with the child. The mesmerizing sound had lulled Emma into thinking she'd left her daughter in safe hands.

Emma skidded on the polished oak floor and stumbled to an embarrassed stop on the navy-and-mauve area rug that covered most of the floor in the study. She sucked in deep breaths through her nose so as not to further disturb the angelic picture of Kerry's dark head snoring softly beneath Drew Gallagher's chin.

He rested one hand on her back and clutched the book in the other. His green eyes looked disoriented through the lenses of his glasses. "I didn't know if you wanted me to let her sleep, or if it was okay to wake her by moving."

Emma's distress ebbed as her breathing caught and jump-started again at the evocative contrast of his blond head so close to Kerry's dark one. Kerry's long hair had snagged on the nubby wool of his sweater and fanned out across his shoulder. She seemed so tiny and delicate, curled against his lanky chest and torso, cradled awkwardly yet with infinite care in the crook of his arm.

Gallagher slipped into so many roles so easily, it seemed. Though this had been an unexpected challenge, he'd pulled off storytelling with expert ease. Emma wondered what other parts he could play with the same finesse. She felt heat in her cheeks, wondering what role, if any, he might play with her beyond tonight. Thankfully, the lone lamp that was on kept her reaction to this softer side of Drew hidden in the shadows.

"Looks like you handled story time just fine." She seized the opportunity to make an exit, needing time to bury those unwanted speculations about her guest. "I'll get her up to bed."

She reached for her daughter as Drew stood and started to hand her over. Kerry mumbled something in her sleep about a princess and rolled into a ball, seeking the warmth that had abandoned her.

"She's dead weight," he whispered. "Let me carry her."

Emma laid Angelica on Kerry's chest and caressed the crown of her head, gently shushing her when she blinked unfocused eyes at her. "It's all right, sweetie. We're taking you to bed."

" 'Kay. G'night."

Once more, Gallagher moved with silent footfalls behind her. Emma peeked over her shoulder going up the stairs, and she marveled at his sinewy strength and his handling of her little girl with such gentleness and respect.

She glided into Kerry's room and turned the lamp beside the bed to its lowest wattage, bathing the room in a gentle glow. She straightened the covers and then folded them back. Gallagher leaned in front of her, placing Kerry on the bed. Inches away, right at eye-level, the knit of Drew's sweater strained with the jut of his shoulder. In one fluid movement, the tension there eased and he straightened.

Graceful strength.

An unbidden image of his arms closing around her with that same controlled power quickened Emma's pulse. The last time she'd been held by a man with any purpose beyond a fond greeting or farewell had been the morning Jonathan left. He'd kissed her for an embarrassing length of time, loving to make her blush, drawing her in close, holding her tightly, securely, tenderly.

That was her last embrace.

She missed being held. She missed being able to surrender her strength.

Drew Gallagher made her want to surrender.

Traitor! The accusation drummed in her head and branded her heart with a capital T. Shocked by her disloyal turn of thought, she retreated.

She tucked the comforter around Kerry, kissed her forehead, and fled out the door without another glance at her dangerous guest. In a way, by inviting him into her home and allowing him to spend time with them, she'd made the subconscious decision that health-wise, virtue-wise, he wasn't a dangerous man—not to little girls, at least.

But he rattled Emma's sense of purpose. He made her think things she had no right thinking. She hadn't wanted a man since Jonathan.

She wanted this one.

As she reached the kitchen, five long fingers wrapped around her elbow and pulled her up short. "Whoa. Did I do something wrong?" His voice held a note of disquiet.

My God. She hadn't heard him coming, hadn't suspected he would come after her. Emma squared her shoulders and turned. She bit the inside seam of her lips to keep her confusion from spilling out. "Nothing's wrong."

The clench of her jaw made her lie obvious. A hard glint replaced the fuzzy focus behind his glasses. He released her arm but moved no further. "Maybe I've overstayed my welcome."

"No." Her cowardly attempt to escape her own thoughts had sent him back into that chilling isolation of his own. He didn't understand. She couldn't explain her sudden need to throw up the iron walls that protected her so well. She couldn't be interested in this man. She shouldn't care that she had hurt him by living up to his expectation that she wouldn't trust him.

And she would not let reawakened hormones stop her from conducting business. "I want to know what you found out about Stan Begosian. Why you think it would be of interest to me."

His cat eyes studied her face, the eyes of a caged predator deciding whether to obey its keeper or seize the chance to escape.

She stood straight and still beneath his scrutiny.

At last he shrugged and stepped away, breaking

the tension that had sucked the usable air from the room. "All right. Business it is. We won't make mention of whatever just happened here."

Emma's chest heaved in a cleansing breath, glad for the reprieve. "Business," she repeated with gratitude. "Here." Forcing herself to behave normally, she crossed to the counter and poured fresh coffee into the two mugs she'd set out earlier. She held one out to Drew. "Black, right?"

"Right."

He took the mug and their fingers touched, burning her from the inside out. Remembering the way a man liked to drink his coffee was simply a matter of good memory and polite etiquette, she reminded herself. It was a tactic she often used with clients and co-workers. So why couldn't she calm those intimate little stirrings at the pit of her stomach?

She snatched her hand away and reached for her own mug. "We'd better get started. It's ten o'clock."

"Lead on, Macduff."

His quote surprised her. Maybe he hated the strain between them as much as she did. A touch of sarcasm might be the right antidote for the tension that assailed them. "Well, at least you're not calling me Lady Macbeth."

"Not yet." Emma spun around, a cutting remark poised on the tip of her tongue. But the hint of humor quirking the corner of his mouth stole her need to even the score.

Emma pressed her lips together to keep from sharing his smile. Most men respected her business acumen. They played hardball, or they walked a wide berth around a woman who controlled as much money and power as she did at LadyTech.

They didn't tease her.

They didn't make her feel soft and silly and feminine.

They weren't supposed to, at any rate. She'd have to send Drew a memo on those rules. She'd better send a copy to herself, too.

She turned, fighting her treacherous longings by pretending they didn't exist.

Drew's husky laughter tormented her conscience all the way into the study.

Drew's mood darkened as the hour passed. Out of curiosity, he'd asked to read the disk from Begosian while Emma pored over the file from the D.A.'s office. *The Journal of James Moriarty* proved to be enlightening, if not entertaining, reading.

The fictional account of Sherlock Holmes's nemesis chronicled an amazing tale of the villain's rebirth. The disclaimer on the first page said the author had chosen that name after reading a collection of short stories and discovering a unique affinity for the brilliant-minded character.

Maybe the length of the day made him edgy and suspicious, but the similarity to his own rebirth from the pages of fiction rang an eerie bell in Drew's limited memory. The sporadic journal began exactly five years ago—the length of time Emma said her husband had been missing.

The length of his own memory.

He pushed his fingers up under his glasses and rubbed his tired eyes.

"Pretty dull stuff, huh?" Emma's throaty voice

settled over his nerves like a soothing caress. His body woke to the sound with a healthy response that overrode his train of thought.

Here in her own home, she'd lost her executive veneer. She wore her hair down, a cascade of deep brown velvet that looked as fine and soft as Kerry's was. In her jeans and those silly fuzzy slippers, curled up on the sofa studying the report, she reminded him of a college coed.

Drew wondered if she'd slip back into her prickly armor if he moved over to the empty space beside her. Probably. Without knowing how, he'd pushed one of her defensive buttons earlier when she ran from Kerry's room. By the time he'd reached her, she had put those fortresses firmly back in place. Emma protected some very deep secrets behind those smoky eyes. As long as he treaded lightly around anything personal, she dropped her guard and revealed a keen intuition and sharp wit. He liked her all soft and open like that.

Maybe he liked her a little too much.

Still, this relaxed companionship seemed a fair trade for burying his desire to discover whether those sable tresses felt as soft to the touch as they looked.

He removed his glasses and leaned back in the chair. "It's not Begosian's style to be so literary. He's more of a picture-book kind of guy."

"So you think he's just a messenger for one of the names in this address book?"

He ran through the list of underworld cronies that had shown up on the papers in Stan Begosian's file cabinet. "Chi Chi Garibaldi works for an outfit out of New York City. Natalie Marple used to be the mistress of a drug king out of New Orleans. Billy Kramer has a Detroit connection."

"Stan Begosian is just local bad news. What would they want with him?"

"What do they want with *you?*" he corrected. "Any idea why criminals from all parts of the country might want to contact you?"

The shrewd intellect in her eyes dimmed. He said nothing further, waiting as she set the file on the coffee table and pulled her knees up to her chin, hugging herself in a classic defensive posture. "My husband ran a task force that targeted the influx of crime into the United States. Arms dealers, drug trafficking, information exchanges. They tackled whatever the government wanted them to."

"Military?"

She shook her head. "Jonathan and his men trained in Marine Intelligence. But he started his own company when he retired from the corps. His men were former operatives working freelance for him. I think they could do more that way."

"With fewer questions asked."

The lost expression he'd seen on her face at LadyTech seeped into her features, aging her youthful face. Drew gripped the corner of the desk to keep from going to her, knowing it wasn't his place to offer her strength or comfort. Nor, he suspected, would such a gesture be welcomed, coming from him. But he'd yet to see her back down from a tough situation, and whatever painful memory she dealt with now met the same resilient strength.

She rewarded his patience with an unexpected revelation. "Jonathan disappeared on his last assignment. The government wrote him off, claimed they knew nothing of his activities. The military said their hands were tied with security issues." Her wistful smile told him she had tapped into a bittersweet memory. "He just wanted to get rid of the bad guys. Make the world a better place for his little girl."

A deep breath shuddered through her. Drew ignored his own advice of caution and crossed to the sofa. She didn't protest when he unclenched her fingers from her knee. Her skin felt as if she'd just come in from the cold. Tracing the delicate length of each finger, he rubbed her hand between both of his, instilling warmth through the soft friction.

"I can see why he'd want to." He encouraged her with a compliment. "Kerry's a treasure."

Emma nodded. She hid the shine of moisture in her eyes by studying his hands at work. "All I've been able to find out is that Jonathan was after an arms dealer nicknamed the Chameleon. According to his men, Jonathan was the only one to see his face. They can't even trace him through fingerprints. I don't know if the Chameleon's on that list or not. I don't even know if he's a man. Jonathan didn't share many details about his work. Said it was a way to protect us."

"Sounds smart." A grudging respect blossomed alongside a bud of jealousy inside him.

"His point man, Hawk Echohawk, told me Jonathan was in pursuit of the Chameleon when they both disappeared. He heard an explosion . . ." Emma turned her hand and latched onto Drew. "I know he's not dead. They found no trace of either one."

Drew gripped her hand with the same strength with which she clung to him. "Em," he said gently. "Sometimes with an explosion—"

"Don't tell me scientific facts." Her head shot up and she shook the hair back from her face. "I've heard them all. Vaporization if you're too close to the impact. The incredible rate of jungle growth that can hide a body in a matter of days. It's not true! None of that was the case." She thumped her chest. "I know it in here. If Jonathan were dead, I'd *know* it." Her fingers curled into a defiant fist. "It makes no sense. I have no proof. But I know he's not dead."

Drew didn't even consider the idea that Jonathan Ramsey didn't want to come home, that he had staged his own death and left his family behind. No man, certainly not one who possessed the degree of honor that Colonel Ramsey commanded, would abandon this beautiful woman and their irresistible daughter.

He reached out and tucked a wayward strand of hair behind her ear. The velvety feel stayed with his fingers when he pulled away. "What incredible faith you have."

Drew had never believed in anything to the degree that this woman believed in her husband.

A foreign impulse swelled in his gut. He was on his feet, and the offer was out of his mouth before he could consider the wisdom of getting involved with another man's wife.

"Let me talk to Begosian. If there's a connection to organized crime, the D.A. would want to know about it, anyway."

Emma swiped her fingers across her eyes, drying

her tears. She stood and followed him to the desk. "You're going to help me?"

"Sir, may I help you?" Her voice rang clear and true in his mind, an elusive memory he couldn't quite remember.

Maybe spending extended time with Emma would be more than pleasurable. Maybe by helping her find answers, he'd find a few of his own.

"Drew?"

He'd never felt so connected to the name he'd chosen as he did now, hearing it from her lips. Skepticism turned to hope when he met her gaze, making him feel a glimmer of the hero her husband must have been. Or rather, the hero he still was.

Drew ejected the disk from the computer and tucked it into his shirt pocket beneath his sweater. The usual rush of tackling a new mystery mingled with something deeper, indefinable. He knew a need to succeed beyond the satisfaction of rising to a challenge. Beyond the need to discover his past.

"I'd like to trace the author of this journal," he said. "Find out who James Moriarty is. Maybe there's a clue in here we haven't figured out yet."

"I can talk to Brodie. Or Kelton Murphy. They both worked with my husband. Maybe one of those names means something to them."

"I don't know this Murphy, but if he's like Maxwell, he won't be too thrilled that we're working together."

The smudges of mascara at the corners of her eyes made her look little older than Kerry. But he saw nothing adolescent in the determination that steeled her shoulders. "I'll hire you."

"To do what?"

"I'm not sure yet. It doesn't matter. But if you're working for me, then they can't question us spending time together."

A spiral of hair had fallen loose across her cheek again. Drew brushed it back, her freckled skin cool and smooth beneath his roughened fingers. "You sure you want to deceive your friends?"

She laid her hand over his, holding him in a rare gesture of trust. "I'm not deceiving them. I'll pay you every penny I have if you can find Jonathan."

Chapter Four

Faith sat on the third step in the drafty stairwell of the rickety brownstone watching over her trickiest assignment. The circle of light she carried with her kept her warm enough, but Drew Gallagher, blending with the shadows of the predawn hour, huddled deep inside his leather jacket.

"You should be home," she reprimanded him gently, knowing he wouldn't hear her. "You deserve a good night's sleep."

She sighed, lifting her bangs with a puff of air. She rested her elbows on her knees and plopped her chin in her hands. This job had proved to be her most difficult case. The temperature around her suddenly dropped, and she shivered. She tilted her face upward, understanding the silent message. "Okay, it's my only case." She sat up straight and spread her *arms wide, beseeching the light from above. "So it's the only case I've ever had.*

The temperature fell in a sudden rush to a subarctic level. Her teeth chattered in contrite apology. "I know, I know, I should have listened to you and minded my own business. I thought I could help."

She relaxed as the heat returned. Soon she could breathe again, surrounded by a glow as soft as a rosy sunset.

Drew Gallagher didn't fare as well, though. He pulled his hands from his pockets and wriggled his fingers, encouraging circulation before burying them inside his jacket again. The banister hid him from sight, but did nothing to stop the winter chill that whistled in through the broken pane on the front door. Taking pity, Faith·left her perch and floated down to him. She wrapped him in a hug he couldn't feel and tried to instill some of her warmth into him.

Alert as always, his gaze darted from the front door in a quick scan of his surroundings. "Yes!" she urged him, waving her hands in front of his face. "Notice me. Listen to me."

But he shrugged his shoulders and turned his head back to the front door.

Faith groaned in frustration. "You don't see me at all, do you?"

A noise rustled behind her, and she crinkled her nose at the putrid odor burning through her sinuses. She turned to identify the acrid stench. The drunk on the inside stoop had rolled over.

"I'll bet you do."

The vagrant's bleary eyes squinted open and looked right at her. His pasty, gap-toothed smile made her cringe. "Hey, honeybunch."

"Shut up." *Drew answered the mistaken come-on with a cold look that made Faith turn away, too.*

"Thank you." *She preened as if his warning had been a gallant defense on her behalf.* "See? You do the right thing. You're a good man." *She tapped his chest.* "But until you believe what's in your heart, you'll never see me. I'll never be able to explain. You'll never understand what you have to do." *Her weary sigh stirred the fall of hair at his shoulder, getting lost in the January breeze.* "I guess I'll keep doing what I do best."

The lights surrounding her blinked. She threw up her hands, chastized like the meddling novice she was.

"Okay, fine. I'm working on it. I will find what I do best. Just give me time." *She floated up through the second and third floors and made her way back to the citadel at the outer reaches to study other events beginning to take shape in her guidebook. She'd been doodling on the first page, only half-listening when they'd explained how this guardian angel guidebook worked. There'd been something about noninterference and guidance through successful rites of passage to earn her wings, too.*

She hadn't realized that wings could be so important. But without them, she'd be stuck here. Alone.

Maybe one day she'd find out how everything worked. Then she could make things right for Kerry.

She'd write her own book about it. Illustrate it herself, and share it with her cohorts. Yeah, once she figured out why humans fought so hard to hang on to life, why love bound two people together through mistakes and miracles, she'd be in demand, not stuck way out in . . .

The lights around her flashed, bleeding first to orange, then a vivid scarlet. She heard the echo of thunder rumbling in the distance.

"I know, I know." Her deep sigh filled the empty expanse. "No books. No wings. Not until I learn to do the job right."

She prayed Drew Gallagher had the kind of time she needed to figure it all out.

Drew shivered. The warm draft of air that had brought feeling back into the tips of his fingers vanished with the momentary awakening of his smelly companion on the stoop.

The Drew Gallagher of the fictional world lived and breathed dumps like this. He passed in and out of the seamy underbelly of the world as if he'd been born to it. Yet he could shave, don a suit and tie and an attitude, and blend just as easily with the upper crust.

The flesh-and-blood Drew Gallagher had taught himself the same skills. But this night, maybe more than ever before, he wondered what he was really like. What was his real name? His real profession? His real neighborhood?

He sure as hell hoped he came from a place far away from this perpetual gloom and squalor. He wanted to come from a place bathed in warmth and light. Where people shook hands and made eye contact. Where they stuck out their necks and helped their neighbor because that person needed help.

Where a woman believed in a man just because she loved him.

Drew shifted, the creak of his leather holster the only sound he made. He wanted to help Emma because he thought he could gain her trust. Because having her indebted to him would make her more inclined to help him find *his* truth.

But his conscience warred with his head. He couldn't move past the tiny kernel of guilt that gnawed at his stomach. He tried to be a good man. He didn't like using her.

But a man had to look out for himself, didn't he? The fictional Drew Gallagher would play this game through to the end. He'd track down her husband, then demand that she rack her brain, submit to hypnosis, do whatever it took to remember her connection to him.

Problem was, the real Drew Gallagher had discovered a liking for Kerry's bubble-bath freshness, and the exotic herbal scent of Emma's hair.

And the idea that he might hurt or fail either one of them sat on his conscience like a lead weight.

The sound of an overbuilt motor revving and sputtering to a stop outside the door brought his focus back to the task at hand. He identified his man by the hurried crunch of slick-soled shoes on the unshoveled sidewalk. Swallowing his questions and his conscience, Drew snagged Stan Begosian by the elbow and steered him to his apartment door without breaking stride.

"Evening, Stan," he said in a low-throated whisper. "Pretty late for a man like you to be out on the town, isn't it?"

The smaller, stocky man quivered in Drew's grip.

"I didn't do nothing wrong. I'm out on bail. I can stay out as late as I want as long as I stay in town."

Drew seized Stan's hand and guided the key into the lock. "I'm just worried about your health. Why don't you invite me in?"

The lock tumbled over, and Drew shoved Stan in ahead of him, closing the door behind them and pocketing the keys.

"Hey, you can't barge in like this. I have rights."

Drew ignored the protest and scavenged around the studio apartment, digging through drawers and opening books. "How'd you make bail money, Stan?"

Begosian huddled in the center of the room, turning to watch Drew's progress. "I don't have to say nothing. You ain't a cop."

Drew let his gaze stray over to Stan's dark, beady eyes. "You're facing two counts of attempted kidnapping and an assault charge. You don't have the kind of money to pay that bond. Who's backing you?"

Stan fidgeted inside his brown tweed coat, and his gaze darted to the kitchenette area. With a feigned interest in the sofa cushions along the way, Drew crossed to the small stove and sink.

"I had some money saved up."

"From what? Selling your dirty pictures?" Drew poked around the pile of pans and plates in the dish drainer. For a cockroach, Stan lived in a remarkably well-kept place.

Stan took a step in his direction, but halted when Drew looked up. "I don't do that kind of stuff no more. I'm in therapy."

"Who pays for that?" A quick examination of the

lone drawer and cabinet revealed nothing unusual. "The D.A. seems to think you're back in business. And quite frankly, you're throwing around a lot of money; that makes me wonder if that's true."

He followed the nervous flutter of Stan's glance a second time. "I tell ya, I'm clean. I just wanted to help out that lady friend of yours."

Drew opened the refrigerator door, but Stan bolted across the room and slammed it shut. Drew scratched a nonexistent itch on his nose, waited for Begosian's focus to shift to the tiny movement, then strong-armed him out of the way. While he explored the bare-bones contents of the fridge, he held Stan by the collar at arm's length. "I don't think you're into helping anybody but yourself. I'll just bet . . ."

He pulled out an old-fashioned metal ice cube tray. Instead of frozen water, he found a plain white envelope anchored beneath the metal dividers. A slow, calculating glare rooted Stan in place after Drew released him to open the envelope.

A scrawled name leaped off the bottom of the check inside. The sixth sense awakened and kicked into overdrive.

"You have a ten-thousand-dollar check here signed by James Moriarty."

"And you got no search warrant!" Stan lunged for the check. Drew sidestepped, and his attacker stumbled past and slammed into the counter.

Drew strolled into the sitting area. "Like you said, I'm not a cop. I don't need a warrant." Begosian backed off from making a physical threat. Drew fluttered the check in the air. "This has made an appearance since the police searched your place. Did Mr. Moriarty pay your bail? Did *he* tell you to give that disk to Emma Ramsey or her daughter?"

"Just the mom." He followed Drew, fixing his covetous gaze on the check. "I was supposed to give it to Mrs. Ramsey and ask for money. I figured the little girl would be easier to talk to."

Drew snatched the scumbag by the collar and hauled him against the wall, pinning his neck and dealing out a bit of the retribution he'd wanted to exact at the museum. "You sure talking's all you had in mind?"

Stan squirmed like a bug pinned in a display. "I swear! I don't do that no more. All I was supposed to do was get the disk to Ramsey and ask for money so it'd look like my own job."

Drew let him dangle. "What does James Moriarty look like?"

"I don't know. I never talked to him. Some lady called me long distance. And then a guy from New York."

"Detroit, too?"

"Yeah." Stan stopped struggling, more awed by Drew's knowledge than by the force of his grip.

"There's no postmark on this envelope. Where's the envelope the check came in?"

"It came in that one." Drew squeezed harder. "Honest! I found it in my mailbox downstairs."

"Then it was hand-delivered."

"Yeah, I guess. Is that important?"

"It means this Moriarty has another local connection. You have any friends?" Stan's eyes swelled to the size of quarters. Drew eased the pressure a fraction, not anxious for his talkative source to pass out on him. A guy with Begosian's history wouldn't make a lot of friends, even in the criminal world. "You said you had more than one call?"

"Yeah. I got a different job each time. Different instructions."

"They all have to do with Emma Ramsey?"

"Not exactly."

Drew altered his grip, tugged, and tossed him onto the sofa. "Make yourself comfortable, Stan, and explain 'not exactly.' "

Emma's purse beeped with an irritating repetition that made her long for the days when she couldn't afford a room to sleep in, much less a cell phone with unlimited calling access. She reached into the outside pocket of her bag and punched the button with practiced efficiency as she put it to her ear. "Emma Ramsey."

"Em. It's Drew Gallagher."

His raspy baritone dispelled her annoyance and shrank the world to the sound of his voice. The confines of her van seemed smaller and warmer. "Hi."

"Where are you?"

"Sitting at a traffic light on Lee's Summit Road wondering why I don't shop closer to home. Kerry's in the backseat engrossed in a computer game." She glanced in the rearview mirror to check the accuracy of her statement. "She waves hi."

The answering beat of silence alerted her to the knowledge that this was more than a friendly call. "Tell her hi back."

She waved her fingers in the air. Kerry smiled and returned to her game. Emma turned the heater down a notch, feeling suddenly a little too comfy, a little too cozy. She had hired Drew to find her missing husband, not help renew her small-talk skills. "Did you find out something?"

"Yeah." A sharp sigh followed his clipped response. "Moriarty's journal looks legit after all."

Emma frowned in surprise. "You mean he's a real person?"

"The name's an alias for a real person. The dates in the journal correspond with crimes that have been committed in New York, New Orleans, and Detroit."

"The places on Begosian's phone bill?"

"Yeah." Instead of enlightening her, his answer only added more confusion to the mystery. "Can I make a copy of that disk? The D.A.'s allowing me a few liberties, as long as I keep him apprised of whatever I find in my investigation."

"If it'll help." His long silences leaped the satellite connection and echoed inside the van. Fewer than twelve hours had passed since he'd left her home the night before. How much work could a man get done between midnight and ten in the morning? Despite her intention to keep their relationship that of employer and employee, she couldn't help but comment. "You sound tired."

"I had a long night."

"Is something wrong?" A car horn blared behind her, alerting her to the green light. She eyeballed the red Suburban in her rearview mirror and thought a choice curse at the driver she couldn't see. The vehicle darted around her once she cleared the intersection. She pressed on the accelerator to keep the brown sedan that pulled in behind her from passing her as well.

"Em? You still there?"

Distracted by the onslaught of Saturday-morning traffic, she found it easier to separate herself from her concern over Drew's sleeping habits. "Sorry. The light changed."

"Look, I need to catch a few hours of sleep. Can you meet me for dinner?"

The offer caught her off guard. "I don't know."

She never went out on weekends. She reserved that time for Kerry. She rarely missed any breakfast or dinner with her daughter. The few times she deigned to meet a man outside the office, there were hundreds of thousands of dollars and contracts or labor demands involved. She never went out on a . . . date.

As if he could read her mind through the hesitancy in her voice, Drew pushed her for a response. "It's just business, Em. I found out a few things. It's a little complicated to get into over the phone."

An absurd rush of disappointment deflated her ego. "Do you want to come over to the house?"

"I don't think so. We need to talk, and I don't want any distractions."

"All right." She eyed the precious cargo in the backseat. "I'll get a sitter."

"Fine. I'll pick you up at six-thirty."

"I'll be ready." It didn't please her to discover that she regretted slipping into her business-as-usual mode with Drew. "Anything else?"

"Your friend Maxwell work on the weekends?"

Another request from left field. Another reason to worry, she suspected. "No. But he would if I asked."

"Good. Tell him to beef up security at LadyTech."

"Why?" Every defensive hackle rose to the fore.

"I think someone is trying to infiltrate your company."

"Do you have a name? Who?"

"James Moriarty."

Drew guided Emma into the little out-of-the-way steakhouse and hung his jacket on a brass hook just inside the door. He didn't argue when she said she wanted to keep her coat. Her conversation had dwindled down to the square set of her shoulders and a few perfunctory yeses and noes.

Once at their table, she sat straight with her purse in her lap and darted sidelong glances at the passing patrons and railroad-themed decor. Was the place not classy enough to meet her standards?

She'd chosen to wear casual gray slacks and a sweater instead of something more formal. Even dressed-down, she carried herself with an understated elegance that garnered intrigued glances. He'd hoped to keep things low-key so they could talk. He didn't want to worry about using the right fork or whether his black turtleneck passed a dress code.

Maybe *he* wasn't up to her standards. He'd been touched by her concern over the phone that morning. Paying visits to ratty neighborhoods wasn't a new thing for him, but having someone worry about getting in late was. A four-hour nap had left him feeling refreshed enough to be able to match wits with Emma. Bantering or business-themed, time spent in her company was quickly becoming an addictive thing.

He liked the challenge of her shrewd mind, and was fascinated by the duality of her character. She was at once killer corporate executive and caring, compassionate nurturer. Her appearance even reflected that contrast, with her tall, strong body and those incredible legs. He closed his eyes for a moment to picture the long, sexy curves hidden beneath the tailored wool flannel she wore. He opened his eyes and looked across the table into the gentle sweetness of her freckled face. She could get a man hotter than an August afternoon, or bring out every primal, protective urge he possessed, depending on which personality she emphasized.

Drew had hoped for the sweet-faced mother tonight. Instead, he realized a tad late, Ms. Tall Dark and Dangerous To His Libido had climbed into the car at six-thirty on the dot.

Fine. He could do cool and impersonal, too. He opened his menu and pretended an interest in the memorized list of items. The first words at the table came from the forty-something waitress with bleached blond hair.

"Gallagher!" She punched his shoulder and cheered him with a smile. "Haven't seen you in ages. How are you gettin' along?"

He folded his menu and smiled. "Fine, thanks, Jody."

She picked up his hand and pinched the skin between his thumb and forefinger. The clicking of her tongue carried to the next table, but he didn't mind. "I don't think so. You get leaner and meaner every time I see you. You eatin' enough red meat?"

He twisted his mouth to keep the grin from spreading. "I'm counting on you to fatten me up."

Jody saluted him with two fingers to her brow, and Drew knew an unexpected satisfaction in seeing her accept the good-hearted mission. People should have a purpose, he thought. They always felt better about themselves and did better work if they understood their purpose.

Every man has his job. And every job is important. He heard the words in his mind. Heard them in his own voice. No, another man's voice. But he spoke the words. He glimpsed a memory of another place and another time. Papers, maps spread before him.

Drew flattened his palms on the table and leaned forward, snatching at the papers, snatching at the dream.

He opened his eyes and saw the gold napkin clutched in his fist. He didn't understand where he was, or what it meant.

"Drew?" Emma's cool fingers touched his fisted hand. "Is something wrong?"

He blinked and looked up. Tiny lines grooved beside her eyes as she frowned. Drew captured her hand in his, grounding himself in the reality of her touch, focusing on the careworn hints of time and caring and sadness in her beautiful face.

"Don't be sad, lady," he reassured her. He hated when she looked so sad. He never wanted to be one of the things that deepened the lines beside her eyes.

"What?" Emma jerked her hand away, and the temporary warmth that had shaded her eyes vanished in a cold snap. "What did you say?"

Drew shook his head, stymied by his own confusion. He didn't have a memory, did he? So how the hell did the past and present get so screwed up in his mind?

He settled back in his chair and seized the first

logical excuse that popped into his head. "Guess I'm more tired than I thought."

Though Emma had finally deigned to speak to him, the way she squirmed in her seat without taking her wary gaze off him didn't bode well for a relaxing dinner.

"You sure you're all right, Mr. Gallagher?" He'd forgotten Jody's presence at the table, consumed with his fractured memory and easing Emma's trepidation.

"Yeah." He shrugged off her concern and ordered a beer. "Whatever you have on tap."

"Right." He'd ruined her exuberance with his inexplicable behavior, but she seemed to take it in stride better than Emma. "How about you, ma'am?"

"Coffee." Her pinched look eased for the waitress's benefit. "And ice water, please."

"Coming right up."

With Jody's departure, Emma caught her bottom lip between her teeth again. Drew recognized the subtle habit. A clear sign of distress.

"Is it all right if I have a drink?" he asked. "I may be on your payroll now, but dinner's on me."

"I'm not worried about the money."

He clasped his hands together on the tabletop. "What are you worried about?"

Her hot gaze snapped to his, then just as quickly froze over. "I don't drink."

"Does it bother you that I do?"

"Your habits are no concern of mine. But if you have more than that one beer before we're done, I'm driving."

He wasn't sure how to explain his opinion about drinking. He'd forgotten enough of his life already;

Julie Miller

it made no sense to indulge a behavior that might make him forget more. "I don't plan to get drunk."

"I'm glad to hear it."

"You gonna tell me why?"

"Are you going to tell me why you called me *lady*?"

Drew backed off, wondering if maybe she was as addled in the head as he. "Isn't it obvious? You've got a lot of class. Of course I'm going to call you a lady."

She clutched her purse like a shield and leaned forward. "Not *a lady*. *Lady*. A nickname. You called me *lady*."

"You want me to call you Legs or Sweetheart?"

"My husband called me Lady."

A long swallow of that cold beer sounded pretty damn good right about now. Maybe he'd just dive in head first. But the desire to make a hasty apology faded with the return of her defensive posture.

"Em, you've been on edge since I pulled into the parking lot. I understand you may not want to socialize with me. But this is a respectable enough place to conduct business. Your nose was out of joint long before I let the lady thing slip. Why?"

Glints of light shimmered in her hair at the quick shake of her head. "Why did you choose this place? Did you talk to Jas or BJ?"

"No. I discovered it a couple years back. Driving around town. I just ended up here. It felt . . . comfortable, when I walked in. I eat here once or twice a month now. The food's good. Simple. Plenty of it." He refused to justify himself further. "Do you always answer personal questions with another question?"

"Jonathan proposed to me here."

100

Her bald statement hung in the air like the final count of a boxing match.

Drew's shoulders sank with the depth of his sigh. He raked his fingers through his hair, shaking loose the tension from his scalp. "Why didn't you say something? There are hundreds of places to eat in Kansas City."

"I didn't think it would matter. But it does. I don't think I should be here with you." Her words tumbled all together. "I'm sorry. I know that sounds terribly rude. All the memories, I thought I could handle it, but . . . I can't."

In a flash of insight, Drew realized that the sadness that hung about her was a perpetual thing. For a brief moment, he'd been a cause of it. But his confusion passed and left him with a clear-minded purpose. He *could* do something to ease the load of worry and responsibility she carried so nobly. He didn't have the background to offer compassion; he didn't have the trust to offer a friendly ear. But he did have the ability to take action, the means to provide information, and the instincts to protect her and the things she cared about.

Drew pulled two bills from his wallet and tossed them on the table. Issuing a silent invitation, he grabbed his jacket and escorted her out the door.

A blast of wind hit them, and Drew shifted to Emma's right side. He placed a guiding hand at the small of her back and shielded her from the force of the frigid air. In silent agreement, they quickened their pace along the sidewalk, then cut across an open lane to reach his black Ram truck.

With the best of P. I. Gallagher's habits ingrained in him, Drew scanned the parking lot for oncoming cars, unwelcome guests, and anything else that might look suspicious. He unlocked the passenger door first and held it open for Emma.

Before he could shut the door, she reached out and clasped his forearm. "I'm sorry. Please don't take this personally."

Her soft touch sensitized his skin through layers of leather and wool. Her gentle voice eased his guilt. Deep inside, her simple gesture took away the harm of his mistake. The raw, empty wound inside him ached with the need to be healed by this woman.

But he looked past her through the driver-side window without acknowledging the effect she had on him.

Two cars down. Tweed coat. Brown sedan. Dark, beady eyes looked away when Stan Begosian realized that Drew had him in his sights.

Drew pushed Emma into the truck and slammed the door. A car engine turned over as he raced around the hood and climbed in.

"What are you doing?" Emma gasped at his rudeness.

"Buckle your seat belt." He turned the key in the ignition. Begosian's brown sedan lurched out of its parking space.

"I always do."

Drew crunched the truck into gear. "Buckle it now!"

Emma obeyed the steel in his command without immediately understanding the urgency. The squeal of tires grabbing for traction on the wet pavement caught her attention an instant before Drew stomped his foot on the accelerator and she slammed back into the seat.

The black velour headrest saved her from a nasty case of whiplash. "What . . . ?"

A faded brown Chrysler sped out of the parking lot, dashed in front of another car, and skipped into the second lane of traffic. Drew spun his truck in two opposite ninety-degree angles, tossing her first into his shoulder, then back against the door. He ignored the clear path of the exit ramp and jumped his truck over the decorative berm that surrounded the restaurant's grounds.

"Hold on."

"Drew!" She gripped the dashboard and shoved her hand above her head to brace herself against the teeth-jarring ride.

"That little weasel," Drew muttered to himself.

Ignoring the whining echo of numerous car horns, he, too, cut across traffic and fell in behind the brown car at a climbing speed already well beyond the thirty-five m.p.h. limit.

He wove in and out of the two northbound lanes of traffic, bounced over an alley curb, and closed in on his prey. Since Drew came up with no answer to her unspoken question, Emma tried to put herself into his position. She traced the line of his unblinking gaze and zeroed in on the object of his pursuit.

What she saw shifted her bewilderment from Drew to the driver of the Chrysler. "I saw that car this morning. Behind me in traffic."

"Figures."

She dropped her grip on the ceiling, her body adjusting to the pitch and roll of the wild ride. "Who is it? Why are you chasing him?"

"Our friend Begosian. We're being spied on,

lady." She snapped her attention to the thin slash of his mouth. The endearment sounded foreign in his voice. But the shock of hearing it stabbed a little less painfully this time. He clenched his face in a disgusted frown and cursed. "Sorry. Emma."

That he would correct himself to spare her pain eased a hurtful place inside. It was a tiny gesture, but its sheltering concern penetrated her defensive reserve, warming her like a hug. It was a silly coincidence to hold against him, anyway. How could he possibly know what Jonathan had called her?

"It's all right." She climbed out of her righteous shell and joined the chase. She untucked her shoulder from its harness and reached across his lap to find his seat belt. With her cheek pressed to his side, she could feel the rapid intake of breath that expanded his rib cage. She inhaled the rich scent of leather and Drew, and knew a sudden strength, an energizing rightness to working side by side with this man. She sat up straight and pulled the belt across his legs and chest and buckled him in. "Don't lose him."

He threw her a quick, questioning look, and she spread her lips into a wry grin. "Can't help it. I'm a mom."

His answering smile gleamed with pride. "You're a trouper." All at once he jerked the steering wheel to the left. Emma leaned to the right to counterbalance the sensation of spinning on two wheels. "Whoa! Hold on!" he said.

"Where's he going?"

Drew glanced to the side. "Ritzy part of town."

Emma clutched her armrest and squeezed nervously. "There are a lot of pedestrians here."

"And more places to hide." Drew jammed on the brake and cursed. His arm shot out, catching her in the stomach and saving her from crashing into the dashboard. "Move it!" he yelled through the windshield.

A red sports car sat perpendicular in front of the truck, inches away from a horrible wreck. The driver traded mute insults with Drew through his closed window. Emma sent up a quick prayer of thanks that no one had been hurt, then followed with an equally brief request for Begosian to run out of gas or drop a carburetor as she watched his sedan turn a corner and disappear from sight.

"Don't panic yet." Drew's voice returned to its low-pitched rasp. "That's a dead-end street. He's got to turn into a parking garage or pull into a nightclub at the end of the block."

"You're sure?"

The red car zipped into the flow of cars and Drew followed at a much safer speed. "Watch on your side," he directed, pulling into the parking garage to search for Stan's car.

"I don't see him."

When they exited back onto the street, Drew pulled into a parking space beside a gambling club with a garish neon sign that said LUCKY'S. "Stay put," Drew commanded, setting the parking brake but leaving the engine running. He unzipped his jacket and reached inside. Despite the heater, Emma shivered when she glimpsed the shiny silver color of his gun.

"What are you going to do?"

He turned to her and squeezed her hand, kneading warmth into her fingers with his and dispelling the chill in her heart with the rasp of his voice. "Since I don't see him climbing any rooftops, I'm assuming he went in there."

She looked at the crowd of people standing in a line outside the spotlighted double doors, waiting to get in. "How will you find him in that mess?"

He brushed a tendril of hair from her face and tucked it behind her ear. The soft fingertips of his leather glove caressed her cheek, calmed her, and left a trail of unexpected warmth in their wake. "He thinks like a cockroach. I can think the same way."

"What if he sees you first?"

"He won't."

A blast of cold air broke the spell that had her believing his confident words. But he was gone before she could voice her resurging doubts. She watched as his distinctive golden head merged with the line of patrons. Though he was a bit taller than most, she could still see him when he passed through to the other side. She watched his fluid progress until he disappeared around the corner of the building. A side door? she wondered. Think like a cockroach. Avoid the light and slink into the darkness.

She half praised him, half worried when she decided he had a set of lock-picking tools on him. He'd be just fine, she told herself. She'd read that cockroaches had the survival skills necessary to survive a nuclear holocaust. Drew could survive this.

She gasped aloud when she saw one of the big, beefy bouncers leave his position at the front door and trail along the brick wall, following Drew's path. Her eyes widened to a painful circumference.

Did roaches know when a trap had been set? How could she warn him? What should she do?

"Make it up as I go," she chided herself. She hid her purse beneath the seat, turned off the engine, and pocketed Drew's keys. She locked the truck behind her, draped her scarf over her ears, and plunged into the crowd.

Flying by the seat of her pants was not her style. She liked to plan. Even better, she liked to make a backup plan. She needed predictability. She craved security.

She peeked around the corner and saw nothing but darkness. The streetlight illuminated just the top floors of the building, enough to reveal that the brass lamp above the side door had burned out. She squinted into the dim shadows, searching for a sign of Drew or the bouncer.

"Hey!" The gruff voice came from the side, not ahead of her. Emma took advantage of the darkness and ducked into the shadows as the brawny security man shouted, not at Drew but at a cherubic-faced teenage girl trying not to be noticed from her place in line. The bouncer grabbed her by the arm and walked her to the curb. "Does your mama know where you are?" She shook her head. He whistled for a cab. "You gotta be twenty-one to get in here, babe. Go home."

A gloved hand clamped onto Emma's shoulder and dragged her back into the alley. A second hand muffled her startled yelp. She quickly recognized Drew's familiar scent and ceased to struggle, but his grip held firm. He half dragged, half carried her back through the propped side doorway.

Inside, a cacophony of music and the louder drone of conversation assaulted her ears. Her eyes adjusted to the light, and she could see they were in a storage area sectioned off by plywood walls and black curtains.

Drew kicked out the doorstop, pushed open the door, and pulled her into a partitioned cubby filled with crated bottles of liquor. He released her to pull the curtain shut behind them.

"Did you see the bouncer?" she whispered, giving voice to her concern. "I thought he spotted you. I thought I could distract him. That girl did instead. I hope she's okay."

Drew wrapped his hands around her shoulders and flattened her against the wall. His eyes glowed with an unearthly light, and she fell silent. The energy of his rage quaked through her bones.

"Dammit, Em. When I tell you to stay put, stay put."

Chapter Five

Drew pressed Emma's shoulders into the wall, angry with her for failing to follow a simple direction and trust his judgment. Angry with himself for the swell of fear that had crashed through him when he saw her slender form silhouetted at the front of the alley. She wasn't waiting, snug and safe, half a block away. She was broadcasting his intention, and putting herself in the unwelcome position of breaking the law right along with him.

"The whole idea is for *you* to pay *me* to do the work." He whispered the terse reminder beside her ear. The scruff of his beard caught in her hair. He twisted his jaw to free himself, pulling the strands across his face, tangling him in their silken bonds and filling his nose with the unique scent of her. The soft jolt of spice and damp January air dissipated his anger like a gentle slap in the face.

In a heartbeat, the electric charge of danger mutated into the sensation of heated awareness. Had he stood this close to her last night? Was that why her scent seemed so familiar, why having her molded so snugly against him felt so right? "Your job is to stay in the background . . . so I don't worry about you."

Did that husky tremor echo from his own voice? Her fingers dug into the suede collar of his jacket. The heels of her palms pushed against his chest, yet her clinging hands wouldn't let go. "I thought you were in trouble. I wanted to help." A shrug of uncertainty belied the ice in her voice. This instinctive physical and emotional attachment might not be one-sided, after all. "This is my investigation as much as yours. I have every right to be here."

He allowed her to put a few inches of distance between them, as confused by the mixed message of cold words and caring hands as she was. But he refused to release her entirely. "Not when it puts you in the line of fire," he said. He slipped his hands up to cup her face, smoothing back the tendrils of her long, dark hair. "Dammit, Em, I can take care of myself. You don't have to worry about me."

"But I do." Even in the shadowy absence of light, he imagined he could see her lush mouth trembling with the realization of what she had admitted. Those three words surprised, humbled, and touched him deep in a heart that had forgotten how to feel such things.

"Ah, Em." As if she could see in the dim recesses of the storage room, she moved her hand to his face and brushed the tips of her gloved fingers across his lips. The softness of the expensive leather made him wish for the softer touch of her skin. Her tender quest to touch, to explore, to comfort, eased a wounded place inside him. Her gentle petting teased the empty corners of his mind with a long-sought-for memory, a caring welcome that he had never known. Her concern, albeit misplaced, her healing touch, albeit unearned, reached deep into his heart, deeper into his soul and made him wish. Made him hope. Made him want something that shouldn't be his, something that rightfully belonged to another man.

But he wished, hoped, and wanted Emma all the same.

Forgetting their purpose, forgetting their location, Drew caught the tip of her glove between his teeth and gave a gentle tug. He heard the whisper of the cashmere lining sliding against her skin. He closed his eyes to savor the sound like a caress to his ears. When her hand was freed, he pocketed her glove and pressed a kiss to her palm. She cupped his chin and rubbed her hand along the roughened stubble of his beard. The ragged catch in her breath vibrated through him. Without light to see her by, she was scent and sound, a feast for the senses.

Drew was a hungry man.

His thighs crowded closer to hers, pinning her to the wall. Her hand rasped along his jaw until her long fingers tunneled into his hair, holding him close, welcoming him in a way he had longed for throughout five lonely years. He angled his mouth and grazed her cheek, supping the smooth arc of a dimple as he blazed a trail of touch and taste in search of her mouth.

"Drew." Her voice was a frenzied plea—to stop

111

this madness or to claim her, he couldn't tell. He barely understood his own need to touch her, hold her, make her his own. He opened his mouth over hers, ready to taste her. Their breaths mingled. His senses quivered in anticipation . . .

A loud crash rattled the wall behind Emma. Drew felt the tremor through her body an instant before he identified the sound of a door slamming in the next room. He cursed under his breath, his whole body protesting the intrusion on the stolen moment. He silenced her with a hand over her mouth and attuned his hearing to the raised voices on the other side of the wall. She, too, went still, except for the rapid rise and fall of her chest brushing against him as she struggled to find her breath.

She wrapped her fingers around his hand and pulled it from her mouth, giving a quick nod to assure him she knew she must be silent.

Drew damned himself a thousand times over for putting her into this mess. But the tight grip she kept on his hand was the only outward sign to betray her fear. He squeezed her hand in silent reassurance, ignoring the regret pounding through his body like an unanswered need, and concentrating on the conversation in the office next door.

"What do you mean he spotted you?" An unknown voice snapped deep and clear through the thin walls. "I gave you a simple job. We can't afford another screw-up."

Drew felt Emma flinch at the harsh reprimand. He turned his thumb into her bare palm and massaged the tender skin there, urging her to stay calm.

He identified a second voice, shaky with fear and

apology, as Stan Begosian's. "I couldn't get to her. He was there."

Drew assumed that *he* was the blockade in question. He felt the strain of a prolonged quiet as Emma dug her fingers into the sleeve of his jacket, crushing the leather in her fist. She pressed herself along his arm and placed her lips at his ear. The stirring of her breath along the sensitive shell whipped through him like a gunshot, distracting him from the conversation next door. In an instant, he breathed easier, with a touch of regret, when he realized she wanted to whisper to him.

"I've heard that voice before."

"Who is it?"

"I'm not sure. It's too muffled through the wall. But the intonation, the rhythm of it, sound familiar."

He angled his head, grazing his lips across her cheek as he sought her ear to whisper in return. "Think hard. If you recognize him, we might discover Moriarty sooner than you think."

Something thunked next door. Maybe the sound of bumping into a piece of furniture. Accidentally? Or was someone shoved?

Drew pressed his ear to the wall.

"He's with her all the time." Drew heard Stan's familiar whine. "Like she hired him. Maybe they're onto us. I could fly there myself. Send back some other clue for you to use."

Just what exactly was Stan up to now? Drew wondered.

"No, you idiot. That's not how the plan works." The voice of authority resonated with patronizing kindness. Drew wondered if Stan could hear the subtle threat woven into the bland tone. "I have other people in place who can do this job if you can't."

"She got the disk like you asked."

"With that private eye's help, not yours. Without the message, it's just a piece of the puzzle. A game without directions. I don't suppose she'll listen to any explanation from you now."

There was a silence, and then Begosian again: "So I won't get paid?"

"Did you say anything to her?"

"I can't even pronounce that place. How am I gonna tell Ms. Ramsey where it is? I failed geology in high school."

"The term is *geography*." A chair slid across the floor, and the wood creaked with the weight of a large man. Drew interpreted the clicking sound that followed as the punch of numbers on a phone. His intincts warned him that Stan should get out now. But sometimes a cockroach got caught in a trap.

"Aw, hell," Drew muttered, breaking his own silence and releasing himself from Emma's grip. He moved to the curtained doorway and hovered there, torn between the hunch that his best lead was about to be terminated and the responsibility to protect her from this grim side of life.

"Should we try to do something?" Her question was equally quiet. He wasn't surprised to feel the heat of her body as she crept up beside him. Whatever fear she had felt before receded behind her overriding desire to find out the truth.

"If I asked you to stay put, would you listen?" He asked the question with a frown, already suspecting her answer.

"You're not leaving me alone this time." Her hushed determination made him smile.

Two sets of footsteps in the hallway propelled Drew back into the corner of the storage room, pushing Emma safely behind him. Without thinking, he'd made his decision. She came first. The job, her answers, and everything else landed a distant second. The newcomers stopped at the office door and entered.

The man in charge next door greeted them with a perfunctory recitation of names. "Roylott. Jackson. Why don't you give Mr. Begosian a ride home, like we discussed earlier."

"Don't bother," said Stan. "I got my car outside."

"It's no trouble. I'll have Jackson drive you in the limo."

"Yes, sir."

Drew strained to hear a name for the man giving the orders. A shuffling sound, maybe a halfhearted struggle on Stan's part, was the only response he heard.

Drew felt Emma squeeze his arm. But she kept her urgent voice hushed. "He's getting away."

Did she have any clue that Begosian might not be escaping at all? He freed himself from her fingers and slipped into the hallway. If luck was with him, he'd get a name or a face to track Begosian's contact. He sneaked up to the black curtain and peered through, but luck had abandoned him. He caught a glimpse of two well-clad male backsides; one man had a good grip on Stan, and they all disappeared through another curtain at the far end of the hall.

A crashing sound, followed by the tinkling of

shattered glass and Emma's startled yelp, spun him around. "Em?"

An open box lay at her feet; a puddle was already spreading on the floor around her. He smelled the tang of whiskey. She met his surprise with a frantic whisper. "I just wanted to get a look at the man with the voice. See if I knew him. I tripped. I didn't mean—"

"Who's there?" A sharp voice and hurried feet homed in on their hiding place. With destiny closing in on them and nowhere to run, Drew reached for Emma. Ignoring the opposing tug of her arm, he pulled harder and heard the crunch of glass beneath her boots as she toppled off balance and collided against his chest.

Still raw from their earlier embrace, Drew cinched his arms around her to still her struggles, and ignored both the stab of frustrated heat deep in his gut and the fist of guilt tightening around his heart.

He brushed a cascade of hair off her face and caught it at her nape, holding her firmly in his grasp. He bent his head to the startled sigh that puffed between her lips. "You can call me every kind of bastard in the morning, but work with me here, okay?"

"What are you—"

He covered her mouth with his, driving the protest back down her throat. He tipped her head back and let his hair fall around their faces, shielding her startled blue eyes from view just as the curtain whisked to one side and light flooded the hallway.

Drew squinted against the sudden glare and pulled Emma tight, smoothing his hands up and down her back. He traced her long contours through the bulk of her coat, learning her shape and appreciating each curve and hollow he came in contact with.

And Emma was a quick study. She joined the charade, going slack and sinking into him. She wound her arms around his neck, further hiding their faces from the speculative eyes of their surprise visitor.

The feral moan that whimpered deep in her throat diverted him from the purpose of this kiss. He tore his mouth from hers and laved his way down her swanlike neck to that warm, pulsing spot at the curve of her throat where the siren's call hummed. Her fingers entwined in his hair, clutching at him, guiding his lips toward that sensitive spot that made her tremble in his arms, then driving his mouth back to hers. Her lips opened beneath him, pliant and seeking. She tasted familiar and perfect, and oh, so right. He thrilled to the exploration of her tongue running along the arc of his teeth and tasting the tender inside of his lip. He was at once tutor and tutored, unknown to any subject save the taste and feel of this wild and wonderful Emma.

He skidded his hand over the swell of her hip to the juncture of her thigh. He cupped her bottom when she bent her knee and rubbed one long, elegant leg against his. The friction of wool against denim, of feminine softness against hard male need, shook him to the very core.

He was still reeling from the impact of their incendiary passion when a foreign hand clamped down on his shoulder. It took every bit of Drew's considerable willpower not to turn and lash out at the offending interruption. As if in a moment out of time, he had forgotten their audience, their precarious position. He'd forgotten that this was an act. For Emma, at least. At some point in the dangerous charade he had left any assumed persona behind and succumbed to the need to be wanted by this woman, to want her. He'd forgotten Drew Gallagher and answered her kiss as the man he once was, the man buried deep inside, the man he had lost in an unknown accident five years in the past.

The man he might never be again.

"Hey, buddy. We call it Lucky's because of the gambling. Behind the bar is off limits to customers. You either get some out front, or you take her home." Drew straightened beneath the hand on his shoulder and pulled away from Emma, catching her hair and letting it fall across her cheek to mask her face.

But his gaze never left her. He never once blinked, fearing he had misread the openness in her expression, the glaze of unsatiated passion that darkened her eyes to a clear, deep blue. Had she been putting on a show to cover their presence in the back hallway? Or had she, too, gotten lost in the moment?

He trailed his fingers down her arm and squeezed her hand before pulling away, transmitting his mute apology.

"C'mon, pal."

He didn't protest when the big man pulled his hand away from Emma. A look of sadness transformed her features, closing her off as if a door had slammed in his face. Drew rallied his common sense and remembered their purpose at the club.

He pulled her beneath the crook of his arm and turned her face into his shoulder, hiding her from both the man he assumed to be a personal bodyguard and anyone else they might encounter. To his knowledge, only Stan Begosian recognized either of them, but Drew thought it wise to conceal Em's face as they walked past the office next door.

She wrapped her arm around his waist and stayed close, prolonging the pretense of being an amorous couple. She seemed amazingly adept at separating real feelings and actions from ones put on for show. The skill didn't sit well with Drew. A woman like Emma shouldn't possess that kind of expertise, the same ability that he'd picked up from years of keeping to himself and working undercover.

Was losing a husband and going on with her life alone motivation enough to learn to shift so quickly from an honest expression of emotion to a cool, false mask? Or had something more happened to this tall, strong beauty to make her so cool-headed and clever?

He glanced through the open office door and disguised his frustrated sigh on a whispered word of encouragement. The room stood empty, and the nameplate bore only a title: MANAGER.

"What'll it be, pal?" the man asked, pushing Drew and Emma into the bar.

Keeping her head bowed, Emma looked at the twisting bodies on the dance floor. A tremor rippled through her, and she settled more heavily against him. "Take me home."

"Whatever you say."

Two steps into the crowd and Drew stopped at a tap on his arm. Angling Emma from view, he turned to the bouncer in the fine-cut wool suit who had discovered them. The man's acne-scarred face creased in a rueful smile. "Hey, sorry about the bad luck, man, but rules are rules. The boss doesn't like surprises in the back room. Good luck."

Drew refused to acknowledge the leering wink. "I'll try to keep my libido in check next time."

He turned to move on, but the big hand closed around his elbow. "Say, don't I know you? You look familiar."

Emma stiffened at Drew's side. He gave her shoulder a reassuring rub, but kept any alarm out of his expression. "I don't think so. I'm new in town."

"Yeah? I'm from out of town myself, but I never forget a face. It'll come to me sooner or later."

"What's your name?" Drew forced the irony from his voice. "Maybe it will jog my memory."

"Clayton Roylott."

He shook the man's hand without revealing his own name. "Clayton," he repeated. "If I think of where we met, I'll give you a call. You have a card?"

"Nah. But you can reach me here at the club. They'll know where to find me if I'm not around."

"I'll do that. Well . . ." Drew inclined his head toward Emma, and Clayton interpreted the message as he intended.

"Say no more. Hope I didn't spoil the mood."

Drew nodded his farewell and guided Emma through the crowd and out the door. Once beyond the line of customers, she shoved him away and sucked in a huge breath of reviving air. He inhaled the brisk January night and let the cold work its way through his own overheated body. She unlocked the passenger door of his truck and handed him the key, refusing his assistance. He stewed in the silence of his guilt, matching her cool demeanor until he drove the truck into the outskirts of her Mission Hills neighborhood.

He couldn't let their evening end like this. He'd invited her out on business, hoped for a relaxing evening in her sweet company. But somehow events had gotten way out of hand. He'd chosen the worst possible restaurant to wine and dine her. Discovered she didn't like the wine part. Chased Begosian. Eavesdropped on a dangerous conversation.

Kissed her.

And he'd driven for twenty minutes with little on his mind but the inexplicable desire to kiss her again.

Not for show. Not for an audience.

For himself.

But he let his consideration focus on her needs. "I never fed you dinner tonight. Want me to drive somewhere and get you a hamburger?"

"I'm not hungry." Her voice rang with the steel ramrod that stiffened her spine. "What do you think they're going to do to Stan?"

All business. Maybe she was even better than he at turning off unwanted emotions. Fine. He'd give her the security of sticking to business. For now. "I'm sure it'll be nothing good."

He turned onto a side street. She stared straight ahead. "What do you think he was supposed to tell me?"

Drew shrugged. "The boss mentioned geography. Stan offered to fly somewhere. Makes me

121

think it's nothing local, or Stan would recognize the name. Where was your husband last seen?"

"Isla Tenebrosa. It's a small country in the Caribbean."

Her matter-of-fact answer stabbed him like a knife in the gut. A very sharp, very jagged knife from his past. He grunted in pain, as if the wound were physical instead of mental. His vision whirled out of focus and he stomped on the brake. He spun off onto the gravel shoulder and killed the engine, too overcome to drive another inch. He wrapped his arms around the steering wheel and rested his forehead on his wrist, willing the dizziness to pass.

No. Don't fight it. Listen. Listen with your heart, not your head.

"Stop saying that!" he snapped at the soft voice that played games inside his mind.

"I didn't say anything." A different voice, equally soft but tinged with a deeper, husky pitch, spoke beside him. Emma's voice.

He dared to open his eyes and saw her backed against the far door. She still sat straight, but a hesitant frown grooved the worry lines beside her eyes. He couldn't quite find it within himself to ease her concern. The coincidence was too perfect, too frightening to ignore. "You said Tenebrosa?"

"It's an island nation east of the Yucatan Peninsula of Mexico."

"I know where Tenebrosa is."

"Most people haven't heard of it. That was the target of Jonathan's last mission. It's a perfect place for illegal activities since it doesn't draw much attention to itself. It has few allies and little strategic importance."

"You've got the travelogue memorized." Her

recitation wasn't too different from what he'd learned in the research he'd done on the island.

"Have you been there?" Her innocent question brought haunting memories flooding back.

Drew's first conscious recollection was waking up in a hospital on Tenebrosa. He'd been full of tubes and needles, and bandaged from his neck to his hips and down most of his right arm. He'd ridden in an ambulance to an airstrip and flown on to Mexico City, where the skin grafts and stitching had continued in a more sterile environment. He'd gone back to the island after that first year, searching for a familiar face, a business person in town who recognized him, a place he felt at home.

He found nothing.

He remembered nothing.

He only knew that his life had started over again five years ago.

On Tenebrosa.

"Drew? Have you been to Tenebrosa?" He heard Emma's insistent voice like a distant echo. "Can you tell me anything about that place?"

Drew ignored the careening abyss of his memories. He ignored the cautious mix of curiosity and concern on Emma's face.

"Nothing you don't already know." The abruptness, of his response silenced her. He started the truck and drove her to her house, seizing on the one aspect of his life that made any sense. His work.

"I'll check out Clayton Roylott; maybe I can get some more names from him."

Emma's hand hovered at the door handle. She probably couldn't wait to get back to her normal suburban life, and as far away from him as she could get. He didn't blame her. He couldn't count the number of times he'd wanted to get away from his life himself.

"You never told me how James Moriarty is a threat to LadyTech." Now her hesitation made sense. She was responsible to her friends and company, and determined to find the truth. Two qualities he couldn't help but admire.

"He paid Begosian ten thousand dollars to buy stock in your company under the name John Clay a few days before he assaulted you at the Nelson Gallery. Any idea why?"

She thought for a moment. "It would be an easy way, and a legal one, to get a report on the company without raising any suspicions. If this Moriarty's trying to get into LadyTech, it's a good place to start. Or if he purchased stock under an alias, he may be trying to buy up a controlling share."

"You might be onto something."

"It's impossible to do, though. Jas, BJ, and I retained fifty-one percent before we put it on the open market."

"Moriarty may not know that."

She nodded. "I'll watch the reports. See if any other big buys come up. Anything else?"

With the variety of hells he'd endured this evening, one golden piece of heaven remained foremost in his mind. "Was it really so horrible that I kissed you?"

The light from her front porch cast a shimmering glow across her alabaster cheek, capturing her down-turned eyes in a smoky shadow. "No."

Her husky admission settled deep inside him, giving comfort to a soul that knew so little of her honest brand of kindness. She swallowed, drawing his gaze like a magnet to the graceful arch of her throat. "I understand that you wanted to hide our identities tonight," she said. "We were caught where we shouldn't have been. I even understand, and take responsibility for that kiss getting out of hand. I wanted . . . I haven't been held that way for a long time. But . . ."

She held up her left hand and twisted it so the light reflected off the wedding band on her third finger. "This is why it can't happen again."

He hardened his gaze on the unnecessary reminder of all that stood between them.

Drew leaned back on his side of the truck cab, physically and emotionally pulling away from the temptation before him. He couldn't give her what she didn't want. And he didn't want what she wouldn't give willingly. "It won't happen again. You leave the dirty work to me, Missus Ramsey." He emphasized her married title, knowing he was just the means to an end for her, and could never be anything more to this particular woman. "I promise to mind my manners better."

She curled her fingers into her palm. "I'll try to stay out of your way and let you work. But call me if you find out anything. I'll leave a pass at the front desk so you can come into the office on Monday without Brodie breathing down your neck."

Drew dredged up a rusty laugh. "Be sure to tell him I'm working for you. I don't see going one-on-one with him and coming out in very good shape."

"I have a feeling you're the kind of man who always lands on his feet."

The hint of a smile curved the corners of her mouth. Any compliment from Emma warmed and strengthened him like high praise. But since the smile never reached her eyes, Drew tamped down on his ego's immediate reaction. He traded an observation with her instead. "You're pretty resilient yourself."

Her eyes widened like the huge buttons on the front of her coat, but they reflected an icy chill instead of the promise of warmth. "Jonathan taught me how to be that way. He saved my life in more ways than I can count."

Then, despite his growing jealousy, Drew was grateful to Emma's missing husband.

"Find him, Drew. I owe you a debt because you rescued my daughter and you rescued me. But I owe my husband a debt, too. Find him soon."

Emma slipped out of the car and hurried to the front door. She unlocked it and disappeared inside before he made any attempt to move. *I owe you a debt*. He supposed that was as close to an admission of gratitude as he would ever get from her. He had no right to hope that she might, one day, feel something more. No right to wish that some woman, equally gentle and strong and bright and beautiful, had the same kind of faith in him.

He slid the truck into gear and left the light of Emma's home to return to his world of darkness. Jonathan Ramsey had better be one hell of a guy to deserve Emma's loyalty.

To deserve Emma, period.

Faith tucked the covers around her young charge and the hand-sewn doll cradled so lovingly in her arms. The doll was a tiny replica of Kerry herself, with brown yarn hair and embroidered blue eyes.

"Oh, dear." She sat on the edge of the bed, her gaze

focused on an unseen point in the distance until Kerry tugged on her sleeve and captured her attention.

"What is it?"

"Things aren't going exactly the way I had in mind. Your mother and Mr. Gallagher aren't working together very well."

"But Drew's nice."

"I know, sweetie." She reached down and smoothed the bangs from Kerry's forehead, absorbing strength from the hopeful blue eyes that looked up at her. Kerry's lip pouted and she looked at her doll. Faith got the message and smoothed yarn bangs as well. "That's what makes it so hard for your mom."

Kerry shrugged her shoulders, enlightening Faith with seven-year-old wisdom. "He's not a very good reader. He made up words that weren't in the book. But I liked his story better. When Mom reads it, the frog turns into a prince. But when Drew told it, the princess turned into a frog!"

Faith's laughter faded before Kerry's. The old fairy tale seemed like a sordid retelling of the horror story she'd inadvertently created for Jonathan Ramsey. Still, she kept her promises. She'd watched over Emma and Kerry because Jonathan had loved them so. She'd dropped clues and created distractions and used every power available to her to reunite the family so horribly torn asunder.

But since little Kerry was the only human she could clearly communicate with, her options were limited. She doubted that Emma or Jonathan would believe the direct approach, anyway, and listen to her explanation of the truth.

No, she had to bargain and scheme and push and

127

pry. And none of those qualities would help her earn her wings.

The nightlight beside the bed shuddered. Faith threw her hands wide and spoke to the light. "That is the idea, isn't it? I learn my lesson? Get my wings?"

"Faith?" A small hand clasped her fingers. "Are you in trouble?"

"Seems I always have been, sweetie."

"I'll put in a good word for you when I say my prayers tomorrow night."

Kerry's innocent trust reminded Faith of the reason she had interfered in the Ramseys' lives in the first place. "Thanks." She squeezed the girl's hand to reassure her. "I hope putting Mr. Gallagher on the case will help your mom find the truth faster."

The girl's big yawn signaled the end of her visit. Faith kissed Kerry's cheek and the little doll tucked in beside her. She gathered herself into a gentle light and floated to the foot of the bed.

"Faith?"

"Hmm?"

"Angelica doesn't have any wings, either."

Faith smiled at the toy's name. "Your doll? That's because she's not an angel, sweetie."

"Will you get your wings when my mom is happy again?"

"That's not up to me."

Kerry rolled onto her side, her eyelids already heavy with sleep. "If you don't get any, I'll make you some. Okay?"

The urge to cry swelled inside her and burned her throat. But she had no time for tears. "I'd like that, Kerry. I'd like that very much. And when I get mine, I'll be sure Angelica gets her wings, too."

" 'Kay."

So much faith for one so small. Faith felt her power grow, strengthened by one little girl's hopes and dreams.

This time, she would not fail. Come . . . oops—she glanced up and apologized before the word slipped out—high water, she would not fail. Of course, that meant working a bit harder, thinking more clearly, planning more carefully.

She drifted to the top of the stairs, and eased Emma's tired tread with an invisible kneading of her shoulders. Emma turned at the comforting gesture, but Faith knew she saw nothing.

Once mother and daughter had said their good nights, Faith hurried from the house and sped toward her last best chance to turn this whole mess around.

Her good intentions were a test she'd failed one too many times, on earth, and at the citadel. She had her work cut out for her.

She'd keep trying until she got it right.

She'd keep trying until someone who could make a difference believed in the truth.

She'd keep trying until Jonathan Ramsey came home.

Chapter Six

Emma sat pretzel-style on the study floor, half buried in the stacks of letters and photo albums. The tissue box beside her had been opened and put to use, though she felt a twinge of guilt to see that the box was still nearly full. Three or four years ago, even six months ago, the box would be half empty. But as the evening outside blackened into the deepest part of night, she discovered she had less of a need to cry, and more of a willingness to say good-bye, to pack these things up with loving care and store them in the attic instead of the easy access of the hall closet.

She turned the page of the photo album in her lap and traced the pictures with careful reverence. Her gaze touched on an image of a windblown Jonathan, standing tall and broad with that ready smile on his face. Bits of leaves and twigs clung to his short, dark hair and bright red sweater. Emma touched her finger to the spot where his hand rested over her tummy in the picture. Her pregnancy with Kerry was just beginning to show. He was home between missions and quite enamored of her rounding figure.

Raking leaves had become an impromptu opportunity for them to roll together in a pile while he kissed her senseless. Jas and her camera had come along just in time to remind them that the backyard was a fairly public place. Even in the photograph, Jonathan's blue eyes twinkled with the promise of more to come, and she remembered him resuming the seduction later that night.

Emma closed her eyes and tried to recapture the joy of that day so long ago. Though ten years her senior, Jonathan had rejoiced like a kid at the prospect of becoming a daddy. God, how he had loved his little girl. Building things for her, collecting trinkets from around the world, writing her little notes even before she was born.

He might have been part of Kerry's life for only two years, but the bond between father and daughter had been full of promise and love. Not at all like Emma's relationship with her father, who'd come home some nights and looked right through her as if she were a stranger.

She pushed the unpleasant thought from her mind and closed the book. Squeezing her eyes shut, she tried to fixate on the memory of making love that night of the picture. Jonathan's hands skimming her legs, his fingers buried in her hair, his kiss . . .

. . . was raw and purely sensual, surprising himself as much as her, judging by the guttural gasp

131

deep in his throat. His beard stubble grazed her skin along the arc of her neck, pricking her with the tantalizing anticipation of the moist warmth of his lips to follow. And when he found that bundle of nerves at the base of her throat, she forgot about everything else except the sensation of enveloping heat closing around her, rising within her. She pressed herself to his solid length, her body awakening from its self-imposed hibernation to the lure of someone stronger, someone harder than she. Awakening to the utterly female rush of needy hands on her back and legs. Awakening to the erotic feel of long blond hair tangled in her bare fingers.

Awakening to Drew Gallagher's passion.

"Oh, God." Her eyes snapped open, and she clapped her hand to her mouth in a wry mimicry of Drew's gloved hand covering her mouth and silencing her. Good God, what had she done?

Last night, he'd meant to keep her quiet so as not to reveal their presence. Twenty-four hours later, she was trying to stifle her own treacherous thoughts. Even now, her skin tingled with heat inside her sweater. She couldn't blame the uncomfortable temperature on the dying embers in the fireplace. Her breathing didn't grow ragged at the memory of the danger she'd escaped last night, but at the memory of her instantaneous need to be kissed and held by a man. A man who thrived on danger. A man who talked tough. A man unlike her husband in every way except one.

He made her feel safe.

Jonathan had smiled and cajoled and bargained and demanded his way through two years of courtship with her, breaking down each defensive barrier, whittling down her wall of distrust, until she realized she could be safe with a man. She could give him her body, her heart, and her soul, and know that all three would be cherished by him.

She'd known Drew Gallagher for all of two days, and already she'd made the mistake of dropping her guard and allowing her body to react to his touch in a basic, elemental, wanton kind of way. That was all it could be, she warned herself. A physical attraction. And she'd given into it because this rough, no-holds-barred, take-no-prisoners man of mystery and darkness had somehow managed to make her feel safe.

"Oh, God." She repeated the little prayer and opened the album once more, staring at Jonathan's picture, willing his image to replace the clearer, fair-haired likeness of Drew Gallagher in her mind.

Spreading her fingers, she traced her wedding ring with her thumb, reminding herself of all it represented. The action couldn't help but remind her how Drew had taken her hand in the back room of Lucky's, squeezed it tight, telling her to be strong. He'd rubbed her palm with the rough pad of his thumb, teasing her senses, earning her trust, sharing his strength.

She had waved the ring in Drew's face last night, warning him to keep an impersonal distance. Why couldn't she follow her own request? Why did she have to be so drawn to him? Why did she feel she needed him, as she had needed no other man before or since Jonathan?

Maybe she should refuse his offer to help find Jonathan, hire someone else. But, on his own, he'd already uncovered more new leads than a cadre of detectives and officials had turned up in three years.

"I can do this," she told herself, rolling the tension from her shoulders and stiffening her spine. "I can work with him as a professional. Keep everything polite and impersonal."

Her pep talk fell on skeptical ears. Her problem with Drew Gallagher was that she'd already let things get way too personal.

"M-Mom?"

She slammed the album closed and spun around on her bottom, startled as if Kerry had somehow read her mind and caught her thinking of a man other than her father.

"Sweetie." She waited for the breathiness to subside from her voice, then reached out to Kerry. "It's after midnight. What are you doing out of bed?"

Kerry plunked down on Emma's lap and wrapped herself in her lavender blanket and her mother's hug. "I w-wanted a drink."

Emma frowned above her daughter's head, wondering what was really going on. "I left your cup of water on the bedside table."

"You w-weren't in your bed." She snuggled closer. "Are you b-being sad?"

"Oh, sweetie." She wrapped herself around Kerry's petite frame and hugged her close. "I'm just fine. What made you think I was sad?"

"Be-c-cause Faith can't get her wings."

Kerry rose and fell with Emma's sigh of frustration. "Your friend Faith has wings?"

"No. She says you have t-t-to be happy before she can get them."

Kerry's verbal language had emerged at a young age. Before the age of two, she'd begun to put together long phrases and complex thoughts without a trace of a stutter. Imaginary friends hadn't existed then, either.

She'd been so young when Jonathan disappeared. Not for the first time, Emma wondered if she had projected her own sadness, her anger and feelings of betrayal, onto Kerry. She'd worked so hard, talked to so many counselors, to keep her daughter from being victimized by her troubles. Kerry might be a tad shy, but she did well in school and had a circle of real friends of all ages. Emma couldn't explain her daughter's handicap; she couldn't cure it. So she chose not to argue about Faith this time, and worked instead on the more tangible problem she could address.

"I'm not sad tonight." Confused, yes. Feeling more guilty than she cared to admit. But not sad. She opened the album on their laps. "I was looking at some pictures of your father." She stopped on the page with Jonathan's formal portrait taken when he'd earned the rank of lieutenant colonel. "Here's your dad. Isn't he handsome? He loves you so much."

Kerry studied the picture. "My d-dad doesn't look like that anymore."

"You're right. He may have gray in his hair now. Or wrinkles. Do you remember what your dad looks like?"

"I know wh-what Daddy looks like."

Emma smiled and hugged her close. "You've seen his picture a lot, haven't you?"

Kerry squiggled free, pushing the album to the floor and kneeling in front of her. Her forehead crinkled into a frown as she studied Emma with a grown-up intensity. Emma pulled the seam of her

135

lips between her teeth, fighting the urge to smile in the face of such a serious expression.

"D-Drew is my daddy."

"What?" Any urge to smile vanished.

"Faith told me. D-D-Drew is my daddy."

She sat at the main desk, greeting him with a smile that radiated from the fresh-scrubbed shine of her freckled face and made him forget the purpose of his visit. Surrounded by tiers of equipment, stacks of paper, and shades of beige from floor to ceiling, she smiled.

She stood out from the drab decor like a poinsettia stands out against snow. She had lustrous dark hair, classic features, and that sweet, sweet smile.

"May I help you?"

"Stand fast, you bastard!" A very different voice intruded, splintering the serene picture in his dreams.

"Stand fast or I'll shoot!"

The grenade pin sailed through the air. He fired his weapon and contorted his body, diving, crashing into his enemy. He was scorched by heat, numbed by pain.

"No!"

Drew thrashed in his sleep as the nightmare took hold.

He wanted it back. He wanted the peace. The momentary glimpse of beauty. He wanted . . .

"Don't listen." Another voice. More of a thought than a sound.

"You crazy sonofa . . ."

"Tenebrosa is a helluva place to die!"

His voice? Or another man's?

Certain death. Kill or be killed.

"Believe with your heart, not your head."

He twisted, fighting to pinpoint the soft-spoken source of the warning.

He'd stared at her too long to be polite, but not long enough to finish cataloguing every beautiful detail of her appearance.

"Sir, may I help you?"

"Emma?" He called to her in his sleep, a croaking plea for something just beyond his reach.

His world exploded in a flash of fire and searing pain, ripping his flesh, tearing at his heart, and plunging his mortal soul into oblivion.

Drew shot up in bed and rubbed his forehead, brushing the stinging sweat from his eyes. The top sheet and blankets pooled around his hips, exposing his torso down to the waist. The remnants of his nightmare flashed through his mind. He shivered.

Dream or vision?

He combed his fingers through the hair at his temples, smoothing the damp strands behind his ears. The jungle, the heat, the chase—the details were always the same. But now Emma Ramsey had appeared to him a second time, her face added to her distinct husky voice, the only reprieve from the indecent torment of his sleep.

"Ah, lady." He punched his pillow as if he could silence the turmoil that spun in the blank hole where his memories should be. "What the hell do you have to do with me?"

The ringing of the phone saved him from having to face sleep again. He snatched it off the nightstand and hit the talk button. "Gallagher."

A moment of static answered the sharpness his voice.

"Drew? Did I wake you?"

An unexpected calm seeped through him at the soft sound of Emma's voice.

"What's wrong?" He snatched his glasses off the nightstand, the pleasure of hearing her voice giving way to instincts that warned him of news he didn't want to hear even before he could see the clock. Two in the morning. She didn't bother with pleasantries, and neither did he. "Em?"

"Can you come over to the house? There's something I need to discuss with you."

"Now?"

His heart went out to her as he heard her swift intake of breath. Damn. He wished he were there to hold her right now. To take her hand again. To support her with his presence, if that would be all she'd accept from him.

"Yes."

"I'll be there in thirty minutes, if not sooner."

Drew paced back and forth in the kitchen, hot, strong coffee warming the mug in his hand. He stopped at the tile counter and raked his fingers through his hair, feeling totally out of his league. "So what do you want me to do? Talk to her?"

Emma matched his pacing on the opposite side of the table. "No. Yes. I don't know." She planted her hands on her hips and tipped her head up to the light of the Williamsburg brass chandelier, revealing the shadows that marred the translucent skin beneath her eyes. "I don't see how she could be so confused. You and Jonathan are nothing alike. He's taller. Dark. Incredibly structured and organized. He lives and breathes the military. You're less . . ."

"Less heroic?" There was nothing like being

compared to another man and coming in second. He dared her to deny her opinion of him.

She met his eyes and his challenge, then dropped her gaze into the shadows. But he felt the intensity of her glare, the sting in her correction. "Less predictable. Less polished. As much as Kerry likes you, you don't strike me as a family man."

Drew swallowed hard and turned away. Hell. He didn't know if he was a family man or not. Maybe if he had lost his family, they were glad to be rid of him. No one had come for him in the Mexican hospital. No one had responded to his picture at police stations across the North American continent. He couldn't imagine anyone looking for him the way Emma pursued her missing husband. Nah, he probably wasn't a family man.

He certainly knew little enough about kids. Kerry's behavior mystified him. She sure was a pistol, though. Pretty as a picture, like her mom. Delicate, and endearing with that speech impediment. But strong and opinionated beyond her years. Like her mom in that department, too.

He lifted his shoulders in a nonchalant shrug, as if Emma's words hadn't stirred up the haunting question of his past. "I wouldn't know."

"You don't know if you're family material? Or you just haven't found the person you want to make a family with yet?"

Backed into a corner, Drew had to decide whether to tell Emma about his amnesia or make up one of the cover stories that came too easily to him these days. He settled for an explanation somewhere in between. "I don't have any family now."

His vague statement left plenty of room for interpretation, and he could imagine Emma speculating on all the possibilities.

"You lost your family?"

The tremulous compassion in her voice carried across the room and breathed new life into his lonely heart. She understood what it was like to have your life ripped away. Maybe better than anyone else could. Drew squeezed his eyes shut at the answering swell of emotion inside him. The skin on his chest and arms tingled with the need to hold her again. His heart ached to open up and share the healing truth he sensed he could find in this woman. "Ah, lady . . ."

He snapped his eyes open, hearing the endearment on his lips the same way Emma must have heard it. As her lost husband would have said it.

He jumped to soothe her. "I'm sorry. I know . . ." But the slip had already cost him the shared moment. The electric current that had bound them for a few moments vanished in the echo of a misspoken word. Drew swallowed his coffee, relishing the burn of the hot liquid in his mouth and throat. He didn't know which hell he preferred, the nightmarish abyss of his forgotten life or the way his heart kept getting twisted up by the husky voice and rare courage of Emma Ramsey.

That she would reach out to him when she suffered her own heartache seemed unjust. That he could spoil her attempt with a single word seemed par for the course.

He shed his confusion, his feelings, and pulled out the edgy self-reliance that had gotten him through the last five years. "I thought I was here to talk about Kerry, not me."

Emma covered her own exposed emotions by

140

crossing to the coffee-maker and pouring a few drops into her already full cup. "You must have said something to her to make her call you Daddy. I think she's experiencing some sort of hero-worship. I'll call her therapist in the morning."

"But you called me tonight. You must want something from me." Drew watched her lift her head up and straighten her spine. He recognized the effort to gird herself against an unpleasant task. He squared his own shoulders, bracing for his defense. "All I did was read her a story and tuck her into bed."

"And rescue her from that 'bad man.'"

"She asked me if I was a good guy."

Emma turned and looked him in the eye, a maternal version of the corporate warrior he'd seen before. "In her mind, you are."

Drew bristled at the underlying implication. To Kerry, he might be a good guy, but Emma didn't believe it. And he couldn't say or do anything to change her opinion. The impression of being attacked for no good cause sprang upon him. The lonely, fortifying posture of being the outsider hardened the set of his jaw and shut down his willingness to reason with her. He'd read and observed how mothers weren't necessarily the most rational of creatures when they thought their children were at risk.

Two hours of tortured sleep, the gnawing emptiness in his mind, and his mixed-up desire for a woman he couldn't have, had hardly put him in the mood to be reasonable or patient. He pulled out the chair at the head of the table and straddled it, leaning over his elbows on the table and staring at the mug he balanced between his hands.

"So how do you want to handle this?" He put the decision in her hands. "You want me to quit the case? Bug out of your life for good so you don't have to deal with me?"

"Quit the case?" She set her mug in the sink and moved a few steps closer. Maybe he hadn't destroyed all her goodwill. Judging by her response, she hadn't considered that option. Yet.

Drew forged ahead, the independent survivor in him determined to force Emma to make a conscious decision to eject him from her life, even though the lost soul in him yearned for her to make the opposite choice and ask him to stay. To openly, irrevocably invite him into her life.

He spelled it out for her. "I'm one hell of an inconvenience. Your friends don't approve of me. I put you in the line of danger. I apparently make your daughter think crazy things. You should put your life back the way it was before you met me."

Emma now stood at the far end of the table, her expression unclear in the shadows cast by the overhead light. To his surprise—or maybe not so surprising, since she was a woman who preferred the direct approach—she breezed past that chair and sat to his immediate left. She matched his posture, resting her elbows on the table and leaning in to share the same circle of light.

"According to what we heard and saw last night, I'd be in danger whether you were around or not. At least with you here, there's someone else to sense the threat before it strikes, or to think on his feet and get us out of it. Begosian would have followed me, anyway. Because of you, we learned something from it."

Whoa. Just when he thought she'd stay whole-

some and superior enough to justify holding a
grudge against her, she threw him a curve. She
actually saw value in the slimier skills he possessed
in such abundant supply. He tried not to read anything personal into it. He'd think of it as a professional compliment, an olive branch thrown out
onto a negotiating table. "We didn't learn very
much."

She counted off items on her fingers. "We have
another name. Clayton Roylott. We have a boss—"

"He's just a voice, Em."

"A voice I may know." She touched his hand and
pulled it down to the tabletop, moving his focus
and securing eye contact with him. "We could go
back to Lucky's and snoop around, try to put a face
to that voice. And we know he has other plans,
other people in place. So someone else will try to
contact me."

Drew set down his coffee cup, alarmed by the
reckless determination gleaming in her eyes.
"You're not going back there."

"Why not? That Clayton thinks he knows you.
Maybe he'll open up and talk. I could mix with the
crowd and see if I recognize anyone."

"Do you understand what kind of people those
men were?"

"They're criminals."

"They're not just petty thieves or gamblers." He
captured her fingers in his. "Did you hear the
directive about Begosian? We'll be reading about
his dead body floating in Brush Creek or tied up on
the river docks in the next day or two."

He'd intended to shock some sense into her with
his harsh words, but he hadn't prepared for his
own reaction to the ebb of color from her cheeks.

Even the gray-blue color of her eyes seemed to blanch at the truth.

Her gaze dropped to the tangle of their fingers on the table. She clutched his hand with the same force he had used to snare her attention. "I know Jonathan dealt with . . . people like that."

Drew reached out and tucked a wayward curl of hair behind her ear. He cupped his hand there, gently turning her focus back to him. "Those are the kind of men we're dealing with. They're the kind of men I deal with. Think about it. Am I the kind of man you want hanging around you and your company? Or your daughter?"

She leaned back beyond his reach. She pulled her lips between her teeth and fought to control her reaction. A kernel of pride by association took root inside him as he watched her regain her poise and think things through. He'd seen men twice as big and twice as tough lose their cool a hell of a lot sooner than Emma.

"Do you want me to fire you?" she asked.

"Isn't that what this is about? Your little girl has fixed her hopes on the wrong man. I think you need to get rid of me. I just want you to know that. I want you to be clear on what you're asking for if you ask me to stay."

"I may be under some stress." Drew risked a grin at her talent for understatement. "But I've been blessed with a good head on my shoulders. I know what I'm asking. I'm asking you to live up to the trust I have in you."

His amusement vanished. "Don't put your faith in me, Em. I might let you down."

She stood, pulling the sleeves of her brick-red

sweater down past her knuckles and curling her fingers inside. She hugged her arms around her stomach as she walked toward the French doors that led onto the deck off the rear of the kitchen, as if preparing herself for the cold she expected to feel through the insulated glass. "I woke you up in the middle of the night, and you drove halfway across town to help me. You're not the same kind of man as Begosian or Roylott or his boss, or even this James Moriarty. You may think you're a man of mystery, but I know what kind of man you are."

Drew followed her. He maintained a respectful distance, but stood close enough to look over her shoulder into the crisp night sky. The snow reflected the light from the back porch, making it impossible to see the stars. But Drew had a feeling Emma was looking at something else altogether, something hidden deep inside of her.

"What kind of man is that?" he prodded.

"A man of honor. I know it. Kerry knows it."

She huddled tighter in her sweater, apparently fighting a chill in the warm kitchen. Drew's gaze settled on the proud set of her shoulders and the tiny quiver along her chin.

Her voice was a husky whisper, as dark and lonely as the night outside the windows. "I never believed in heroes until I met Jonathan. My father . . . was an abusive alcoholic. My mother never had the strength to leave him, and I . . . I couldn't leave her to face his senseless rages all alone."

He hadn't seen this coming. The admission that she came from such a background struck him in the gut like a sucker punch. "Did he hit you, too?"

Her tight-lipped silence, which locked away so many emotions, gave him the answer he didn't want to hear. "Oh, Emma."

She raised a hand to the nape of her neck and massaged the skin above her collar. He recognized the clinical detachment in her voice as the defensive mechanism it was, distancing her from painful memories. "We never had a lot of money, so I worked all through high school. My father burned my scholarship applications. I missed the deadlines for my freshman year. I was too ashamed to admit what had happened, so I took on a second job and tried to raise tuition money that way."

"He didn't want you to leave, either."

"One night I came home from the hospital where I worked as a floor clerk." She rolled her neck, trying to ease a tension borne from deep inside her. "My mom had fallen down the stairs, according to my father."

Drew breathed in deeply through his nose and out through compressed lips, quelling the rage building inside him. She combed her fingers through the hair at her right temple. He recognized the nervous expression of energy, the subconscious escape valve she allowed herself to keep the awful memories from overflowing and taking over. "You don't have to tell me this," he offered, wanting to ease her pain.

"I want you to understand where I'm coming from." She gathered all her hair at her nape, clenching and unclenching it in her fist. "Mom had a broken neck. I called for help. By the time the paramedics arrived, my father had passed out in

146

his recliner. The police couldn't wake him. He'd had some sort of cerebral hemorrhage."

Her posture still hadn't bowed, but she dug her fingers into her hair with a more brutal force, trying to shake it free from imaginary constraints.

Drew might not have the right, but he had the need to go to her. He gently pushed her fingers aside and gathered her hair in his hands, shaking it free and fanning it, loose, down her back. He closed his hands over her shoulders and dipped his nose to the crown of her head, inhaling the fresh, clean scent of her, hoping she could feel the same purity in herself. He kneaded her flesh lightly, imparting what portion of his strength she would accept.

"God, Em. You lost them both that night?"

She leaned back into his caress. "At the ripe old age of eighteen. I was finally free. But I was still lost. I could survive. But I couldn't live." Some of the tension within her eased. "Then I met Jonathan. He was visiting a friend at the hospital where I worked. He was so tall and handsome in his uniform."

"He taught you how to live again?"

"He taught me how to trust. And how sometimes you have to risk your faith to find what you really need." A soft laugh vibrated through her. "I wasn't always a willing student, mind you. But he refused to give up on me."

"That's why you won't give up on him?" She turned to face him, her eyes focused on the placket of his shirt. She smoothed the T-shirt beneath the opening and fastened the next button. He flattened his hands over hers, stilling them against his chest. "Em?"

She lifted her sad eyes, far braver than she gave herself credit for. "I need you to help my daughter the way Jonathan helped me. You can do that by finding her father. Before she forgets him entirely. Sooner, rather than later or never. By any means necessary. I'm willing to put my faith in you to do that."

"In other words, you want me to tap into my less noble attributes, make use of my, um . . . connections."

"Will you?"

The hope shining in her eyes proved an irresistible enemy to his common sense. He wrapped his fingers around hers and leaned closer, promising to find a man for the woman he was in danger of falling in love with himself. "I already said I would." He paused. "But *you* won't."

"Dammit, Drew. I know I can help."

"By getting yourself hurt?!" He ignored his own sense of impending loss and concentrated on seeing the situation from Emma's perspective. "If you think Kerry has problems now, think about what an injury to you would do to her. Think of how losing your parents affected you." He released her and ran his fingers through his hair, ashamed that he had used such personal information to make his point. "I'm sorry. That wasn't fair."

"No. It was."

She surprised him by lifting two fingers and straightening his rumpled hair, pulling it from the center of his head and smoothing it behind his ear, soothing his temper, easing his regret.

"Maybe it's okay for Kerry to think of you as a

father figure. I could have used a man of honor like you growing up."

Despite the comfort he found in her gentle touch, Drew pulled away. "You'd better cut the 'man of honor' stuff. I'll do my job, that's all. I don't want to see that kid get hurt."

"And you don't think that makes you a man of honor? Defending her? Defending me?"

Her praise made him uneasy. She'd opened up a painful secret while he allowed a lie to sit between them. Maybe it was for the best that he didn't tell her about his past; she didn't need any more grief to bear.

Drew understood the challenge she'd laid before him. The tightness around his heart understood all too clearly what he had to do to help her and Kerry. He had to protect them. He had to find her husband.

And then he had to give her up and never be a part of her life again.

"Drew?"

Her voice pushed aside the pain in his heart and propelled him into action. "I think our best chance at catching a break is for me to shadow you. Be with you constantly. Not too noticeably, I don't want to scare anybody away, but I'd like to lurk in the background. That way, if Moriarty should try to contact you or LadyTech again, I'll have the jump on him." He shifted uneasily, knowing he had to say this but fearing the answer he knew she should give him. "Still, if you'd rather not have me around Kerry, I can explain what's going on to your friend Maxwell. He could keep an eye on things here, or assign someone you trust to stay with you."

"I trust you."

Three simple words. They washed over Drew like a balm to his soul. Nightmares be damned. Maybe he *was* going crazy. Maybe he was setting himself up for pure torture, spending time with Emma when he wanted her so badly. Despite a mutual attraction, he knew she was determined to remain loyal to her husband. The notion might sit tough on his libido, but it made him respect the hell out of her.

He struggled to say the right thing, to live up to her expectations of him. "It could make things awkward for Kerry, having me around so much."

Emma smiled, a weary, beautiful curve on her lips. "I'd rather she were friends with you than with an invisible wingless friend who gives her bad advice."

"Wingless?" Drew frowned. "What do you mean?"

"You'll have to get the story from her. But unless her therapist tells me differently, I think the best way to help her through this is to help me. She already feels a bond with you. Maybe if she sees you working to find Jonathan, she'll get past the idea that you're her father, and simply accept that you're our friend."

Their friend.

Emma excused herself to check on Kerry. He followed her into the hallway and watched her climb the stairs, the hem of her long sweater catching on the curve of her bottom, tempting him with its graceful sway up each and every step. His body heated in an immediate response to her tall, cool elegance.

But he was more concerned about the tiny fissures cracking open around his guarded heart.

Their friend? He didn't have many friends in this edition of his life. He should be rejoicing at the prospect of adding Emma and Kerry to the short list. But he couldn't shake the selfish burn in his gut that told him finding Jonathan Ramsey might mean losing so much more.

Chapter Seven

Emma checked her watch for the fourteenth time in fifteen minutes. She rolled her chair back from her desk and crossed the wine-colored carpeting in her office to the wet bar where she poured herself a glass of orange juice from the mini-fridge. She took a drink, set the glass on the counter, and walked away.

Work seemed like such an inconvenience this morning. She'd wanted to cancel her meetings, hand over reports to be reviewed to other executives, and drive Kerry after her appointment straight home instead of to school. For the first time in a year and a half of monthly counseling sessions, Kerry had babbled with delight at the prospect of her daddy coming home, instead of evading questions about missing a father figure in her life.

Emma crossed her arms and raised her hand to her chin, tapping in a distracted rhythm with her thumb. She remembered the fantasy she'd created as a young girl. It was a fantasy where a good, kind man came home every evening at six o'clock, asked about school, and complimented her mother on the spotless house and delicious meals she'd created on a tight budget. That fantasy father would tuck Emma into bed, kiss her cheek, and she'd sleep through the entire night without the harsh awakening of crass words yelled in anger, screams that shook the walls of the house, or her mother's quiet sobbing drifting up the stairs to her room.

Kerry had created a similar fantasy around Drew.

But Drew Gallagher was no fantasy. He was flesh and blood, secrets and sinewy strength. He wasn't a family man. He wasn't father material. Yet it seemed both the Ramsey women were looking to him to be their savior.

Emma had grown up in a cruel reality and had given up on finding a man to fit into her skewed view of the world. Until Jonathan. He'd taught her to believe in men again, helped her get to know the men he called friends until they became her friends, too. His memories had sustained a more positive view of the world even after his disappearance.

She owed *him* her loyalty, her gratitude. She couldn't look to a new man to take his place.

What worried Emma the most wasn't that Kerry saw Drew as a rescuer who could make her seven-year-old world feel safe and secure, but that she herself saw Drew as a rescuer, too. He took her battered, closed-off heart and forced her to feel again. But he was all wrong for her, she knew that.

Hell. She was still a married woman. She knew that, too.

But his rangy body and burnished good looks stirred longings in her she'd wondered if she could ever feel again. The steel in his soft-spoken voice soothed her in ways words alone could not. And the heat that shimmered in his emerald-green eyes when he looked at her melted the ice that shielded her heart.

She was so damn lonely. So lost.

But she felt alive in Drew's arms. Connected. Her instincts to trust him felt alien. Before, she'd trusted only one man with her darkest secrets. Jonathan. But now, just as easily as Kerry gave Drew her trust, Emma gave it, too.

That she could so readily betray Jonathan's memory just to feel safe, just to feel womanly, just to feel human again, scared the hell out of her. Her conscience nagged her with the same sense of impending doom that used to keep her awake at night and give her ulcers as she'd waited to find out when her father's rages would arise.

The firm knock on her door startled her from regret back to frantic impatience. She dashed across the room and swung the door open wide, refusing to question the instant relief she felt at seeing Drew framed in the doorway.

"Good morning." His gaze narrowed as it fell upon the breathless rise and fall of her chest. "Are we still on?"

She nodded, and he strolled in without further comment on her odd state. Grateful for the respite to collect her wits and resume rational thinking, Emma closed the door and watched him set a black leather satchel on the floor beside one of the loveseats.

She scarcely recognized him as the same scrub-bearded lion who had come to her door at two-thirty that morning. By ten a.m., he'd transformed himself into a corporate version of the mystery man she knew. The black suit he wore fit his broad shoulders and lean flanks as if it had been custom-made for him. A crisp, white oxford shirt and paisley tie added a touch of traditional style, while his glasses and sleek ponytail gave his appearance a contemporary flair.

"Do I pass muster?" The temperature in the room went up ten quick degrees when he turned and caught her admiring the back view of his trim-fitting trousers.

She had the good grace to blush. "With flying colors." She picked up her juice and poured a second glass for him. "You've done this before, haven't you?"

"Work undercover?" He sat on the loveseat opposite her. "Yeah. Seems to be a talent of mine, blending in with whatever the scenery might be. Sort of like a chameleon, I guess."

"Chameleon?" Her hand shook and she hurried to set her glass on the coffee table between them before spilling her drink.

"Oh, God." Drew plunked his glass down and shot to his feet. "Sorry. Poor choice of words." He circled the room like a caged lion, stopping when he caught sight of Jonathan's picture on her desk. He drew in a deep breath. With just a few steps, he stood in front of her. He took her hands and pulled her to her feet. His mouth thinned before her eyes.

"I can't start carrying a list of names and topics to avoid when I'm around you."

She looked through the tips of her lashes into his intense green gaze. "I'm the one who needs to toughen up," she assured him. She took the message to heart. "I don't want you to second-guess your actions because you're worried about how they might affect me."

"I can't help worrying."

A loose lock of hair had escaped from the clip at her neck. He tucked it behind her ear, the brush of his fingertips a sweet caress on her cheek. The touch felt soothing, intimate, right.

Wrong!

She chided herself for how easily she gave in to his protective strength. She tilted her face away from his fingers, but she stood her ground. Staying close to Drew without touching him provided a compromise of sorts for her traitorous body and lonely heart. She spoke with an authority in which she wanted to believe. "I won't fall to pieces on you. That was just a knee-jerk reaction to that man's name."

"I know you're tough, Em. You're probably the strongest person I've ever met." His voice dropped to a husky pitch. "But you've been through so much. You hold it all together with grace and determination for Kerry's sake, or maybe just to keep your sanity. But I've seen what it costs you. I don't want to make it any harder on you."

"You won't." She crossed to her desk and slipped into the taupe jacket she wore with her herringbone tweed skirt. Putting on her work garb might armor her against handsome private eyes and guilty consciences, as well as the usual schmooz-ing clients and tedious meetings. "So, what's on the agenda today?"

He watched her a moment before answering. "You tell me. I want you to keep your daily routine. If Moriarty *is* trying to get his teeth into LadyTech, or you, I don't want to do anything to put him off."

"You don't?" Emma paused at the last button of her jacket. "Isn't the idea to protect us?"

Drew laughed, and the low-pitched, masculine tone shimmied along her spine like a physical touch, belying her concern. "I haven't lost my mar-bles yet. But we need him to make another move in order to catch him. We foiled his initial plan. But he's invested too much trying to get to you already to give up. I'm counting on him to put a Plan B into action."

The game began to make sense to her. "It's not all that different from a business deal. If you're not approachable, an investor won't make the effort to contact you."

"Exactly." His conspiratorial smile warmed her like a shared secret. "But then we have to be smart enough, and prepared for any surprises, to close the deal."

Business she understood. Let Moriarty show his hand first. "I just go through my day as scheduled and wait for Plan B to happen?"

"Something like that." He went back to the loveseat and reached inside his black satchel. She heard a tiny click before he straightened. "I'll leave this transceiver here, out of the way. I can monitor any conversations you have without actually being on the scene."

"Is that legal?"

"Did you hire me to follow all the rules?" he countered.

Emma flashed back on five years of going through every legitimate channel available to track down her husband. She'd found nothing. Drew's cagey, cutthroat intelligence provided an avenue she hadn't yet tried. His presence gave her something even stronger.

Hope.

She answered his taunt with a symbolic squaring of her posture. "Do I have to do anything to make it transmit?"

His approving nod brought out some of that strength he seemed to think she had in such abundant supply. "It's voice-activated. It'll pick up anything above a whisper in this room."

The telephone on her desk beeped, energizing her like the gunshot at the start of a race. She pushed a button. "Yes, Caitlin."

"Your ten-fifteen's here."

"Thank you. Show him up." She turned to Drew, finding a degree of comfort in the normalcy of a business meeting. "Wyatt Carlisle and his attorney. I'm conducting negotiations on a buyout opportunity with his company, Consolidated Technologies. Possibly getting us a better foothold in the Detroit market. I'm not too sure about the deal, though. Reports show only a moderate profit for the last three quarters, and suddenly he's selling so many computers he can't keep them in stock."

"Is that unusual to have such a large turnaround?"

"Not for a fledgling company." She'd pored over

the data on Carlisle for weeks before agreeing to meet face to face. The recent turnaround in Consolidated left her wondering if the final figures had been doctored to make the buyout more appealing. "This guy's been in the business twenty years."

"It sounds like he hit the right market."

"It sounds too good to be true."

Drew smiled, and the rare gift warmed her inside. She liked talking business with him, having him listen and respect her expertise. His investing his time in this simple conversation made her feel appreciated on a level that had nothing to do with business, and everything to do with being a woman.

"I'd say trust your instincts."

Her thoughts moved a world away from business to a matter much closer to her heart. "I do trust them, Drew. I know you'll do whatever you can to find Jonathan. And to help Kerry."

Her heartfelt encouragement seemed to rattle his polished exterior for a moment. But then he shrugged and moved toward the door, as if her faith in him didn't matter; as if he didn't believe it.

"Just keep it cool today. Conduct your meeting as usual. I'll be on the second floor, checking out my new office and doing a bit of eavesdropping."

Emma stopped Drew at the door, a simple touch on his arm enough to make him turn. "I know this is hard for you. That we have . . ." She looked for a word that could explain the complexity of the attraction between them and came up short. "You won't quit because of me, will you?"

He covered her hand where it rested on his coat sleeve. His callused touch gave her warmth, strength, and the promise of something she wanted to seize with both hands and hold on to forever.

"I won't quit." His raspy promise filled the stillness of the room. It sank deep into her heart and reminded her of a different time, a different man.

But the promise was the same.

A light knock on the door pushed them apart before she could question the half-formed feeling. She straightened her jacket and hair, but Drew's promise remained with her. She needed time to think about it, but practicality won out over wistful thinking. She buried that need beneath her workplace armor and opened the door to her guests. "Mr. Carlisle."

⋅ She shook his fleshy hand, unconsciously comparing it to Drew's firm grip. Carlisle indicated the gaunt, eagle-eyed man standing behind him. "My associate, Daniel Forsythe."

"Mr. Forsythe." She had a clear view of him over the top of Carlisle's short, stout figure, and in the forefront of her vision she saw Carlisle swell up and try to appear taller.

"I thought this was a private meeting." She bristled at the tone of Carlisle's voice. Great. The man had no charm, and he was self-important to boot. Her worry over the mysterious James Moriarty waned in her foreboding over the rest of her day.

The snide comment had no outward effect on Drew. He smiled as he shook hands with both men and introduced himself. "Drew Gallagher. Project consultant. I'm just on my way out. Nice to meet you."

Carlisle did not return the sentiment. Emma tamped down the feeling of injustice that flared within her, saying nothing while the man scoped out her office, then sprawled on one of the loveseats. With an apologetic smile, she closed the door on her administrative assistant, Caitlin, and Drew.

As she poured each of her guests a cup of coffee, she wondered how Drew handled undercover work. She wasn't even pretending to be anyone else, and already she faced a challenge in controlling her animosity against Wyatt Carlisle without letting it show.

How did Drew keep his feelings hidden? The resentment he must have felt when she wouldn't let him in her front door that first night; the interrupted passion after being discovered in the back room at Lucky's; how much could he hide behind those intense cat eyes and glib taunts? How many secrets did Drew Gallagher possess?

"Are we having a meeting, or what?"

Carlisle's impatient request cut short Emma's speculation and ate away at her goodwill like acid. She picked up the silver tray and smiled anyway. She could buy and sell his company ten times over. And she might do it, just to teach him a lesson.

What she couldn't do was make too much of her fascination with Drew. She couldn't grow any more dependent on him. She couldn't keep fantasizing about the feel of his arms around her, or the feverish press of his lips against hers.

What she couldn't, mustn't, do was fall in love with him.

Knowing she had to remind herself of that fact frightened her more than the prospect of never finding Jonathan at all.

* * *

161

Drew stuck his finger into the knot of his tie and loosened the cinch from around his neck. The LadyTech building had a suite of guest offices on the second floor, down the hall from the board room. Emma had chosen an office of simple design for him, decorated in charcoal and burgundy, with a streamlined mahogany desk and a lone charcoal-gray sofa in front of the window. What it lacked in creature comforts, it made up for in a clear view of the main parking lot and outbuildings behind the office center. At his request, BJ had loaded the room with hardware.

He sat in front of a computer system with more technology than his namesake, the fictitious Drew Gallagher, could ever dream of using on a case. He ran a search on the names of investors, and sub-searched the names of record on corporate invest-ments. He logged onto the Internet and found a website on Sir Arthur Conan Doyle so he could read up on Holmes's nemesis, James Moriarty, and get a list of characters' names that might be used as aliases for buying stock.

He tapped into LadyTech's personnel records and pulled up Emma's file. He buried the twinge of guilt that ate at him beneath the excuse that Emma had once offered to give him that same information in exchange for the disk with Mori-arty's journal.

In a matter of minutes he learned that she'd grown up in the nearby college town of Warrens-burg, Missouri. Her father had been a mechanic, though no place of work had been listed. Drew guessed the man either hadn't been able to hold a job because of his drinking, or Emma hadn't wanted to keep any detailed records on him. Her mother was listed as a homemaker. Emma had worked from the age of twelve, when she hired out to clean neighbors' houses. At sixteen, she'd worked as a waitress, and at seventeen, she took the job she'd mentioned at the local hospital.

She'd worked her whole life, it seemed. Drew frowned at the knowledge. She hadn't been allowed to be a kid, to party with her buddies in high school or college. According to her birth record, Em was only thirty-two years old. She carried herself with a maturity far beyond her years.

Drew wished he could fix that for her, give her time off to spend time with her daughter. Safeguard her company so she wouldn't have so much responsibility. Find her hus . . .

He swore beneath his breath. *He* wanted to be the man to help her, support her, share her burden.

Love her.

He breathed deeply, calling on the wisdom of his sensei to help him relax and accept the truth.

She didn't love him. She couldn't love him.

She wouldn't want to think about loving him if she found out he was still snooping into her past, taking advantage of her heart-wrenching situation to help himself find the truth of his past.

He hit the print button to copy her work history and rose to his feet. He stretched his arms in a wide circle, brought his palms together and lowered them to chest level, centering his energy and searching for a peaceful resolution for his nagging conscience.

Breathing evenly and concentrating on a calming mantra, he heard the door open and close with only a whisper of sound. Without altering his position, he glanced between slitted eyelids at the menacing hulk who had invited himself inside.

"Maxwell."

He endured the security chief's wary assessment, like a young wolf tolerates the scrutiny of the pack leader. The big man crossed to the sofa and made himself at home. "I see you found a new way to get into LadyTech."

Drew completed his exercise before opening his eyes and changing his stance. He pushed his rolled-up sleeves past his elbows and sat, mimicking Brodie Maxwell's deceptively relaxed position. "I have Emma's permission."

"I know she hired you. I just came to see that you're doing your job and nothing more. My friends and I promised Jonathan that we'd protect his wife and daughter."

"If you don't believe I have Emma's best interests at heart, why haven't you thrown me out of here?"

An expression resembling a smile changed the landscape of Brodie's face. He leaned forward, elbows on knees, and clasped his boxing-glove-sized hands together. "Believe me, I would have already if I had my way. But Emma's very persuasive. She thinks you're onto something."

So Emma had gone to bat for him. Drew hid his surprise—and pleasure—at the admission by rising to his feet and dipping his hands into his pockets. His casual stance was a conscious, superficial show like that of the warrior seated across the room. "So, did you have me checked out?"

Brodie nodded. Drew expected as much, if the man was any good at his job. And Drew suspected that he was very good. "The D.A. says you're tenacious and smart. That you think like a criminal."

"Is that a good report or a bad one?"

The giant didn't answer. "Here." He pulled a folded sheaf of paper from his pocket and handed it to Drew. "I cross-checked those names you gave Emma from Begosian's phone bill. I concentrated on areas of contact we made with the Chameleon. Everything about him is speculation, mind you. There are no fingerprints or identifying photographs of the man."

"The only one who can identify him is Jonathan Ramsey. I know the story."

Brodie nodded, not revealing his opinion about Emma sharing such information with him. "My unit worked mostly out of the country, but we have traced direct pipelines of arms sales into New Orleans, New York, and Detroit. If the Chameleon's alive, it's possible he'd pressure those contacts to reach Emma, without coming into the country himself. That's my story. You bring me up to speed on what you've found out so far."

Drew laid the list of familiar names on the desk and walked to the window, dropping his guard a fraction. Brodie seemed like the kind of man he could work with. Straightforward. Sure of himself. They didn't have to like each other, but they shared a mutual respect. And an interest in Emma.

"James Moriarty is an alias that someone, whom I suspect has a lot of money and influence, is using to create several ties to Emma. I've run across the names of at least two of Sherlock Holmes's villains who've bought modest but sizable shares of LadyTech stock."

"If enough front men buy shares, whoever is backing them gains a controlling interest."

Drew slid his gaze to the big man. "I see you're smart, too."

Brodie unfolded his body and turned to stand next to Drew. Side by side, they watched the comings and goings of the employees outside. "It's not the first time someone's tried to get ahold of LadyTech."

The deep, toneless rumble captured Drew's full attention. "Through BJ?"

"Yeah. It's an old story." Brodie's massive chest rose and fell as he dismissed whatever unpleasant memory had gripped him. The man wasn't just tough. He cared. A whole hell of a lot, Drew suspected. He'd be an ideal ally. The kind of soldier Drew would want backing him up in a fight. "You think this James Moriarty could be the Chameleon?"

The query didn't surprise Drew. It was the first logical theory that he, too, had come up with. But he'd done his homework. He'd worked over everything he'd seen and heard so far in his mind a dozen times, coming up with a dozen different answers. But the street smarts in his gut told him which answer was the best.

And it wouldn't make him popular at LadyTech.

"You want to know what I think?" He took the risk of trying his idea out on someone else before he presented it to Emma.

"Not especially. But it's polite to ask."

Drew thought about laughing at Brodie's comment, but there was nothing humorous in what he was about to say. "I think James Moriarty is your friend Jonathan."

The dead silence in the room put Drew on instant alert. He pulled his hands from his pockets and shifted to the balls of his feet. He braced for the giant's reaction. It was frosty, as he'd expected. "Your sense of humor doesn't do much for me, Gallagher."

"Put your emotional attachments aside and think for a minute. Moriarty knows too much about Emma and her company to be a total stranger. And the journal on that disk?" He waited for Brodie to look him in the eye. "It begins five years ago, on the island of Tenebrosa. The place where your buddy disappeared."

Drew flinched as he watched Brodie's barely contained temper. "Jonathan would never hurt Emma. Or LadyTech."

"The man's been gone five years. People change."

Maxwell moved surprisingly fast for a big man. Before his next breath, he'd hauled Drew up by the collar and pinned him to the wall. "Not Jonathan Ramsey."

Drew didn't struggle, knowing he could never overpower the man's brute strength. He gasped against the massive forearm pressed to his gullet. "Maybe something happened in that explosion."

Brodie's craggy face filled with an angry hope. "If he could have come home, he would."

"Ease up, Chief." Drew touched two fingers to either side of the larger man's wrist and twisted. Maxwell swore as his arm went limp and Drew freed himself.

Drew put a respectful distance between them and watched Brodie shake his arm, trying to restore feeling to his hand. He had learned that trick the hard way, at the hands of his master. He knew it would take a good ten to fifteen minutes for Brodie to feel the tips of his fingers again.

"What did you call me?"

Drew shook his head, not understanding the threat in Brodie's voice. "Chief."

The look in those icy gray eyes made Drew question the term himself. He fought to make the memory happen, but nothing made any sense. He grasped for a rational explanation. "Emma called you the security chief. I guess I picked it up from that."

"I was a chief gunnery sergeant in the Marines," said Brodie. "Everyone called me Chief."

"Small world, hmm?"

Drew held his ground and watched Brodie evaluate his remark. The big man's nod didn't fool Drew into thinking he'd won him over. Brodie walked to the door, still rubbing his wrist. "All right. You take the lead in this investigation. I'll watch your back because Emma asked me to. But I'm calling in some friends of mine. They have connections that might prove useful."

"And you want a second opinion on me."

Brodie's eyes gleamed at Drew's perception. "If any one of them doubts you, too, you're through."

Drew met him at the door, refusing to grant him the upper hand. "Sounds fair." He had bargained long enough. He slipped into an authoritative mode that called for action. "Now here's what I need from you. A round-the-clock monitor on Kerry. If I'm not there, someone else should be."

"Done."

"Good." Drew pulled in a deep breath and smoothed the emotion out of his voice before he made his next request. "Tonight I'm going to

Lucky's Bar and Casino to follow up on a hunch I have. I want to rattle a few cages, see if I can force Moriarty to show his hand. Emma thinks she can help. I *don't* want her there."

He didn't want her in the line of danger if he pushed too hard and things got out of hand.

Brodie nodded, reading his mind. "All three LadyTech women are stubborn. It's best to have them watch each other. I'll put Beej on that one." He opened the door and stepped into the hall. But he stopped and turned, presenting a menacing threat instead of the staunch ally Drew had wanted. "You're wrong about Jonathan, you know."

Drew tasted bitterness in his mouth as he closed the door after him. "For Emma's sake, I hope I am."

Drew's headache beat in tiny pinpricks along the base of his skull in torturous precision. Had his mental anguish transformed into physical pain? Since meeting Emma, his nighttime visions had become more frequent. He gave one short laugh at the grim thought that at least he could enjoy some variety to his nightmares now.

No longer limited to a chase and explosion in the jungle, he could now sample other horrific images, other dangers. The soft female voice that echoed in the recesses of his conscious mind kept warning him to think with his heart. What the hell did that mean? The only thing that made sense to him anymore was Emma.

Her sexy voice whispered through his memory even now as he sought respite from the long afternoon. A cup of coffee might be the last thing he needed for his headache, but the walk to the

LadyTech break room gave him a chance to stretch his legs and get out of his office.

Dinner and sleep would be a healthier option. But even after a working lunch, Emma was still in meetings with Carlisle, and the list of false stock purchasers had grown longer. He wanted to consult with her, weed out any legitimate names from the list of villains. Test his theory about Moriarty's real identity.

Hell, he just wanted to be with her. To see her sweet smile. To inhale the fresh scent of her hair. To pull the shades in her office and find out whether she had any other erogenous zones as acutely responsive as the soft indentation at her throat.

The prospect of doing the research left a lazy smile on his features, which lingered as he pulled a cup from the dispenser and reached for the coffee.

"My God, she's a tough broad." Wyatt Carlisle and his lawyer sauntered into the break room, sharing a relieved laugh at Emma's expense. "You think there's anything about Consolidated she *hasn't* asked us? I bet she's a witch in bed. Nah. I bet she's hard on us because she doesn't get it hard anywhere else."

Drew crushed the styrofoam cup in his fist. He read the letters of the brand name on the glass coffee pot in his right hand, controlling the impulse to break it across Carlisle's face.

So the pudgy CEO was a chauvinistic lowlife. Emma's concerns had been about the legitimacy of his profit margin. She was so damn driven to keep everything legal, honest, and aboveboard. But Drew didn't think Carlisle's business practices needed watching; he wanted to know about the man himself.

Drew schooled his protective temper and decided that a bit of fade-into-the-woodwork listening would be appropriate. Just play the flunky.

He poured himself a cup of fresh coffee and busied himself with cleaning up his mess at the counter, while Wyatt and Daniel Forsythe worked around him. Wyatt took four sugars. Drew averted his face to hide his scowl. So that's how Carlisle got the stomach for all his sweet-talking.

"I think you need to back off a bit, Wyatt," warned Forsythe, pulling out a chair and sitting at the glass-topped table. "Or she won't go for the deal."

"Here ya go." Drew nodded and accepted the wrappers Wyatt handed him to put in the trash. *Good*, thought Drew. *If the bum thinks I'm unimportant, he'll feel free to talk his heart out.*

Wyatt picked up a cinnamon roll that had been sitting out since early that morning and sat in a chair across from Forsythe. "I'm not worried, Daniel," he said. "If I'm too nice, she'll get suspicious. She likes playin' hardball. If you know what I mean."

"She knows her stuff. She questioned everything we padded."

Wyatt grunted. "She's got too much time on her hands. Now, there's a babe who needs to get laid. Wouldn't you like to do the Iron Maiden? Just once? Knock the stuffing out of her? I could stand to have those legs wrapped around me." The bile in Drew's stomach turned over with barely contained rage. The idea of that scum touching, the idea that he'd even talk about touching, Emma seared through him with an angry vengeance.

He forced his shoulders to remain relaxed as he glanced over to see Wyatt licking icing off his fingers with a satisfied smile. Forsythe studied his coffee cup, either bored or disgusted with his boss's line of talk.

Fine. So Drew only needed the strength to toss one bastard through the plate-glass window overlooking the garden.

"Wyatt, watch your mouth." Forsythe had looked up from his coffee. Drew turned away and pretended to study the selection of snacks in a vending machine. "LadyTech's big enough to swallow up and spit out Consolidated a dozen times over. You're lucky she's even considering paying top dollar for your company."

Carlisle frowned and tossed his roll on the table. "I don't want to sell. But I wasn't given a choice, and you know it."

Now, there was an interesting tidbit of information. Drew noted Wyatt's forced motivation in his mental log, right next to the notation that said the scumbag should never be allowed to even look at a female, much less mention a lady's name again.

"Wyatt . . ." For the first time since entering, Drew felt the focus of eyes upon him. But Forsythe was too late in trying to shut up his client.

"If he wasn't paying me good money to do this, I wouldn't have a thing to do with the Iron Maiden."

Drew tossed his coffee cup into the trash and turned, giving the men his best Cheshire cat smile. "No red meat. I really wanted to sink my teeth into something today."

He looked at the half-eaten roll in the middle of

the table and shook his head. He gave the lawyer a cursory glance, then stared right at Wyatt Carlisle, memorizing every line in that cheese-puff face. "Gentlemen."

He nodded once and swept out of the room, imagining the silence before Wyatt started chastising his lawyer for warning him off in front of witnesses.

So Carlisle and Consolidated Technologies were just a front for someone else. Emma had suspected something already when she studied Consolidated's fourth-quarter profits. Drew climbed the stairs and wondered if his word was good enough for her to stall negotiations on the buyout until he could check out where Carlisle had gotten the money to pad his accounts.

Drew slowed his pace, less worried about exposing Moriarty and saving LadyTech from a potential loss than about a problem that hit him much closer to home. Some problems required patience and savvy and days of investigation. Others required immediate action, like protecting himself when Brodie'd cut off his windpipe, or scum like Wyatt Carlisle who were allowed to walk the planet.

He'd seen Forsythe's locked briefcase in one of the guest offices which Emma's visitors were using as their base away from home. Drew needed answers.

And the best way to get an answer was to go straight to the horse's mouth.

Chapter Eight

Drew sat in the dark room and rested his body. He propped his legs up on the desk and leaned back in the chair, studying the outline of his shoes. He'd picked the lock on Forsythe's briefcase and found about what he expected—documents full of legalese, a report on LadyTech, and—not too surprising—a cashier's check from one James Moriarty.

At first the check, made out to Consolidated Technologies, gave Drew a charge of adrenaline. The pieces to this disconnected map were beginning to fall into place. And all roads led to Emma and LadyTech.

But Drew's victory was short-lived. Leaving the check and locking the briefcase behind him, he sat down to think. What kind of lawyer carried around proof that the company he worked for wasn't on the up-and-up? His impression of Daniel Forsythe was of a sharp legal counsel, way too smart to bring such evidence on the site of the company with which he was negotiating a deal.

Drew might be good at his job, but this was too easy. Relying on the telltale clench of his stomach, he suspected that this was some kind of setup. Bread crumbs through a forest of mystery and danger leading him right where someone wanted him to go.

Wyatt Carlisle was a different story. He reminded Drew of Stan Begosian. Though different in size and shape, the man was a weasely two-bit crook. They both had weaknesses which a tougher criminal like Moriarty could exploit. Just as they, in turn, exploited their own victims.

A rustling sound in the hall diverted him from his thoughts. Drew's focus zeroed in on the door-knob as it turned. The light snapped on, the door opened, and Drew enjoyed a rush of satisfaction at the startled look on Wyatt Carlisle's face.

"What are you doing in here?" he asked.

Drew entertained himself by watching Carlisle adjust his tie and the sleeves of his jacket, then fiddle with his collar and go back to the tie again. Now, this was a moment worth savoring, seeing Mr. Cheese-puff squirm.

"You like Emma Ramsey, don't you, Carlisle?" Drew inspected his fingernails, as if discussing nothing more important than the weather.

Wyatt huffed over to the desk and stood on the opposite side. "I get it. You're the guy she's doin'. I didn't mean anything by that stuff in the break room. It's just guy talk. You know."

When Carlisle's prattling ran out of steam, Drew

finally stood. Even in a relaxed stance, he towered over the other man. He didn't raise his voice or make a fist or even lean toward him. He touched the frame of his glasses with his index finger, straightening them on his nose and drawing Wyatt's attention to Drew's narrowed eyes.

"The next time you feel the need to share your crude fantasies about Emma"—the pudgy man caught his breath and stepped back, as if Drew had threatened to beat the snot out of him—"don't."

Wyatt sputtered, searching for a snappy comeback, searching for anything to say, looking like the fool he was. Drew walked to the door. When he heard the unguarded sigh of relief behind him, Drew turned. "Oh, and Carlisle? Tell Moriarty I'm onto him."

Carlisle's visible flinch, and the drain of color from his pasty face, were the only proof Drew needed to know he was on the right trail.

Emma cursed, calling herself every name she'd ever heard her father use, after lying to BJ and sneaking out of the restaurant where they'd gone for an impromptu moms' night out. She was no fool. She knew she'd been invited out to keep her occupied while Drew returned to Lucky's to check out Clayton Roylott and his cronies.

By the time BJ would figure out the deception, the taxi Emma had called from the restroom would have taken her several blocks away. By the time BJ could get to the house and relieve Brodie of babysitting duties to come after her, she'd be just a nameless patron blending in at Lucky's.

She cursed again, more gently this time, alternately blaming and loving Drew's failed attempt to keep her away from a potentially risky situation. It was a risk she was willing to take if it meant finding a link to Jonathan.

With the smaller Monday-night crowd, she had no trouble getting in and finding a secluded booth in a corner where she could watch the people coming in the front door, as well as the curtain behind the bar that masked the hallway leading to the back rooms.

As she waited for her diet soda to arrive, she studied the growing crowd. The dance floor was smaller than she remembered. Maybe that was just an illusion brought on by her need to simply get out of there last Saturday night, and get away from Drew and all the frightening things he made her feel.

She looked for the distinctive shade of his blond hair, but didn't see it. From her position, she could only see the first two tables at the entrance to the gambling area. No Drew there, either. She supposed she could take a walk and explore further, but she had a hunch that anything interesting would happen behind that black curtain.

A polite waiter brought her drink and waited for her to taste it before taking her money and leaving. Emma took another sip and checked out the rest of the staff in their white shirts and black vests and armbands. Each of them looked too young to have been the man she'd heard the other night.

Maybe he was someone she'd done business with herself. But none of the clients she could think of had a bar listed in their portfolio. And if that man was simply a customer with back-room privileges, she'd have no way to connect him to Lucky's.

What could she do to find out the man's name? Or get a look at his face? There must be something more productive than just sitting there and waiting for the right man to walk by. What would Drew do in this situation?

He'd take action, Em decided. He'd make something happen. She could make something happen, too. If she could just get into those back offices.

"You by yourself tonight?" A gray double-breasted suit appeared in her side vision a moment before she felt the light touch on her shoulder.

Startled from her thoughts, Emma's hand shook, and soda sloshed over the sides of the glass. She mopped the spill with the beverage napkin, but it was too soaked to dry her fingers. She set down her glass and fumbled for a tissue in her purse.

"Here. Allow me." A crisp, white handkerchief dangled before her eyes. She followed the line of the man's arm up and looked into the face of Clayton Roylott.

A shimmer of fear moved through her, followed by a stronger feeling of opportunity presenting itself. She couldn't immediately tell if he recognized her or not, but the gleam of appreciation in his eyes was unmistakable. If he remembered her and considered her trouble, he didn't care. While Emma swallowed her distaste at the realization that she could use her feminine attributes to get what she wanted, she silently applauded her foresight to wear her hair down and dress in the clingy cream-colored sweater dress that hugged her body like a second skin.

"Thank you." She accepted his handkerchief and wiped her hand, making herself smile when he slipped into the seat on the opposite side of the booth. She held up the cola-stained cloth. "I hope I haven't ruined it."

"Cloth is cheap. Coming to a beautiful woman's aid is priceless. Keep it." Despite his pockmarked face and oily line, he was a compelling man, olive-complected with large brown eyes and jet-black hair. He wore it short, with nary a lock out of place. How could a woman be tempted to touch that hair-sprayed coiffure? Her fingers suddenly burned at the memory of burying themselves in Drew's silky mane. She made a fist in her lap, trying to dispel the disturbing sensation and ignore the comparison. She needed to stay in the moment, to stay in character.

Act interested, she advised herself. "It's nice to see that chivalry isn't dead." She wanted to gag on the cutesy line, but it had the intended effect on her guest.

He beamed with pleasure and extended his hand across the table. "Clayton Roylott. We met Saturday, but I didn't catch your name."

So he did remember her. "Emma . . ." She nearly said *Ramsey* and almost choked at the blunder. *Real smooth*, she chided herself. If he knew the men who worked with Stan Begosian, he would surely know her name. But she froze the slight smile on her face, and doctored her maiden name to cover the slip. "Emily Kane."

He held her hand longer than necessary. When she pulled away, he leaned back and asked if she wanted a cigarette. She turned down his offer and waited while he lit his own and exhaled a cloud of smoke away from the table without ever taking his eyes from her. She crossed her legs one way, then the other, hiding her desire to squirm beneath his never-ending scrutiny. If he remembered her, he must remember Drew as well. Their little performance in the hallway should have clued him in that she belonged to another man. But Roylott's interest indicated it didn't make any difference to him.

"So what brings you to Lucky's?" he asked.

Emma tried to think of the right questions to ask to elicit information about the man's boss, the man who had threatened Begosian. Until the right idea came, she'd simply have to play along. "I'm looking for someone."

"Me, I hope."

How could she do this without arousing his suspicions? She saw a woman at the next table tracing her finger around the rim of her glass. Emma picked up her glass and copied the absentminded stroking. Roylott's attention shifted to the glass, away from her face. He'd be less apt to catch her in a lie if he didn't focus on her eyes.

"Meeting you again is a pleasant surprise, and maybe you can help me," she said.

His attention moved to the cleavage behind the glass. "You know how I feel about damsels in distress."

She willed herself not to empty her churning stomach. *Keep it cool, Emma. That's what you do best.* "Do you work here, Mr. Roylott?"

"Clayton. It's more like I work out of here. I use it as a base in the Midwest." Male braggadocio kicked in when he started talking about his job success. "I have business in a lot of cities across the country."

Emma calmed herself a bit. Other than the leering fascination in his eyes, this wasn't all that different from a business meeting. "What kind of work do you do?"

"Now, do you really want to talk business?"

She set down her drink and leaned toward him. "I'm fascinated by it."

He snuffed his cigarette in the ashtray and reached for her hand. "Then let's talk on the dance floor."

Now Emma cursed her choice of clothes. Clayton held her close enough for her to feel the imprint of his jacket buttons. The palm of his right hand slipped further down her back with each new measure of the slow dance tune. Before the song reached the coda, his hand was at her hip with his fingers spread toward her bottom.

She tried to keep from bolting by focusing on the busy bartenders behind them. By focusing on what the boss's voice had sounded like. By focusing on Jonathan's image. But nothing seemed to dispel the crawling sense of discomfort that crept across her skin. Forgetting the importance of staying in character, Emma grabbed his wandering hand and returned it to the small of her back. At his grunt of displeasure, she reminded him, "You said we'd talk business, remember?"

As if to punish her for denying his hand open range privileges, he tighted his arm at her waist and pulled her even closer, lifting her onto her toes so that her face was level with his. "I have lots of money and lots of power. That's all you need to know."

Images of her father's controlling anger sprang to mind, and Emma instinctively pushed against him. "I was more interested in who you work for."

He pressed his forehead to hers, and for one

God-awful moment she thought he might kiss her. Instead, he drilled his gaze into hers, and Emma went stone cold still. Only now, looking into Clayton's eyes, did she truly understand what Drew had meant when he'd said these men were criminals.

Fear and common sense and the memories of surviving her father's wrath made her suddenly compliant, and not at all challenging. She dropped her gaze to his chin. "That is, if you don't mind me asking."

That's better. She got the message as clearly as if he'd spoken the words out loud. Her meek request seemed to calm Clayton's anger. She showed no outward reaction this time when he moved his hand down to her rear and swayed to the music once more. "His name's Moriarty. It's not his real name. But that's all you need to know. Other than that I make real good money with him."

Moriarty! He knew the man behind the journal and the stock buys and Stan Begosian's stalking terror? She needed a real name, a face to go with the information. But she wasn't sure how much longer she could play this part and let Clayton paw her.

"I'd like to meet this man of opportunity."

"Tonight all you need is me, babe."

How could Drew do this kind of work? How could he subvert his tastes and values and feelings and play along with the bad guys without destroying himself? What kind of job had she asked him to do for her? Shrinking inside at only one night of working undercover, she could barely understand what kind of character and dedication it required of a man to *mix it up* with these lowlifes like Drew did. He could he become like these people and still walk away a hero? How could he play such a part and come out unscathed?

Maybe he hadn't.

Drew said he had no family now. Had they been the price he'd paid to do his job?

She squeezed her eyes shut when Clayton nuzzled her ear. "Let's take this into my office."

"The back room?" Yes, she told herself. She needed to see what was in that back room. Surely, she could find a heavy object to knock him senseless with if things got out of hand.

"Come with me." He kissed her cheek before pulling back, and Emma tried to smile.

"Mind if I cut in?"

A wave of cleansing relief washed over her at the distinct rasp of Drew's voice.

"Yeah." Clayton stepped back to face the man who had moved, unnoticed, behind him. "We have business we're going to discuss."

"No. I don't think you do."

Tall and lean, dressed in black from neck to toe, with hair slicked back into that all-business ponytail, and gemlike eyes set on maximum intimidation, Drew Gallagher was her dark knight in shining armor.

Roylott shifted back and forth on his feet as the depth of Drew's displeasure registered. Silently cheering, Emma made no protest when Roylott took her arm and pushed her toward Drew. "I didn't realize you were here. I was just keeping her company. Hey, anything you want from the bar is on me."

"Thanks." She heard no real gratitude in Drew's response. The possessive note in his voice left no room for further conversation. Roylott nodded and slipped away into the crowd.

When he was out of earshot, Emma let out the breath she'd been holding and threw her arms around Drew's neck, at the moment more relieved to see him and escape Roylott's degrading touch than she was to receive any new clues about Moriarty.

"Thank God," she whispered, pressing her face to his neck and clinging to him as if he were an anchor. "Thank God you came."

Drew wrapped his arms around her, shielding her from all the Roylotts of the world. She felt a shudder ripple through him before he eased a little space between them, took her hand, and resumed the dance. That tiny revelation of suppressed emotion thrilled her, touched her heart. He'd been scared for her. What he couldn't let the cockroaches of the world see, he shared with her. Emma changed her grip so that she was holding *him* reassuring *him*, of her safety. "I'm all right, Drew."

"You just don't listen, do you. No matter what I say, you're determined to get yourself into the middle of this mess." He fanned his fingers at the small of her back and held her close, his thighs brushing against hers with each step. Roylott had held her closer than this, but with Drew's gentle touch she felt cherished. With his mouth bent close to her ear, she felt safe.

She closed her eyes and savored the fluid movement of a man and woman who fit together as perfectly as anyone she'd ever known.

"Okay. We're going to dance our way over to your table, grab your purse, and I'm taking you home." The curt command was hardly the sweet nothing she had expected to hear.

Emma leaned back against his arm, confused by the conflicting message of his touch and voice. "No, you're not. I'm glad you rescued me from his groping hands, but Clayton likes me. He's willing to talk. He said he works for Moriarty."

"Emma." He whirled her into his arms as another couple spun past within earshot. "You can take that man all the way to your bed, and he's still not going to tell you what you want to know. He doesn't have the answer."

"What? How dare you!" She pushed at his chest, angry at his words, angry that he might be right, angry at herself for not knowing the rules of the game. But Drew's arm didn't budge.

His tone, however, softened into a gentle apology. "I'm sorry. That was out of line. It's a hard way of telling you the truth."

Emma's rebellion faded with the admission. "I guess I didn't really believe you when you talked about these men. If they want LadyTech, they won't give up easily."

"If Moriarty wants *you*, he won't give that up easily, either."

She nodded and allowed Drew to steer their path toward the table. "So you don't think Clayton knows who Moriarty is?"

"Not his real identity. But I think *I* might."

"Really?" Emma stopped, a frisson of anticipation boosting her hope. Drew barreled into her, but he quickly caught her in his arms and kept them from falling.

The corners of his mouth eased into a smile, as if he knew what this information could mean to her.

"I went through the files in that office. Yes, you distracting Roylott bought me some uninterrupted
time to do the job right." His praise made the
creepy memory of Clayton's touch recede. "You
want to guess how many times the name James
Moriarty comes up? I pulled four good sets of fingerprints. I'll run them through the D.A.'s office.
We'll find his identity that way. Until then, I don't
want to speculate and raise your hopes. I want you
out of here. Now."

"You know who belongs to the voice I recognized?"

Drew frowned. His hands tightened once, twice,
on her shoulders. His sudden hesitation worried
her. "What are you afraid to say to me?"

"Sonofabitch."

Drew and Emma both froze at the laughing
expletive. Clayton had returned, his face wreathed
in good humor. He slapped Drew on the shoulder.
"I figured out where I know you from."

Drew turned slightly, angling his shoulder
between herself and Clayton. "I don't think—"

"Sure. We worked a couple of jobs together
down in Miami. Seven, eight years ago. Your hair's
different, and we both have a few more wrinkles.
No wonder I didn't recognize you."

When Drew didn't respond, Emma jumped in. "I
didn't know you'd been to Miami."

Drew's silence didn't bother Clayton. "Yeah,
Cam and I hung out together for about a year.
Well, I worked for him, of course." He put his
hands up in surrender, and the sincerity of his
apology made her believe that the two men really
did know each other. "Sorry about before. If I had

186

known she was yours . . . I mean, I thought she was
for hire. Stupid mistake, of course."

For hire? Her concern gave way to indignation.
"You thought . . . I was a . . . prostitute?"

"No. No, absolutely not." His dark eyes darted
from her to Drew. "Poor choice of words on my
part." She realized he was apologizing to Drew for
the insult, not to her. He was apologizing for
insulting Drew's woman. Smooth charm cast
aside, the man groveled for Drew's forgiveness.

Emma felt the blood rush down to her toes,
making her light-headed. *My God.* Clayton thought
Drew was some kind of criminal. More than that,
that he was someone of importance in the criminal
world.

Just what type of work had Drew done when he
was bumming around the country, as he'd told her,
before coming to Kansas City? She prayed it had
been an undercover assignment of some kind. She
prayed she hadn't pinned her hopes on the very
kind of man her husband had tried to eliminate.

What was the name Clayton had used? "Cam?"
she asked, stepping to his side and looking into his
face to prompt Drew from his continuing silence.

"Oh, sure," Drew said to Roylott. "Clayton. You
were using a different name down there, right?"

She could tell he was lying! He didn't remember
a thing. His eyes had lost their sharp focus. Their
usual cat-eye gleam had dimmed.

Clayton nodded, as if discovering an old friend
at a class reunion. "Scotty. Everybody called me
Scotty. Roylott's a name out of a book. Thought I'd
go literary."

"A Sherlock Holmes book?" Some of the glint

returned. Drew was skipping over whatever had just transpired. This was the sly detective, following a lead on his investigation. "Is that your idea or your boss's?"

"His."

"This guy you're working for now. Is he around? I might have a deal for him." Emma marveled at Drew's smooth transition from caring defender to confused man to clever criminal. Which one was the real Drew?

"Nah. He had some business to take care of. Flew out of the country this morning. You can work with me, if you want. The boss is always looking for good help."

Drew closed his hand around Emma's elbow. "Maybe later. Let me get the lady home first."

Emma pulled free, more than curious about Drew's past. She had quickly discovered that the easiest way to lie was to tell a half-truth. "Nonsense. You know I've been running my own business for years. You can talk in front of me."

"And you know how I feel about mixing work and pleasure." He gave her a look that mocked her own determination. This was not a battle she could win, yet. "I'll get your purse and coat."

She conceded the skirmish but not the victory. In the short time that Drew was gone, she tugged on Clayton's sleeve. With Drew's territorial rights protecting her, she no longer feared his advances. "So you knew Cam down in Miami?"

"Yeah. We met on a job. But he never stays in one place too long, if you know what I mean."

Emma had no idea. But she smiled anyway, pretending to agree, bluffing her way through this conversation. "Tell me about it."

Clayton puffed out his chest and nodded in admiration. "He's a mystery man, that one. He insisted we all use nicknames."

Was this her chance? She pressed her lips together, stalling the impulse to shake more useful information out of him. "What nickname was he using then?"

"Like I said, he didn't stay around too long."

Damn the dolt! He'd been well trained in giving ambiguous answers. "But you're sure you knew him?"

"Oh, yeah. When you're the best in the business, nobody forgets you."

Drew unlocked the door to his apartment and pushed it open for Emma. The arctic chill in her voice when he'd helped her with her coat at Lucky's warned him that something had changed between them. When she'd said, "I want to go someplace private where we can talk," he'd agreed. He was ready to go head to head with Miss Cool, Calm and Collected.

"Of all the fool stunts, Emma . . ." He locked the door and hung their coats on the coatrack. If she for one instant thought he'd been glad to see her endangering that beautiful swan neck of hers by flouting common sense and going to Lucky's—even flirting with a known racketeer like Clayton Roylott—he intended to change her way of thinking.

She rubbed her arms as if the apartment chilled her. Maybe, he thought ironically, she had created that chill herself. "Let's talk about being a fool." She turned on him. "Is that what you think I am? A fool? Are you and Roylott working on some con to get my money?"

Her attack shook some of the wind from his anger. He had no grounds to defend himself. The idea that Roylott had known him in Miami, seven or eight years ago, before the accident, ate a fearful hole in his gut. Obviously, Emma didn't like hearing about that possibility, either.

While it might explain his affinity for the kind of work he did, he didn't like it. For five years, he'd worried that he'd left a family behind, had hurt good friends, had left a job unfinished.

He hadn't considered that he'd left a life of organized crime.

He pulled off the rubber band that held his hair in place and ran his fingers through it, massaging the base of his skull, trying to ease the tension he felt. He stuffed the band in his pocket and strolled into the kitchen, just now giving thought to the appearance of his place. He wasn't much for keeping house, but then there wasn't much house to keep. His bed was made, the dishes were clean. But the bare brick walls and sparsity of furniture that had once made the openness so appealing to him, now echoed with an embarrassing loneliness. The brutal barrenness revealed a lack of a past or connection to anything or anyone of importance.

Could he explain his amnesia to Emma? Or would she see it, like Roylott's reference to this "Cam" in Miami, as just another lie?

"Make yourself at home." He offered the invitation by rote. "I'll put some coffee on."

Emma, despite the frostbite of her temperament, looked soft and stunning. Her dress clung to each long curve of her body and stopped short a couple of inches above her knees, revealing a long stretch of knee and calf, and her delicate ankles were set off to sexy perfection by the tall heels she wore. No wonder Roylott couldn't keep his hands to himself. It required every bit of Drew's considerable willpower to respect the walls she'd thrown up between them.

Just looking at her, he wanted her. But he would not break Emma's rules. At the moment, winning back the trust he had lost seemed much more important than staking any possessive claim on her body.

Drew flipped the switch on the coffeemaker and settled onto the sofa. He rehearsed all the ways he could explain his loss of memory. Each beginning sounded irrational or insane. He bought himself some time by watching Emma's silent inspection of his things and waited for her to speak first. She tested the spongy strength of his exercise mat with her toe, even punched his kick bag once. But when she got to his overflowing bookshelf, she stopped to explore, fingering her way through textbooks and fiction titles.

Too late, Drew realized the discovery she had made.

She pulled a dog-eared paperback from the shelf and turned, brandishing it before her like judgment itself. "What kind of sick game are you playing?"

He rose to his feet, sensing it was too late to defend himself, but desperate to try anyway. "It's no game, Em. I can explain."

She advanced on him, a furious frost maiden with a glacial bite to her voice. "Drew Gallagher isn't your real name. You got it from these books! It's just another part you're playing."

"Emma." He put up his hands to placate her, but she refused to retreat.

They stood toe-to-toe. She looked him straight in the eye, her angry breath mingling with his. Drew braced himself for her accusation. "Talk to me, Cam." The name sounded wrong on her lips. It sounded foreign in his memory. "Just what kind of work is it you do? Roylott practically gave himself a hernia bowing and scraping to you because he's afraid of your wrath."

"What?" He stared at her through narrowed eyes. Maybe he hadn't heard her right.

"It's a simple question. Just who the hell are you?"

"I don't know."

Drew slumped onto the sofa, the depth of her distrust and disappointment an impossible weight to bear.

She paced back and forth, a righteous prosecutor digging the truth from her prime suspect. "You don't know? You don't know if you're a hit man or drug runner? Are you a crime lord? An arms dealer? Or are you some cheesy private eye? Or are you just some sick man who gets his kicks by putting me through hell?"

Drew grabbed her wrist as she walked by, halting her accusations, forcing her to stop and listen. "I honestly don't know . . . who I am."

She jerked her hand away, avoiding his touch with a vengeance. "Drew? Cam? I knew you were a good liar. But are you so sick that you'd lie to yourself, too?"

She clutched the book to her chest with both hands. A fine sheen of tears glittered in her eyes. He'd done that to her. Maybe he *was* sick. Maybe he should have walked away from Emma Ramsey at the very beginning. Using her for his own benefit had brought her to this. By teaming up with him, she probably felt as if she'd colluded with the enemy.

No wonder the angels hadn't seen fit to help him find his past.

Not when his lies had made Emma feel like this.

He stood, wanting to hold her, wanting to help her. But she backed away. Drew didn't pursue.

He offered her the only solace he could give her. The truth.

"Five years ago I was in an accident. I suffered burns over a third of my body and sustained a head injury that . . ." He raked his fingers through his hair, wishing he had a better excuse, wishing he had something more tangible to share.

"I have amnesia. I don't know who I am or where I come from or what I did before I woke up in a hospital five years ago." He walked around her to the bookshelf and glared at the forty or so novels through exhausted eyes. "I took the name Drew Gallagher because I liked the character. It seemed as good a decision as any at the time. It had a better ring to it than John Doe."

"Why didn't you tell me this before?"

He actually laughed at the soft-spoken question. "Oh, I don't know. It never came up in conversation."

She moved up beside him, still clutching the paperback in front of her like a shield. But the effort to stand on more equal ground gave him the encouragement he hadn't realized he needed. "When you said you thought you knew me, that was just a come on line, wasn't it?"

"No." This would truly sound crazy, but he owed her a complete explanation. "I get snatches of my past in dreams." He skipped over the demons that tortured his sleep, and seized on the one shining light he'd known in five years. "I've seen your face. Heard your voice. I remember you. I met you in an office once."

"That's why you asked me all those questions. You wanted to know where we'd met." She reached past him and returned the book to the shelf.

Another notch had opened in her defensive walls. Another chance for him to . . . to what? She was as married a woman as any he'd ever known. Married to another man. And she thought he was a criminal. What the hell did he think he had to offer a woman like Emma anyway?

"Well, we haven't met," she said. "I hate to say it, but I'd remember you. A lot more clearly than Clayton Roylott does. I'd remember your eyes if I'd ever seen them before."

Drew went to the kitchen and poured coffee. He needed something to occupy his hands so he wouldn't reach out to her. He had no right to touch her. No right to make her remember the connection that flared between them whenever they defied rules and logic and dropped their guard. No right at all.

"I remember your voice." He went on to explain his haunting vision, and tried to express the rare clarity he felt in that one snippet of a memory. "It speaks to me in my dreams as sexy and memorable as when you're right here with me."

She joined him in the kitchen. He devoured her living image with his eyes, believing that his memory was as real as the flesh-and-blood woman standing before him. She picked up her mug, but like him, didn't drink. "What do I say in your dream?"

"You ask if you can help me. You're sitting at a desk behind a counter, and you say, 'May I help you?' "

"What else?"

He hesitated. "That's all I know."

"You don't remember anything else about your past?"

Of course, she'd challenge him. Admitting how much of his life he had lost sounded ludicrous to his own ears. And telling her about the grenade and explosion, the death-hunt through the jungle, would only solidify her belief that he was some sort of heinous criminal.

Her brow furrowed as if she were thinking of her own past, as if she were actually trying to help him. "I worked a lot of secretarial jobs."

"I know. I checked it out."

"I see." She exhaled a heavy sigh, and Drew knew that her momentary assistance had ended. "So you spied on me. You took advantage of my situation to get close to me."

He set his mug on the table, calming a flare of anger at her refusal to believe in him. "If I just wanted to use you, Em, I wouldn't be helping you."

"Are you really helping me? Or are you like James Moriarty, playing a game with my company and my life?"

"I'm not like him."

"How do you know?" She slammed her mug on the counter and stalked out, her long legs carrying her all the way to the front door before he caught up to her and spun her around.

"Dammit, Em, you have to judge me by the man

I am now. Not cast me out because of someone you think I used to be."

She struggled against his grip on her arms, but he refused to let go. "How am I supposed to do that?" she asked.

"If you really think I'm capable of extortion and racketeering and God knows what else, like Roylott, why would you come here, alone, to my apartment?"

Everything about her went still, except for the rapid rise and fall of her chest that matched his own heated breathing. "I'm looking for evidence to back up his story. He's involved with Moriarty, and maybe you are, too."

He saw through her tough talk to the vulnerable woman inside. He dared her to be as honest as he'd been. "Try again."

Her eyes searched his for seconds that lasted into eons. She caught her lip between her teeth, fighting against whatever emotion she trapped inside. "Maybe I want you to prove me wrong."

He brushed his thumb against her lips, easing the strain there. "You said I was a man of honor."

"You denied it."

"You told me things about growing up I don't think you've shared with many people. You trust me."

She trembled beneath his hand. "That was a mistake."

He smoothed her hair behind her ear, shushing her like a wounded bird, letting her know that her secret would always be safe with him. A tear welled in the corner of her eye, and Drew's voice dropped to a hoarse whisper at the sight. "Your daughter believes in me."

She moved her hands to his chest and wound her fingers into the collar of his shirt, reaching for him, yet pushing him away. "She's seven years old. How does she know what to believe in?"

Drew framed her face between his hands and tilted it to his, forcing her to read the candid admission in his eyes. "Dammit, Em. I care about you. Maybe I'm even falling in love with you. That has to count for something."

"Love?" she repeated, staring wide-eyed as if he were a madman. "It counts for nothing. Not when you're a man who doesn't tell the truth."

Chapter Nine

Emma crushed the crisp cotton of Drew's shirt in her fists, angry at him for daring to say such a thing. Angrier at herself for wanting it to be true. "Love?" She challenged him again. "What do you know about love?"

She expected him to give her a flowery description of their physical attraction. She expected an angst-filled outpouring about a man searching for something or someone to belong to. She expected the story of a fateful connection between two people who understood each other like no one else could.

She didn't expect, "Not much."

He moved his hands to cover hers, clinging to her for a breathless moment before he pried her fingers loose and walked away. She hugged her arms in front of her, mourning the sudden loss of his body heat, chilled from within and without. She leaned back against the steel door, needing some kind of support for her shaky resolve. "What do you mean?" she asked. "How can you feel something if you don't know what it is?"

Drew was a man in pain. A pain as deep and tragic as any she had ever known. The demons had shone clear and cunning in the depths of his world-weary eyes. She stayed at the door, part of her wanting to go to him, to offer comfort in words or a touch. But part of her held back, the part that was afraid of giving, the part that was afraid of opening up her heart and losing everything all over again.

He retreated to the row of windows at the far side of his apartment. It was only twenty or thirty feet away, yet the distance between them felt like miles. He opened a window and breathed in deeply. His shoulders rose, then sank in weary resignation.

"I don't remember what anything good or positive feels like. I know injustice, and heart-stopping fear that wakes me in a cold sweat in the middle of the night. I knew that same fear tonight when I saw you in Roylott's arms. I was jealous as hell, and scared to death I couldn't get you out of there, that he would use you, hurt you."

The barren apartment echoed with the ensuing silence. He had admitted more than he'd wanted to already. Maybe he'd even surprised himself as much as he surprised her.

The idea of someone caring, the idea of someone wanting to protect her—not just physically, but emotionally—was an aphrodisiac she could succumb to all too easily. But she couldn't afford to be weak. Not with Kerry, Jonathan, and the LadyTech empire depending on her.

She hadn't survived an adolescence full of terror because she had no strength. She hadn't stayed at her mother's side and offered her support because she lacked courage. She didn't endure losing the man she loved by giving up.

"You don't know how tempted I am to argue with you." She chose her words carefully, walking a fine line between compassion and emotional survival. "You talk tough. But there's a depth of caring in you that I think you underestimate. I've seen it in the way you treat Kerry, and I've seen it with me a dozen times.

"But it's not your job to take care of me that way." The weariness of her spirit weighed her down and anchored her to the floor. "It's not your place."

"I know." He turned, and she felt the glowing intensity of his catlike gaze reaching out across all those miles of lies and regret. His wistful smile touched a sad chord in her heart. "Your husband is the luckiest man in the world. I hope he knows what you're going through for him."

"I know there's someone for you, Drew; someone waiting to . . ." Her voice trailed off as she heard the words the way he must have. Who might be waiting for him? *I have no family now*, he'd told her. She'd assumed he'd gone through a divorce, or had lost his loved ones in some tragedy.

Earlier, she'd been too caught up in her temper and suspicions to notice the subtle details of the place he called home. The spacious layout had all the necessary amenities: furniture, appliances, workout equipment. But now she realized what was missing.

Photographs. Souvenirs. Handmade items.

All the gifts and mementos a person collected over the years. She had Kerry's handprints from her first day at preschool hanging in her bedroom. Family photographs with Jonathan. Diplomas from college and graduate school. Even the afghan and doilies her mother had crocheted.

Those objects gave her a tangible reminder every day of her life of all that was important to her, all that she had accomplished, all that life could be.

He had no such faith to sustain him, no remembered promises to give him hope.

Drew had nothing.

Nothing but his misplaced feelings for her.

"You really don't have a past." Her stunned acceptance of his crazy story carried across the room.

"I could be that man Roylott knew." He offered up the possibility like a bargaining chip, an offer on the table that she could either accept or reject.

His unspoken request stirred her heart. It tugged at her conscience and tapped into her rational mind. She made herself think of the unspeakable relief she'd felt when he'd rescued her from Roylott, of the tender care she'd witnessed when he held her sleeping child in his arms, of the way he made her senses come alive with just the simplest touch or the most passionate kiss. *That* was the man she knew.

Believing in those facts instead of a known criminal's assertion, she rejected the idea that he could be so self-serving and cruel. She took a step toward him. "I know evil, Drew. I grew up with a man whose illness killed his conscience. I saw and heard all the ways a man could terrorize those who were weaker and at his mercy."

"In my forgotten life, I might be like that."

"You are nothing like my father." That was one truth she believed with all her heart. "You have a conscience. Or else we wouldn't be having this discussion. You would never hurt Kerry or me."

"No, I wouldn't." That concession to the man he was now seemed to give him some measure of absolution. He, too, risked taking a step. He covered two feet of floor space, and miles and miles of the suspicion and regret yawning between them. "Do you still want me to help find your husband? To protect you and Kerry? I'll understand if you don't." He rattled off options with detached speed. "I can give you names of some good private detectives. I'll turn over everything I've found so far. Or you could check with Maxwell. He'll hire someone you can trust. Your friend Maxwell would probably like that."

She considered his offer for a moment, but quickly discarded the idea. "I don't know what kind of man you used to be, Drew. But I know what kind of man you are now. I still think you're the only one who can bring Jonathan home. Nothing's changed there."

And yet everything had changed between them.

Drew pushed up his glasses and rubbed his eyes. The guest room in Emma's house had a more homey feel than his own apartment: queen-sized bed, plush appointments, his own private bath. The duffelbag packed with his things looked small and lost in the walk-in closet. Two hours of pouring over reports from the D.A.'s office should have put him to sleep by now. But he sat there on the bed, dressed in his beat-up black jeans and a T-shirt, pillows propped against the headboard, wide awake.

What had possessed him to say those things to Emma? Fear? Desperation? He'd really lost it, talking about things he hadn't thought through yet. It had been hard enough to talk about his amnesia; even harder to concede the notion that Clayton Roylott really might know him. But love? Where had that come from? He shouldn't have those kinds of feelings for her. Couldn't.

A good, healthy lust for the woman was one thing. Feeling compassion for her plight made him human, and he desperately wanted to believe he still had some humanity left in him. He could even rationalize the fear he felt for her safety. She was a client, after all. If he didn't keep her safe, he wasn't doing his job.

But love?

He closed the folder in his lap and shook his head at the new level of craziness that was consuming him. Yeah, maybe he hadn't been thinking as clearly as he should have. He had no way to disprove Roylott's claim that they'd worked together in Florida. But Emma's suspicions had blindsided him. She'd always questioned which side of the law he belonged to. But he'd been caught in the lie of his identity. Caught red-handed with the deceptive motive of using her to find his past. He had no way to earn back Emma's trust, except by completing the job for her. But even that might not be enough.

She wasn't his to lose, and yet he mourned the

loss all the same. She needed him. For now. But he would be out of his mind if he thought she'd ever accept those feelings from him.

"Looks like you're stuck with work, Gallagher," he chided himself. He was back to square one as far as discovering his past was concerned. Emma didn't know him. His job might be a lonely companion, but right now it was the only thing that gave him a reason to keep going.

He set aside the file and pulled out his notepad to review what he knew so far. Moriarty was buying up LadyTech stock under front men with names from Sherlock Holmes mysteries. Did the man think of himself as the reincarnation of that fictitious villain? If so, who did he see as his archrival, Holmes? Was it Emma? Drew himself felt like the detective going head-to-head on this case.

Moriarty had tried on at least three separate occasions to contact Emma directly. He influenced crime families across the country. He'd written a journal whose beginning matched the dates and places of Jonathan Ramsey's disappearance. Were there clues coded into that journal that Drew hadn't recognized before?

And why did his gut insist on connecting Jonathan himself to James Moriarty?

His notepad and glasses joined the folder beside him on the bed. He pressed his thumb and forefinger to the bridge of his nose, fighting to ease the tension that refused to subside.

He'd sent the four sets of prints he'd taken from the office at Lucky's to a contact in the Highway Patrol. Forty-eight hours seemed like an interminable wait for answers. In the meantime, gambling on the nickname Scotty, Drew had traced an arrest record for a man named Clayton Scott. Not that it had told him much. The con-man-slash-bully dabbled in a lot of questionable business ventures. He'd only been convicted on minor charges; all his major crimes had been pleaded down or dismissed.

Roylott might talk big, but he was just a middle man. Like Stan Begosian and Wyatt Carlisle, Roylott was simply a means to an end. But what exactly was the end? What was James Moriarty up to?

"D-Drew?" The sleepy little yawn of Kerry's voice startled him.

He knocked the papers onto the floor, scrambling to swing his legs over the side of the bed and get to his feet. He never made it.

"Drew!" Dragging her doll behind her, Kerry woke as if it were Christmas Day and sailed across the room. She launched herself into his arms, knocking him back on his seat. Chubby fingers cinched around his neck. "You c-came back."

Glancing around the room as if a hidden list of instructions on how to handle this situation would suddenly present itself, Drew caught her up in one arm and patted her head with the other.

"Hey, punkin," he greeted her at last. "What are you doing up in the middle of the night?"

"I had a b-bad dream." She loosened her grip only to settle more comfortably in his lap.

He knew the feeling. "Let me get your mom, okay?"

"Sh-she's not in her room. I checked." She sat back to look at him. Her eyes rounded. "D-don't you want to s-see us?"

"Of course I do."

"Good." She released a child-pitched sigh and snuggled against him. She laid the doll on his chest, too, and squirmed impatiently until at last Drew understood and closed his arms around both tiny treasures.

Such a little bundle of opinion and energy. Drew smiled to himself at the incredible trust Kerry gave him. Without understanding why, her willingness to relax, and the simple idea that a hug could make things better for her, fortified his spirit as little else could.

He gave her a squeeze and elicited a soft giggle. He had no earthly idea what to do next. Call Emma? Put Kerry back to bed? Just hold her until she got up and left on her own?

As if the inanimate objects of the room understood his dilemma, the light beside his bed dimmed, casting the room into sleepy shadow. He attributed the brown-out to the time of night, the lingering winter, and the drain on the city's power supply.

He heard a frustrated sigh that was not his own. Kerry's shoulders hadn't moved, except with her even breathing. Emma wasn't standing at the doorway, so Drew wondered if he had imagined the sound.

Kerry stirred and lifted her head, gazing out at a distant point in the darkness. "I don't want to talk about it," she said. Though drowsy, she articulated the words with the clarity of a soft bell. "Okay. If you say so."

"Whoa there, champ." The difference in her speech didn't register until she'd spoken a second time. Drew's big hands dwarfed her tiny shoulders as he pushed her away to look into her face. "Who're you talking to?"

"Faith." She blinked big, blue, innocent eyes. "Sh-she says I have to t-tell you 'bout my dream."

Drew looked from her to the unseen Faith, and back again. He felt confusion furrow a tense line across his forehead. "How come you didn't stutter?"

As soon as he said it, he wished he hadn't. She was just a kid. A tiny one, at that. She probably was extremely self-conscious about her speech impediment. Pointing it out like the curious detective he was might shoot holes in her self-esteem.

But Kerry was not only vocal, she was resilient. She answered his question with the same efficient tone her mother used when conducting business. "T-Faith's my fr-iend. She never leaves me, 'cept when I'm s-sleeping."

"Is Faith the one who told you I was your daddy?"

She nodded.

"You know I don't look anything like him, don't you? He has dark hair. Darker than yours." He pulled a strand of his own hair. "Mine's blonde."

"I know." Kerry reached up and touched it, too. "Y-yours is longer, too. But Faith s-says you're the same."

"Do you believe everything she tells you?"

She nodded with absolute loyalty. "Angels always t-tell the t-truth."

"And you talk to this ... angel without any problem?"

"I g-guess."

For the first time, Drew tried to see Emma's situation from Kerry's point-of-view. She'd been abandoned as a little girl by a father she could barely remember. The girl's mother wore her sadness like a shield, and carried her fading hope like a badge of honor.

Even though Kerry came first in Emma's life, he saw a similarity in each of the lives of the Ramsey women. Though Emma might not have been the focus of her father's rage, she couldn't help but be affected by it. Though Kerry had nothing to do with Emma's sad loneliness, she, too, couldn't help but be influenced by the demands Emma made on herself.

An imaginary friend who stayed by her as a steady guide made sense.

Taking a small leap of trust himself, Drew decided to accept Kerry's friend. For Kerry's sake.

He changed his grip to a comforting hug around the girl's shoulders and let her snuggle against him once more. "So what does Faith want you to tell me about your dream?" he asked.

Kerry sniffed and turned her nose into his chest. He didn't mind. "There's a m-man who c-comes to my house."

"Me?" Drew went rigid, wondering if he had unintentionally worked his way into her dreams and frightened her.

"No. He's bigger th-than you." Drew slowly exhaled and let himself relax, off the hook, but still concerned. "He t-takes Mommy away f-from me."

An angry resentment made him frown. Even in dreams, he didn't like the idea of anyone or anything frightening this little girl. He gave her shoulder a reassuring squeeze. "You know your mom loves you more than anything, punkin. You two are a team. She wouldn't let anybody take her away from you."

"He's n-not nice." She huddled closer, and Drew hugged her tight.

"*I* won't let anyone take her away from you, either." He made the promise without thinking, only feeling. He told her what she needed to hear, and heard the words himself with a sense of absolute rightness.

The bedside lamp brightened to its full strength. He narrowed his eyes against the sudden glare, and questioned its timing. But before he could make anything of the unusual coincidence, a ball of yarn tapped against his chin.

He pulled back and squinted at the embroidered doll's face staring at him. Kerry yawned. "Angelica's tired," she said.

Drew bit the inside of his cheek to keep from smiling at the droopy-eyed, seven-year-old mother figure in his lap. "Then we'd better put her to bed."

He scooped up both girl and doll and tossed them onto his shoulder like a sack of potatoes as he stood. Kerry giggled in his ear, breathless and surprised by the brief sensation of safe flight. "Daddy!"

Drew shushed her and carried her into the hall, bending his knees and dipping her up and down, prolonging the late-night carnival ride to her room. "You'd better call me Drew, punkin. So your mom doesn't worry."

" 'Kay."

"Promise?" The heady sensation of this girl's adoration had to take a backseat to common sense and his concern for Emma.

"It'll be our se-secret."

With a dramatic flourish, he swept her off his shoulder and laid her on her bed, almost tempted to chuckle right along with her as he tucked the covers up under her chin. "Good night, punkin."

"You c-can give me a g'night kiss if you want, Drew." Honored by the invitation, Drew smiled. He bent low over the bed and brushed a gentle kiss across her forehead. When he started to pull away, she caught him by the neck and whispered in his ear, "Daddy."

She released him with a flurry of hushed giggles and turned away, curling up into a ball around her soft stuffed doll. Drew straightened, a slow grin spreading across his mouth at their shared secret. Emma would probably cringe to hear Kerry call him that, but he liked it. He felt necessary, special, and—for a few short moments in the middle of the night—loved.

Before that rare good feeling could overwhelm him into thinking it meant anything more than temporary gratitude or infatuation, Drew left the room. He'd better find Emma to see why she, too, refused to stay in bed and sleep.

The idea that he could carry her to bed and give her a kiss to calm her fears created a wry twist of laughter in his throat. She'd slap his face. Fire him. Worse he'd feel as guilty as hell.

Guilty. Guilty. Guilty.

The word echoed in his head, a judge pronouncing sentence on him for feeling things he shouldn't—about another man's wife and another man's child. He descended the stairs with a light, noiseless tread. By the time he reached the downstairs hallway, his buoyed spirits had sunk again.

He coveted another man's life. He wanted Emma and Kerry for his own. Even if he remembered his life from before, he'd want this one instead. The Ramsey women had cracked a chink in his solitary armor and wended their way straight into his heart.

"She had a nightmare?" Emma took the stairs two at a time. Drew followed more slowly behind her. She caught her breath as she entered her daughter's room, not wanting the sound of her panic to startle and waken Kerry.

As she neared the bed, she could see she'd overreacted. Kerry slept soundly, spread-eagled in contented slumber. Emma smoothed the hair from Kerry's forehead and gave her a kiss. She straightened the covers and stepped away. "You keep an eye on her, okay?" she whispered to the wide-eyed doll tucked snugly beside her.

She slipped quietly out of the room and pulled the door shut. Drew stood outside his own room, an expectant look on his face. "She okay?" he asked.

Emma nodded. "Perfect."

Standing in the shadowed hallway, dressed in her silk pajamas and quilted robe, with fuzzy blue slippers warming her toes, she felt an intimate connection to Drew. Maybe it was the shared concern over Kerry's welfare. Maybe it was her tired brain reacting to the sight of his well-worn jeans hugging muscled thighs and lean hips. Maybe it was the aching hole in her heart that wanted to accept his care and concern, and recapture the absolute trust she'd had in him earlier in the day.

But she couldn't talk about those things. She

couldn't share those feelings with Drew. So she fell back on the one topic that had never failed her. "I've studied every number in the Consolidated proposal. I've decided to reject Wyatt Carlisle's offer."

Drew seemed to take the abrupt change of topic in unquestioning stride. "Good. The man crawled out of a swamp. You're better off without him."

His succinct appraisal of Carlisle triggered a smile. His agreement with her assessment reinforced her confidence in her decision. "Did you see those eyebrows of his?" she asked, slipping into a normal conversation that relaxed her, reassured her. The kind of simple, silly conversation she hadn't shared with a man in years. "They reminded me of fuzzy caterpillars. I sat there talking buyout all day long, and all I could think of was, when are those eyebrows going to get up and crawl across his face?"

Drew's answering smile glinted in the dim light. "You amaze me, Emma. You have a lot on your plate, but you handle it all with style and class." His smile disappeared. He hooked his fingers into the front pockets of his jeans and studied the floor for a moment before looking at her. "I'm sorry if I said anything tonight that made you uncomfortable. I don't want to add to your burden."

"You didn't." She expressed her remorse with a sigh. In an instant, the facade of their shared moment of congenial companionship dropped to reveal the strain between them. "You had to be honest. I appreciate that."

"I just want you to know that I'll do everything in my power to help you." He straightened up, snapping to attention with lithe, controlled grace. "Then I'll walk away. There won't be any trouble when your husband comes home."

She should have liked the sound of that, *when your husband comes home*. Drew said the words as if it were only a matter of time before they came true. She hugged her arms across her stomach, easing the sudden sorrow she felt. Drew would leave her. As soon as Jonathan returned, this new friend would be lost to her forever.

"Did I ruin your case by talking to Roylott tonight?"

"No. Moriarty's smart. He knows we know about the buyouts. We may even have forced him to show his hand sooner than he wanted."

"Make him go to Plan C, huh?"

"Yeah. Keep him off balance so we have some advantage." He turned his wrist and pushed a button on his watch. "Well, it's almost three in the morning."

Emma nodded. Even his simple declaration of the time sounded like a good-bye. "Thank you for watching out for Kerry."

"My pleasure." Drew's soft voice blended with the night. Its low-pitched rasp caressed her ears and brought goose bumps to her skin.

She fought the good fight of mind over body, told herself it was pointless to react to him this way. Pointless to wish he weren't standing so far away. Pointless to imagine he'd really meant it when he'd said he was falling in love with her.

Because, despite her loyalty to Jonathan, despite the suspicions about Drew's past, she was falling in love with him, too.

"Good night." She broke the eye contact between them, embarrassed to realize that she'd been staring.

" 'Night, Em."

She heard the door to his room click shut and settled in her bed for the night. But sleep was an elusive thing. For years she had despaired of ever finding a man, ever allowing herself to drop her guard enough to let one close to her heart. Then she'd met Jonathan.

And now she knew Drew Gallagher.

As she drifted to sleep, feelings of betrayal mixed with longings to be held and loved and comforted. Guilt at her growing feelings for Drew warred with guilt at denying his feelings for her.

Two good men. Very different, yet stirring so many of the same needs and desires in her.

Yes. A quiet voice whispered its way into her half-dozing mind.

Emma opened her eyes, expecting to see Kerry standing at her bedside, wanting to crawl in beside her. But there was no little girl with nightmares or cold feet. She squinted into the darkness, but sensed no one there. With a tired sigh, she rolled over and tried once more to find sleep.

Listen to your heart. She heard the voice again. More of an imprint on her subconscious mind.

"My heart loves Jonathan," she mumbled to herself, telling her subconscious to shut down and go to sleep.

No. That's your head talking. Listen . . . The dream voice stopped abruptly. *I have to go to him now. He needs me. He needs you, too.*

"What?" Emma sat up in bed. She pushed her hair back from her face, wondering who had spoken to her, only half remembering the strange argument from her dreams.

"Stand fast!"

"Hmm?" Emma snapped her eyes open, instantly and fully awake. Who had spoken? Was it Kerry?

"No!"

Drew's deep-pitched moan reverberated through the still house, striking her heart with a chilling sense of fear and foreboding.

When he cried out a third time, she stepped into her slippers and hurried down the hall, pulling on her robe. "Drew?"

"You bastard!" He wailed like a man in pain. She ran past Kerry's closed door and pushed open Drew's.

"Drew!" she called to him in a sharp whisper.

"We'll both die!"

She stubbed her toe on the corner of the bed, feeling her way to the lamp on the table beside him. Her curse at the throbbing pain died in her throat when she flipped on the light. Drew lay on his stomach, thrashing in his sleep. The covers had twisted around his legs. A pillow that should have lain beneath his head had been pummeled and tossed aside.

"Stop saying that." His voice broke on a strangled moan.

Emma bit her lip, wondering what kind of demon possessed him. "Drew." She said his name quietly, hoping he could hear. "Drew." She said his name a bit louder. She touched his bare shoulder. The fever in his skin seared her fingertips, and she snatched them back.

He'd said he had dreams. But she never imagined he meant horrific nightmares that sounded like torture to her ears. "Dammit, Drew, wake up!"

She pushed past her shock and concern and grabbed his shoulder again. She shook him. Hard. She dove on top of the bed, ducking as his arm flew out, striking out at her or the image in his dream, or maybe both. He rolled over and sat up. His eyes opened but were glazed over with a wild look of madness. He dropped his jaw open and sucked in huge gulps of air.

"Drew?" Lying flat on the mattress in case he lashed out again, Emma studied him. His chest rose and fell in a rapid rhythm. His skin glistened with sweat. She reached out and grazed her fingers along his flank. "Are you all right?"

"Get out." His terse whisper was more of a vibration than a sound.

She climbed up on her hands and knees, trying to make eye contact. "You were having a nightmare."

"I said get out!"

She scrambled back on her haunches, avoiding the sudden movement of his shoulder as he turned on her. A brief memory of her father's harsh commands made her hug her arms around herself. But she cried out for a different reason altogether.

The lamp light revealed a shiny pattern of scars that mottled his torso and disappeared beneath the furry patch of golden hair at the center of his chest. The blotches of scar tissue curved up over his right shoulder, and veed beneath the waistband of his black pants. "Oh, my God. Drew."

In a heartbeat the rage left him. "I'm sorry."

He rolled off the opposite side of the bed quicker than she could catch a steadying breath. By the time she got to her feet, he was halfway down the stairs. She leaned over the railing and watched him disappear into the kitchen. The back door opened and closed.

Barefoot, bare-chested, he'd gone out into the night.

God, how he must have suffered both physical pain and mental anguish. And yet he'd survived. He'd pieced together a life for himself and kept going. And somewhere along his hellish journey, he found time to rescue little girls and make big girls turn to him for safety and support.

Giving him time to work through his nightmare, giving herself time to decide what to do, she checked on Kerry. Then she returned to pull the blanket from his bed and went down the stairs after him.

After slipping her coat over her shoulders, she followed him outside onto the back porch. He stood like an ancient Eastern warrior, his legs braced apart, hands fisted at his hips, eyes tipped up to the fading light of the moon.

His long hair caught on the breeze and danced around his chiseled jaw. He held himself with such strength, such heartbreaking, solitary strength.

She inhaled the crisp air and caught the scent of him. Strong, yes, but still very human. "Spring may be on its way, but it's still thirty degrees outside tonight."

His face showed no reaction. "I didn't scare Kerry, did I?"

Emma gentled her voice, wanting him to hear her strength and reassurance even if he would not see it. "No. She's sound asleep."

"I'm sorry I woke you." Again he put someone else before his own needs.

"I'm glad you did."

"Why?" He gave a derisive laugh and glanced over his shoulder, finally looking at her and revealing the deep lines of fatigue and regret at his eyes and mouth. "So you could share my nightmare? Don't you have enough bad memories without adding mine on top?"

She simply smiled and let his self-loathing run its course. "Here." She draped the blanket around his shoulders. She arched an eyebrow when he started to shrug it off. "Humor me."

She moved behind him and held the blanket there herself. He flinched at her touch, but didn't pull away. Standing as tall as his shoulder, she turned her head and leaned into him, resting her cheek against his back. He held himself rigid beneath her embrace. As if he had no right to accept her comfort.

She apologized for making him think that way.

She stepped closer, aligning her body to his, exchanging warmth, trading understanding. They stood together in silence for several minutes until he shuddered. It started at his shoulders, moved down through his back and into his legs. In that instant, he relaxed his guard, and she wound her arms around his shoulders, hugging him from behind.

Now that she had broken through the distance that separated them, she dared to smile. "You'll catch cold out here. Come inside."

He laid his hand over hers near the base of his throat. "No, it feels good. Seems like I can never wake up enough to make the nightmare go away."

"The one I'm in?"

"Oh, lady, there's nothing nightmarish about

you in my dreams." He pulled her hands away and turned, his voice and expression immediately contrite. "Sorry. Seems to be a habit I can't break."

Emma noticed he still held her hands. Elegant muscle and sinewed strength. She liked the feel of his hands, a rasp of sensation across her softer skin. The same way his husky voice emphasized the differences between them. She was actually getting used to the sound of "lady" in that deep, gravelly voice.

She looked up into his eyes and smiled. "You have enough to think about. As long as you're not calling me 'Iron Maiden,' I don't mind. Not really."

He reached up and stroked her cheek, the essence of a smile on his face. "You are one class act. A real lady every step of the way. Just because you're tenacious and have crackerjack business sense doesn't mean you're not sexy and pretty and . . ." He dropped his hand and looked away, retreating from the unspoken territory where she'd asked him not to trespass.

His compliment warmed her all the same. She crossed her arms and looked at him with amused suspicion. "Are you the reason Wyatt Carlisle shaped up after lunch?"

"He minded his manners then, didn't he?"

"Yes. But I'm still not buying his company. I made that decision even before you told me about Moriarty's check. I prefer to do business with a man of integrity."

"Good. I don't want you messing with the likes of Carlisle."

Their shared smiles lightened the atmosphere surrounding them. The eerie quality that made his eyes gleam like emeralds returned, reassuring her that he had recovered from the terror of his dreams.

Maybe now it was safe to ask. "What happened to you? How did you get burned?"

He shrugged, as if having cheated death was no big deal. "I don't remember. The doctors said the pattern of damaged tissue and the severity of the burns indicate an explosion. They said it was a miracle I survived. Shrapnel that close to the heart should have killed me."

It would be a tragedy if anything happened to this man's big, open heart. Though his methods might be a bit nontraditional, he felt things and expressed his caring in ways she was only beginning to understand. "Well, I for one am glad you survived. And I can think of at least one other lady who's glad you're here, too."

Drew smiled like a doting uncle. And she knew he would be fine. "Kerry's a pistol, all right."

The distant chime of the doorbell interrupted their rare camaraderie. Drew opened the French doors and followed Emma inside. He shed the blanket and quickened his pace, reaching the door first and peeking through the peephole. The wary set of his shoulders eased a fraction as he turned to her.

"It's Maxwell. What does he want at this time of night?"

With a frown of curiosity, she stepped around him and opened the door. Brodie's gray gaze settled on her, then moved beyond her, turning to ice as he took in the half-dressed Drew.

"What's wrong?" She asked the question before Brodie could make any comment that would force her to defend Drew.

He stepped inside without shutting the door. "Stan Begosian's body has turned up. He's parked in a car outside LadyTech."

"Oh, my God." She felt the strengthening grip of Drew's hand on her shoulder. "Won't the police take care of it?"

Brodie nodded. "They're already there. I brought BJ with me. She'll stay with Kerry." He paused a moment, frightening her more than she cared to admit. His glance included Drew. "But I think you'd both better come see this."

Chapter Ten

Help me, Emma.
I tried to reach you in the only way I can. By computer. I smuggled a disk out with some of Moriarty's files. But he's discovered my trick. I've been a prisoner for too long, forced to work for a man I despise.
Please help me.

That handwritten note in Jonathan's strong, familiar scrawl was stapled to another message, neatly typed and much more ominous.

My dear Mrs. Ramsey:
I have valued your husband's assistance these past few years. But I find him harder to control by the day. For the lion's share of LadyTech,

222

Mrs. Ramsey, I'll send him home in one fairly healthy piece.
  If not, I'll send him home in pieces.
  Await my call on February 1st.
                                        James Moriarty

For the untold time that day, Emma reread the ransom note that had been pinned to poor Stan Begosian's coat.

"Three days?" She crumpled the paper in her fist and tossed it onto her desk. The chestnut-haired man sitting there, Kelton Murphy, unfolded the note and smoothed it out flat. She raked her fingers through her hair, nearly mindless with frustration. "Why wait three days?"

Though it had been a rhetorical question, Kel answered her anyway. "He knows it takes a while to arrange a stock transfer. He's giving you time to meet his demands."

"I can't change that much stock through normal channels in three days." She paced to the window and looked outside, feeling like a caged guard dog, wanting to lash out to protect what was her own, and going mad because she couldn't. "He might as well have demanded it on the spot, and not given us any time to help Jonathan."

She sucked in her breath and cringed at her ashen reflection in the window. "I didn't mean that."

Brodie crossed the room and squeezed her arm in a show of support. "We know, Em. Remember, Jas and BJ have agreed to turn over whatever part of their stock is necessary to give you fifty-one percent. All we need is a legal document to bind the

223

transfer. If Moriarty wants real stock certificates, he'll just have to wait."

"You're not really going to pay that bastard's ransom, are you?" A third man, Rafe Del Rio, with dark brown hair and mischievous eyes, rolled to his feet from the nearest loveseat. "He stole five years of your life, and the best man I ever served with. If anything, he owes you."

A fourth man, a big, broad-shouldered Native American named Hawk Echohawk, stood quietly to one side. "Emma, are you sure this ransom note is legitimate?" he asked.

She turned slowly, studying each of her guests as her gaze passed by. These were the men Jonathan had served with. His hand-picked team of experts. His closest friends.

They were quite possibly the only people in the world who could truly understand what losing Jonathan felt like to her. She had no desire to give them false hope, but then she believed with all her heart that Drew Gallagher had made this happen. He'd done his homework. He'd butted heads. His closing in on James Moriarty was what had made this happen.

"It's legit."

If poor, misguided Stan hadn't been sacrificed as the bearer of Moriarty's message, she had no doubt that the criminal would have contacted her in another way. Through the club at Lucky's. Or through Wyatt Carlisle.

Kel Murphy, as usual, regrouped and kept them all on track. "So what is it you want us to do?" he asked.

Area law enforcement, in coordination with Interpol, had tapped her phones at home and work, and set up a system to monitor her cell phone. Their aim was to trace the kidnapper back to his international lair and put him out of commission without giving him anything he wanted. Emma didn't like the idea of gambling with her husband's life. She didn't like gambling with her friends' futures, either. "I don't want Jas and Beej to sacrifice what they've worked so hard for."

"Tell them that," reminded Brodie. "They offered."

"I know." The unfailing friendship of her two college-roommates-turned-business-partners had proved a blessing many times over. She knew they'd help her in any way she asked. But right now, what she needed most were their prayers and support. And a round the clock friend to stay with Kerry. Jas had cut short her West Coast trip and flown back to stay with Kerry and Katie Maxwell while Brodie and BJ helped Emma.

"They won't have to give up anything." Emma breathed in deeply, still coming to terms with the brief suggestion that Drew had made to her earlier. "I'm not going to pay the ransom."

"Good girl." Rafe's bright voice carried above the instant discussion that Emma's statement aroused.

Kel's gruff admonition silenced them all. "I don't think she's doing it to please you."

Rafe threw up his hands and stalked to the desk. "Well, think about it, smart guy. If Moriarty wanted to exchange the colonel for control of LadyTech, why didn't he contact Em sooner?"

Kel's deadpan seriousness had long been a contrast to Rafe's effusive demeanor. "My concern is, what would he want to use the colonel for? Why keep him this long?"

"We know Jonathan is not trading state secrets. He'd die before betraying his country."

"Rafe." Brodie's sharp rebuke ended their bickering.

"Sorry, Em." Rafe and Kel apologized in unison.

Hugging her arms together, she shrugged, conceding their point. "No, you're right. Jonathan's a patriot. I think Moriarty's a common criminal, not some spy or subversive."

Kel pointed out the obvious. "You can sell info to unfriendly countries for big bucks."

Brodie contradicted the argument. "He's been out of commission five years. They'd want current information. I think she's right. Whatever he's using Jonathan for has to do with money, not politics."

Emma raised her voice. "None of that's important now. We just need to bring him home."

At that moment, the door opened. BJ walked in with a handful of computer printouts. Drew followed a step behind. The room fell silent when he paused in the doorway. Tall, bronzed, and needing a shave from his full night's work, he drew Emma's gaze like a beacon. Behind his glasses, his weary eyes gleamed with intelligence and confidence.

She'd pinned her hopes on this man. She prayed he was about to deliver.

He swept his gaze around the room, taking in the four unique, powerful men who eyed him with curiosity and suspicion. When he looked at her, he smiled. Emma's heart took on new life and beat with a quicker tempo at the silent reassurance.

The smile vanished. He closed the door and aimed an accusatory glance at Brodie. "So this is the inquisition you promised me."

BJ frowned up at her husband. "What's he talking about?"

Drew took the papers from her and crossed to the coffee table. "It's okay, Beej. He's only trying to protect you from the bad guys."

"Well, when I see one, I'll let him know, okay?"

She followed Drew to the table and helped clear away coffee cups. He spread out the papers as Emma and the others gathered around.

"What did you find?" Emma slipped in at Drew's right and touched his elbow, impatient for answers when she sensed they were so close to finding them.

Drew covered her hand where it rested on his arm, giving her a squeeze that lasted just long enough for her to sense the questioning looks of the four other men. He released her without apology or explanation and leaned over the table. "With BJ's help I think we broke a code in Moriarty's diary, which we now know was penned by Jonathan. It's a map. If you follow the place names like compass points, and interpret the dates as latitude and longitude, it pinpoints the spot where I believe he's being held."

"And the usefulness of that knowledge is . . . ?" Kel questioned.

Brodie crossed his arms, flexing his shoulders and creating an imposing silhouette. "This is the P.I. I was talking about. Drew Gallagher. He's got some theories of his own."

Emma bristled at the underlying hostility in her friend's tone. She doubted that Drew could miss the subtle challenge to prove himself, but she silently applauded him for not rising to the hidden taunt.

If anything, he seemed to relax, taking command of the room by refusing to be baited. "We have a three-day window of opportunity before Moriarty claims his payoff."

Rafe knelt at the table and studied the numbers more closely. "Are you suggesting what I think you are?"

Drew hooked his thumbs into his pockets and lay down a challenge of his own. "I don't know. Are you guys as good as Emma says?"

She looked at each man around the table. "I know you have lives of your own. But if you could help . . ."

Rafe grinned. His smile was charming, but his eyes were hard as steel. "Em, if you want us to go down and get him, say the word."

Kel's acceptance was a bit more cautious. He looked at Drew. "You're sure this man has the colonel? We've been on wild goose chases before."

She felt Drew's attention turn to her. She tilted her head, questioning his stark look. But those gem eyes shuttered before she could decipher their meaning. He answered Kel with that supreme confidence of his. "I know where Jonathan Ramsey is."

"Then count me in," Kel said.

Hawk had always been an enigma to Emma, a gentle man with strange powers she didn't understand. "These coordinates put us on Tenebrosa. I've been there recently. Jonathan was not there."

Drew looked at Hawk, then looked again, as if recalling something for an instant, and then forgetting it just as quickly. She recognized the quick expansion of his chest as a calming technique. Whatever thought had crossed his mind must have disturbed him.

"Drew?" She counted on him to see this through. But if he had any doubts, she didn't want to be responsible for putting any one of these men in danger.

But he shook off both her concern and his own to answer Hawk. "Actually, I believe Moriarty has a villa on a small island off Tenebrosa. It's more of an atoll really. It's not on any proper map. Of course, I don't know exactly where it is on the island, or what kind of security and manpower he has in place."

Hawk simply nodded, apparently satisfied. "Get me on the island and I'll find out what we're up against."

"Maxwell?"

Emma looked to the big man. She swallowed her words of regret when she saw BJ curl her arm through his, offering her husband her love and support in his decision.

The two exchanged a meaningful glance before he spoke. "I wasn't there when the colonel disappeared. But I'm damn straight gonna see that he comes home."

"Thank you," Emma whispered, her gratitude going out to both Brodie and BJ.

Drew nodded. "I'll go with you to coordinate the rescue. I seem to have made myself an expert on this Moriarty." He made a point of engaging each man's eyes before leaving. "I'll draw up a timetable and get back to you as soon as I have the details."

As he turned, he took Emma by the elbow and guided her to the door with him. He bent his head to whisper out of earshot. "I'll bring him home to you, Em. Just like I promised."

She conquered the urge to wrap him up in a hug.

He seemed so alone. A man with only his nightmares to keep him company. Even with everyone signing on to his plan, he seemed somehow alone. "I'm sorry about them," she began, noting that her friends were even now giving them anxious stares.

He shushed her with a gentle brush of his fingers across her cheek. "Don't apologize. I've faced tougher crowds."

"But if you have to depend on each other—"

"It's okay." He smoothed a lock of hair behind her ear, purposely ignoring the curious looks that she could not. "They wouldn't worry about me if they didn't love you so much. I find it reassuring to know that they'll be around to take care of you when I'm not."

A fist of panic seized her. "What do you mean?"

"Em."

With the hesitant whisper of her name, she understood. She wouldn't see him again after the mission. If it was a success, Jonathan would be back in her life, and this man who said he loved her would have no rightful place in it. And if the mission wasn't a success . . .

The fist tightened.

"You be careful," she demanded. It had never occurred to her that her heart might break twice, losing both good men in her life.

He bent his head to whisper into her ear. "Don't worry, lady." The nickname sounded like an endearment. She absorbed its caress without a trace of remorse. "Andrew Gallagher always lands on his feet."

And then he was gone and the door had closed behind him. She hugged herself tightly, trying to keep an overwhelming sense of impending doom at bay. Once Drew left, the others grew animated again.

She heard Rafe's voice first. "Seems like old times. I'm still earning a living at this. But are you boys ready for action?"

Kel's skeptical voice came next. "Are you sure he's on the up-and-up? Can we trust his information?"

Hawk answered. "I didn't sense any subterfuge in him. He's genuinely trying to help Emma."

"We all are." That was Brodie, sounding dubious about Drew.

Friends or not, hearing their talk incensed her. With a shortage of rest and patience to control her anger, she lashed out. "How dare you treat him like that!" She spun around and advanced on the startled group, chastising them with each and every step. "Drew's not the enemy. He's uncovered every connection to Jonathan we have so far. He's the man I hired to bring him home. As far as I'm concerned, you either listen to him—or you go home yourselves."

Brodie put up his hands in mock surrender, pressing at the air in an attempt to placate her. "Em, how much do you really know about this guy?"

"I know enough."

"He has this bizarre idea that Jonathan and Moriarty are the same person."

"That's enough! He's just impersonating him to escape." She stopped advancing only when BJ stepped in front of her husband.

"Emma," she cautioned, a voice of reason in a fog of fatigue and twisted feelings of love for two men. "We're all here to help Jonathan."

Emma stopped and glanced around at the sympathetic glances. Good God. Didn't anyone understand how hard this was for her?

One man did.

She shut her eyes and pictured Drew's compassionate grin. With a conscious effort, she pushed his image aside and recalled Jonathan's beaming smile on their wedding day. Then she snapped her eyes open and accused them all.

"What's wrong with you? Are you worried about my loyalty to Jonathan? Well, don't question it. Ever!"

The answering silence was filled with the heartbeat of each man in the room. Properly chastened like a group of errant teenage boys, instead of the savvy former Marines they were, they moved past her defense of Drew and their own doubts and went to work.

Forty-eight hours later, Drew hunched over the hand-drawn map Kel Murphy had scrounged for him, marking the armed patrols, electrified fences, and watchtower of Moriarty's compound, all according to Hawk's reconnaissance report. Four of them sat in a nest created of broken palm fronds, ammunition, and high-tech equipment, while Brodie patrolled the area.

The tropical heat beaded sweat across the black and green camouflage paint streaked across Drew's face. Kel had "borrowed" a yacht from a friend, along with the map, and they had anchored it a couple of miles offshore and rafted in to what Rafe had jokingly dubbed Hell's Island.

If Drew had a camera, he'd take a snapshot and send it in to illustrate the cover of the next Drew Gallagher adventure. Except Gallagher's fictitious world had suddenly taken on a very real, very dangerous edge.

"Two dogs and their handlers patrol the grounds at any one time, it looks like," said Hawk. "The rest of the security is in the guard tower or inside the villa itself."

Drew listened to the Indian's quiet voice and was again struck by an odd sensation of familiarity. Just like two days ago in Emma's office when those dark eyes had studied him so intently. He'd seen those eyes before. He knew his voice. Somewhere, in another place, another time, he'd looked into those eyes and made a request.

For what? When? Where? The tiny knife-point of a headache pricked him behind his eyes. He pinched his nose between his thumb and forefinger and breathed deeply. The timing couldn't be worse for a blocked memory to try and show itself.

"Gallagher." He snapped his eyes open and looked into Kel's face. "You with us?"

Drew nodded, filed away that hint of recognition to be studied another day, and resumed the briefing. "What kind of tech do they have?" he asked.

Hawk pointed to the map. "There's a heliport here. The fences and radar are controlled in the tower. Munitions are back here in what probably used to be servants' quarters."

Rafe, already tinkering with some little black box gizmo in his hands, leaned forward. "I'll take out the tower and work my way to the heliport. We might need a quicker way to escape than on foot."

"Right," said Drew. "If Brodie puts the guards out of commission, that leaves Hawk, Kel, and me to get into the house and find the colonel."

Kel shook his head. "I'd slow you down." He

slapped his right leg. Drew had noticed the man's perpetual limp, but had discarded it as any real handicap; the man had a commanding demeanor that kept Rafe in line and the rest of them focused on the task at hand. He'd already proven to be an invaluable resouce by procuring equipment, transportation, and travel papers within a twenty-four-hour time frame. He was a real right-hand man.

"All right," Drew said. Kel gave him a curt nod. Of thanks? Or was it just the okay to continue? Drew took the hint. "You get back to the ship. Do what you can to keep any other boats from leaving the island."

"Done. What do you want us to do if we run into Moriarty? Arrest him? Kill him?"

"I don't think there is a James Moriarty."

"What?"

Now was not the time to explain his suspicions about the elaborate ruse of Moriarty's true identity. He'd get Jonathan home first, and then pray he was wrong—for Emma's sake.

"Let's say it's just a feeling I have." Drew looked to the others. After brief consideration, they accepted his explanation and awaited the rest of their instructions. "That leaves Hawk and me. We'll get inside as soon as we can to locate the colonel. We'll radio in if we come up empty-handed."

"The second floor has keyhole windows," added Hawk. "Too skinny for a man to get in or out of."

Drew folded up the map. "Unless we find a jail cell proper, that's where we'll start our search."

He looked around at each man, even Brodie standing at a distance. This felt right. Familiar. Maybe because it was the best thing he could do for Emma and Kerry. Maybe just because it felt good to see the grudging gleam of respect in their eyes.

"Let's do it, then," he ordered. "The fireworks should begin at nineteen hundred hours."

Drew lay on his belly in the mud, trying to picture Emma with her long, long legs that looked too sexy for a corporate executive in those sensible above-the-knee skirts. He pictured her sweet, calming smile and the clear intelligence in her eyes. He concentrated harder on the image of her dressed in a clingy, cuddly robe, leaning over her dark-haired little girl and brushing a kiss across that tiny angel's cheek.

He tried to remember all the mental snapshots of Emma and Kerry he'd made over the past few days, in an effort to thrust aside the mind-numbing visions that threatened to overtake him.

Lying in wait in the jungle, breathing in the perfume and humidity of tropical air, holding a rifle in his hands, all reminded him of something awful. A terrifying pursuit. A kill-or-be-killed mentality.

He turned on his side and curled into a ball, racking his entire body with the need to make those memories recede. He needed Emma with him now. A simple word. A gentle touch. A smile across a room. She made the nightmares disappear. He could hold on to his sanity because of her. He had a reason to live and find his way home because of her.

"Emma." He breathed her name on a prayer.

She hears you. She knows. That soft voice entered his brain once more.

Drew swore violently and sat up, jerking himself into clear consciousness. "Leave me alone! Do you hear me?"

Knowing the futility of fighting madness, he calmed his temper. He closed his eyes and spoke in hushed tones for nobody but the jungle and the voice in his head to hear. "I love her. You know that?"

I know. It made sense that the voice should answer.

"She needs her husband, though. And Kerry needs a real daddy. I promised."

A mango sailed through the air and thunked him on the side of the head. "Hey!"

He shifted to his haunches with his rifle aimed to fire. But peering into the trees and ferns, he saw nothing. No one. He glanced up. The nearest mango tree was a good twenty feet away. Even if the fruit had fallen it wouldn't have carried that far. It seemed as if someone had thrown it at him.

"Trying to knock sense into my head." He scanned the tree line, looking for a mischievous monkey or a clumsy sloth. Someone was with him, watching him. Yet he didn't sense any real threat. More of a sense of . . . "Frustration?" he asked quietly.

"I really am losing it." He shook his head and checked his watch, chiding himself for losing the focus of this mission. Nineteen hundred hours.

Right on cue, the guardhouse exploded, lighting the early-night sky with flaming debris. It triggered a chain reaction of miniature lightning bolts along the chain link fence, blowing out electronic relay stations like popping lightbulbs around the perimeter.

"Go, Rafe." He praised his compatriot, then shouldered his rifle to scale and drop over the defunct fence.

He crouched low to the ground to get his bearings on the compound. He saw a flash of green uniform racing from shadow to shadow at the back of the house, and knew Brodie was well on his way to subduing the guards.

Drew pushed aside everything but the idea of finding Jonathan Ramsey and getting him out of there in one piece. He'd done plenty of odd jobs in his work as a private investigator, but he'd never been part of a strike team like this one. Yet he fell into the role as easily as if he'd been playing it his whole life. He dodged from cover to cover, kicked in a side door, and entered the kitchen of Moriarty's villa.

A big, burly cook pulled a knife on him, but Drew subdued him easily. He kicked the knife away and left the unconscious man on the floor. Now he could hear the whistles and explosions of a firefight in the compound, and wondered how much resistance Rafe and Brodie had encountered outside.

"I'm in," he radioed over his shoulder mike to Hawk. The Indian was already on the second floor, combing the villa room to room.

Drew rounded the corner to the stairs and encountered two more guards. The bulky men, dressed in tropic-weight suits, provided little resistance to Drew's rifle. True, he had surprised them, but one of the two men should have gotten the drop on him, and neither man had fired his weapon.

He ignored the nagging, half-formed suspicion

that sprang to mind, and ascended the stairs without a sound. Hawk had the east wing, so Drew headed west. Hugging the wall, he pushed open the doors, one by one.

The fourth door was wrenched from his hand, pulling him off balance. A fist with a knife swung down, catching him on the wrist and knocking his rifle to the floor. He ignored the fiery stream of pain in his arm and barreled into his attacker. The man should have been downed, but his solid build deflected the brunt of the blow, and he merely stumbled back a few steps. Drew crouched low, caught the arm with the knife the second time it descended, twisted, and flipped the man onto his back. A quick blow to the man's chin left him unconscious.

Drew knelt over him. In the fight, the man's jacket had ripped. Drew picked up the knife and cut the cloth further, revealing a bulletproof vest. Were Moriarty's men always this prepared? On a secluded tropical island not known to standardized maps, did they get many armed attacks? Or . . .

"Are you expecting us?" Drew whispered the query out loud.

A really bad feeling churned in his gut. Was this all a setup?

He'd gone through this before. Meeting a man who never showed. Being setup. A chase through the jungle. Seeing a man's face for one instant in time before a grenade pin sailed through the air . . .

"No!" He clenched his teeth so tight his jaw ached. He would not succumb to that dream now.

Any pause now could mean the failure of their mission. He would not let his past get in the way of Emma's future.

Climbing to his feet, he grabbed his rifle and kicked in the next door. It was an empty room. He swung around and kicked in the next.

Cigar smoke hung in the air. He entered, gun first, angling back and forth to check every corner for another guard. He saw only one man in the room, sitting in an office chair in front of the narrow window. He studied the back of the man's dark head as he slowly closed in on him. He sat so still. If this was Jonathan, and if he was injured or killed in the raid, Emma would have his head. Hell, he'd hand it to her on a silver platter himself if he screwed this up for her.

He almost laughed out loud at that weird thought. Coming around the side of the desk, he could see that the man's arms had been tied to the chair. With his rifle aimed at the man's head, Drew spoke. "Jonathan Ramsey?"

With some effort, the man swiveled the chair around. The man had a black eye and a bloody lip, but when he lifted his face, Drew nearly came undone. The hair color and cut were different, the eye color was different, the angles on their faces were different, yet Drew had the sensation of looking in a mirror.

He could only stare. He could scarcely breathe.

The captive's good eye rounded in shock. He stared right back.

"My God," he whispered through parched lips. "Did Emma send you?"

Drew blinked rapidly, trying to dispel the image

before his eyes, trying to make sense of the image in his brain.

"Are you here to take me home?" The man spoke again, but the sound barely registered.

"Colonel." A stronger voice snapped through Drew's brain like a gunshot, waking him from his delusion. Hawk crossed the room and pulled a big knife. In two quick strokes he cut the prisoner free.

This older, beaten-down version of the man in the picture on Emma's desk tried to smile. "Hawk. Thank God. Are the others here?"

A quick nod. "You okay, Drew?" Hawk asked over his shoulder as he helped Jonathan Ramsey to his feet.

"What?" Drew asked.

Hawk glanced down at the blood on Drew's wrist. "It's nothing." Drew fought through the muddy confusion in his brain and picked up Hawk's rifle. "We'd better get to the chopper and out to the boat. I don't want to have to explain any of this to the authorities."

Drew dispatched two more men en route to the helipad, leading the way as Hawk half supported, half carried the weakened Jonathan across the compound. As soon as they were aboard, Brodie ran out of the servants' quarters and jumped into the chopper. "Go! Now!" he ordered.

In a tornado of wind gusts, the helicopter rose from the ground, putting distance between them and Moriarty's villa. As Rafe angled the chopper and headed toward the ocean, a second explosion on the ground rocked their ascent. But Rafe's steady hand piloted them safely away from the burning munitions storage shed.

"Nice work, Chief!" shouted Rafe. "They sure

won't be following us now." He grinned over his shoulder to the man buckled in the middle of the bench seat behind him. "You okay, Colonel?"

Jonathan nodded, his eyes closed. "I'm fine now, Del Rio." He opened his eyes and thanked each of them in turn. "Hawk. Brodie. Didn't Kelton Murphy make it?"

Rafe turned his attention back to his flying. "He's already on the boat, waitin' to take us home."

"Home." Jonathan seemed to savor the word on his tongue. "It sounds good. Emma and Kerry?"

Drew gave him his full attention, and silently wondered if this shadow of a man was still Emma's larger-than-life hero. He wondered if he measured up to the love and loyalty she'd held in her heart for five long, lonely years.

"They'll be happy to see you." Drew answered the question himself.

Jonathan turned to Drew, turned far enough around so he could look at him with his uninjured eye. "Who are you?" he asked.

"A friend of Emma's."

He held his inspecting gaze, and Drew wondered if he realized the kind of feelings he had for Emma and Kerry. Those blue eyes, so like Kerry's, narrowed with a steel glint. And something like . . . laughter . . . glowed there.

Drew flashed back in time to another place, a different set of eyes. But the look was the same.

Before he could make any sense of it, before he could say anything else, Jonathan turned away.

Drew pulled out the first-aid kit and doctored the gash on his wrist in silence. Couldn't anyone else sense something strange about this man? he wondered. He sank into silence as the other four men reacquainted themselves. Didn't anyone else have the same suspicion he had about this rescue?

Maybe his opinion was clouded by the knowledge that taking Jonathan home meant losing Emma forever.

But these men were seasoned soldiers. Veteran warriors. They knew how to size up a man or a situation at a glance. Didn't they understand the same thing he did?

This mission had been way too easy.

And he had a sneaking suspicion that he alone knew exactly why James Moriarty hadn't been at the villa.

He was sitting in this helicopter, right beside Drew.

Chapter Eleven

Jonathan was coming home!

After all this time, the love of her life was coming home.

Nerves mixed with excitement. Had he changed? He must be a different, harder man after years as a hostage. Had Moriarty broken his indomitable spirit?

She herself had changed, she knew. She'd become more assertive, more confident. She was raising a beautiful, smart little girl. And she had helped turn LadyTech into a multimillion-dollar corporation.

Would he still see her as his lady?

Would he still be her hero?

Emma craned her neck to see around the crowd of people in the concourse at Kansas City International Airport. Did this many people always travel to and from Mexico City? Why couldn't they find other ports of call to conduct business and take winter vacations?

She had a husband coming home!

The flight's arrival had been announced some minutes ago, but the plane was full and the passengers were taking their own sweet time to unload their gear and deplane. She paced back and forth in a three-step pattern, never taking her eyes from the gate. Kerry played contentedly in the chairs with Jas and baby Katie, while BJ stood close by, as eager to welcome her own husband home from a dangerous journey as Emma was eager to welcome . . . two men.

She stopped in her tracks.

Just the thought that her loyalties were divided between Jonathan and Drew was enough to make her question her heart. What about Drew? He'd risked his life to bring Jonathan home. He'd done so much. He'd helped her in so many ways.

Not all her thoughts had been for her husband.

How could she justify her feelings for Drew?

She'd barely slept in two days, and she had the shadows beneath her eyes to prove it. When Kel wired and said he'd gotten them on an earlier flight, she'd given up all thoughts of rest or food. She had put on a dress that Jonathan had liked, bundled up Kerry, and raced to the airport. Six hours of waiting had now stretched her nerves to the breaking point.

She was all raw, exhausted and heartsick, desperate to see Jonathan and reclaim their love. The coffee Jas had bought for her only further upset an already nervous stomach. She needed to see him.

Hold him in her arms. She needed him to come home.

But she'd grown to need Drew, too.

One by one, or in romantic pairs, passengers filed down the jetway and through the gate. Grown children greeted older parents. Friends hugged. Businessmen hurried through without acknowledging anyone in the crowd. She held her breath, looking . . . searching.

Drew emerged first, a vision of world-weary fatigue in his trim jeans and black leather jacket. He scanned the crowd until his gaze caught hers. She took a step toward him, feeling an urgent response in her heart that matched the hungry look in his eyes.

He swung his duffel bag up over his shoulder and she saw the white gauze bandage on his wrist. He'd been hurt! Her hesitant step became two bold ones. She pushed through a gathering of well-wishers and froze at the suddenly shuttered look in his eyes.

"Drew?" She mouthed his name.

He turned his head and she followed his gaze. Rafe and Hawk emerged. She smiled in thanks to each. Then Kel Murphy limped out. He gave her a curt nod. Brodie arrived next. He scooped up BJ when she ran to him and they greeted each other as if they'd been parted for weeks.

And then she saw him

He was as tall as she remembered. His shoulders were not quite so broad as they used to be. He still walked with the erect carriage of a career military man. His dark hair had sprouted silver wings at the temples. And his handsome blue eyes were marred by a bruise and some swelling.

He stopped when he saw her. Drank her in from head to toe. "Emma."

Tears welled in her eyes, blurring her vision. Suddenly the distance between them vanished, and she ran into his arms. "Jonathan."

He crushed her mouth beneath his, driving her lips against her teeth, then plunging his tongue inside. It was as if he were trying to recapture five years of loneliness and separation in one single kiss.

Emma shrank from the force of his lips, turning her face away and burying her face in his neck. "I missed you so." She wept against his skin, needing simply to be held. "Welcome home, sweetheart."

"Believe me, it's good to be home." He shifted his hold on her and ran his hands up and down her back. He cupped the curve of her hips, skimmed the swell of her breasts. It was hardly much in the way of comfort, but perhaps after five years of captivity he'd forgotten how to read her silent requests. Once, he'd loved public displays of affection and emotion. Maybe his eagerness to touch and explore her now stemmed from that, a need to publicly proclaim his love for her. But instead of reassuring her, the bold caresses in front of a watchful audience made her feel even more awkward.

She pulled his groping hands down to a neutral position at her waist and backed up a step. She lifted her fingers to frame his face. The cut near his mouth and his black eye worried her, but beyond that, he seemed to be in relatively healthy physical condition. More than likely, the scars from his experience would be mental and emotional, buried inside. "You're all right?" she asked.

"I'm in one piece, if that's what you mean." He pulled her hands away but clasped them between their chests. He looked down to study their entwined fingers before looking back to her. "I spent a long time in a hospital. But I've healed. Much to my surprise, my bill was paid by a man who called himself Moriarty. At first, I agreed to work for him to pay off my debt. But too late, I realized I was being held prisoner instead."

"You didn't call me first?" she asked, crestfallen to learn she hadn't been foremost in his thoughts as he'd been in hers. She immediately apologized. Who knew what he'd been through? Maybe he'd even suffered amnesia for a while, like Drew. "I'm sorry."

"It's all right. I couldn't call you. Moriarty monitored my every move. It wasn't until he put me to work on his computer system that I devised a way to contact you. I don't suppose you sold a bit of stock lately."

"You're behind the stock buys?"

He nodded and smiled proudly. Proud? The Jonathan she knew had been an easygoing, self-effacing man. Comfortable in his own skin, confident in his abilities. But he never had to brag about it. This was not how she'd expected his homecoming to unfold. This was a time for welcomes and loving, not asking questions or raising concerns.

"I worked through his computer network. Thought if I raised enough suspicion, you'd take the hint. I knew I could count on a rescue."

"What about Stan Begosian and Wyatt Carlisle?"

He shook his head. "I don't know those names."

"But they know James Moriarty. Or knew him. Stan Begosian's dead."

247

He cupped her shoulders, the hound-dog look he gave urging her to change the subject. "Emma. Sweetheart. All I know is I'm glad to be home after so long."

He pulled her close and kissed her again. She tried valiantly to kiss him back. The Jonathan she knew had been a patient man. He'd always backed off until she felt comfortable with a situation. He'd never pushed her until she was ready to move on. Maybe he'd lost some of that patience after five years.

Unfortunately, she discovered, she needed his patience now more than ever. Flattening her palms on his chest, she pushed him away. She covered the abrupt end of the kiss by turning and reaching for Kerry.

"Here I am, hogging the spotlight," she said, smiling. "Come here, sweetie, and say hi to your dad."

With a gentle nudge from Jas, Kerry came forward. She clutched her doll in front of her like a shield and stared up at Jonathan with wide blue eyes. Emma knelt beside her, took Kerry's hand, and extended it toward her father. "Here, sweetie. Remember the pictures? This is your daddy."

As soon as her hand was released, Kerry added it to the grip on her doll. She sidled up next to Emma and hid half her face in the pleats of her mother's skirt. Emma had wondered how this meeting would go. Jonathan was a stranger to Kerry, after all. But she'd counted on a father's love for his little girl to prevail and make this work.

"Hey, there, little lady." Jonathan crossed his arms in front of his chest and winked at Kerry.

Then he turned and looked around at their dearest friends. "Say, what does a man have to do to get a square meal around here? Nothing with beans and tortillas. I've eaten enough of those to last me a lifetime."

That was it? A wink and a cute line? A flash of blond hair distracted her from the corner of her eye. Drew had moved from his spot at the fringe of the group and was looking straight at Kerry. Emma urged Jonathan to show Kerry the same interest.

"She's a little shy."

"No problem." He laughed out loud, the old Jonathan laugh. "We'll work it out one of these days."

"Sure," she conceded. "This has been a big day for her as well as you and me. Maybe when we get her back into familiar surroundings she'll relax a bit."

"Fine by me." He grabbed Emma's chin and planted another kiss on her lips. "Shall we go home?"

Emma nodded and said a quick, silent prayer. Maybe familiar surroundings would relax her a bit, too. "By all means."

By mutual agreement, the entire entourage of men, spouses, children, and friends moved out to the main concourse and walked toward the parking lot.

Everyone closed around Jonathan. Everyone except Drew. He turned and headed in the opposite direction. Depositing Kerry with Jas, Emma stepped out of the group and cut him off. As before, he stopped when he felt just a touch at his elbow. She faced him now, but struggled to bring her gaze above the collar of his jacket to look him in the eye.

She inhaled a steadying breath and dredged up all her courage to begin this difficult conversation. She raised her chin and got lost in those incredibly unique eyes. "Thank you." She couldn't find the words to say any more until she caught sight of the bandage on his arm. "You're hurt."

He shrugged off her concern. "Believe me, I've had worse."

"You kept your promise. You brought him home."

The leather of his jacket creaked as he shifted his stance. "I'll send you a bill for my services."

"What?"

"I'd have done it for free, but"—he raked his fingers through his hair, looking as awkward about the discussion of money as she felt—"I don't want you to think you owe me anything."

She frowned. "I owe you everything."

"No." His firm denial skidded along her nerve endings and lodged in a painful place near her heart. "You owe that little girl and yourself a real chance to be happy again. Maybe next time I run into you, you won't look so sad."

"I *won't* see you again, will I?" A hotter sheen of tears than those she had shed earlier burned her eyes. She had known it would come to this. Still, she couldn't bear the thought of Drew never being a part of her life. He had come to mean so much to her in such a short time.

"I just want you to be happy," he said. A tear spilled free. He reached out and brushed a finger across her cheek, carrying the tear with it. He achieved a smile she could not find in herself. "Take care of the pistol, okay? And that doll of hers, too."

He tucked his fingers behind her ear and cradled her cheek in his palm. A fire glowed, bright and glorious, in his emerald eyes. Then it died out.

"Good-bye, Emma."

She turned to watch him walk away, a lonely figure in black. She blinked the tears from her eyes so she wouldn't miss a single step of his retreating figure. The swing of wheat-blond hair down to his shoulders. The easy stride of that lanky frame. The air of a disconnected soul that hung around him like a cloak.

The hand at her elbow startled her before the voice spoke in her ear. "Everything all right?"

She turned and looked into her husband's cool blue eyes. "He figured out where you were being held."

He glanced at Drew. "Is that so?"

"It's because of him that you're home."

He looked at her. "Then I owe him big-time, don't I?" Jonathan closed his fingers around her arm and pulled her into step beside him. "Frankly, I don't trust the guy."

She wrenched her arm free, reminding him that she was not a woman to be bullied in any way. And her opinion was not to be taken lightly. "I hope you thanked him."

Jonathan sighed heavily, as if he found this conversation tiresome. "C'mon, sweetheart. I want to go home."

He linked his arm through hers, and she walked by his side to catch up with the others. "Home," she repeated, wondering if the joy she had expected to feel upon his return would show itself there. "It sounds good."

She only wished Drew Gallagher had such a place to go to.

Drew sat in his kitchen, nursing his third beer of the night. Emma wouldn't approve of him drinking so much. Not for three nights straight. But then, Emma wasn't around to care one way or the other how he took care of himself. Or didn't.

He gathered up the cards from the table and shuffled them. He took another swig of beer, saluted the tingle at the center of his forehead that told him he was on the first step to oblivion, then set the bottle out of reach in the sink.

He lay down another solitaire hand on the table and blindly considered which would be the greater torture—succumbing to sleep and facing the nightmares, or staying awake and spending every waking moment thinking about Emma.

His mind replayed the message that had been waiting on his answering machine when he got home from the airport after saying good-bye to her. *"Hey, Drew."* It was Jack Tucker from the Highway Patrol crime lab. *"Got the fingerprint match-ups you wanted. Four clear sets. Clayton Scott and Stan Begosian, like you suspected. A local thug named Arnold Jackson. The fourth was a little harder to track down. Took your suggestion and found it on the military database."*

Drew echoed the name the technician had given. "Jonathan Ramsey."

Jack had gone on to ask if there were any loose ends on his missing-persons case he'd like Jack to wrap up for him. Drew had called back to thank him, but "forgot" to mention that he had stepped outside the law a bit to retrieve Ramsey himself. Besides, he wasn't quite sure how to explain the colonel's prints being found in Kansas City when he supposedly was being held hostage in the Caribbean.

Drew didn't like the possible explanations at all.

The fourth man in that room at Lucky's had been the boss, not a prisoner. Emma had recognized something familiar in his voice when he'd given the order to take care of Begosian. But she hadn't identified him then because those weren't the sort of words she was used to hearing from her husband.

And where were Moriarty's prints? Nowhere. Because *there was no Moriarty*. That fourth man had to have been Jonathan Ramsey. He'd bet his life on it.

What kind of man played such cruel games on his wife? Drew didn't see anything heroic in putting her through that kind of hell.

Jonathan had the means and opportunity to terrorize Emma and take over large chunks of her company. But he didn't seem to have a motive. As her husband, he'd already have rights to the company. Even without owning stock, he'd have the benefits of her wealth. Without a motive, Drew had no case to take to Jack Tucker, the D.A., or anybody.

And he surely had no right to take his story to Emma. Hadn't she suffered enough?

He flicked a card across the table with frustrated fury. "Hi, Em. It's Drew," he said mockingly to himself. "Say, that man who had you so scared? It's your husband." He shot another card with pinpoint accuracy. "You know that hero you worship? He's changed a bit. Remember how he used to save lives?" He tossed a card and missed the pile. "Now he takes 'em."

He wondered if Emma or any of Jonathan's friends had noticed a difference in his personality. Torture or hypnosis could do that to a man—make him different inside, make him sick. The man may have been abused recently, but he hadn't been misused over an extended period of time. His muscles were strong. He stood straight. There had been no outward, lasting indication of severe trauma. "Why the masquerade?"

The scattered cards had no answer.

Drew leaned back in his chair and crossed his arms over his face, shielding his eyes from the light above him. Was he, Drew Gallagher, really so different? He was a changed man from five years ago. He now played a role. Maybe there was something unique about Isla Tenebrosa, some frightening convergence of evil spirits and false hopes that altered a man's personality. Like Jonathan Ramsey. Or robbed him of his personality altogether. Like Drew himself.

With the beer so close, Drew reached back for it. Maybe tonight was the night to break his rule. He could get wasted and not have to deal with torturous thoughts about himself or Ramsey or Emma. But before he grasped the bottle, it fell over in the sink and broke.

He left his hand outstretched and watched the golden liquid run down the drain. He glanced up, then down at the broken glass and grimaced.

"I know. Now the voice is going to talk in my

head and tell me it's saving me from being my own worst enemy."

But no voice came.

The phone rang instead.

Drew considered letting it roll over to the answering machine. After all, the good people of the world would all be asleep by this time of night. But a sixth sense, an instinct more profound than any voice in his head, propelled him across the room.

Something was wrong.

He snatched up the receiver on the fourth ring. "Gallagher."

"Drew?"

Emma!

A wave of longing crashed through him. Just hearing her voice calmed him, soothed him, made him want to be near her. A second swell of guilt followed closely behind.

She didn't belong to him.

She never had.

She never could.

"What's wrong?" he asked, in lieu of polite conversation that might prolong the sound of her voice. Besides, he didn't want to ask how things were going for her. Any answer would be crushing.

"It's Kerry."

A stab of fear replaced any selfish concern he'd been feeling. "Is she hurt?"

"No." Her terse response lessened his immediate worry, but he knew there was something more. "I can't get her to sleep. I've fought it for two nights, but I'm afraid she's going to make herself sick."

"Has she seen a doctor?"

"Dr. Klein said it's the adjustment to having Jonathan home. I've tried to put familiar things around her, keep her to her routine. But she clings to me constantly. When I let her go, she cries until exhaustion claims her."

Drew swore. Of all the people to be hurt by this mess . . .

Emma waited for his outburst to subside and went on. "She's asked for you. I know you don't want to have anything to do with me. But if you have some time, I . . . she . . . would appreciate it."

He scraped his hand across his scraggly beard. He looked like hell and felt even worse.

But Emma needed him. Kerry needed him.

"What about your husband?"

"He wants to do what's best for Kerry, too."

Is that why he'd kept his distance from her at the airport? Because it was *best* for Kerry?

"Drew, will you come to the house? I know it's late."

"All right. For the pistol."

Despite his best intentions, despite the heartache, saying no to those two ladies was a thing he could not do.

To Drew's surprise, Jonathan answered the door. The two men evaluated each other like rival rams vying for supremacy of the herd. Understanding that this was not his territory, Drew looked away first. Only then did Jonathan invite him in.

"I realize it's late," said Jonathan. "Don't worry, though, buddy. I'll pay you for your time."

"Don't insult me. Helping Kerry isn't a job. And I'm not your buddy."

Jonathan's lips thinned into an understanding

smile. Neither man needed to endure the pretense of friendship. Jonathan didn't bother to take Drew's coat; he simply turned and walked down the hall, speaking as if he expected Drew to follow. Perhaps a man of his military rank excepted others to fall in line like that. Drew tamped down his irritation and followed anyway.

"I'm glad you're here," said Jonathan. "The kid won't leave Emma alone. They're both exhausted."

Drew buried his hands in the pockets of his jacket, restraining the urge to flatten the man in his own house. But he didn't curb his tongue. "The kid has a name, you know."

Jonathan halted at the base of the stairs. From here Drew could hear Kerry's low, keening moans. Her weeping sounded like the cry of an injured animal. Emma must be beside herself with worry.

Drew put his foot on the first step, but Jonathan braced his arm across the balustrade and blocked his path. "Don't presume to tell me how to run my family. Kerry won't let me near her. Think how that's hurting me. My own daughter."

Drew knew how Jonathan would feel. Maybe he'd judged Jonathan too harshly. Perhaps his suspicion and dislike for the man had more to do with jealousy than with any more noble motivation. "That must be rough."

"It is." He headed up the stairs once more, and Drew fell into step behind him. The closer he got, the more heart-wrenching Kerry's cries became. Her voice cracked with hoarse overuse.

When they entered the master bedroom, Drew forgot the reason for this late-night visit. Emma sat in a rocking chair with Kerry curled in her lap. Angelica and that lavender blanket were part of the mix, too. Kerry's face was pink and puffy, her eyes nearly shut. But Emma . . .

Her skin white as milk, she rocked back and forth, humming a little patternless tune. The fine blue veins normally visible beneath her closed eyes had darkened like smudges of eye shadow. Yet her face was scrubbed clean, telling him those shadows were real.

A tug on his sleeve stopped him in mid step. Jonathan whispered a command in his ear. "You're here to see the kid, not my wife. Remember that."

Had he betrayed so much in a single look?

Drew simply nodded and waited while Jonathan spoke to his wife. "Emma." Her eyes snapped open. "Look who's here."

"Drew." The hope she gave that one word cascaded through him, stripping him of his armor, leaving him feeling raw and exposed—and hopelessly in love with this woman he could not have.

Kerry roused a second later. Too weak to climb down, she simply stretched out her arms to him.

"Hey, punkin." Unable to resist her silent plea, Drew spared Emma a glance and scooped the girl up in his arms, blanket and all. "Will you let me tuck you into bed tonight?"

She nodded and clung to him, tiny fists grabbing fingerfuls of leather jacket as he carried her out into the hall. She turned her face away from Jonathan as they passed him and whimpered into Drew's neck.

Drew said nothing. He simply carried her to her room and closed the door behind them. "So. What are you doing to get your mom so worried?" he asked, taking her to the bed and tucking her beneath the covers. He sat on the edge beside her, folding the lavender blanket in half and tucking it with equal care around Angelica.

She rolled on her side to face him. "The b-bad man f-from my dreams is here."

The nightmare again. What kind of unjust world let a little girl be terrified by dreams as frightening to her as his were to him? He shrugged his shoulders, unsure why Kerry or Emma or even Jonathan thought he could help with a situation like this. "Your dad is here now. He'll protect you and your mom."

Kerry shook her head, agitating herself and the covers around her. "Uh-uh. He's the b-bad man. Mom's g-gonna leave me now, and Faith an' Angelica will never get their w-wings."

Drew frowned. He put the sheet and bedspread back in order, searching his brain for the right reference for seven-year-old logic and coming up empty-handed. "Your dad loves you a lot." He figured this explanation was as good as any. "But since he's been away, he hasn't had much practice taking care of little princesses."

Kerry sniffed and widened her puffy eyes beneath an arched brow reminiscent of her mother. "You m-mean he doesn't l-like me b-because he doesn't know how?"

Doesn't like her? Kerry's observation stabbed through him with a surprising force. What must it be like to be a child and think a parent doesn't like her? He gave a brief thought to the child or children he might have unknowingly abandoned. But that prick of guilt gave way to a much more real sense of injustice that this bright little girl should feel so unwanted.

He unzipped his jacket and settled more comfortably on the bed, meeting the question in her gaze with an equally serious look. "Maybe you have to teach him, the same way you taught me how to read a story. You have to be brave and work hard, and help him be a good dad."

She sat up. "B-but you're my daddy."

"No, punkin. I'm not." He took her by the shoulders and gave her a gentle squeeze. She felt so fragile and delicate in his hands. Her trust felt equally fragile and precious, and the responsibility of living up to it humbled him. He must have done something worthwhile in one of his past lives to receive such a gift from her. "But I will be your friend. And I would be honored if one day you give me a kiss and turn yourself into a frog, and we can hop off and live on my lily-pad together."

A tiny laugh snorted through her nose. She rolled her eyes and shook her head, looking remarkably grown up, and making Drew smile. She tilted her focus up to a point beyond his left shoulder. "You see? He doesn't know how the story goes."

Drew released her and looked over his shoulder, expecting to see Emma. But the door was closed and the light from the bedside lamp didn't reach that part of the room. The evenness of her speech registered. He turned back to Kerry. "You're talking to your friend Faith again, aren't you?"

She nodded. "She says I should l-listen to you and be brave. Sh-she says it will work out." She looked to that unseen point again, then back to Drew. "She hopes."

He didn't know whether to attribute this sudden

capitulation to her conscience, his reassurance, or blind luck. But he'd take this calm, confident little bundle of beauty over the teary-eyed girl who'd seemed so miserable any day.

Drew pulled his wallet from his back pocket and fished out one of his business cards. He pressed it into her small hands. "This has my phone numbers and address on it. I want you to work really hard to get to know your dad. Teach him about Angelica and hugs and bedtime stories. I want you to try, because your mom needs you to. She loves you more than anything." He replaced his wallet and noted that his rapt audience hadn't moved. "If you get scared, talk to your mom. Or you can call me."

She picked up her doll and hid his card inside the folds of its calico dress. Then, with the darting speed of a child, she climbed up on her knees and threw her arms around Drew's neck. "Don't you be scared, either," she said. "Faith says she keeps m-messin' up. But she'll get it right."

Giving in to the unexpected impulse, Drew hugged her tight. "I keep messing up, too," he whispered, clenching his jaw to stanch the overwhelming emotion swelling inside him. "I'll keep trying until I get it right, too."

He released her and stood up. When she settled back under the covers, he pulled the bedspread up to her chin and pressed a kiss to her cheek. "You take care of yourself, okay, punkin?" And since he no longer had the privilege, he added, "Take care of your mom, too."

"I will."

Drew straightened and smiled down at her, giving back every bit of the adoring look in her eyes. "You think you can sleep now?"

She nodded. "G'night, Daddy." A huge yawn punctuated her answer. "I mean, Drew."

"Good night, punkin." He hesitated before leaving her. Emma would have his hide for what he was about to say. "This friend of yours, Faith?"

"Um-hmm?"

He spoke quickly, smiling at how fast fatigue caught up to her. "I think it's okay if you believe in her. I can't be around much when you're teaching your dad about being a dad. But if she makes you feel safe, you go ahead and talk to her."

Kerry's face wreathed into a smile, even as her eyes drifted shut. "Faith likes you, too."

His mission complete, Drew switched off the lamp and turned to the door. An after image of light floated through the corner of his vision, stealing from the doorway to Kerry's bed. He spun around to follow it, but saw nothing but a sleeping girl. "I'm really losing it," he muttered, dismissing the flash as a trick of the softly glowing nightlight, or an imprint on his retinas from the lamp.

Only the image had looked strangely like . . . a woman.

He pressed the heels of his palms to his eyes and shook his head. "I'm *really* losing it."

Drew opened the door and stepped into the hallway, pulling the door closed with utter silence. He wasn't startled to turn and see Emma standing there, her shadowed eyes curiously bright. "Is she all right?"

His gaze dropped to her fluttering fingers,

clutching and unclutching the collar of her robe. He reached out and covered her hands with one of his. Her nervous tremor stilled beneath his touch, and he smiled. "The pistol's fine. I told her she could call me if she needed to talk, but that she needed to work things out with her dad."

Emma's face blossomed in a valiant smile. "Thank you."

"You look exhausted. You better hit the sack, too."

A dark shadow loomed up behind her. Drew released her hand and looked over her shoulder at her husband. "I'll see you out," Jonathan said.

Emma turned, an embarrassed flush staining her cheeks. Embarrassed to be caught holding hands with Drew? Or embarrassed by her husband's rude dismissive tone? "Jonathan . . ."

"Sweetheart. Drew's right." He pulled her to him and kissed her forehead. "You go get some sleep."

Drew could see the snap of fire in her eyes. Her lips parted as if to protest. Instead, she pressed them together. He recognized the tight control she exerted on herself, and wondered why she didn't lash out at him. She would have told Drew exactly what she thought.

"Good night, Drew."

" 'Night, Em."

Both men watched her, graceful even though dead on her feet, until she disappeared behind her bedroom door. With Emma and Kerry out of sight, they didn't waste pleasantries on each other. Drew took the steps at an easy pace, while Jonathan followed more resolutely behind him.

At the bottom of the staircase, Drew turned the

tables and stopped, bracing his hand on the balustrade and turning on Jonathan. "Why don't you try acting like a father instead of letting Em carry the whole burden of parenting that little girl? Pick her up. Hold her. Talk to her. She's going to be smarter than the rest of us put together."

Jonathan crossed his arms and glared down at him. "Well, that's not your concern, now is it?"

Drew grabbed him by the collar and pulled him down to his level. "I don't know what game you're playing, Moriarty. But I have proof, fingerprints, that show you were in Lucky's Bar the other night, not held prisoner in the Caribbean. You can have somebody beat you around the face a time or two, or pad your goons with bulletproof vests, but you don't fool me." He paused for a breath, time enough to cool his delivery if not his fury. "I haven't told Emma. But I will. If you don't treat them right, I will."

Jonathan laughed, an evil sound that chilled Drew to the bone. "Those fingerprints prove I'm Jonathan Ramsey, Lieutenant Colonel, USMC Retired." Drew didn't resist when the colonel removed his hands from his collar. "Now. Do you want to leave before I tell you who *you* really are, Mr. Gallagher?"

Drew backed off a step, giving himself a physical space to ward off an attack of any kind. "How could you possibly know?"

"Five years ago, in the jungles of Isla Tenebrosa, *you* tried to kill me."

"That was the Chameleon. Ask Hawk. He was there. No one knows what the Chameleon looks like."

An idea awakened inside Drew, leading him toward the truth he'd sought for so long, tightening him in its wretched grip like a noose.

Jonathan Ramsey smiled, a grin as full of hate as any perpetrated by Sherlock Holmes's archnemesis. *"I do."*

Chapter Twelve

Emma returned to a routine of sorts, more for
Kerry's sake than her own. She drove Kerry to
school, then went on to LadyTech. "Be careful
what you wish for," the old adage warned. She
finally had her husband home.

And she didn't think she could feel much worse.

She sorted through the stack of messages on her
desk, wanting to ignore each and every one. The
work she'd once found so invigorating now seemed
an imposition. She had problems at home she
needed to fix. But employees and investors and
friends were counting on her; she wouldn't let
them down.

A week had passed since Drew had come to the
house to help Kerry through Jonathan's return. A
week had passed since she'd felt secure. A week

since she'd felt it was completely safe to drop her guard.

The oddest things seemed to bother Jonathan. Things he wouldn't have noticed before, things he would have laughed at or dealt with and moved on.

She'd asked him to go through his clothes she had stored in the attic to see what he wanted to keep, what he might need to replace. He'd rifled through the trunks, left the clothes in a mess, and told her to get rid of everything. "Even the uniforms?" she'd asked. "No, of course not!" he'd snapped at her before barricading himself in the study with the computer.

Hawk had stopped by with his new wife, Sarah, to introduce her to his old friend, and offered to take them to dinner. They'd stayed all of twenty minutes before Jonathan had chased them out with a false excuse of having a prior commitment.

And the thing that seemed most out of character for the man she remembered was the way he treated Kerry. Or rather, the way he ignored her.

Emma picked up the photo on her desk taken that morning long ago when she and Kerry had welcomed him home from a mission. He'd refused to set Kerry down, holding her even when a former commanding officer stepped up to shake his hand.

Now he acted as if she were a stranger to him.

Poor girl. She marched up to him every night with her blanket in tow and asked him to read her a story. He'd found an excuse to get out of it every time but one. Emma had come running when he'd yelled her name from the study last Saturday. Kerry had cornered him on the couch. She curled up beside him, holding a book in her hands and resolutely trying to read to him. But not until Emma joined them did he relax and listen.

Emma set down the picture without giving it the loving caress that had become an ingrained habit over the years. She couldn't help but recall her memory of Drew sitting with Kerry in his lap, totally out of his element, yet willing to accept the responsibility of caring for a child.

She inhaled deeply and took a sip of coffee, trying to clear all such comparisons from her mind. She shouldn't spend her time missing Drew when she needed to concentrate her energy on helping Jonathan readjust to free, civilian life.

Still, her hand hovered above the phone. She wondered what case Drew might be working on now. She missed the challenging gleam in those emerald eyes, daring her to be as smart and resourceful as she knew how to be. She missed the comforting reassurance of his hand brushing her cheek. She missed the heady sound of his heart-baring confession, *I'm falling in love with you*.

When she felt her own knuckles brushing her cheek, she curled her fingers into a fist and forced her mind back to this moment and the task at hand.

She punched a button on her computer and began dictating a memo to Caitlin. "Computer, record. Staff memo, dated February fourteenth, regarding Takahashi Industries . . ."

A firm rap at the door distracted her an instant before it opened. She barely had time to hit the pause command and rise to her feet before Jonathan swept into the room with a bouquet of long-stemmed red roses.

"Good morning, sweetheart!"

He wore a double-breasted suit of charcoal-gray flannel. He created a dashing figure with his dark hair, handsome face, and mischievous smile. He seemed so like the Jonathan of old that she walked around the desk to greet him. She eyed the dramatic presentation of flowers in his hand. "What's going on?"

He bowed with a flourish that filled the office with the cloying scent of roses. "It's Valentine's Day, my dear." He laid the bouquet in her outstretched hands and kissed her before she had a chance to respond. "I asked Brodie and BJ to take Kerry tonight so I can take you out to dinner and we can have a romantic evening at home." He nuzzled the shell of her ear. "Or we can skip the dinner part."

Flustered by the invitation, concerned about the plans for Kerry, and distracted by the persevering flick of his tongue, she ducked her head and carried the roses to the wet bar. Suddenly she found it difficult to breathe. But her heart wasn't pounding in her chest with anticipation. It seemed to have sunk somewhere in the vicinity of her stomach. She ran some water and placed the stems in the sink. "These are beautiful. I don't have a vase large enough for all of them. Let me buzz Caitlin and see—"

He cut off her rambling by sidling up behind her and wrapping his arms around her waist. "Forget the flowers. I'll bring you champagne. Chocolates. Anything your heart desires to show you how much I love you."

When he pushed her hair aside and kissed the back of her neck, she gripped the edge of the sink and bit her lip. This was her husband, after all.

They loved each other! So why did she cringe each time he touched her? Why didn't it feel right?

She'd kissed Drew one time—one time!—and she'd felt more alive and sexy and desirable than she did with her own husband's recent repeated attempts to seduce her.

Thinking about Drew while her husband held her destroyed her good intentions to be patient with Jonathan. She pushed at his hands and shrugged him off. She gave him a shaky smile as he released her and crossed the room. "Please, Jonathan. I hardly think work is the place for that sort of thing."

He followed her to the sitting area, undaunted by her rejection judging by the glint in his deep blue eyes. "I can wait, sweetheart. I'd forgotten how beautiful you are. I've been alone for so long. . . . But I can wait until tonight."

He slid his gaze along the length of her, somehow making her feel dirty. It wasn't love she saw in his eyes, but lust. She knew men had certain urges. Hell, she had them herself. But Jonathan's desires had always been prompted by something more emotional. She'd always felt that *she* was more important, not her body.

"Yes, well," she fiddled with the buttons of her jacket, "I'll see you tonight, then."

"Is something wrong?" He sat on a loveseat and patted the cushion beside him.

Yes! Thank God. This was the husband she knew. Sensitive. Willing to listen.

She perched beside him, wrapped her arm through his, and tried to figure out how to begin. "I guess I wasn't prepared for the adjustment it would take to get used to the physical part of our relationship again. I've been alone a long time, too. I guess I need a little time and patience."

"You want to be with me, don't you?" His eyes narrowed, reflecting confusion at her explanation.

"Yes, I do," she reassured him.

"You love me, don't you?"

"Of course."

He rose to his feet, dismissing the conversation before it had ever really started. "Good. We have reservations at seven. Wear something to show off those gorgeous legs of yours."

"Jonathan . . ." She stood, giving vent to her temper, and to the doubts she'd held in check for too long. "We need to talk. Get reacquainted. Decide how to help Kerry. It's not like you to get up and walk out when we have problems we need to fix."

His expression grew serious. "You're right. I've been gone too long to just take up where we left off."

She breathed a little easier. "Exactly."

"Then we'll get reacquainted tonight." He leaned in and pressed a quick kiss to her mouth. "I'll help you through this. Don't worry."

"Don't worry?"

He strode to the door and opened it. "I need to run. BJ's setting me up with a computer in my office, and I want her to show me how to navigate my way through the LadyTech system."

Emma's shock at his abrupt behavior prevented her from getting the conversation back on track. "Are you sure this is the kind of work you want to do? You never really liked sitting in an office before."

He praised her with a smile. "I want to find out just how successful you've been in my absence. See if I can help by taking some of the management duties off your shoulders. You'd like to spend more time with Kerry, wouldn't you?"

"Yes. But we've barely discussed this." She followed him to the open door. "Are you sure you want to go back to work so soon?"

He caught her by the chin and tipped her face to his. "Sweetheart, I may never be able to go back to the kind of work I did before. I've had my fill of guns and violence. And don't you want to know what our enemy wanted with LadyTech? Who better to check on Moriarty's plans than a man held prisoner by him for five years?"

His bleak statement shamed her. "No one but you, I guess. I'm sorry."

"Don't worry about it." He chucked her lightly on the chin, a love-tap that triggered memories that the Jonathan she knew would never intentionally remind her of.

"Jonathan—"

But he didn't let her discuss that, either.

"I'll see you tonight."

He waltzed down the hall to his new office with the oblique title of Administrative Executive. Emma raked her fingers through her hair and breathed deeply. The oversweet smell of the roses hit her and gave her a headache.

Or maybe the scent merely compounded the aftershocks of Jonathan's visit.

"Help me get through this," she prayed to the guardian spirit she hoped was watching over her. In a moment of crystal-clear hindsight, she realized she'd had someone watching over her.

A guardian named Drew Gallagher.

But she'd paid his bill and sent him away.

* * *

Darn it!

"She almost had it! She came so close!" Faith pointed both arms at Emma, who sank into her chair and buried herself in her work once more. "She almost had it."

She dropped her arms to her sides and rolled her eyes upward.

"She said the words. Can't I talk to her now?"

She muttered something beneath her breath, knowing that every word and thought was overheard. "All right. I'm sorry. She probably wouldn't believe me." Her bangs rose in the air as she puffed out a sigh. "But she asked for help."

Faith planted her hands on her hips and circled Emma's desk. "What am I going to do with you people?"

She dug her invisible fingers into the tense muscles of Emma's shoulders. Emma angled her head, but since she couldn't see her, she dismissed the sensation. At least she'd decided to relax and accept the inexplicable massage from an unknown friend.

Faith kneaded harder. "You won't trust your instincts. Gallagher won't trust his heart. And that Jonathan. He doesn't listen to anybody but himself."

Her voice trailed off as a new thought hit her. "Or does he?"

She clapped her hands together in joy. "Of course! That's why this isn't working."

All those years ago, at the citadel of the outer reaches, she'd struck a bargain with Jonathan Ramsey. She'd been swayed by pictures and prayers and heartfelt pleas.

But her bargain had been with Jonathan Ramsey. Not the Chameleon. She was spending her time helping the wrong man. One man was her enemy. He was Jonathan's enemy. Emma and Kerry's enemy, too.

Faith tapped her palm on her forehead, wishing she'd had the sense to think of this sooner. Her job was to protect the Ramsey family, watch over them with patience and care. She'd reunited them, but it wasn't working out the way she intended.

But the Chameleon wasn't her charge. She had hoped that the second chance at life would make him a better man. Being with Emma and Kerry should have shown him how beautiful and positive life could be. But the man was unchangeable.

Just because he'd reentered the world at the same time Jonathan did didn't make him her responsibility. She didn't have to follow the rules with him.

"Of course. That's what I'll do."

The electrical power in Emma's office snapped off, then surged back on again. Faith watched Emma check her computer right away, then frown and lean in closer to read the flashing message there out loud.

" 'You don't follow the rules anyway' " Emma picked up the phone and punched in a number. "What's going on?"

Faith pushed her sleeves up past her elbows and headed out, with new determination driving her. She ignored the words that flashed on and off on Emma's computer.

Faith knew the message was meant for her, but she ignored it. "I'm gonna make things right for you, Emma Ramsey. I promise."

Thunder pounded through Drew's brain. He rolled over onto his stomach, buried his head beneath a pillow, and prayed that the sound would go away.

It thundered again. Drew cursed and sat bolt upright, then cursed again when the bright sun hit his eyes. He blinked the world into semifocus and discovered there was no storm outside.

When he heard the sound a third time, he realized someone was beating on his door. "Coming!"

He thought he yelled the response. But the wad of stuffing that filled his head after last night's dive into self-pity—with the help of Jack Daniels and a few beers—might just have reflected the sound back into his own ears.

His visitor knocked one more time before Drew could find his glasses and climb out of bed. He opened the door without thinking, without putting anything on besides his pants, without a care for who might be on the other side.

"Good afternoon, Mr. Gallagher." Hawk Echohawk's imposing silhouette blended with the shadows of the hallway. But Drew could see he wore a sheepskin coat over his jeans, and he could see that the mysterious Indian meant business. "You look like hell, my friend."

Drew shook his head and started to shut the door. "I don't believe I'm your friend."

A big, black military boot prevented the door from closing. Drew wasn't in the best of shape to defend himself, so he shrugged and opened the door wide. He supposed he had this reckoning at the hands of Jonathan Ramsey's friends coming to him, anyway. He just wished he had a clearer mind to deal with it. He stepped back. "Come in, if you feel the need to."

He pulled out a chair at the kitchen table and plopped down in it. He heard the click of the door lock behind him like the crunch of a gravel pronouncing a guilty verdict.

Hawk moved silently, and he moved fast. By the time Drew knew he was behind him, he'd circled the table and sat on the opposite side. Drew squinted, trying to read the intention in those fathomless dark eyes.

"I don't have time to do much explaining," said Hawk. "But it's enough to know that I sense things about people. When I read your aura at the LadyTech building, and again on Moriarty's island, I sensed that you are not who you claim to be."

Had Ramsey told his friends his claim? That he, Drew, was the Chameleon? No. If Hawk thought that Drew was responsible for gun-running and murder, he wouldn't be sitting down now for a chat. Drew shrugged this meeting off as coincidental. "I work undercover a lot. It's easy to get that impression."

The Indian's stoic silence told him that story didn't fly.

"How do you know Andrew Gallagher's not my real name?"

Hawk's expression changed into something that might be an amused smile. He got up and sorted through the dirty dishes in the sink and picked up the coffee pot. Once he had that started, he disappeared into the bathroom and emerged moments later. He tossed Drew a towel and took off his coat. "Sober yourself up," said Hawk. "I want to hire you."

"To do what?"

"I want you to run a background check on someone."

Drew couldn't believe this. This man should be his enemy, not his employer. He should be offering a choice of punishment instead of coffee and work. "Who do you want me to investigate?"

"You."

"So, will you file charges against Moriarty?" asked Jonathan, fixing his tie in front of their full-length mirror.

Emma hooked her pearl-and-onyx earrings through her ears and tried not to think what a weird conversation he had started as they put on the finishing touches to go on their date. But at least he was talking to her. "I already have. Against Wyatt Carlisle, too."

"Any idea what this Moriarty looks like?"

Emma nearly laughed. First he promised her wine and roses; now he grilled her about LadyTech instead of romance. "Drew had this crazy idea that *you* were Moriarty."

"Did he, now?" Apparently this topic bothered him a great deal, because he suddenly appeared beside her in the dresser mirror. And she saw no trace of humor in his expression. "Just how well do you know this Gallagher? You seem to trust him with an awful lot of personal business."

Emma frowned. The need to defend Drew from the implied accusation swelled inside her. "He's a good man. He came through for me when no one else could."

"You have feelings for him, don't you?"

Only then did it register that she had taken another man's side against her husband. She tried to play down the urgency of her defense with a more rational argument. "He's a friend. To Kerry and me. He saved your life. You should be grateful to him, too."

"Are you certain it's just gratitude you feel?"

She turned to face the real man instead of the reflection. She adjusted his tie needlessly, straightened his collar, and allowed her hands to linger on his chest. Avoiding the subject meant avoiding a deeper inspection of her own feelings for Drew. "Look. Can we just go to dinner? We need time together, you and me. Let's forget everything else and concentrate on tonight."

She felt the scrutiny of his wary blue eyes. And since she wanted this reunion to work, needed it to work, she lifted her face to meet that gaze. She let her loyalty to him shine through, telling him better than with words that he was the man she loved. Stretching on tiptoe, she pressed her lips to his, offering a gentle kiss, a promise of things to come.

In the instant it took to close her eyes, she felt the tension in him leave. Then his hands cupped her shoulders and he deepened the kiss. She obliged him by encircling his neck and running her fingers into his hair. He slid his hands down her back to her waist and pulled her flush against him.

He abandoned her mouth and kissed a trail along her jaw to her ear. "I told you we didn't need dinner tonight," he whispered before taking a nip at her earlobe. Her earring clicked against his teeth, and she stiffened, hearing the almost inaudible sound like a clang in her ear.

Emma schooled herself not to pull away, but she dragged her hands back down to his chest, wedging a bit of breathing space between them. "But

I'm hungry." She whispered the soft protest, seeking an understandable excuse to put him off.

His roaming hands swept to her shoulders once more, pushing aside the spaghetti straps of her black dress, and tasting the uncovered spot with his lips and tongue. "I'm hungry, too." His tone held a very different meaning. "Sweetheart . . ."

Emma squirmed in his embrace. If he wanted to arouse her, why didn't he do or say any of the things he knew she liked? As she tilted her shoulder away from his lips, she asked, "Why don't you call me 'Lady' anymore?"

"What?" He took advantage of her position and dipped his mouth to kiss the swell of her breast, revealed by the fallen strap. Her breath came in rapid pants as she fought off the unconscious panic he created by kissing his way along the vee of her neckline toward the shadowy cleft between her breasts.

"You used to always call me 'lady.' It was a pet name." She laughed, hearing it sound a bit forced in her own ears. "Despite where I came from, you always said I had class, that you'd never think of me as anything but a lady."

"Do you have to talk so much?" Backing up his words, he raised his head and claimed her mouth in a fiercely possessive kiss. The sound in her ear intensified as alarm rang throughout her entire body.

She braced her feet and pushed against his chest, turning her head away when his hold on her tightened. "You remember that, don't you?"

"Enough talk already. Kiss me."

She heard nothing gentle or pleading in his command. Felt nothing gentle or seductive in his touch as he tightened his grip and lifted her off the floor. She twisted and kicked, uncaring that this was her husband she was hurting. He carried her to the bed. Her foot tangled with his, and he fell with her, landing on top and trapping her.

"Stop it, Jonathan!" she hissed. She stabbed at his face with her fingers as he nipped at her shoulder and rolled his hips over hers. "Get off me!"

He shifted slightly, palmed her breast. He grabbed the neckline of her dress and started to pull. But the change in balance freed her whole arm. "Jonathan!"

She smashed his nose with the heel of her palm, just the way he had taught her to defend herself all those years ago. His head snapped back. He scrambled to his knees on the bed, holding his face in both hands and screaming an awful string of curses.

Emma tried to roll away from him, but his knee anchored the hem of her dress. She sat up and yanked at the binding material. She felt it give, heard a rip and a pop, and she was free.

Almost.

Jonathan grabbed her by the chin, folded his palm around her jaw, and jerked her face up to his. "What the hell do you think you're doing?"

Emma shoved at his chest and pushed him away. He stumbled off the bed on one side, and she crawled off the other. "I asked you to stop."

"I'm your husband."

"No, you're not!" She pulled her straps back on to her shoulders and straightened her skirt. "The man I married would never behave this way. I don't know you anymore. You're not like the man I fell in love with. You've changed."

"Have I?" he challenged. The growl in his voice was still menacing despite the grip he kept on his nose. "It's that Gallagher, isn't it? He's not a friend of yours. He was your lover, wasn't he?"

"No! I've always been faithful to you." She clenched her fists in front of her, cursing fate and chameleons and the passage of time. "You're the only man I've ever been with."

"You may be a knockout package on stilts, sweetheart, but as far as I'm concerned, you're a cold fish. So much for the welcome home." He turned to the mirror to inspect the damage to his face.

"How dare you?" She rounded the bed, advancing on him with the strength of righteous indignation to guide her. She tugged on his sleeve, jerked hard to get him to face her. "First you reject your daughter, then you treat me like nothing more than a sex object."

"Oh, no, I value your business expertise, too."

His callous response twisted her heart like a corkscrew. She released him and crossed her arms in front of her, shielding herself from another crippling attack on everything she'd believed in for so long. "What about love, Jonathan? I love you. I have always loved you."

He slid his gaze over her body in a way that made her sick to her stomach. "Then prove it."

Anger gave her strength. "Get out! Pack your things and go to a hotel."

"No. I'll move into the guest bedroom. But I'm not moving out. I know my rights."

"Your rights?" Shock at his cool, cutting tone gave way to clear, rational thought. She matched his cold tone note for note. "At your request, this house is in my name. You always wanted us provided for, remember? As far as I'm concerned, you're a trespasser now." She held it together a few moments longer, long enough to grab her coat and purse from a side chair and march down the stairs with ramrod determination. "I want you out of here by the time I get back, or I'll call the police."

She quickened her pace when she heard him on the steps behind her. "Dammit, Emma. You can't do this to me. I suffered for five years."

She opened the front door, stopped, wheeled about, and glared at him. Her heart broke open and shattered into thousands of tiny pieces, one for every teardrop she had ever shed on his behalf.

"I suffered, too."

She stepped outside. She heard him curse and try to follow her. But the door flew out of her hand. "Emma!"

Without touching it, the dead bolt locked behind her.

He pounded on the door, rattled the doorknob. Emma put her long legs to good use and ran to the van.

She heard a woman's voice behind her, clear as a thought in her head. *Take that, you creep!*

When she glanced over her shoulder, she saw nothing and no one. Her rational mind might wonder about it later, but right now she simply offered her thanks, started the engine, and sped off into the night.

* * *

Drew studied the thick file on the table in front of him and took another sip from his bottle of water. The ache in his head had dulled to a tolerable level. He even relished the telltale signs of eye strain as at least a productive abuse of his body.

He'd taken Hawk Echohawk's challenge at face value, and had resurrected his investigation into his own past. Without revealing how much he knew, Hawk had said he'd guessed Drew suffered from amnesia. Drew hadn't questioned the Indian's perception. Something about those midnight-dark eyes made him think Hawk could see things that most men couldn't.

He flipped the page and read yet another of Kel Murphy's accounts of crimes attributed to the unidentified Chameleon. Stealing guns and other types of weaponry and selling them to the highest international bidder—that seemed to be his mainstay. The man who had escaped any photo, fingerprints, or artist's rendering had also dabbled in the drug trade. And along with his marketing of munitions, he was credited for conveying a sensitive secret or two from government to government. The man supplied revolutions and, according to Kel and Hawk, incited a few himself in order to make a profit.

Drew closed the file and sank back in his chair.

And he himself might be this Chameleon.

The name Cam, remembered by Clayton Roylott, was close enough to Chameleon to be an identification.

Jonathan Ramsey said he was a match.

But Hawk had shared two very interesting pieces of information with Drew. First, he assured Drew that he didn't believe he *could* be the Chameleon.

283

Hawk had said he would be able to sense underlying criminal motives, a past history in Drew which he did not. And second, those very traits Hawk said were missing in Drew he'd found in someone else.

Jonathan Ramsey.

"You don't trust your friend?" Drew had challenged him.

Hawk would not be baited. "Do your job, Mr. Gallagher. Anyone with a connection to Isla Tenebrosa during the same time frame we were there is too big a coincidence to ignore."

"You think my history can explain anything?"

"I want to know why you were in Tenebrosa, and what happened to you there."

Drew rose to his feet and cleaned up the remains of his takeout dinner. "What happened?" His sharp laugh reflected little humor and a great deal of frustration. "I almost died is what happened."

Not for the first time, he wondered if he'd have been better off if he had died. He was a man without a memory, a man without a clue, a man without a past.

And a man without much of a future if he couldn't prove that he wasn't the Chameleon.

He'd sent his fingerprints to Kel Murphy for an international check, suspecting they'd come back unidentified as they had in the past. The natives in Tenebrosa either didn't know him or wouldn't admit to it. How the hell was he supposed to help Hawk or Jonathan or anybody else when he couldn't even help himself?

Where was that voice in his head to guide him now?

Drew peeled off his shirt and kicked off his shoes and walked over to his workout mat. Running through his kata would help clear his mind, empty it of the nightmares that plagued his sleep. At least he could rest in oblivion until the physical exhaustion wore off. After that, sweet dreams were up for grabs.

He pushed open the windows, took his position, and bowed.

Halfway through the second set, he heard a knock at the door. With his left arm extended and his right hand fisted at his chest, he paused. The intrusion sifted through his consciousness, canceling out the peace he had not quite attained. Ignoring the second knock, he exhaled deeply, returned to his original position, and bowed again.

He slipped the dead bolt open before the third knock. "How the hell do you expect me to find what you want in one day . . ."

His temper evaporated at the unexpected visitor. "Emma."

The first thing he noticed were the deep lines from strain that grooved the pale skin beside her eyes. The second thing he noticed were the tiny bruises at either side of her jaw. Five bruises. In the shape and scope of a man's fingers.

A white-hot poker of protective rage burned through him at the knowledge she'd been hurt. "Son of a—"

"Drew." Keeping a tight rein on a ragged sob, she stepped forward, buried her face in his neck, and burst into tears.

With one arm shielding her, he guided her inside the apartment and locked the door behind her. Then he turned and surrounded her in his embrace. He tunneled his fingers into her hair and rubbed his cheek against hers.

"What happened? Are you all right? Kerry?"

"She's with BJ tonight." He felt a hot tear scorch his skin as it cooled from his workout. "Just hold me, Drew. Hold me tight. Kiss me." She lifted her mouth in an irresistible temptation, asking for what he was so willing to give. "Kiss me."

He looked into her clear blue eyes, saw the need etched there, felt an answering need inside himself to give all she asked for and more. He angled her face and claimed her lips, gently at first, seeking the conscious acknowledgment of her request.

She opened beneath him, and he seized the offer, deepening the kiss. She moaned in her throat, tunneled her fingers into his hair, anchored herself to his probing mouth.

Drew swept her away into a world of his making. A world of security. A world of trust.

The world of his love.

Chapter Thirteen

Emma gloried in the possessive claim of Drew's mouth on hers. He tasted familiar and intoxicating. She felt no fear in the needy exploration of his hands on her back, her bottom, and tangled in the length of her hair. She knew no hesitation when he pushed her coat off her shoulders, dipped his arm behind her knees, and scooped her up against his chest.

Her pain and powerlessness vanished in the instant her fingers touched the damaged skin on his shoulder. He was such a unique man. Lonely. Just. Brave. Jonathan's suffering had changed him into a man she didn't know, a man she could no longer trust. Drew bore his suffering with dignity. He wore it like a badge of honor, evidence of his strength, proof of his ability to endure.

He wore his scars on his skin. They hadn't touched his soul.

She hugged her arms around him and pressed a kiss to that fearful mark on his shoulder. He carried her to his bed and laid her down with urgent care. He knelt beside her, holding back, skimming her body with a look of cherished adoration.

He made her feel so different than Jonathan did. With Drew she could be strong. Proud of her strength. She could be equal. As she'd been with the old Jonathan.

Her body thrummed with the anticipatory thrill of promise shining in his eyes. She had been primed for this moment since the night he'd kissed her at Lucky's. Then, she had consciously denied the need he aroused in her. Tonight she accepted it, and gave that need free rein.

She reached for him, and he came to her with willing haste. He lay half on top, half beside her. The unyielding strength of his muscled chest butted against the softer contours of her arm and breast. One lean, powerful thigh pinned her legs, and she felt his heat rising against her hip.

He brushed his fingers across her cheek in that loving way of his, then traced the path with his warm, firm mouth. He drew his thumb down the line of her throat, and she arched her neck, giving greater access to his lips and tongue which followed the pattern of his hand.

He found that bundle of nerves in the hollow of her throat and then kissed her with exquisite thoroughness. A muscle clenched low in her belly. "Yes," she moaned, seeking the mindless pleasure he could provide. "Like that."

"Ah, Emma." His husky words rasped against her skin. "You're so beautiful. So damn beautiful."

He moved over the top of her, and she took his weight, losing herself in the differences between them. She demanded and he gave. She clutched his shoulders, dragged her fingertips down his back. She felt the hitch in his breath as her nails found a sensitive spot near the base of his spine. She felt powerful. Sexy. An equal partner in this embrace.

His shoulder flexed against her breast, hard male against soft female. The tiny shock kindled a flame that he stoked into a blazing wildfire when he caught her knee and bent her leg beside his hip. He glided his hand along the length of her thigh. The whisper of silk and callused palm opened a wealth of sensation in every pore. As he pushed aside her dress and slip, and neared that most sensitive part of her, she clenched her legs together, adjusting to the corkscrew of sensation spiraling down to her core.

His hand closed over her an instant before his mouth closed on her breast. He pressed his palm against her, and she cried out on that long-held breath. She clutched him to her as the heat of his tongue stroked her through the knotted caress of shantung silk.

She stretched beneath him, seeking relief from the pressure building inside her. She felt his need press into her thigh. Her belly tightened another notch, and the fire neared its flash point. She dipped her long fingers inside the waist of his pants and felt the sheen of sweat and powerful muscle as she grasped his buttocks. "Drew," she pleaded, wanting more, wanting all of him.

He slid his hand up under her dress to the waist-band of her hose and pulled. She lifted her hips, struggling with him to free herself to the promise of skin on skin, and so much more. Feeling the rasp of his palms along her legs, all the way down to the tips of her toes, he peeled off the hose and tossed them aside. Before she could analyze her pounding heartbeat, before she could second-guess her wary catch of breath, he was on top of her again, running his hand along the inside of her thigh, spreading her legs, reaching higher. She sank her fingers into his hair and tugged his mouth back to hers.

She hadn't felt this free, this out of control in years. Jonathan hadn't made her feel this way, not this new Jonathan, at any rate. "No." The thought escaped, but she denied it. Her fingers gathered the silky tendrils of his hair in a bunch.

"Hey."

She'd pulled his hair. She'd tugged too hard and pulled his hair. "I'm sorry." She kissed a second apology. "Don't stop. Please don't stop."

His hand stilled on her hip, tangled in the hem of her dress. He found the ripped seam.

"Em?"

He held the torn corner of her skirt between his fingers for her inspection. She felt the change in his body, the ragged tension, the forced with-drawal. She knew she had lost the moment before it had ever fully been hers.

"No. Don't leave me," she said. He raised himself up on his elbows above her. She laced her fingers behind his neck, wanting him back, needing him. "I want to forget."

"Forget what?" The scowl on his face gentled when he looked into her eyes. "Lady, tell me what happened. Tell me what's wrong."

More than the fire of his passion, more than the power of his embrace, the gentle brush of Drew's fingers across her cheek undid her. Heat stung her eyes, flooded them with tears, then spilled over onto her cheek and across his hand.

She sat up, tried to roll away. "I'm sorry. I shouldn't have used you like that. I wasn't thinking. I only wanted to feel. I'm sorry."

She wiped at the moisture on her face, but his hand was already there. His fingers caught each drop, carried it away, until the dam broke inside her and the tears came too swiftly for any kind touch. "Oh, God," she sobbed. "I can't stand . . . I can't be with him."

Drew gathered her into his arms, settled her beside him on the bed. He cupped her head and turned her face into the crook of his neck. "Ah, lady. Sh-h-h." He rocked her back and forth as the tears flowed unchecked. "Sh-h-h."

Emma wept for all she had hoped for, all she had lost.

She wept for broken dreams and foolish resolutions and shattered hearts.

She wept for brave men betrayed by their past and loyal women haunted by their future.

She cried until her head hurt and her sinuses ached. She cried until her throat felt raw. She cried until she could cry no more.

And Drew held her. He held her long into the early hours of the morning, long past the time her tears had dried up and her body continued to

291

quake in weary, bone-shaking sobs. He held her snug in his arms until her body surrendered to exhaustion and she drifted into a dreamless sleep.

Drew slept through the night with Emma in his arms. He stirred just a time or two, to straighten her dress around her and to cover her with a blanket.

Though his body ached with unfulfilled need, he slept the sleep of those at peace, the kind of sleep he couldn't remember.

She had needed him, in a way that couldn't be neatly explained by lust or circumstance. Something had frightened her terribly, shaken her to the very core. Though he railed against the most likely suspect, the one man who could hurt her the most, she hadn't come to him to fight that battle for her.

She had come seeking a sanctuary.

Emma had finally let go. Her will battered down, her faith exhausted, she'd lost that cool reserve that made her so strong and had let go of all the pain and fear and heartache she buried inside her.

He awoke with Emma tucked to his side, her arm slung across his chest. Her hair fanned in a profusion of sable-rich glory across his arm and the pillow behind her.

Drew hugged her tight, pressed a kiss to her forehead, and silently thanked her for the honor. When the strain of a lifetime had become too much to bear, when she no longer had the strength to protect herself, she had come to *him*.

He crawled out of bed and tucked the blanket around her. He wanted her to sleep and regain her strength. As he stood over her, he frowned. The bruises on her face stood out stark on her freckled alabaster skin. He remembered the ragged edge of her torn dress and wondered just what that bastard had done.

Knowing Emma, she had put up one hell of a fight.

Keeping that thought foremost in his mind so he wouldn't tear the place apart, he showered and dressed. He was pouring himself a glass of milk when Emma wandered into the kitchen. Though statuesque as ever, she seemed small and vulnerable with the blanket hugged around her, covering her from shoulders to ankles.

"Good morning." He offered the gentle greeting with a smile. "How are you feeling?"

With one hand gripping the blanket at her throat, she pulled her hair free and shook it loose around her shoulders. The resulting cascade framed her face in a dark cloud. Barefoot and without makeup, she looked a far cry from the cool, confident corporate-exec facade she normally showed the world. "I want to apologize."

"For what?"

Her gaze snapped to his, wide and questioning. "For barging in on you last night. For not finishing what we started." She tucked a curl of hair behind her ear and huddled into an even more closed posture. "For taking advantage of your good nature."

"*My* good nature?" He laughed and drank a long swallow of the wholesome milk. "Lady, I thought you liked me for my less sterling qualities."

She stepped to the table, opposite him, gripped the back of a chair, and gave him a stern look. "You may have questionable talents that help with your work, but you're a good man. You could have

293

taken advantage of my hysteria last night, but you didn't. I needed a friend more than I needed a lover, and you were there for me."

"Taken advantage?" He narrowed his eyes at her choice of words. "Is that what this is all about?"

She shrank inside the blanket. Everything stern or strong seeped from her pale features.

Drew pulled a platter from the microwave and set it in the center of the table. Then he pulled a mug from the cabinet. "Coffee or milk?"

"I beg your pardon?"

He set the mug on the table in front of her. "Coffee or milk? Which do you want with your breakfast?" She eyed the toast and scrambled eggs he'd set on the table and made a polite but thanks-but-no-thanks face. She was too upset to eat.

"You shouldn't have gone to the trouble."

"I planned to eat anyway." He ignored the defensive dodge of her shoulders when he moved around her and pulled out the chair for her. "Sit." He touched his fingers to the indentation of her waist and guided her to her seat. "Last night you needed to vent. This morning we need to talk."

He felt her gaze rise to him and follow him around the table. When he sat, she sought his eyes. He offered her a supportive smile and set about eating his eggs and toast. For several minutes, she simply watched him in silence. He waited for her to fill him in on whatever had happened to make calm, rational Emma Ramsey go through an emotional upheaval like the one he'd witnessed last night.

"I called my lawyer yesterday evening. Interrupted his dinner." This was not what he'd expected to hear, but he schooled his curiosity and took another drink of milk, waiting for her to elaborate. "I filed for a divorce from Jonathan."

The food in his mouth went sour. He dropped his toast on to the plate and shoved it to the middle of the table. "Did he hurt you?"

"Not the way you mean." There were numerous ways a person could get hurt in an abusive relationship. Physically. Mentally. Emotionally. None were acceptable in Drew's book. Not with any woman. Especially not with Emma.

He donned a more detached demeanor, assumed the role of a dispassionate counselor. Letting her see his anger wouldn't encourage her to talk. Sharing his opinion of the sort of justice he wanted to wreak on the husband to whom she had fought so hard to be loyal, wouldn't help Emma. "He's been home for less than a month. Divorce seems like a drastic step if you're not getting along."

She lifted her shoulders, but seeing them tremble made a mockery of her show of strength. "I should have done it sooner."

Drew asked the question he wasn't sure he wanted to hear the answer to. "Did something happen last night to force this decision?"

Her gaze darted to his, then down to her plate. She picked up a slice of toast and toyed with it. "He was a little aggressive; a bit needy." She dropped the uneaten food. "I left before he could really scare me. I'm sure things have calmed down by now."

Her rote recitation appalled him. Is that how her mother had sounded when she'd been abused?

"Don't defend him to me."

"I'm not. I . . . he . . ." She sought his gaze with a frantic need. "It wasn't just last night. He's . . . he's not himself." She loosened her grip on her woolen shield and fisted her hand in front of her. "He's so demanding. I hoped he'd come home the same man I once knew. I expected that maybe he would be more subdued after being held prisoner. That he'd have problems to work through. But this Jonathan is . . . strong."

She settled back in her chair, as if surprised by her own revelation. Drew rested his elbows on the table and leaned forward, maintaining the shorter distance between them. "Strong?" he questioned.

"He makes demands. He expects them to be followed, without any discussion. If there's a problem with Kerry, he just tells me to take care of it. He didn't like the office I gave him at LadyTech, so he conned the staff into taking everything out and moving it into a bigger room. He said he wanted to be closer to me, but I didn't buy it. He treats me like I'm some kind of prize he's entitled to."

While Emma's temper built into a small inferno, Drew forced himself to remain cool and detached. He considered it one of his finest acting jobs, since all he really wanted to do was grab his gun and his truck keys and track down Ramsey. No one, not even her husband, had the right to play with Emma's self-confidence and destroy her trust like this. "Could it be his military background? He's probably used to giving orders."

"He never gave one to me before now."

Drew tried to come up with another rational explanation for Jonathan's behavior. He couldn't.

Emma dropped her focus to her hands in her lap. "My father was like that. He'd make demands. He'd want his dinner cooked a certain way, want me home right after school. He'd tell Mom to wear a certain dress, but if it was in the laundry, he'd . . ." Drew waited with forced silence while she caught her breath and worked through the memory that assailed her. "You could never please him. Sometimes he'd just stalk off, get in his car, and leave. Go drink with his friends. Sometimes . . ."

Drew didn't want to imagine what Emma's father had done on the times when he didn't leave the house. "Em . . ." Unable to keep his distance any longer, he stood and circled the table. He pulled her to her feet and wrapped her up in his arms, blanket and all.

She turned her face into the juncture of his neck and jaw and simply let herself be held. But she didn't cry. She was summoning her scattered strength, absorbing a bit of his, and building up her own spirit. Drew inhaled with deep pride. A delicious scent teased his nose, a scent of herbal freshness that was uniquely Emma. She would not be beaten. Not by history, not by time, not by a shattered love.

Several moments passed before she spoke again. "Jonathan knew about my father. He knew my fears about ending up like my mother. He was always patient, even when it wasn't convenient for him. He taught me that I could have a different opinion, I could argue my side and it would be okay."

She pushed back against his arms, and he altered his hold so she could look into his face. She dug her fingers into the worn cotton of his black sweatshirt, pleading with him, with herself, for understanding. "I can't explain it, Drew. A man's character doesn't change, no matter what he's been through. That man may have Jonathan's face, but"—she looked up into his eyes—"he's not my husband."

Emma drove her van down the long boulevards of Kansas City and through the grand old homes of her own neighborhood with a growing feeling of emptiness. Last night had drained her, emotionally and physically. She'd emptied herself of emotion, her love and trust shattered by the man who had once taught her those two very things.

She knew an inescapable sense of doom, the resignation of going to do a tough job simply because it needed to be done. She had never shied away from difficult tasks. But she dreaded the coming days all the same.

Still, hope sprang anew. She wasn't foolish enough to delude herself into thinking that going through with the divorce proceedings would be easy. But spring was just around the corner with its promise of rebirth and new life. She wanted to leave the winter season of her life behind her, those bleak years she'd pined for Jonathan's return, those last few months when she'd denied the need in her restless heart to move on with her life, these last horrifying weeks when she was given the chance to be reunited with her love, and the last two days when she'd finally admitted that the love she'd known no longer existed.

With a bit of rest behind her, and the fresh perception of a new day, she realized how cheated she felt. She'd given her heart and soul to Jonathan. She'd rebelled tooth and nail at first, but finally she'd come to believe that two people in love could risk their hearts and because they loved, know their hearts would be safe.

Now she knew better.

She'd risk her love on Kerry, and nothing more. No one else.

And despite the tempting haven of Drew's arms, she wouldn't even trust the dark knight who followed behind her in his pickup truck. Drew had feelings for her, he'd admitted as much. And she cared about him. They shared an intense physical attraction. He held her with care, listened with patience, prodded her to action, and reminded her of the kind of man she had once loved.

But she would never love again.

The smart woman in her knew that risking her heart on a man like Drew, a man of mystery, a man who lied with ease, a man who could be anyone he chose to be, would be a mistake.

She rarely made mistakes.

She never made the same one twice.

Emma pulled into her driveway. She sat in the van and waited for Drew to park his truck and escort her inside the house. She studied her reflection in the rearview mirror. She wasn't proud of taking advantage of his caring nature, but when he'd insisted on seeing her home, insisted on checking the house to make sure Jonathan had no intention of retaliating, she had said yes.

She wanted to be strong enough to say no to him. But the pale strain on her fresh-scrubbed face revealed the truth, that she was just an outer shell of strength. She couldn't bluff her way through a confrontation with Jonathan right now. And though she hated to admit it, she was more than relieved that Drew had been persistent enough to override her protests.

A sharp tap on her window startled her from her introspection. She took a steadying breath, grabbed her purse, and climbed out.

"His car's in the garage." Drew had moved quickly, always on guard, always protective.

"All right, then. Let's get this over with."

His hand on her arm stopped her. "You don't have to do this, Em. I can go in and help him find his way out the door."

She smiled at the dead-serious scowl on his face. She imagined he'd intimidated quite a number of people with that expression. She patted his hand and dismissed his offer. "No, thanks. I'd like to leave some of the house in one piece."

His lips curved into an answering smile, but that wary alertness never left his eyes. He released her. "Then lead on, Macduff."

The normalcy of that teasing remark, a Shakespearean reference to their first evening together all those nights ago, gave Emma a much-needed boost of confidence. But that flashback to a happier time faded as they neared the front door.

Drew followed her up the steps to the front porch. He removed the glasses he'd worn for driving and stuffed them into his pocket. Then he reached inside his jacket. She'd watched him strap on his gun before they left his apartment. Then, she had assumed it was his standard everyday gear. Now, she wondered.

She stopped at the door before inserting her key. "Are you expecting trouble?" she asked.

"I always expect trouble." It wasn't a glib come-

300

back this time. The obvious wariness in his expression told her he meant it.

Her questionable self-assurance took a nosedive. Emma gritted her teeth and unlocked the door. Her confidence didn't matter. She had a job to do, and somehow she'd just have to get it done.

They hadn't even gotten the door closed when Jonathan marched out of the study and confronted them in the hallway. "Emma. Finally. I've been worried sick about you."

The words of concern hit her like an accusation. She planted her heels and held her ground, though she reeled inside. "Were you?" she managed to ask without a quiver in her voice.

He looked like hell. He needed a shave. His clothes were untucked and wrinkled, as if he'd slept in them. Emma knew a moment of concern. Maybe he *had* been worried about her. She nearly stepped forward, reaching out to straighten his inverted collar. But he fisted his hands on his hips and smiled. That chilling baring of his teeth voided any remorse on her part.

His eyes dismissed her for the moment, and he turned the full brunt of his displeasure on the man standing behind her. "I see you brought your bodyguard with you. So you left me and went straight to another man's bed, right? That won't look very good in court, sweetheart."

She felt Drew surge forward, saw the answering shift in balance in Jonathan's legs. Instinctively, Emma turned to the man she knew would listen to her.

"Drew." He halted a breath away from her. The front of his jacket grazed her outstretched fingers. She could feel the heat of him, banked at her request. But judging by the rage that simmered in his eyes, she knew that his patience was tied at the starting gate with a very flimsy rope.

"How can you insult your own wife?" Drew challenged.

"Do you know who you've been sleeping with, my dear?" Jonathan seemed to delight in Drew's flash of temper.

Emma spun around again. She lifted a supplicating hand to Jonathan, desperate to strike a bargain before a bad situation deteriorated into something she couldn't handle.

"I asked you to leave. Drew works for me. He's just here to see that you pack your things and move out as soon as possible."

"Sooner," warned Drew.

Jonathan blinked and shifted his gaze from Drew to Emma. Idly she wondered how she had ever thought those blue eyes charming or handsome. "I already got a call from your lawyer this morning. You didn't waste any time, did you?"

Emma stepped back at the sharp derision in his words. Guilt struck her like a punch in the gut. "I'm sorry. I wanted to tell you first."

"Well, if you were a little less busy consorting with the enemy, maybe you could have."

Emma pressed her hands to her temples and shook her head, trying to clear her mind of his words that made no sense. "What do you mean, consorting with the enemy? Drew's a friend. A good one."

She added the latter in Drew's defense, and found herself tamping down the desire to defend him in more unequivocal terms.

Jonathan laughed. The smug sound of superiority jangled her nerves and sparked shards of doubt in her mind.

"You sure you want me to leave you alone with Gallagher?" He taunted them both. "That's not his real name, you know."

"I know." She squared her shoulders, bracing herself for whatever bombshell Jonathan was toying with.

"Drop it, Ramsey." Drew's low-pitched warning hovered in the air. "You're clouding the issue. The lady wants you to pack up and haul your keister out of here."

"I'd call the police if I were you, Emma." Jonathan walked to the hall closet and pulled out his coat. He slid it onto his shoulders and buttoned it with painstakingly slow attention to detail.

"I'll call them to remove you from the premises." This time, she issued the warning.

The monster who was her husband pulled out a suitcase and unhooked a filled garment bag that hung from the rod. He slung the bag over his shoulder and grinned at her. "That private eye you're putting all your trust in is a fraud, sweetheart."

"You sure you're not just catching your own reflection in the mirror?" She wanted this to be over. She wanted to wake up and find out this whole nightmare was ended.

"Let's see who the villain is here, shall we?" His taunts nicked a hole in her dwindling resolve. "I'm the husband who's been missing for five years, wounded in the line of duty, held against my will. And you're the wife who's what? Sleeping with the hired help?"

"That's it, Ramsey." Drew's clipped response overrode her shock. "Get out."

Drew whipped around Emma, snatched the suitcase, and shoved it at Jonathan's chest, knocking him off balance. In the same swift movement, he pushed Jonathan into the wall and trapped him there. The suitcase wedged between them seemed to be the only thing keeping Drew from wrapping his hands around her husband's throat.

"Drew." She stepped toward them, unsure of which man she wanted to protect.

He shoved the suitcase up under Jonathan's chin. "Tell her anything you want about me, Ramsey. But you hurt her once more and I'll—"

"Bad timing, hmm?" BJ asked the question from behind Emma.

With the door standing open, there'd been no need to knock. Before Emma had a chance to explain, Brodie had picked up Drew and slung him against the opposite wall, pinning him there, straight-armed, with a hand at his throat.

"What the hell's going on?" Brodie asked.

Emma ran to Drew. "Let him go." She tugged on Brodie's arm, but he wouldn't budge. Inwardly cursing the overabundance of heroes all ready to protect her from perceived threats, she slipped between Drew and Brodie and forced his attention. "I said let him go."

"Big guy, please." Brodie blinked at BJ's throaty request.

"BJ?" Emma pleaded. She knew the one person Brodie would listen to without question was his wife.

BJ spoke again. "Honey. Not with Kerry here."

"Sweetie," Emma breathed. The blood in her head rushed to her feet. She'd been so caught up in averting the fight that she hadn't even noticed

Kerry standing with BJ. Now she couldn't miss the wide-eyed shock in her daughter's eyes. "Everything's okay," she said.

She heard the useless lie with the same disbelief as was reflected in her daughter's face. "Your father and I had an argument. Drew tried to help me, and Brodie misunderstood." Emma turned her plea to Brodie. "Please let him go."

Only Drew and Jonathan remained impassive amidst the fear and confusion and concern.

Emma felt Drew's even breathing behind her, shallow under Brodie's grip, yet calm. Calculating.

"Don't do that pinch thing again." Emma heard a relenting rumble in Brodie's deep voice. She dared to hope. "I'll let you go."

"I wouldn't be so quick," said Jonathan. "Remember all those months we spent tracking the Chameleon? Remember how we'd get a lead, track him, and then he'd disappear?"

"Yeah." Brodie angled his head toward Jonathan, clearly perplexed by the shift in topic.

Jonathan picked up his suitcase, shouldered the garment bag, and smiled. "How does it feel to hold him right in your hands?"

Emma attacked the next day at work with a fervor normally reserved for meeting deadlines on negotiations and contracts. Fortunately, no such deals were riding on the line, because, despite achieving the physical fatigue she strove for, she couldn't keep her mind focused on LadyTech.

After Jonathan dropped his bombshell last night, he'd simply smiled and left. Brodie had released Drew. Kerry had run through the crowd of stunned adults and barricaded herself in her room.

Drew himself had simply straightened his jacket, offered his apologies without any defense, whispered a cool, "You know where to find me if you want to press charges," and left. The night swallowed him up, leaving Emma to face the stunned sympathy of her friends and discover a shockingly disloyal truth buried deep inside her heart.

She loved Drew Gallagher.

Good intentions and firm resolutions had become a moot point somewhere along the line. When Jonathan had maligned him, and Brodie had threatened him, she'd jumped to Drew's defense against her own husband.

She'd fallen in love with the very man who may have tried to kill Jonathan.

And it felt right.

No matter how uncharacteristic Jonathan's behavior had grown, she still owed him the respect of their marriage vow. She should believe his accusation. And yet she felt a more powerful pull toward that mysterious private detective who would not defend himself against that accusation.

Drew felt more like her husband than the man she had married.

Her computer screen flashed, startling her. She'd just turned the machine off, finishing her dictation for the day. She must have forgotten to turn off the monitor.

But when she reached out to push the power button, the words scrolling across the screen caught her eye.

See with your heart. Not your eyes.
Believe with your heart.

She leaned forward, puzzled. "What?"

Maybe her fatigue was getting the better of her. Maybe she'd exhausted herself to the point of hallucination.

"It's almost as if someone's trying to tell me something."

She shook her head at the illogical idea and hit the monitor button. The machine flashed on.

Not off. It had been off.

She'd just now turned it on.

Emma glanced around the room, expecting to see some sort of prankster laughing at her expense. She saw no one. And she wasn't ready to believe in ghosts.

But the creepy feeling of an impossible communication stayed with her. "Go home, Emma," she admonished herself for foolish thinking.

She grabbed her coat, gloves, and hat from the closet. Winter had not been left behind. The recent drop in temperature and light, and the steady snowfall outside attested to that. So much for an early spring.

She bundled up and headed out the door to pick up Kerry from her after-school care program. Her love for her daughter was the only constant in this whole mess. The one future hope she could still cling to.

"Believe with your heart." She repeated the message out loud as she descended the stairs to the parking lot. She saw little logic in the events that had transpired the past few weeks.

A man without memories who said he remembered her. A husband who was not her husband back from the dead. A daughter who listened to invisible friends.

Emma welcomed the cold blast of air that hit her when she left the building. She needed to return her world to rational order. Then maybe, just maybe, she could push aside that little part of her brain that actually thought that message on her computer made sense.

Chapter Fourteen

Faith and Kerry sat on the top floor, peeking through the balcony railing to watch the scene unfolding on the first floor below them.

Emma threw up her hands on either side of her shoulders and tromped into the kitchen. "You need to discuss this through our lawyers, Jonathan."

Faith seethed in frustration as that . . . man . . . followed her. He'd been messing up everything from the first day he set foot in their lives. "I think we can be civil. This is too important to leave to lawyers," he said.

The voices faded, and Faith turned to the dark-haired girl sitting in such attentive silence beside her. She wrapped an arm around Kerry's shoulders and gave her a hug, concerned over the little gears spinning inside her mind that gave the dialogue of

*the two adults a seven-year-old interpretation.
"Whatchya thinking, sweetie?"*

*For a moment Kerry didn't answer. "He's the bad
man."*

"From your dream. I know." Faith held her close.

*Kerry's gaze fixed on the archway into the kitchen,
waiting to see her mother emerge. "He wants to take
Mom away from me."*

*"No, he doesn't," Faith said. She knew that much
was true. He had no interest in separating Emma
from her daughter. He did, however, have an
increasing interest in separating her from her company. And, to Faith's chagrin, he'd already done a
thorough job of separating Emma from her trust in
the endurance of love.*

*"It's not mine to give you." Emma crossed from
the kitchen into the study, her shoulders squared. "I
told you. The fifty-one percent of stock we kept off
the market is split three ways. You're only entitled to
half of seventeen percent."*

*"That's a foolish way to run a business."
Jonathan's voice carried from the kitchen. Kerry
huddled tight around her doll, retreating from the
anger in her father's voice. She sank even further
when he appeared in the hallway. "What if you and
Jas and B J have a falling out? You lose control of
your company. You lose Kerry's inheritance."*

"That's not why you want LadyTech."

*The dialogue became muffled as they moved
beyond earshot.*

*Faith had done her best to communicate with
Jonathan Ramsey, but thus far she'd had no success. Heck. She hadn't had any success with this
mission since . . . She looked up before the lights
could blink. "I know. I've never had any success."*

"He makes you sad, doesn't he?" Kerry tilted up her long face. "He makes Mom sad, too."

"I thought I was doing the right thing." Faith apologized to Kerry for the umpteenth insufficient time.

"I know. My dad was gonna die, but you figured out a way to save him. Only your plan isn't working out the way you wanted it to." Kerry climbed up on Faith's knees and gave her a hug, then sat back on her haunches and spoke with the voice of experience. "Duddy says we have to try real hard."

Faith scrunched her face, worried about what Kerry was leading up to. "Which daddy is that?"

Kerry rolled her eyes and shook her head. "My real daddy, of course. Don't worry, Faith. I have a plan, too."

Faith's concern bumped up a notch to alarm. "You do?"

Her pint-sized companion nodded, and a conspiratorial gleam filled her eyes. She reached beneath the hem of Angelica's dress and pulled out a business card. Faith recognized the name on the card at once. Drew Gallagher.

"You're going to hire a private investigator?" joked Faith.

"No, silly. Mom doesn't want to leave me, right?"

"Right." Faith dragged out the word, and wished desperately that the girl had an adult to talk to instead of herself—a well-meaning but definitely misguided angel.

This time, the hallway light did blink. No wonder she could communicate with Kerry. Despite the difference in their ages and their planes of existence, they thought and acted alike. "Tell me this plan of yours."

"I'm going to leave, and then she'll have to come

stay with me." Such incredible logic. Such a dangerous thing to do.

"Are you telling your mom where you're going?"

"No. 'Cause she'll tell me I need to stay home, and
then she won't leave."

Kerry hurried into her room and pulled out a little
suitcase from her closet. She opened it and turned it
over on the bed, dumping out a complete wardrobe
of doll clothes. Faith prayed that Emma would come
upstairs right about now.

No such luck.

She watched the methodical efficiency of Kerry's
childish hands stuffing the doll clothes under the
bed, out of sight. Faith knew that the lack of hesitation in the little girl's movements indicated she'd
already given some thought to this plan. Kerry went
to her dresser and closet and selected an assortment
of necessary travel items. Her piggy bank, her lavender blanket, a toothbrush, a book of fairy tales, her
new snow boots, and Angelica.

She closed the suitcase and latched it, then pulled
her mother's cell phone from beneath her pillow.

"Kerry?"

The girl punched in Drew's number and waited.
Faith was chilled with foreboding, and wished she
could turn into flesh and blood and shake some
sense into her. After a minute, Kerry sighed and
turned off the phone.

"I quess I'll just have to walk."

"Kerry." Faith had never been anything but kind to
her little charge, but she pulled out every last bit of
authority she had ever possessed in this life, and the
previous one. "This is not a good idea. It's dangerous. Your mom will be scared."

312

Kerry put on her coat and stuck the phone in her pocket. "Mom's scared already."

Damn. Oh, damn, Oh, damn.

Faith knew she'd pay for each of those curses, but right now she didn't know what else to do. She swept down into the study and shouted Emma's name. No response. She blew on the flames in the fireplace, hoping the swift surge of heat and light would catch the woman's attention. Emma turned, but quickly dismissed the odd flare-up.

Kerry sneaked past the study door, and Faith darted after her. Kerry opened and closed the front door with a perfect silence that thundered in Faith's ears.

Faith made one last effort to send a message to Emma. She was growing adept at manipulating those man-made computers, so she flew across the keyboard and booted a message onto the screen. She didn't wait to see if Emma would read it. Right now Emma sounded like she was in the middle of throwing Jonathan out.

Again.

Faith couldn't stay to help her this time. A little girl alone in the twilight in a big city when temperatures were dropping was a bigger priority. She floated along like the snowflakes, keeping Kerry company as she trekked down the sidewalk.

Faith prayed Emma would be observant enough to read the message she had left in time.

Drew traipsed up the stairs to his apartment. He rolled his shoulders beneath his jacket, trying to dispel the chill that had been with him long before he'd stepped out into this last stand of winter.

He'd spent the day in the district attorney's office, going through virtually every shred of evidence that might prove he wasn't the Chameleon. And failing. Known appearances of the Chameleon corresponded with Drew's hazy memories of the accident and recovery in Tenebrosa and Mexico. There were no fingerprints on file to disprove Jonathan Ramsey's accusation.

He'd had little success trying to prove who he was. He was having even less success trying to prove who he wasn't.

He hated to disappoint Hawk Echohawk. He wanted to believe the Indian's instincts. But the truth all seemed to point to the fact that he'd been in the jungle that day with Jonathan Ramsey. Like him, Drew had suffered the burns and shrapnel wounds of a grenade. There weren't many such injuries on that tiny jungle island. For two men to be so wounded during the same time period pointed to one devastating truth.

He, alias Drew Gallagher, once known as Cam, was an international terrorist with ties to all parts of the world, wanted by governments on three continents.

He was the Chameleon.

"Amnesia's not a bad way to go into hiding. A little extreme, but all the profiles say I'm incredibly clever, and willing to do anything to elude the authorities." He tried the joke on himself, but the humor fell flat.

On the drive home from the D.A.'s office, he'd debated whether to turn himself in at a police station or check himself into a mental ward. In the end, he opted for neither. He had one final option to check into. Clayton Roylott. The man didn't

claim to know much about "Cam," but more than
likely, with a little persuasion he could introduce
Drew to some other connections who might be
able to tell him more about his past.

The likely truth shamed him. But more impor-
tantly, he knew the truth would devastate Emma.
Not that she wanted to have anything to do with
him, anyway. But at least he hoped to clear his
name and make a graceful departure from her life.

Now it seemed the only honorable option left
him was to build the case that Jonathan Ramsey
hadn't been able to. A case that would hold up in
court, and put him behind bars where he belonged.

He pulled off his gloves as he reached his floor,
and took out the keys to his apartment. As he
neared his door, he noticed a package sitting
beside it. As a matter of caution, he unzipped his
jacket and reached inside to unsnap his holster.

A few steps further, the package moved. A length
of dark hair tumbled out from beneath a stocking
cap. Drew quickened his pace as recognition
kicked in. "Kerry? What the heck?"

"Daddy!"

Drew braced himself and caught the flying bundle. She clung to his neck like a second skin, and
he shifted her weight to his left arm. With his right
he pulled his cell phone from his pocket and
punched in a number he now knew by heart.

It was answered before the end of the first ring.
"Kerry?"

The barely disguised fear in Emma's frantic
voice turned his blood to ice. He didn't bother with
greetings or reassurances, or even ask why.

"It's Drew. I think I found something you're
missing."

* * *

Drew leaned his shoulder against the doorway to his kitchen and watched Emma tuck the blanket around Kerry's sleeping form. She kissed her little girl and hovered over her a minute longer, straightening her hair and positioning her doll in the crook of her arm. Drew thought he'd never seen anything so beautiful as the tender interaction between the dark-haired beauty and her daughter.

"I hope the sofa's okay," he said when Emma straightened and turned to him. "She was asleep on it before I could get the bed made."

"She's fine." Emma's fatigue haunted the husky timbre of her voice. "I don't know how to thank you. When I saw that she'd run away . . ."

Drew ushered her into the kitchen and to the waiting cups of coffee they always seemed to share. "She's a resourceful kid. Showed my card to the taxi driver and told him to drive her home to her dad's place. It must have cost a small fortune."

"She inherited her mother's business sense. I'm sure she had quite a stash in her piggy bank." She sat down, but instead of picking up the coffee, she rubbed her hands along her upper arms, hugging herself. "Did she say why she ran away? She overheard Jonathan and me fighting."

He didn't like the sound of that. But then, he didn't have the right to care one way or another. "She said something about a plan. I got the idea she and Faith cooked it up."

"Great. Anything could have happened to her. She's only seven years old; she's been through so much already. I suppose she said that Faith promised to protect her." She shoved her fingers into her hair and captured it in a fist at her nape. The frustrated movement bared the sculpted grace of her chin and the swanlike arc of her throat. Drew swallowed hard and turned to the counter. This was hardly the time for his body to kick into overdrive.

"Faith's always with her except when Kerry's asleep," he said.

"She told you that?"

"Yeah." He set his cup in the sink and shoved his hands into his pockets. He knew nothing about parenting, but sensed that Emma needed to know every detail possible in order to deal with Kerry's behavior. He swallowed his pride and his dreams and shared the information he'd gleaned from Kerry. "She's got this idea that you and I are supposed to be together. I know that's crazy. She seemed to think that you'd go wherever she was." He glanced over his shoulder at Emma, gauging her reaction. "So she came here."

He watched her stand. Even that simple action was a thing of beauty. Proud posture, long-limbed grace. "Is it really such a crazy idea?"

Her question surprised him. "Emma..." He wanted to warn her away from dangerous territory with words, but his vocabulary momentarily escaped him.

That left him only one other option. Escaping his thoughts with a gut-deep sigh, he left the kitchen and headed for the front door. With her long legs, she quickly caught up to him as he slipped into his jacket.

"Where are you going?"

The jacket felt hot. She was dressed simply, in jeans and an oversized sweater that masked her long, lithe figure. But his heart still thumped in his chest. It was a silly little fantasy, the one steaming his thoughts right then. He and Emma alone together for the night. Her guard eroded by relief over Kerry's safety. Her apparent willingness to overlook his transgressions was a balm—and a heady aphrodisiac—to his battered soul.

"There's only one bed, Emma."

She moved behind him and tugged at the shoulders of his jacket. "I'm not putting you out of your own home."

He shrugged the leather out of her hands and pulled it back on. "This is too cozy for me. I don't begrudge you the security of staying with Kerry tonight, but don't ask me to be nobler than I am. If you're sleeping in my bed, I can't."

And then she did the most incredible thing. She hugged him from behind. Her arms came around his waist and she laid her cheek against his shoulder. Drew's breath caught on a ragged gasp as she pressed herself close in a gesture of healing and forgiveness.

"Don't go," she said simply.

He tried to do the right thing. He tried to disentangle himself and walk away. But when his hands touched hers, they stayed. He tipped his head back and inhaled the fresh scent of her hair. In his musty world of darkness and half-truths, the smell and feel of Emma breathed a bit of life into his tortured soul.

His arms resting over hers belied his words. "I can't stay. I want you in ways you're not prepared to handle right now." She trembled behind him, and he felt the same ripple of awareness shimmy down his spine. "You're not a one-night stand, Emma. You need the kind of trust you can't find in

your heart for a man like me. And right now, I
can't prove to you that I'm anything more than—"

"I know what Jonathan said. I don't believe it."
Her arms tightened around him, and he felt the
tips of her breasts brand him through the layers of
clothing between them.

He craved her support, but he didn't buy her
words. "Lady, you have no proof."

"Maybe I don't need any."

Drew finally found the strength to extricate himself from her arms, but he couldn't quite release
her entirely. He captured her hands when he
turned around and admonished her, "You're
smarter than that."

Her gaze settled on his mouth. "I don't feel very
smart these days."

The longing in her eyes matched the need inside
him. His lips parted as he felt her visual caress like
a stroke of her tongue. Suddenly the jacket he wore
was way too hot. Without taking his gaze from her
tightly compressed lips, he unhooked the zipper
and shed the leather garment to his feet.

He moved slowly, savoring these moments of
trust and desire, holding back lest his powerful
need frighten her away. He framed her jaw
between his hands, and took a moment to admire
the smooth, cool perfection of her skin before dipping his head and pressing a kiss to the corner of
her mouth.

"You handle anything that comes your way with
class"—he kissed her again at the opposite corner—
"dignity"—he ran his tongue along the seam of her
lips, coaxing them to open "—and determination."

On a heavy sigh that sank deep into Drew's soul,

319

Emma opened for him. He moved his mouth over hers, tasting her warmth, drinking her in like a reviving balm pouring over faded dreams and distant hopes. She spread her hands flat against his chest, dug her fingertips into his shoulders, and pulled herself closer.

She angled her lips, sampling all the ways their mouths could come together, teasing him with each discovery of something new.

Drew kneaded his hands down her arms and across her back. He found the hem of her sweater and worked his way underneath. At the first touch of bare skin, he gasped into her mouth. He moved his hands up her back, spanning the elegant expanse of skin and muscle. A groan lodged somewhere inside his chest when his trailing hands discovered she wore no bra.

He worked his hands to the front, reaching up and finding her breasts' small, proud peaks. He brushed his thumbs across the distended nipples, heard her breath catch. The purring in her throat drew his lips to that spot. He boldly palmed her breasts and relished the reflexive clench of her hips against his thigh.

She was explosive beneath his hands and mouth, primed tinder waiting for a spark. The heat rose within him, flint and stone coming together to create a miraculous flame.

She skidded her hands down his flanks and around his back, dropping down to grab and squeeze his buttocks through his jeans.

The heat inside him pulsed to his groin.

"Touch me, lady," he begged her, his voice a gruff rasp in his throat.

Of one accord, he lifted her sweater and she

pulled off his sweatshirt. Freed of the cumbersome garments, he pulled her back into her arms and claimed her mouth, branding her with the same intensity with which her breasts singed his hard chest.

Her hands clutched at his back. He felt the erotic dig of short nails along his spine. When she found that indentation at the base and dragged her fingers across it, he stretched against her with a keening cry.

"Emma." He pleaded and warned her all at the same time. He was near the limit of his endurance, ready to explode, yet something about standing just inside his front door didn't seem right.

This was Emma. His lady. The woman he loved.

He could barely speak through his deep, rapid breaths, could barely concentrate with the wandering exploration of her hands. Still, he summoned what was left of his will and snatched her wrists. He spread her palms flat on his chest and trapped her bewitching fingers there. He looked into her eyes, made sure the fog of passion had cleared enough for her to listen.

"We're standing in the middle of my living room. Kerry might wake up."

Courageous even in this, she never looked away from his searching gaze. Her cheeks blushed a becoming shade of pink, but she never looked away.

"I don't want to stop. The only time I feel whole and safe and happy is when I lose myself in you." She glanced around his bare apartment, probably seeing the lack of enclosed spaces with the same dismay he did. But then an idea lit up her eyes and she backed away, catching his hand in hers and drawing him along. He followed her willingly, a moth drawn to a beautiful flame.

She led him straight into the bathroom. Hardly the romantic rendezvous he had envisioned, but one that grew decidedly more alluring when she bent over the tub and ran the water for the shower. Drew kept his gaze on the never-ending curve of legs and derriere snugged in soft denim while he fumbled to lock the door behind him.

She turned and unsnapped her jeans. Drew followed the movement of her hand downward as she unzipped them. "Don't be noble, Drew. This is what I want."

"You're sure?" he asked one more time, preferring to live with the pain of stopping now than with the regret of wishing they had stopped. "God, lady, be sure."

She stepped out of her boots, jeans, and panties and walked toward him, a tall, proud, beautiful amazon. He bucked beneath the brush of her fingers on his stomach when she reached for the snap of his jeans. "I'm sure."

With their clothing cast aside and the sound of water to mask their uneven breathing and ragged sighs, they stepped into the shower and became a twisting union of seeking hands and mouths, anxious to touch, eager to explore, yearning to give, and helpless to take.

He supped at her throat and suckled her breast. She kissed his scars and brushed her hand along his aching shaft.

"Oh, God, Drew. Now, please. Now."

He lifted her and drove her back against the tile wall, sinking into her with unleashed freedom. Those long, long legs of hers wrapped around his hips, hooked at the ankles, and pulled him impossibly closer.

And then the spark struck the match and he carried them, together, into an explosive release of love and passion. It was a single moment, uniquely carved out of time, without a past or a future—just a single moment, perfect in every way.

Because in that moment, Drew understood what the voice in his head had been trying to say.

Believe with your heart.

He had no way in hell to prove it, but Drew remembered everything.

Emma woke the next morning to the sound of rich male laughter blended with the delighted giggles of a rested and rambunctious little girl. The pleasant ache in her body, celibate for five years and unused to the demands of a healthy man and her own reckless needs, tempted her to stay in the warm cocoon of Drew's bed.

Their joining last night had been wild, desperate, and so full of chained-up need that she blushed even now. She hadn't realized she could be so uninhibited, daring enough to take charge when Drew had given her the opportunity to stop. The sheer joy and mindless release she'd experienced seemed almost . . . sinful.

She rolled onto her side and curled into a ball in a useless attempt to shield herself from her own thoughts. What had she done? Legally, she was still a married woman. She had never made love to any man besides her husband.

Yet she had given herself willingly, determinedly, to Drew.

In the chaos that had followed Jonathan's

return, she had sought the one haven that felt right to her. Drew's doubts about his past, his doubts about his own character, had spoken to that womanly part of her that possessed the unique power to heal a man. Even if only for a few stolen moments.

But could he give her that one thing she needed most? The security of a loving heart?

Or were these moments of time and place the only security fate would allow?

A fake growling noise and Kerry's high-pitched squeal brought Emma back to reality and the responsibilities at hand. She sat up in bed and noticed that the sweater and jeans she had left strewn about Drew's apartment had been folded and placed at the foot of the bed for her.

She made quick use of the considerate gesture. She freshened up and dressed, then tiptoed into the main room in her stockinged feet. Her "good morning" died in her throat at the amazing scene before her.

The morning sun, made brighter by the snow outside, shone in through the windows, reflecting off the bronzed glory of Drew's chest and golden mane of hair. He wore nothing but a pair of black cotton pants, such as martial artists wore. His body moved in a ballet of controlled precision—extended arms, clenched fists, the bunching of muscles across his back, the flex of powerful thighs.

Emma made a conscious effort to close her gaping mouth.

What made the scene even more amazing was the sight of the dark-haired girl, who stood no higher than Drew's waist, mimicking the moves beside him.

When Drew turned to his left and kicked, Kerry turned, too. But her leg didn't reach the hanging bag. Without breaking his rhythm, Drew swung her up into his arms and she smacked the bag with her foot, hitting a joy button that released another stream of giggles.

When Drew set Kerry down, he saw Emma. She took a half-step back, feeling the discomfort of being caught spying. But Drew's strange eyes glowed with a warm welcome. He crossed the mat with a purposeful stride and dipped his head to kiss her fully, possessively, and not nearly long enough, on the mouth. "Good morning, lady."

He'd touched her only with his mouth, but she stood paralyzed, stunned by the instant and intense flowering she felt deep inside her belly. "Good morning," she finally managed to answer on a breathless whisper.

"Mom!" Kerry ran over, breathless with excitement, and Emma knelt to wrap her in a hug. "Drew's teaching me how to do the ka-ka, like he does."

"That's kata, pistol." Kerry lifted her face, beaming at her new teacher. Emma made note of the mutual adoration as she straightened.

"Have either of you eaten breakfast?" she asked, and then shook off their exaggerated groans with a smile of her own. "Exercise is good, but you have to eat, too."

"Mom." Kerry tugged at Emma's hand for her full attention. "The best part is kicking the bag. You can hit it with your fist, too. But the best part is jumping up and swinging around . . ."

Kerry ran off to demonstrate.

Drew picked up a towel and draped it around his

neck, using the end to dab the sweat at his temples. "Help yourself to whatever's in the kitchen. I'm gonna jump in the shower."

The meaningful drop of pitch in his voice went without her comment.

"She's not stuttering," she said.

Drew angled his body to look over his shoulder and see the same miracle she did. "Has that happened before?"

"No. She's stuttered ever since we learned her father wasn't coming home. But today . . ."

While she stared in mute wonder, Drew bristled beside her. She saw his body language go through a subtle change, from her daughter's confident, playful hero back to the closed-off loner she had always known him to be. He gently brushed his fingers across her cheek, tucking her hair behind her ear. "Her father's coming back to her, Em, I promise."

She frowned. "What are you talking about? He did come home, and it was a disaster." She turned her head and pressed a quick kiss into his palm before he pulled his hand away. "I'm grateful to you for all you did to find and rescue Jonathan. But you can't work miracles, Drew. Don't make promises you can't keep."

He splayed his hands at his hips and shook his head, looking everywhere in the room but at her. When he did finally recapture her gaze, she saw a look of cold-blooded determination. "Don't give up hope yet, Emma. I promise to make things right for you."

"Drew . . ."

She didn't want those kinds of promises from him. But he left her before she could explain.

Last night had been grand and glorious. She wasn't prudish enough to pretend she hadn't enjoyed being with him. She wasn't dishonest enough to pretend she hadn't needed every minute of it. But she was smart enough to draw the line at blind devotion to duty, or whatever seeds of guilt still plagued Drew enough to make him promise such impossible things.

Emma and Kerry had cereal and juice while Drew showered. When he walked into the kitchen for a slice of toast and a cup of coffee, she noticed a different kind of confidence in his stride, the look of a man who was comfortable in his own skin.

With the toast wedged between his teeth, he went to the closet and unlocked his gun and holster. He slipped it over his shoulders and strapped it into place. Next he pulled on his bomber jacket and zipped it up. The methodical straightening of his cuffs and collar reminded her of Jonathan putting on his uniform and going out to do battle.

She left Kerry at the table, scooping rings of cereal onto her spoon. "Drew?" The absolute purposefulness of his actions made her edgy. The comforting smell of leather and aftershave calmed her a bit. But she still found his actions suspicious. "Where are you going?"

"To find out the truth, once and for all."

"What truth?"

He reached out and cupped her cheek. The poignant look in his eyes made her worry about whatever emotions roiled within him. "You never gave up on Jonathan, did you?" he asked.

"I couldn't. I thought I loved him."

"I know it's hard to ask of you, but"—he inhaled deeply, lifting his chest, and squared his shoulders on the exhale—"try to hold on to a little bit of faith in him. Will you do that for me?"

"Drew, you're not making any sense."

"Just a little bit longer. Please."

Chapter Fifteen

Lucky's was a pretty dead place in the middle of
the day. A few diehards had already found their
way to the roulette table, and a couple of men in
suits sat at the bar with a bowl of pretzels between
them, nursing what Drew suspected was their
lunch.

But he was interested in neither games nor sus-
tenance. He wanted answers.

He removed his glasses and stuck them inside
the pocket of his black chambray shirt, beneath his
bomber jacket. It was a simple enough gesture, but
it allowed him the unseen opportunity to unsnap
his holster and check the position of his gun for
easy access. Though he rarely used the weapon, he
had a feeling he might need it today. And it always
helped to put on a good show.

His intended audience arrived, right on cue.

"Cam." Buttoning his double-breasted blazer over a bulge that Drew recognized to be another gun, Clayton Roylott strode out from behind the bar with his hand extended in welcome. Drew shook hands and let Clayton slap his shoulder as they greeted each other like old friends. "Good to see you again." The man was already steering Drew toward a secluded table out front and signaling the bartender. "Let me buy you a drink."

Drew slid into the booth across from Roylott and declined. "It's a little early for me. I stopped by to ask you a couple of questions."

Clayton rubbed his hands together in greedy anticipation. "Got a job lined up for me?"

Drew assumed a relaxed pose, leaning into the corner, guarding his back, and appearing nonchalant. "You have a new boss now. I'm sure he has plans for you."

"What is this, some kind of joke? A test?" His silly grin betrayed a note of panic as he looked back and forth around the bar. "I did everything Moriarty told me. He said he got his instructions straight through you. That's why I was so surprised to see you before. I didn't think you were out working the field yourself anymore."

"That's right." Drew told the truth in a way that wasn't quite the truth. "I'm retired from that kind of work."

"So what's this about? Hey, you're not still mad about me hittin' on your girlfriend?"

He said nothing, letting Clayton stew a moment in fear of his wrath.

Correction. In fear of the Chameleon's wrath.

Drew bit down on his lip to kill the smile that wanted to form. He'd wager he could give Clayton a heart attack right about now if he could simply reveal the truth. But he expected that complicated explanation would be beyond Roylott's ken.

"Cam?"

He would let him worry long enough to make him unsettled, reactive. More likely to let something slip. He pulled a photograph from his pocket, the one he'd slipped from Emma's purse earlier that morning. It was a picture of her pregnant with Kerry, with bits of autumn leaves clinging to her sweater and hair. A picture with a tall, dark-haired man standing behind her, possessively claiming what was rightfully his.

"Is this Moriarty?" asked Drew, pushing the photo across the table.

Clayton looked down, then up, his eyes wide with surprise. "What's he doin' with your girl?"

He'd take that as a yes.

Drew pocketed the picture before Clayton's hands could touch it. "Tell me exactly what he hired you to do."

"You think he stiffed you? You know I'll make it right, don't you?"

What a sycophant. He found it odd, this man's bizarre brand of conscience that made it a crime to flirt with his boss's woman, but said it was okay to bilk innocent people out of their hard-earned money and murder two-bit dirtbags like Stan Begosian. Drew wished he had the handcuffs from the glove compartment of his truck to slap on Roylott. This guy needed to be hauled in to do some serious time in jail.

But Drew had other plans for him first.

"Did he tell you to pay Stan Begosian ten thousand dollars to buy LadyTech Corporation stock?"

"Yeah. I paid him to deliver the disk thing, too."

"Do you know he tried to give that disk to the woman in this picture?"

"He said Emma Ramsey. Your lady told me her name was Emily." The similarity of names seemed to escape him. "You mean he's trying to do something to your woman?" Clayton backed up in his seat, waving his arms in front of him. "I swear I didn't know about that. All I did was hire the guy and transfer the funds."

Thank you. Drew wanted to say the words out loud. But an effusive thanks for confirming his suspicions would destroy the ultracool persona Clayton expected him to play.

He took a stab at tying together more loose ends. "Did Moriarty use contacts out of New York and Detroit to buy up LadyTech stock?"

"I don't know. He operates out of the Caribbean. But you knew that, right? He said that's where you hired him."

Drew remembered the jungle rescue at Moriarty's villa. His suspicions that the job had been orchestrated from the start fell into logical order. Jonathan had pretended to be Moriarty, had lured his old buddies in for the "rescue" to reunite him with a grateful Emma. She, in turn, would welcome him with open arms and turn over what he hadn't yet bought of her company.

Drew's hand tightened into a fist at the idea of that madman touching Emma, kissing her, trying to take her to bed. He'd used her loyalty. Abused her vulnerability. But the anger coursing through him, firing his blood, cooled at the knowledge that Emma was strong. Her instincts had told her to refuse the man masquerading as her husband, and she had. What an amazing wife he had.

He relaxed his fist, but not before Clayton noticed it.

"Moriarty *did* stiff you, didn't he?"

"Let's say he's operating without my approval." Drew slid to the front of the booth, ready to leave. "I don't suppose you know where I can find him?"

"Don't bother. I found you."

Drew froze at the telltale click that preceded Jonathan Ramsey's low-pitched warning.

Despite the Sig-Hauer at his temple, Drew knew a stunning sense of calm. He knew the true enemy now. He could face him on equal footing for a change, without the brick wall of amnesia shielding him from the truth.

"Take his gun, Clayton."

Drew's host seemed as stunned as if the gun had been pointed at *his* head. He possessed a great deal of respect for—more like healthy fear of—both men. Clayton clearly didn't know which boss to follow. "I don't get it. If you two want to duke it out over some woman, maybe you'd better take it off my turf."

Jonathan groaned with displeasure. "Don't suggest anything to me. You're an easily manipulated idiot, at best." The gun stayed level at Drew's head, while Jonathan confounded Clayton even further. "What if I told you that woman was my wife? That 'Cam' here was trying to steal her. Would you be so eager to sit down and make nice conversation with him?"

Drew said nothing. He let Clayton wallow in his confusion. "What about retaliation?"

"I'm the only retaliation you need to worry about." Jonathan stepped back and pointed the gun at Drew's chest. "Now take his weapon and pull the car around front."

Several minutes later, with his hands tied together in the backseat of Clayton Roylott's limo, Drew turned to the well-dressed man still sporting his gun as an accessory beside him. "Isn't Moriarty a predictable name for a villain to be using?"

"I've pitted my wits against better than you before. It seemed like an amusing compliment to my abilities."

Drew remembered that ego. He'd profiled it himself. How many times had he tracked the man to his latest operation, only to find him gone without a trace? His ego might be the one thing greater than his cleverness. He filed that information away for a later opportunity.

He looked out the back window and noticed a black sedan following them. He put that information on file, too.

"Do you know what happened in the jungle on Tenebrosa?" He asked the question as calmly as if they were going for a pleasant drive in the country instead of journeying toward his imminent execution.

"Oh, yes," said Jonathan. "And I gather you now know, too. Regaining your memory isn't going to help you explain anything, though, is it?"

The taunt hit its mark. Drew could feel the reality in his heart. He could know the facts in his brain, but unless he ran into a telepath, he had no way to communicate that truth to the outside world.

"How long have you known?" he asked, subdued but not defeated.

"That you and I are not who we appear to be? Almost from the first." Jonathan settled back in his seat and told the whole incredible story, knowing Drew was the only man on earth who would believe it, and planning that he wouldn't be alive to repeat the tale.

"Once I regained consciousness in a godforsaken hospital in the middle of nowhere, looked into the mirror, and saw your face, I figured out what had happened. I contacted some friends, mentioned plastic surgery as a plausible excuse for the different look, and they accepted me back in my rightful position.

"I had a bit of a setback with your face, however."

Drew couldn't resist a touch of sarcasm. "Sorry for the inconvenience. I always liked my strong jawline myself." He lifted his bound hands up to his chin, indicating the cleft in the middle of Jonathan's chin. "Your chin's easier to shave, though."

Jonathan found the comparison amusing. Then his focus returned. "I had perfected the art of working undercover. I never left any traceable clues. You, however, in your bumbling, patriotic way, had a set of fingerprints and a recognizable face. It took me a while to figure out how best to put your assets to use. And then I realized what an opportunity your wife presented to me. I've never been one to pass up an opportunity. Like the one I'm seizing today."

Drew no longer found the story entertaining. Every muscle in his body steeled with suspicion at the reference to Emma. "What are you talking about?"

Jonathan checked his watch. "Emma's lawyer should be picking her up for a late lunch right about now. She'll be tied up in that meeting for an hour or more. Kerry is at dance lessons."

The implied threat boiled through Drew's blood. "Yousonofabitch."

"I finally found something that girl is good for."

Drew lurched forward, but the gun barrel rammed tight under his throat stopped him cold. He jerked his chin up and twisted away from the threat. He breathed in deeply, urging his body to remain unmoving even though protective rage thundered in his veins.

Jonathan pushed a button in the ceiling control panel, and the limo turned off the state highway onto a twisting gravel road. "My wife won't give me what I want. So I'll take it from her. And just in case you'd planned to pull off some kind of miracle like you did on Tenebrosa, I don't want you around to interfere.

"I thought you were dead once, until I saw you face to face at my villa. My whole career, you've been an annoying inconvenience. Who'd have thought you would be leading *my* rescue."

"I did it for Emma." Drew wanted the bastard to understand there was no other reason in the world good enough to keep him alive.

"Well, then, she'll be pleased when she hears I've gotten rid of that clever Chameleon forever." He leaned in, delighted with his own ingenuity. "And I know damn well that there's no evidence to prove that I'm really him—stuck in the wrong body."

"No *physical* evidence," Drew countered.

"What other kind stands up in a court of law?"

Drew was far more interested in proving the truth to Emma, in giving her the evidence of all that lay in his heart.

If he got the chance.

The limo pulled to a stop off the side of the road. Drew recognized the abandoned rock quarries that had long since filled with water and turned into deep man-made lakes. Now, with the recent cold snap, the lakes would be frozen over with a thin layer of ice. But someone could break a hole through the surface, dump a body into the water, and let Mother Nature hide the deed beneath a layer of newly formed ice.

The door opened beside Drew, and Roylott waved him out with a gun. Refusing his offer to help, Drew swung his legs out and stood beside the long car. A second man, a stocky thug who Drew recognized as Stan Begosian's escort at Lucky's, walked up behind him and held him at gunpoint while Clayton stuck his head back inside the limo to consult with Jonathan.

Clayton's voice was muffled, but the grim order came through loud and clear. "Shoot him. Tie him up, and throw him in the quarry. I don't want his body found."

Roylott straightened, uncomfortable with the task, yet unwilling to disobey. "Yes, sir."

"Jackson will drive you back to town in his car. Don't fail me."

Clayton closed the door, and the driver U-turned the limo around them. "Ramsey!" Drew shouted. Ten feet down the road, the limo stopped.

Jonathan's window opened automatically, and he looked out, curious to hear Drew's last words. Drew didn't disappoint.

"If I get my hands on you again . . . plan on dying."

Jonathan smiled at the threat. He angled two fingers at his brow and gave Drew a mock military salute, then rolled up the window and the limo pulled away.

When Clayton leveled his gun at his prisoner, Drew snuck a look at the man's Rolex. One p.m.

"Let's go, Jackson."

The thick-necked man behind Drew jabbed his gun into Drew's ribs and prodded him forward. He fell into step behind Clayton. They formed an odd parade, two men dressed in well-cut suits and dress coats flanking a jeans-clad civilian wearing leather and long hair.

He tried to see his watch beneath his sleeve as they climbed over a pile of debris rock and down into the quarry. But the twisting motion to free his wrist earned him a second jab in the ribs. Drew grimaced but kept walking.

Fortunately, he had dressed for warmth that morning in his black work boots. The lug soles gave him traction on the snow-covered, sometimes icy rocks, while Clayton struggled to keep his footing in his slick-soled loafers. Jackson huffed and puffed with exertion behind him.

When they reached a plateau of relatively flat stone some twenty feet above the water line, Roylott stopped. He glanced over the edge, then back at Drew and Jackson. "This is as good a place as any.

"Sorry about this, Cam," Clayton apologized.

Drew shifted to the balls of his feet and gritted his teeth in a false smile. "Me, too."

He jammed his elbow into Jackson's gut, rammed his doubled fists into his gaping jaw. Startled by the attack, Jackson stumbled, dropping his gun into a crevice between the rocks.

Drew didn't wait for Clayton to make the decision to shoot. He lowered his shoulder and rammed him, knocking him off balance and sending his weapon flying off the ledge into the water below. Jackson ran up behind him, but Drew kicked out, hitting him in the chest with enough force to knock him off his feet. He crashed to the rocks, silent.

Clayton had squatted down, stretching his arm between the rocks to try to retrieve Jackson's gun. Drew looped his arms around his neck from behind and pulled up, strangling him with the knots that bound his wrists. Clayton's hands flailed in a token struggle, but within a minute, Drew had cut off his oxygen long enough for the man to pass out.

He didn't waste a moment checking for a pulse or savoring his triumph. He gasped hard, controlling his breath from the exertion, keeping himself from expelling too much oxygen and getting lightheaded. He ran to Jackson's crumpled body and searched through his pockets. He pulled out his keys and a pocket-sized hunting knife.

He paused only a moment to check his watch. One-twenty. "Damn."

Twenty minutes was a long enough head start for Jonathan Ramsey to get to Emma or Kerry first.

Drew hurried across the rocks, leaping where he had climbed before, trying to make up time.

Time.

The one element that had been stolen from him

five years ago by an inexplicable twist of fate. Time with his daughter and friends. Time with the woman he loved.

He popped open the knife and sawed at his bindings when he hit flat ground. He'd cut himself free by the time he climbed into Jackson's car.

He had five years of a lost life that he intended to make up to those he loved.

But Ramsey had a twenty-minute head start.

Not Ramsey, Drew thought, starting the engine and spinning gravel behind his wheels as he raced onto the road.

The Chameleon. In Jonathan Ramsey's body. In *his* body.

The Chameleon had also had a twenty-minute head start on him down in the jungles of Tenebrosa. He'd run him down that time. He'd left the rest of his team behind when the opportunity had presented itself. He'd tracked the criminal down. Caught him in the heart of the jungle.

He'd blown himself to hell, losing everything.

In twenty minutes, he could lose everything all over again.

"Dammit, Jonathan, let her go! I'll give you whatever you want."

Emma's angry voice, tinged with a panic she refused to give in to, reached Drew through the trapdoor leading to the roof of the LadyTech building.

He climbed the ladder that took him from the top floor to the roof, cursing each rung as if it were a mile that separated him from Kerry and Emma. He'd wasted precious minutes calling Brodie and putting him on alert. He'd practically terrorized

Kerry's dance teacher, demanding to know where his daughter was.

To hear that she'd been picked up by her "father" had eroded the last of Drew's cool reserve.

Finally, sheer luck and an insistent voice inside his head had steered him to LadyTech. *"Up!"* the voice had whispered, like an angel hovering at his shoulder. *"Go up. Quickly."*

He'd driven the car on to the front sidewalk and ran into the building. He'd mounted the stairs two and three at a time. Now, he caught the top rung and pushed open the trapdoor. An icy wind hit him as he climbed on to the roof.

But that was nothing compared to the chill of seeing Jonathan Ramsey holding Kerry by the wrist and dragging her perilously close to the edge of the roof.

He stopped and laughed when he saw Drew. "Well, look who's here. You just refuse to die, don't you?"

"Drew!" Emma spared him a glance over her shoulder, her smoky eyes sharp with fear. Her breath came in short, shallow gasps, judging by the tiny clouds that puffed from her mouth in the cold air.

Her long hair whipped around her face as she turned her focus back to their precious daughter. "Kerry, sweetie. See? It's gonna be all right. Drew's here."

He stalked, quiet as a big cat, up beside her. He reached out and squeezed her shoulder in reassurance.

"What do you want, Ramsey?" challenged Drew.

"How about a happy reunion with my wife, and title to half of all she owns?"

"Never, you bastard." Emma might be terrified for Kerry, but she hadn't bowed out of this fight yet.

God, she was a magnificent woman. No wonder he loved her so much.

"Don't be too hasty, sweetheart. I'm the one with the power here."

Drew took advantage of the interchange and made eye contact with Kerry. She clutched Angelica tightly to her chest. Her big blue eyes swelled with fear, but she wasn't crying. She winked back at him, telling Drew she was able to think and react. Good.

Suddenly Jonathan lifted Kerry by the wrist and dangled her over the edge of the roof, three stories above the paved parking lot below.

"Kerry!" Emma screamed.

"Don't struggle!" warned Drew, rushing forward. If she were to swing or kick, it could loosen Jonathan's grip on her.

"Back off!" At Ramsey's words, Drew froze in his tracks. Kerry was just out of reach. "It's cold up here," the villain sneered. "My fingers might grow numb."

Drew felt Emma's hands at his elbow, pulling him back. He put up both hands to placate Jonathan. "Put her back on the roof, and let's talk."

Kerry, eyes squeezed shut against her terror, hovered in the air a moment longer before Jonathan set her down in front of him. He wrapped an arm around her shoulders to keep her there.

"Tell us what you want," Drew prompted. His oath to kill this man had just become the sole purpose of the rest of his life.

"Fifty-one percent of LadyTech. I already own a

respectable portion of it, but I need a controlling interest."

"It's just a business." Emma pleaded with him, her eyes still on Kerry. "Take it."

"Don't sell yourself short, sweetheart. You've built quite an empire, with technology reaching into all parts of the world. Think how easily I could transport information, rearrange funds, all within the boundaries of the law and international trade agreements. You've set up everything I need."

Emma shook her head, and Drew found himself admiring her once again. She'd been victimized by two horrible men in her lifetime, and still she came back fighting. "They don't allow criminals to run corporate empires. You'll be arrested in a heartbeat."

"I'm no criminal." Jonathan smiled. "I'm Lieutenant Colonel Jonathan Ramsey, American hero. They'll be flocking to congratulate me on my success." He turned his focus to Drew. "And once the authorities have recorded your broken body as that of the notorious Chameleon—with my helpful identification—there will be no one left to challenge me. No one to believe your bizarre story."

"What's he talking about?" Emma asked. Drew felt her gaze slide to him for an instant, then back to Kerry.

So it came down to this. He had to explain himself to Emma on a frozen rooftop while the life of his child sat like a bargaining chip on a negotiating table.

Drew exhaled deeply, watched the cold air turn his breath to vapor. The story he told held even less substance.

"I'm your husband. I'm Jonathan," he said simply. "He's the Chameleon. He has my body. I don't know how." He sought Emma's probing gaze, let the love that had brought him back to the world of living shine in his eyes. "It's me, lady. It's me."

A hushed voice rang sweet and clear in the cold, crisp air. "I believe in you, Daddy."

Emma's frown eased, and she backed up her daughter's words.

"I believe you."

The sun broke through the clouds, catching patches of ice with its light and reflecting with a blinding intensity into Drew's eyes. He raised his hand to his forehead to shield his gaze from its brilliance.

Emma, too, had turned her head to protect herself from the bright light. Kerry had buried her face in Angelica's hair.

Jonathan alone seemed oblivious to the light.

"Isn't this touching?" he mocked. "At any rate, this sappy reunion won't mean anything in court. I can prove *my* identity beyond a shadow of a doubt. Can you?"

At first, Drew didn't realize the question was intended for him. He was still caught up in the light, mesmerized by the way the long shafts of sunlight seemed to gather in a ball and grow in size above Jonathan's head.

He didn't get a chance to answer. "My lawyer has drawn up a document calling for the immediate restructuring of your company. You'll buy back whatever shares you need, turn over your own, and make me senior partner in LadyTech."

"Fine." Emma murmured her agreement, transfixed by the gathering light, unable to look directly at Jonathan anymore. "Just let her go."

"Not until you sign the document. It would have been much easier if you'd simply accepted me as your husband, given what was due me." Jonathan rambled, unheeding, as the brilliance behind him began to lengthen and grow. "I even tried to have a little fun with you. It seemed like such a shame to let your beauty go to waste."

The nasty taunt of Jonathan's words registered, and Drew tore his gaze from the light. His glare must have shown his fury, for Jonathan jerked Kerry away, mere inches from a plunge to certain death.

"Let her go." Drew's voice was cold.

Jonathan laughed. "I'm feeling an incredible sense of déjà vu, aren't you? You've found me out, discovered my true identity yet again, and you're still powerless to stop me."

The light took the shape of flowing robes and hair, and Drew recognized a friendly face from long ago. "I don't think so."

All at once, Jonathan turned, seeing the light for the first time, seeing the woman standing behind him. "What the . . ."

Drew charged forward as Jonathan's startled retreat knocked Kerry over the edge.

A lifetime flashed before his eyes, and his heart hammered in his chest. He dove forward, snatching a fistful of coat, and slammed into the retaining wall. Kerry screamed as the pendulum effect swung her back into the wall. Angelica flew out of her hands.

But in the next breath, Emma was there, tall and strong. She grabbed Kerry by the arm and pulled her onto the roof and into her arms. Battered and bleeding, Drew pushed himself to his feet, reached out for his family, and jackknifed backward as a hand jerked his coat.

"Drew!"

Emma's scream pierced his fog of fear as clearly as she had pierced his tortured dreams. He spun around and grappled with his nemesis. It seemed he stared into the very face of evil.

But Jonathan was already falling. He had latched his hands onto Drew's jacket. Now he laughed, insane with fear. "We'll both die again, Colonel!"

The two men tumbled over the edge. The white light swooped down, captured one of the men in its arms, and all three crashed to the earth below.

Chapter Sixteen

"Dear Lord, please. I can't go through this twice. I love him so. Please help him. Please."

"I owe that man my life a dozen times over. This is partly my fault. Give him a chance."

"Em deserves to know love again. Make them a family."

"I don't go in for this kind of stuff. But if somebody's listening . . . do the right thing."

"Bring him back to us."

"He's a good man. Help him. Make him well."

"These people are hurting. Please give them comfort. Please give them what they need."

"This isn't fair, and you know it."

"Faith? Help my daddy. Please?"

Faith sat in the pew beside Kerry and listened to the prayers of a faithful wife, anxious friends, and hard-

ened men who had seen too much of life. She heard the honest expressions of anger, fear, and love. But most of all, the innocent plea of a trusting little girl made her heart ache and filled her with a determination to do what she could.

There was only one answer to all of their prayers, and she had the power to grant it.

But she didn't have the permission.

A warm whisper of light suddenly suffused Faith's unseen perch. She tipped her face to the rosy glow above her and quirked her brow into a skeptical arc. "Isn't that cheating?"

The light pulsed through her, filling her with heat, hope, and possibilities. "I can do that?" she asked, her doubt transformed into a smile.

When the light flickered again, she pressed a kiss to the crown of Kerry's head and added a quick prayer of her own.

"This time, I promise to get it right."

Drew drifted through the gray fog, blind and deaf to the beeps and prods and hushed voices outside his hospital room.

Inside of him, vibrant memories and waking dreams kept him company in the eerie nothingness surrounding him.

Long, dark hair. Rich and sensual. Falling through his fingers like heavy silk. A husky voice, whispering to him in the darkest part of the night. Legs. So long and fine, a man couldn't even begin to describe them.

Sparkling laughter. Hero worship in clear blue eyes. Tiny, chubby fingers grasping his larger finger with the determination of a drill sergeant and the trust of a little girl for her daddy.

Such warmth and promise.

Home.

A distant memory. So close, yet so far out of reach.

Oh, how he wanted to go home.

Help me! he cried in his mind. *Please, I've been gone too long. I want to go home.*

A high-pitched, erratic beep pierced the fog, burned a staccato intrusion inside his brain. He caught his breath but couldn't exhale. The air in his lungs grew stale. Every muscle in his body clenched. He screamed out in protest but there was no sound.

A loud explosion detonated in his mind. A searing pain pierced his chest. He was falling, falling Then . . .

"Drew?"

A quiet voice whispered through the chaos. The hurtful sounds, the mindless pain receded. "Drew?"

The sensation of floating relaxed his body, and suddenly he could breathe again. He inhaled deeply, feeling a cleansing draft of air. As he exhaled, he opened his inner eyes to the growing light beside him.

The light pinkened and took shape. It was that of a beautiful woman. Not his Emma, but someone equally gentle. She laid her hand over both of his and smiled. "It's all right, Drew."

"I know you." She seemed familiar, yet he couldn't remember where they'd met.

"I've been with you a long time, Mr. Gallagher. Or should I call you Colonel Ramsey?"

"I'm Jonathan . . ."

349

He looked away and thought a moment. Drew? That name felt as comfortable as an old friend. But he'd called himself Jonathan.

"Jonathan." He rolled the name around his tongue, let it sink into his bones. Felt it resonate through the core of his being. "I'm Jonathan Ramsey."

He looked at the creamy-haired woman, bathed in a serene light that seemed to penetrate his skin and clear away the remnants of the fog. "You're the voice in my dreams."

In the back of his mind he heard the muffled sounds of urgent voices, smelled the sterile tang of stainless steel and antiseptic. But he was drawn to the light and her gentle smile. "Where am I? How long have I been here?"

"Your present body is in a hospital bed. The doctors and nurses are fighting to bring you back to the living."

"But I'm already dead." He shook his head, half a memory away from understanding. "I've been here before. The jungle . . . and a grenade."

"Those memories are part of your life, too." She squeezed his hand to ease his confusion. "Time works in funny ways here. The last time we met was five earthly years ago."

"*Before* the hospital in Tenebrosa." He ground the words through his teeth. Memories flooded a painful rush of knowledge and anger and regret into the recesses of his mind. "This is a different hospital.

"I died before. On a mission. I left my men behind to pursue . . ." He drilled her with a look, knew that he had looked at her this hard and furiously once before. "You're an angel. You sent me back. Into the Chameleon's body."

Her face creased with a look of profound sorrow. "I made an unforgivable mistake. And I have done all I can to make it up to you. I haven't been allowed to interfere directly, but I have watched over you and yours ever since."

"You're Kerry's friend."

Her frown eased. "Yes, for as long as she believes in me. I'm your friend, too."

The sweetness of her voice moved like a balm through his soul. The rush of anger at the injustice, at the years he'd been robbed of, gave way to a stunning realization. "I fell in love with Emma all over again. First as Jonathan Ramsey, then as Drew Gallagher." He wiped the harshness from his voice. "You led me to her, didn't you?"

"I tried to make amends."

The incomprehensible was starting to make sense. "Those instincts of mine that kept bringing me back to her . . . you were guiding me."

"I had to read a lot of Drew Gallagher books to figure out how your mind worked."

He almost laughed at the odd idea of an ethereal being reading an old paperback novel. Had he really created a fictional personality for himself? Or had he simply chosen a character with a set of values and a heart that matched his own?

The angel spoke again. "I knew Jonathan Ramsey would find his way back to the people he loved. And I knew you'd keep your promise to take care of the Chameleon. He was an evil man who knew no repentance. His second chance at life was more evil than his first. I thought he might be . . . differ ent. Fortunately, he didn't survive the fall as you barely did. Now he has been properly dealt with; you've righted a wrong that I created. Now I'm allowed to repay the favor."

A thin thread of hope lurched through his body, connecting him from this lighted plane back down to earth.

"I'm not going to die?"

"Emma, Kerry, and your friends are praying very hard that you don't."

"But Moriarty, whoever he is, took my body. And he's dead. How can I . . . ?"

She shushed him, and he felt her gentle command like a hug of reassurance. "Have faith in the power of love, Colonel. You and Emma are soul mates. You've loved each other from the moment your spirits first touched. A shrapnel wound or a blow to the head can never change that. Not even an angel's mistake can change that. A different body can never diminish the love you and Emma share."

"What are you saying? Can you send me back?"

"All you have to do is ask."

"I'm asking. I'm praying. Faith—that's your name, isn't it?—I want to go back. Please. Send me back."

"That's all I needed to hear."

Emma blinked, and a hot tear slid down her icy cheek. Her feet had gone numb from kneeling for so long. Kerry nestled at her side, dozing on and off at the late hour. And someone always held Emma's hand on the other side. BJ, Jas, Brodie, Hawk, or Rafe. Even Kel. Their friendship was a blessing Emma had always cherished but never fully appreciated until this night. Occasionally, someone would urge her to take a short nap or get something to eat. But Emma stayed where she was. As long as she maintained her vigil at the hospital's chapel rail, she had hope that Drew would survive.

She loved him. As perfectly as she had loved Jonathan. And her guilt was no longer an issue, because deep in her heart she believed what her darling Kerry had known all along. Drew Gallagher was a good man. Her man. Their man.

Drew Gallagher and Jonathan Ramsey shared the same spirit. Their faces might be different, but their hearts were the same. Drew's honor, his sense of duty, were Jonathan's.

Her heart sank like a leaden weight in her chest at the prospect of losing the man she loved all over again.

"Please, God," she whispered, pouring her heart and soul into those two words. Kerry stirred beside her, and Emma automatically hugged her closer. "It's all right, sweetie. Faith's with us. She's helped us before and she'll help us again. I believe in miracles."

A brush of something soft whispered across her cheek, drying the tear there. The unseen caress jolted through Emma's body, rousing her from her exhaustion.

In the still minutes before midnight, Emma felt the miracle of love reborn. Of a love that never dies.

She felt it in the tingle of her skin. She felt it in the pounding beat of her heart. She felt it deep in the grateful release of fear from her soul.

She turned where she knelt and saw him at the

back of the hospital chapel. A battered and glorious warrior strode toward her with catlike grace and a fierce intelligence resting on his proud shoulders. She saw so much love, so much hope, shining in the emerald depths of Drew Gallagher's eyes.

Drew saw so much love, so much hope shining in the smoky blue depths of Emma's eyes that he nearly stumbled in his determination to reach her and share the miracle Faith had given him. He knew he'd never tire of watching Em unfold her long, sinuous body with that innate strength and elegance she possessed.

He heard the gasps and thanks and stunned whispers of his friends as he passed by them, but he had eyes only for Emma. For his wife.

Free of pain, his eager strides took him closer, close enough to see the sheen of tears in her eyes, close enough to see the trembling in her shoulders, close enough to . . .

"Daddy!"

Drew braced his feet to catch the airborne figure of the only other female to ever capture his heart. He hugged Kerry in his arms and planted a kiss at the crown of her beautiful, sable-dark hair. "Punkin," he whispered. "I love you. I thank you and Faith for believing in me."

She squeezed his neck and laughed. "See? I told you she was real." Kerry leaned back, and Drew pressed his lips together to keep from grinning at the serious expression on her face. "We can all be a family now, right?"

Emma's soft voice checked his answer. "The doctors said there'd been too much damage." She reached out and touched his chest, brushed her fingertips across his lips, threaded her fingers into the long hair at his shoulder. "Are you real?"

He lifted his gaze from her searching hand to the skeptical light in Emma's awestruck expression. "I'm real." He swallowed past the tremor in his voice. "I know it's impossible to believe, but it's me . . . Jonathan."

A tear spilled over her eyelid. He feathered his fingers across her cheek and into the hair at her temple. He caught the tear with his thumb and brushed it away. "Don't cry on me, lady."

A brave smile trembled across her mouth. She rubbed her cheek into his hand and whispered, "I believe. Welcome home."

Dampness burned in his eyes as he leaned forward and kissed her. Their lips touched, and a feeling of absolute rightness swept through him. Her soft mouth opened, and the gesture of comfort became a greedy exchange of need. He felt her hands at his waist and he drew her into the crook of his arm, still kissing her, loving her with his heart wide open.

Several eons too soon, she ended the kiss. Doubt squeezed his heart in its fist. Could she not see him, love him, for the man he was inside?

He remembered countless battles, perilous missions, dangerous cases he'd endured. But nothing he had ever experienced in Jonathan Ramsey's body or Drew Gallagher's matched the fear gnawing at him now. Had he fought his way back from death to her a second time only to be pushed to arm's length?

"Emma?"

She wrapped her arms around his waist and snuggled close, easing his fear a bit. "I have a question to ask," she said.

"What's that?" An eternity passed by in a beat of silence.

"Do I call you Drew or Jonathan?"

"Just say you love me and the rest will work itself out."

He didn't dare breathe.

"I love you."

He released his apprehension on a whoop of joy.

With his daughter in one arm, he lifted his wife in the other and spun them around. With Kerry's giggles of joy serving as a backdrop, he lost himself in the youthful beauty of Emma's wide smile.

When he set her on her feet, she stretched the length of his side, waking every male nerve in his body. She brushed her fingers along his jaw, studying his mouth, making him crazy with want. Then she cupped his cheek and turned his face to hers. She looked into his eyes, into his heart, into his soul, and pressed a kiss to his lips.

"I love you," she repeated, and the last of his doubts crumbled away.

"I love *you*," he echoed, claiming her mouth and making her his.

Some moments later, keeping Emma tucked to his side, Drew greeted his old friends with laughs and hugs and prolonged handshakes. He looked into Hawk's familiar, fathomless eyes and grinned. "I've got one hell of a story to tell you, shadow man."

"I thought you might."

It was thanks enough for believing in him.

Brodie's firm grip nearly crushed his hand. "I'm sorry I doubted you."

"I'm not." The big man's eyes widened in surprise. "I counted on you to take care of my family in my absence. You protected them like they were your own. There aren't many men I'd trust with that responsibility."

"So, Colonel. Are you gonna tell us what happened?" Rafe Del Rio asked the question they all wanted to hear.

Emma took over before he could answer. "It has something to do with switching bodies and love everlasting." The confidence in her voice reflected a real belief, not that corporate boardroom show Drew had learned to distinguish in her husky voice. "And a guardian angel who never gave up on us."

"Daddy, look!" The wonderment in Kerry's voice drew the attention of both her parents and the other adults. He followed the direction of her pointing finger and saw her love-worn, hand-sewn doll sitting on the rail at the front of the church. A mysterious hand had crafted a new addition to the doll's body.

"Angelica's got wings," said Emma, her awestruck whisper a caress to Drew's ear.

Drew looked down at his daughter and exchanged a knowing wink.

"It's called faith, my love." Drew beamed at the doll's miraculous appearance and knew the doll's namesake had finally received her wings as well.

"Faith. What a perfect name for an angel," Emma said.

Startled by the accuracy of her comment, he looked down and saw a knowing, Mona Lisa smile.

Maybe she *did* know what she was talking about.

Drew laughed and hugged Emma and Kerry to either side, basking in their circle of love. "Absolutely perfect."

FRIENDS

Miss Kerry Doreen Ramsey

cordially invites you

to attend

the Renewal of Marriage Vows

between

her mom and dad,

Emma Carol Ramsey

and

Andrew Gallagher Ramsey,

Saturday, April 15th,

at their home.

No gifts, please.

Your enduring faith in us is gift enough.

(However, bring your favorite bedtime story.

We will be celebrating late into the night!)

Shadow of the Hawk

Julie Miller

Sarah McCormick has one last shot at adventure. Resigned to the life of a spinster, the prim schoolteacher plans to lead five teenage girls to the shadowy isle of Tenebrosa. There, in a tropical paradise, they will study an ancient people and perhaps learn something about themselves. But a mountain of a man upsets her plans—a handsome Indian named Hawk who claims she and her students will be in peril. And when the virile ex-marine swears to protect them, Sarah wonders which is in jeopardy—her body or her heart. Hawk has seen the shy schoolmarm cut a man to ribbons with her sharp tongue, and he is haunted by visions of schooling her lush, surprisingly soft lips in passion. Now, threatened by an evil as old as Tenebrosa itself, Hawk knows that her kiss can stave off the shadows and their love can light the way to paradise.

___52322-1 $4.99 US/$5.99 CAN

KIMBERLY RAYE
FAITHLESS ANGEL

Faith Jansen has closed the door on life and love. After the death of her young ward, she is determined not to let anyone into her little house again. So when she finds Jesse Savage standing on her stoop, a strange light in his eyes, she turns the lock against him. But Jesse returns to her home each morning, gardening tools in hand. Despite her resolution never to reach out again, she finds herself drawing closer to him. So when she finds herself deep in the desert night with him, the doors of desire are flung open, and the light of something deeper is let loose to flood her heart and lead her to a heaven only two can share.

___52296-9 $5.50 US/$6.50 CAN

Something Wild

Kimberly Raye

Dependent only upon twentieth-century conveniences, Tara Martin seeks to make a name for herself as a top-notch photojournalist. But when a plea from her best friend sends her off into the Smoky Mountains to snap a sasquatch, a twisted ankle leaves her in a precarious position—and when she looks up, she sees the biggest foot she's ever seen. Tara learns that the big foot belongs to an even bigger man—with a colossal heart and a body to die for. And that man, who was raised alone in the wilds of Appalachia, will teach Tara that what she needs is something wild.

___52272-1 $5.50 US/$6.50 CAN

Dorchester Publishing Co., Inc.
P.O. Box 6640
Wayne, PA 19087-8640

Please add $1.75 for shipping and handling for the first book and $.50 for each book thereafter. NY, NYC, and PA residents, please add appropriate sales tax. No cash, stamps, or C.O.D.s. All orders shipped within 6 weeks via postal service book rate. Canadian orders require $2.00 extra postage and must be paid in U.S. dollars through a U.S. banking facility.

Name_____
Address_____
City_____State_____Zip_____
I have enclosed $_____ in payment for the checked book(s).
Payment <u>must</u> accompany all orders. ❏ Please send a free catalog.
        CHECK OUT OUR WEBSITE! www.dorchesterpub.com

STRANGER ON THE MOUNTAIN
Linda O. Johnston

The mountain lion disappeared from Eskaway Mountain over a hundred years ago; according to legend, the cat disappeared when an Indian princess lost her only love to cruel fate. According to myth, love will not come to her descendants until the mountain lion returns. Dawn Perry has lived all her life at the foot of Eskaway Mountain, and although she has not been lucky in love, she refuses to believe in myths and legends—or in the mountain lion that lately the townsfolk claim to have seen. So when she finds herself drawn to newcomer Jonah Campion, she takes to the mountain trails to clear her head and close her heart. Only she isn't alone, for watching her with gold-green eyes is the stranger on the mountain.

__52301-9 $4.99 US/$5.99 CAN

Dorchester Publishing Co., Inc.
P.O. Box 6640
Wayne, PA 19087-8640

An Angel's Touch

Heavenly Persuasion

Lorraine Henderson

Lovely Jessica McAllister vows to honor her dying sister's final request. Determined to raise orphaned Maria as if she were her own daughter, Jessica never thinks she'll run into trouble in the form of the child's uncle, handsome winery-owner Benjamin Whittacker.

Benjamin is all man, and as headstrong as Jessica when it comes to deciding what is best for Maria. As sparks fly between the two, their fight for custody turns into a struggle to deny their own burning attraction.

Left to their own devices, the willful twosome may never discover their blossoming love. But Benjamin and Jessica are not alone. With one determined little girl—and her very special angelic helper—the stubborn duo just might be forced to acknowledge a love truly made in heaven.

_52069-9 $5.99 US/$7.99 CAN

Dorchester Publishing Co., Inc.
P.O. Box 6640
Wayne, PA 19087-8640

Please add $1.75 for shipping and handling for the first book and $.50 for each book thereafter. NY, NYC, and PA residents, please add appropriate sales tax. No cash, stamps, or C.O.D.s. All orders shipped within 6 weeks via postal service book rate. Canadian orders require $2.00 extra postage and must be paid in U.S. dollars through a U.S. banking facility.

Name_____
Address_____
City_____ State_____ Zip_____
I have enclosed $_____ in payment for the checked book(s).
Payment <u>must</u> accompany all orders. ❏ Please send a free catalog.

Dreams Of An Eagle
Lori Handeland

After losing everything in the War Between the States, including her husband and young daughter, Genny McGuire is haunted by the dream of a white eagle who takes her to the heights of happiness, then leaves her in despair. Frightened, yet compelled to learn the truth behind what she believes is a prophesy, Genny heads for the untamed land of Bakerstown, Texas—and comes face-to-face with Keenan Eagle, a half-breed bounty hunter as astonishingly handsome as he is dangerous.

___52276-4 $5.50 US/$6.50 CAN

Dorchester Publishing Co., Inc.
P.O. Box 6640
Wayne, PA 19087-8640

Please add $1.75 for shipping and handling for the first book and $.50 for each book thereafter. NY, NYC, and PA residents, please add appropriate sales tax. No cash, stamps, or C.O.D.s. All orders shipped within 6 weeks via postal service book rate. Canadian orders require $2.00 extra postage and must be paid in U.S. dollars through a U.S. banking facility.

Name_____

Address_____

City_____ State_____ Zip_____

I have enclosed $_____ in payment for the checked book(s).

Payment <u>must</u> accompany all orders. ☐ Please send a free catalog.

CHECK OUT OUR WEBSITE! www.dorchesterpub.com

THE LOVE POTION

SANDRA HILL

Get Ready . . . For the Time of Your Life!

A love potion in a jelly bean? Fame and fortune are surely only a swallow away when Dr. Sylvie Fontaine discovers a chemical formula guaranteed to attract the opposite sex. Though her own love life is purely hypothetical, the shy chemist's professional future is assured . . . as soon as she can find a human guinea pig. The only problem is the wrong man has swallowed Sylvie's love potion. Bad boy Lucien LeDeux is more than she can handle even before he's dosed with the Jelly Bean Fix. The wildly virile lawyer is the last person she'd choose to subject to the scientific method. When the dust settles, Sylvie and Luc have the answers to some burning questions—Can a man die of testosterone overload? Can a straight-laced female lose every single one of her inhibitions?—and they learn that old-fashioned romance is still the best catalyst for love.

___52349-3 $5.99 US/$6.99 CAN

A Case Of Nerves

Angie Kay

Standing on the moors of Scotland, Alec Lachlan could have stepped right off of the battlefield of 1746 Culloden. Decked out in full Scottish regalia, Alec looks like every woman's dream, but is one woman's fantasy. Kate MacGillvray doesn't expect to be swept off her feet by the strangely familiar green eyed Scot. But she is a sucker for a man in a kilt; after all, her heroes have always been Highlanders. Wrapped in Alec's strong arms, Kate knows she has met him before—centuries before. And she isn't about to argue if Fate decides to give them a second chance at a love that Bonnie Prince Charlie and a civil war interrupted over two centuries earlier.

___52312-4 $5.50 US/$6.50 CAN

Dorchester Publishing Co., Inc.
P.O. Box 6640
Wayne, PA 19087-8640

Please add $1.75 for shipping and handling for the first book and $.50 for each book thereafter. NY, NYC, and PA residents, please add appropriate sales tax. No cash, stamps, or C.O.D.s. All orders shipped within 6 weeks via postal service book rate. Canadian orders require $2.00 extra postage and must be paid in U.S. dollars through a U.S. banking facility.

Name_____
Address_____
City_____State_____Zip_____
I have enclosed $_____in payment for the checked book(s).
Payment <u>must</u> accompany all orders. ❏ Please send a free catalog.
           CHECK OUT OUR WEBSITE! www.dorchesterpub.com